SHADOW GUARDIAN

AN O'BRIEN TALE

STACEY REYNOLDS

This book is dedicated to the HOEcakes. My band of semper sisters.

OTHER BOOKS BY STACEY REYNOLDS

Raven of the Sea: An O'Brien Tale

A Lantern in the Dark: An O'Brien Tale

Fio: An O'Brien Novella

River Angels: An O'Brien Tales

The Wishing Bridge: An O'Brien Tale

The Irish Midwife: An O'Brien Tale

Dark Irish: An O'Brien Novella

Burning Embers: An O'Brien Tale

His Wild Irish Rose: De Clare Legacy

CHARACTER LIST

List of Characters from the O'Brien Tales series:

Sean O'Brien- Married to Sorcha (Mullen), father to Aidan, Michael, Brigid, Patrick, Liam, Seany (Sean Jr.), brother of William (deceased) and Maeve, son of Aoife and David. Retired and Reserve Garda officer. Native to Doolin, Co. Clare, Ireland.

Sorcha O'Brien- Maiden name of Mullen. Daughter of Michael and Edith Mullen. Sister of John (deceased). Native to Belfast, Northern Ireland. Married to Sean O'Brien with whom she has six children and eight grandchildren. A nurse midwife for over thirty years.

Michael O'Brien- Son of Sean and Sorcha, married to Branna (O'Mara), three children Brian, Halley, and Ian. Rescue swimmer for the Irish Coast Guard. Twin to Brigid.

Branna (O'Mara) O'Brien- American, married to Michael. Orphaned when her father was killed in the 2nd Battle of Fallujah (Major Brian O'Mara, USMC) and then lost her mother, Meghan (Kelly) O'Mara to breast cancer six years later. Mother to Brian, Halley, and Ian. Real Estate investor.

Captain Aidan O'Brien, Royal Irish Regiment- Son and eldest child of Sean and Sorcha O'Brien. Married to Alanna (Falk). Father of two children, David (Davey) and Isla. Serves active duty in the Royal Irish Regiment and currently living in Shropshire, England.

Alanna (Falk) O'Brien- American, married to Aidan, daughter of Hans Falk and Felicity Richards (divorced). Stepdaughter of Doctor Mary Flynn of Co. Clare. Mother to Davey and Isla. Best friend to Branna. Clinical Psychologist working with British military families battling PTSD and traumatic brain injuries.

Brigid (O'Brien) Murphy- Daughter of Sean and Sorcha, Michael's twin, married to Finn Murphy. Mother to Cora, Colin, and Declan.

Finn Murphy- Husband to Brigid. Father of Cora, Colin, and Declan. I.T. expert who works in Ennis but does consulting work with the Garda on occasion.

Cora Murphy- Daughter of Brigid and Finn. Has emerging gifts of pre-cognition and other psychic abilities. Oldest grandchild of Sean and Sorcha.

Patrick O'Brien- Son of Sean and Sorcha. Married to Caitlyn (Nagle). Currently residing in Dublin after joining the Garda.

Caitlyn (Nagle) O'Brien- Daughter of Ronan and Bernadette Nagle, sister to Madeline and Mary. Married to Patrick. Early education teacher. English as a second language teacher for small children. No children of her own as she has fertility issues. Native to Co. Clare.

Dr. Liam O'Brien- Second youngest child of Sean and Sorcha. Currently in medical school.

Sean (Seany) O'Brien Jr.- Youngest child of Sean and Sorcha. Serving with the fire services in Dublin. Trained paramedic and fireman. Unmarried and no children.

Tadgh O'Brien- Only son of William (deceased) and Katie (Donoghue) Nephew of Sean and Sorcha.

Dr. Mary Flynn-Falk- Retired M.D., wife of Hans Falk. Stepmother to Alanna O'Brien and Captain Erik Falk, USMC.

Sgt. Major Hans Falk, USMC Ret.- American, father of Alanna and Erik. Married to Doc Mary. Retired from the United States Marine Corps.

Maeve (O'Brien) Carrington- Daughter of David and Aoife. Wife to Nolan, mother to Cian and Cormac. Sister of Sean.

Katie (Donoghue) O'Brien- Native to Inis Oirr, Aran Islands. Widow of William O'Brien. Mother of Tadgh O'Brien.

Aoife (Kerr) O'Brien- Wife of David O'Brien, mother of Sean, William, and Maeve. Originally from Co. Donegal.

David O'Brien- Husband of Aoife, father of Sean, William, and Maeve. The oldest living patriarch of the O'Brien family.

Michael Mullen- Native to Belfast, Northern Ireland, married to Edith (Kavanagh). Father of Sorcha and John.

Edith (Kavanagh) Mullen- Married to Michael Mullen, mother of Sorcha and John.

Lt. Izzy Collier, USN- Doctor/Surgeon in the United States Navy. Originally born in Wilcox, Arizona. Close friend to Alanna O'Brien.

Eve Doherty: From County Cork. Liam's girlfriend at Trinity College.

Jenny- Daytime barmaid at Gus O'Connor's Pub.

*When I die, Dublin will be written in my heart...**James Joyce***

PROLOGUE

<h2>𝒶n Garda Síochána
      Dublin Metropolitan Region Headquarters</h2>

TADGH O'BRIEN STARED down at his detectives credentia
willing to believe it. He'd pinch himself if the room
crowded. He'd left his simple life in County Clare over tl
ago, taking a shot at becoming a police officer like his f
uncle, and on the heels of his cousin Patrick. Although he
Dublin many times to see his cousin Liam, now a medica
he'd been unprepared for the size and chaos of the Iris
Dublin proper was broken up into several districts, all ι
Trinity College, where Liam went to school, was in Dubl
was where he and Patrick had found an apartment, which
This new job was walking distance to work now. Getting to
other districts had taken many nights of studying Dublin m
were the Dublin districts going all the way up from D
Dublin 24, odd and even depending on which side of the
resided. Then there were the other names. Finglas, Ringser
county areas that were out of the city limits, like Sword:

Laoghaire. It was a lot to remember, but he'd eventually gotten a feel for the city, and it was finally beginning to feel like home.

Being a new detective, hot off the assembly line from Uniformed Crime Investigations, he had a desk that was ass deep in a pool of other new detectives who didn't rate an office yet. Region Headquarters, no less. Although he'd scored the highest marks on the detective's exam, that wasn't what actually gained him the promotion. It was a solid arrest on a particularly horrible set of assholes who were targeting joggers and walkers at the University, knocking them down, and stealing their electronics, wallets, whatever they had on them.

He'd been county champion in secondary school for running the 1500M. When he'd gone to the university in Limerick, he'd also competed for the first two years. So, when those little pricks hit their next victim, he'd been ready. Even in combat boots, he'd caught one of them and thrown the little bastard right into the back of his buddy, causing both to go head first into the lake at St. Stephen's Green. The tourists loved it, and soon the little video was viral. He'd taken a bit of teasing about it from the other men. He came into the locker room to find that they'd jimmied his lock, put little wings on his boots, and hung a cape over his uniform.

The muggers had varied their locations, but the pattern wasn't hard to figure out if you put some time into it. And for some reason, they liked to hit on Mondays and Wednesdays. Shitbird evening out, apparently.

The Garda had been taking a flogging in the press for weeks about not apprehending the two fiends, and it didn't help that one of the victims had been the daughter of a local politician. When Tadgh had asked to be assigned to help with the case, the plump, fifty-something Sergeant, who was almost to his pension, was more than happy to oblige.

That little victory in his file, along with his test scores, meant that as soon as he hit the required three year mark with the Garda, he could put in for a transfer to the Detective Unit. Damn. His father would've been proud. His Uncle Sean had actually teared up on the phone, when he told him. Even his mother, Katie, had been excited for

him, though she'd initially resisted the idea of this career path. Yes, both Tadgh and Patrick were on the fast track. Not bad for two small-town boys from Doolin.

"O'Brien! Where the hell are ye, man?" Sergeant John Tierney, his direct boss, was looking over the sea of desks. He put an eyeball on him, waved a file, and motioned him over. "I've got your assignment. You aren't going to believe this shit."

* * *

FBI FIELD OFFICE -DEARBORN, Michigan

Special Agent Charlie Ryan stared into her empty coffee cup and willed it to refill itself. She'd been up for 36...no wait, shit, 40 hours straight. Another freaking raid. She'd done eighteen months of this game. After getting poached out of the Cleveland Police Department by the FBI, three and a half years ago, she'd done her initial time as a rookie Special Agent in the fraud unit. Snore.

Miami had been nice, if you liked sunny days and sweltering humidity. The beaches were amazing. She just hated starting over. She'd just shed the rookie status at the PD, and although it was a prudent career move, the first two years had been back into the *rookie pay your dues* seat again with the feds. Two years doing identity theft, bank fraud, and other equally boring SLJs (Shitty Little Jobs).

When she'd accepted the position with the International Human Rights Crime division of the FBI, she'd been ecstatic. She was willing to put up with the construction barrels, shitty weather and the shittier attitudes that were ingrained in the people of Dearborn, Michigan. She'd grown up in Cleveland; worked for CPD. She understood these people.

However, this job was wearing on her. Dearborn was a major resettlement area for Muslim refugees. Although most of them were good, law abiding, family-oriented people, there were a fair number of douchebags as well. The radical end of the Brotherhood was alive and kicking in Dearborn, and they were recruiting like crazy. Their targets? Young, disenchanted youth. Young Muslim boys who thought that America was going to be like Disneyland. Another group ripe for recruiting was young, white girls who wanted to piss off their parents. They wanted to become ISIS brides so they could take selfies in their new abaya and hijab and could post them on Instagram. Jesus, Joseph, and Mary.

They'd just raided the home of a thirty-something year old Yemeni couple that had been stockpiling weapons and reaching out to the youth in the local mosque. Junior high kids, for God's sake. They also had an eighteen year old Bangladeshi woman living with them that was clearly a slave...sorry, a *housemaid.* Funny how her door locked from the outside. She was pants pissing scared when they'd unlocked that door, and she was suffering from malnutrition. There was a lock on the fridge and pantry as well. *Damn it.* Charlie rubbed the bridge of her nose, trying to erase those gaunt cheeks and frantic eyes.

Most of the time she left work pissed off. Sometimes she left sad. It ebbed and flowed with the drastic season changes. Urban Michigan sucked in early spring, construction barrels and mud being the two highlights of every day. The summers were muggy and hot, but it was beautiful in the autumn, like now. The deciduous trees were spectacular, but as the temperature dropped and winter approached, it would be overshadowed by a frigid tangle of angry commuters who made too little money and drove too long to get to their place of work. The good news was that you could drive out of the city and hit some of the most beautiful scenery in the entire U.S. The Great Lakes never lost their appeal, even in the snowy depths of winter.

Her stomach growled, but she was getting tired of Turkish takeout and hitting the hot dog trucks for dinner. She needed a good steak. She needed a long bath. She needed a date. Someone who didn't know what she did for a living and wouldn't try to nail her on the first date. Someone normal, like a UPS man or a chef. Yeah, a chef who made really good steak.

What she really needed was a vacation. Somewhere exotic and friendly. Maybe the Bahamas, or Italy. Somewhere with fun nightlife, lots of water, and handsome dance partners. She didn't even care if she went alone. She started packing up her briefcase to head home.

She looked at her watch, 13:00. Shit. Her mental clock was off. It was the middle of the day. Maybe she should eat? Go see a travel agent? They still had travel agents, right? She wanted someone else to do the work, book the trip to specific desires, provide some steamy romance novel for the plane ride, and push her into a cab. Yeah, that would be nice.

CHAPTER 1

DUBLIN, IRELAND

"Okay, explain to me again why we are driving into the dodgy end of Dublin to some gym." Tadgh asked. His tone was light, joking, but Alanna answered.

"Izzy is training. She's got a competition coming up. She is also hell bent on visiting dojangs in every country she visits. Don't worry. She should be ready to go. If not, maybe we will get to watch her open a can of whoop ass on someone."

The two carloads of O'Briens parked in the lot of a Hapkido dojang. They all piled out and into the building. The receptionist was an older Asian looking woman who introduced herself, bowing slightly. "This is my son's training facility. He is busy with your friend, but I can show you to the observation area where we usually let the parents stay and watch."

Tadgh, Liam, Eve, Aidan, and Alanna all filed up the stairs with Sean Jr. taking up the rear. They spread out onto a platform that was glassed in with two-way glass. They could see the training area. Just as the sparring mates came into view, they saw a young woman with a long, sandy braid and intense brow get thrown, ass over teakettle, onto the rubbery mat. The instructor had an arm bar over her throat and she waged a little battle, turning purple, feet digging in, until she finally submitted and tapped out.

"Holy hell," Liam muttered, his arm around his girlfriend. "Maybe she needs to postpone the competition."

Alanna's mouth turned up. "Just watch." Just as she said it, they were circling. Her friend Izzy darted in, taking the offensive. She took the lapels of the instructor's dobak and pulled him off balance just as she swept the leg. Down they both went, but she didn't let go. He rolled her on her back, but she weaved her legs around his ribs just as she twisted the dobak lapels up and in, cutting off his air on two fronts. He began to waiver and she visibly tightened. He dug his elbows into her thighs and they popped open, releasing his ribcage.

Liam chuckled. "Nerve compression. Nice. Hurts like a shot of electricity in your arse and your instinct is to let go." They watched as the two grappled, and she pushed off her one foot to swing over him as she kept that grip on his uniform. Then she was opposite him, but ear to ear, feet pointing to opposite walls. She had him, with his shoulders both pinned to the mat. Boom.

The two jumped up, bowed, and started laughing as they fist bumped. The other students were clapping. The master motioned for another student to come and said something they couldn't hear. They watched as Izzy and the other man went to a rack and removed two wooden staffs. The other students paired off and the instructor allowed some music. *Momma Said Knock You Out* by LL Cool J started booming over the speakers and Alanna laughed. "Guess they let her pick the playlist." After a bit of clackety-clack on the wooden staffs, gut jabs, and smooth moves, the session was over. The group walked down to the mats and Izzy looked at the clock.

"Oh, man! I am sorry. I lost track of time!" She bowed to her instructor again and ran toward the locker room.

"She gets a little focused. Luckily, she's low maintenance. She won't be long," Alanna assured them. Tadgh was talking to the instructor and Liam and Seany were cracking jokes about dying between a woman's squeezing thighs being better than getting cracked in the head with a big stick.

Sure enough, a few minutes later Izzy came out of the locker room at a full slide. Worn Levis cut-off mid thigh, a tight U.S. Navy t-shirt that was tucked into a big leather belt and rodeo style buckle, and no shoes. She'd obviously taken a combat shower with her hair still up. She didn't say anything. She just looked at Eve and Alanna. Cute sandals, jewelry, club attire. Then she looked at herself. "One more minute."

The men watched with fascination as this female ritual was engaged. Alanna jumped behind her, plucking the tie from her hair. Eve dug in her bag and pulled out a lipstick. All while la femme de ass-kicker was sliding on cowboy boots. Hair cascaded everywhere. She flipped her head upside down as Alanna combed it with her fingers, Izzy using the lipstick at the same time. Eve was spraying her with some sort of glittery perfume so her arms and legs had a sparkly sheen. Then she threw her head up and started tying a knot in her t-shirt, exposing her mid drift. She pulled the jeans down on her hips to expose more of the olive skin and feminine torso. Seany and Tadgh let out a simultaneous breath, appreciating the effort. She bent over, dug something out of her bag, and plopped a raggy cowboy hat on her head. She smiled, threw her bag over her shoulder, and said, "Let's roll." She threw her arm around Alanna on the way out.

* * *

"So, you're training? Does that explain the no alcohol?" Sean Jr. leaned toward Izzy, stars in his eyes. Tadgh as well. The club was slow, due to an autumn lull in the tourist season.

"Nah, it's more dehydration prevention from that long-ass plane ride. I'm not a big drinker, but I like a little bourbon on occasion. Did you like the show? He's a tough instructor. It's fun to travel to another dojang and have some random instructor kick your butt." She was smiling.

"Oh, aye. Although you gave as good as you got." Seany said. Liam and Eve were listening, comfortably tangled in one another. Alanna

9

and Aidan had gone to meet James and Alex and the rest of the family at the door to show them where everyone was sitting.

They had met James and Alex in Doolin several years ago, while the two men were on holiday. Branna befriended them at a local pub, the rest of the family following suit, and the two men always touched base when they visited from England.

Eve said, "It was quite something to watch you take on a full grown man. You're very strong. I think I'd like to learn some of those moves."

Izzy nodded her head. "You should, definitely. I would love to teach you, but I'm not here much longer. I can set it up, though, even if it's just a bit of self defense. Every woman should know how to defend herself. They could cater it to your dancing to avoid injuries. I've had to scale back a lot due to my line of work. No punching."

Liam laughed at that. "Piano player?"

She wiggled her fingers inward at each other. "Scalpels and needles are my instruments."

Liam sat up straighter at that. "Are ye a doctor, then?"

Izzy nodded. "Yes. Did you think I was swabbing the deck in the Navy?" she grinned. "I'm a surgeon. The Navy has a great medical community. I went in as an officer when I graduated from medical school. I did my residency with the Navy, partly in a combat zone, and now I'm stationed at the Naval hospital in Portsmouth, Virginia in the trauma unit. My commitment ends next year."

She leaned in to Seany. "I'm a little older than I look, sweetie. I'm pretty sure I have a decade on you."

He just smiled, winking at her. "You look just about perfect, love." Izzy laughed, shaking her head.

Tadgh chimed in, then. "Will you get out? Go into the private sector?"

She shrugged. "Don't know. I love the military, but I really don't know. I'm still working that out in my head. What about you, Liam? Alanna said you're almost done? What's your specialty?"

Liam took a sip of his beer. "Internal Medicine with a splash of Infectious Disease."

Izzy laughed. "From what I know of infectious diseases, it usually only takes a splash. Good for you. Any plans?"

Liam cleared his throat, shooting a look at Eve who had gone still. "Well, I took a scholarship from the church. I'm supposed to be doing a medical mission in the late spring. It will be a six month commitment but it will count toward my residency. I've done a year already, and I could actually extend it to a year and finish at the mission hospital. Apparently, they need doctors pretty badly and are willing to take rookies, but I'll just stay the six months." He looked at Eve and squeezed her shoulders. "I don't want to be gone that long."

Izzy nodded. "Yeah, funny how that money comes with strings. But, you take the King's coin, you do the King's bidding. Where's the mission?"

"I have three choices. The Sudan, Kazakhstan, or Manaus." Izzy dropped her bottle of mineral water away from her mouth.

"You lucky bastard. If you tell me you picked anywhere but Brazil I will smack you with this bottle." This made Eve giggle and the men chuckle. "Come on, like you aren't dying to get frisky with your little microscope and some dengue fever slides on the Amazon River. Agh, I am so jealous!" Liam was raising his brows over his drink, smiling. That's when the rest of the crowd showed up.

After hugs were exchanged and introductions made, they all settled to the tables they'd grouped together. Unlike their local pubs, this place came with a team of cocktail waitresses ready to serve. One in particular seemed to like the end of the table that held Seany, Tadgh, James, and Alex all sitting together with no rings and no women. Seany swiftly ordered a round of drinks for the group, including a Tullamore Dew for Izzy. "Just try it. If you like bourbon, you'll like Dew. And Eve, you need to take the night off as well. One drink isn't going to dim your twinkle toes."

Eve sighed and Tadgh slid over her Moscow Mule. "See there, love. A sprig of mint. So if you think about it, it's just a salad with a lot of dressing."

Eve snorted. "All right, all right. Far be it for me to dull the celebration." Then she looked down and noticed that neither Brigid nor

Branna had a drink. "What's this, then? You two aren't drinking?" They both stiffened, but Aidan came to the rescue.

Aidan stood up, clinking a spoon to his drink. "Attention, we've got some toasts tonight! Get your drinks." Everyone turned and took drinks in hand, listening to the eldest brother's commanding voice. "We've had a few big events these last couple of months and this is our one shot at celebrating together, so let's list them off, aye? Age before beauty and all, I'd like to first drink to Tadgh's big promotion." The entire group raised their glasses, the men giving a whoop. Tadgh blushed at the praise. "He'll be taking that big brain, with his big bollocks riding shotgun, to the Detectives Unit at the Garda headquarters in Dublin!" Seany, Michael, Patrick, and Liam all banged on the table. Then they all took a sip.

"Next is my pretty, little brother Patrick who is finally out of traffic enforcement and starting the National Security Surveillance Unit on the Armed Response Team. A long title for a total ass-kicker job, and I couldn't be more proud of him." Aidan went over to Patrick and enveloped him in a tight man hug. With a thump on his back, he said. "I'm so proud of you brother. Watch your back." Patrick sat down and put his arm around his wife. Then he whispered in her ear. It didn't go unnoticed.

Then Tadgh jumped up. "Next but not least, the baby of the group. Seany, stand up." Sean Jr. stood up, putting his fingers through his hair nervously. "Our little baby boy has landed himself a job with fire services. He'll start training next week!" Then Seany was swarmed by his big brothers, including Tadgh, who had always been more of a brother than a cousin.

"Nice. Just fire, or EMT?" It was Izzy who asked.

"Fire first, then I can apply for EMT training after I clear probation. I'm just glad to have the position. Two years at university doing the EMT studies will put me ahead of the crowd if I decide to go that way. For now, I'll be smoke-eating with the rest of the barbarians." His smile was huge, like the boy turned man who couldn't wait to prove himself in his chosen field.

James and Alex had been watching all of this, cheering along with

the group, when James finally chimed in. "Crikey, all this at o
Next will be births and engagements." Brigid winced slightly, lool
at Branna and then at Caitlyn. Caitlyn was pale, but compo:
James's face fell as Alex nudged him. "Christ, did I just step in it
someone getting divorced or something?" It was Caitlyn who clea
her throat.

She stood, and Tadgh noticed the fragile smile on her face. So ve
fragile compared to the girl that had done a spritely march down t
aisle to her O'Brien mate. Patrick squeezed her hand from the se
next to her, offering comfort and acknowledging her strength. SH
said softly, "Well, now. Is it one or both of you?" She said this to Brigi
and Branna. Brigid smiled sadly as Finn spoke up. "She's carryin
another lad."

The whole group gasped with joy. Brigid smiled, remembering
how happy Cora and Colin had been to find out about a new baby.

Then Branna spoke gently. "We've just started trying for a third."
Michael held her close, kissing her temple. Branna had delivered
twins, Halley and Brian, but it hadn't been without complications.
The twins were three years old, and after the ordeal the pregnancy
and delivery had been, they hadn't felt safe for a while, thinking of
another pregnancy. So they'd given Branna's body time to heal.
Michael watched as Alanna squeezed Branna's arm and exchanged
glances with Aidan. Aidan and Alanna had just had their second child
a few months ago, little Isla, who was nestled between Granny Mary
and her Grandpa Hans, back in Doolin. Davey, their first, was
delighted to have a baby sister, and not be the youngest grandchild
anymore.

"I guess little Isla will have some more playmates," Caitlyn said,
smiling. Tadgh watched her as she raised her glass like a goddamn
trooper. "To the ever expanding O'Brien clan, and another beautiful
O'Brien man on the way." She gave a nod to Finn and Brigid, and
Brigid stood up and hugged her as the others drank.

Tadgh's throat was thick with emotion. For lots of reasons, not the
least of which was poor Caitlyn. Two miscarriages in three years, with
a lion's share of disappointment in between. She sat next to Patrick

whose eyes never left hers. He took her chin in his hand and kissed her mouth, rubbing his lips back and forth. Tadgh was close enough to feel the intimacy, and to hear the heart breaking words. *Don't worry, love. We're enough. You and I are enough.*

As if the DJ instinctively knew that the tension in the room needed breaking, the dance music kicked up a notch. He watched Izzy finish off her Tullamore and hop out of her seat. She looked at James. "Do you mind if I borrow the Italian?"

James cracked off a laugh. "He loves to dance, go right ahead."

All of the O'Brien men watched as the ladies piled onto the dance floor. Hair swinging, asses churning. Izzy, though... holy Hell. The song was from that badly dressed little perv, Robin Thicke. *Blurred Lines.* Even the married men weren't immune. Izzy might be a big, important surgeon for the U.S. Navy, and an ass-kicker on the side, but her most compelling talent at the moment was her hips.

"Fucking crikey, she's enough to make me flip back over the fence. I better watch Alex." The laughter rumbled through the group, until she got serious. The hip rolls and ass twerks were a sight to see, like Polynesian Hula meets Latin American Salsa. Aidan laughed as he saw Seany and Tadgh turn their heads sideways in unison, watching Izzy's ass from a new angle.

"Do you think she fancies younger men?" Seany asked. Then Tadgh made his move right as Seany tried to get up, shoving past him, knocking him back down to a seated position, and scurried toward the dance floor. Seany laughed, cursing him with a few choice obscenities, then followed hot on his tail. Pretty soon they were all dancing, Eve's long limbs and lithe dancer's body wrapped around Liam's. The couples all smoothing their hands over each other. Izzy hanging with the boys-only club. The night was filled with laughter and the celebration of new beginnings.

* * *

THE SCENE at Patrick and Caitlyn's flat the next morning was comical to be sure. O'Brien men strewn throughout the living spaces with

pillows and spare blankets. There were empty water glasses that Brigid and Branna had distributed to the boozers, along with a half empty bottle of aspirin. The women, all sober, had crammed into the two bedrooms, vowing that if Izzy wasn't getting any action, no one would. This, of course, prompted both Seany and Tadgh to offer up their services, causing Brigid to cuff them both behind the ear.

"As much as I'd love to be the jelly in an O'Brien man sandwich, I'm married to my job, boys. But I appreciate the offer," Izzy replied in her no nonsense way. Grinning as the two competed playfully for her affections.

Now, in the late morning, Brigid was at the coffee pot, making it strong enough to tackle the party crowd. Branna was at the stove, making french toast and bangers. Caitlyn was putting out a stack of plates and flatware and starting the kettle for tea. Liam and Eve had gone back to their own flats and so had Tadgh. He and Patrick had to work the next morning, so they'd been sensible enough to stop at two drinks.

"I wish you would have told me," Caitlyn said. The girls all turned to look at her, but it was Brigid who sighed.

"I know, deirfiúr. We just thought we'd wait. Make sure everything was okay."

Caitlyn grinned, "Aye, I understand that well enough. And maybe you were hoping if you waited long enough, I'd have some good news as well?"

Brigid shook her head. "No, not at all. There's no pressure from us. God knows you have enough of that going on in your own mind. We're here for you, Caitlyn. Until we're old and grey and wearing big granny knickers. There aren't any expectations."

"I know that. I do. And I don't expect you to keep good news under your hat, out of fear of hurting me. It's not you that's hurting me, darlin'. This trouble I've had? It just is. I love my nieces and nephews more than anything. Honestly, they're the only comfort you can offer me. A life full of children, even if I didn't bear them. They're the children of my heart. 'Tis a blessing, this news." She walked to Brigid and lay her hand on her abdomen. "Another O'Brien man... nothing but good can come from it. May he get his mother's eyes and his father's temper."

Brigid coughed on a laugh. "Amen to that, sister." She put her hand over Caitlyn's. Then Branna and Alanna were there, and they circled their arms, putting their heads together. They were so wrapped up in the sister love that they didn't see Izzy.

She got down on all fours, crawled across the kitchen floor, and popped her head in between a set of legs, looking up at the circle of women. "I can't believe you bitches are having an estrogen-fest without me!" The girls sprang apart, startled and giggling. Then they made a dogpile on the floor, mauling Izzy with hugs and kisses.

As Michael, Finn, Seany and Aidan peered around the kitchen wall, they were baffled at the display in front of them. Giggling lasses rolling all over the floor, limbs and hair and cackling voices. "Did you need us to get the oil and bikinis, then?" Finn said with a brow lifted. They all looked at him and the hysterics started up again.

"Ye need to get our sister out of the mix if you think we're going to enjoy that show," Seany said with a shudder.

CHAPTER 2

*T*adgh sat at the table, surrounded by bigwigs in the Garda, higher ranking detectives, and a few odd men out, like himself. He also noticed an Arabic looking man with sharp, dark eyes who was about his age. The only real surprise was the Lord Mayor of Dublin. Tadgh controlled his breathing and quelled the impulse to squirm. All of these bosses were giving him the sweats. Apparently the politician, the one so grateful for him catching the muggers who had assaulted his daughter, had specifically asked for him to be on this task force. He wasn't sure what the task force was supposed to be doing, but whatever the hell it was, it was big. It didn't have a name, because they were keeping everything out of the press. For now, anyway. This shit always leaked.

"Thank you all for being on time. We've a bit to cover this morning, no time to be pissing about with late-comers. Sergeant Detective Collins, dim the lights if you would."

The man had introduced himself as the Deputy Commissioner (DC) in Charge of Operations, Bill Sullivan. He started the slide show off with no sugar coating or preamble. The group of officers cursed under their breath, Tadgh let out a hiss. Female murder victim, young, Caucasian, petite, glassy eyes. The hair stood up all over Tadgh's body.

"The victim is Jessica Friar from Minnesota. Went missing from Dublin 4 two weeks ago, found dumped up north near the river two days later." He changed the photo to her face. Beaten, cut. Then another slide flipped to her hands, combative wounds. She'd fought. But there were also rope burns. Tadgh's stomach rolled as he thought of their dear, beautiful Alanna. When she'd come to Ireland with Aidan and met the family three years ago, the slight residual burn marks from tape had been on her wrists, and ligature marks on her throat. Luckily for them, that bastard had been killed in prison. Apparently the woman that he'd almost beaten to death had been affiliated with a local motorcycle gang. Score one for biker justice. As he looked at the changing slides, he cleared his throat, looked away with closed eyes, composed himself, and looked back.

"Cause of death, torture. Specifically, strangulation. That was after he, or they, had worked on her for a while. The finger marks, hand size, and allover brute force of the violence leads the coroner to believe the killer, or killers, are male. There were also definite signs of sexual assault, including DNA left on the body. We have all of that being processed and analyzed. Now, the next thing I am going to show you must not, under any circumstances, leave this room. It goes without saying that you will shut your gobs completely when it comes to this case. We are keeping this under the radar with the media until we can get a handle on this sick fecker. But this detail is absolutely classified, even with other officers." He clicked the computer and the next slide came up. More animated hissing and cursing. She'd been carved up at the inner portion of her right arm, at the soft flesh that would press against her ribcage.

"What in the fecking hell is that?" Tadgh said. He shouldn't be talking out of turn since he was the junior guy in the room, but he was feeling angry and a bit vicious at the moment. It wasn't the Dep. Commissioner that answered. It was the dark, quiet man across from Tadgh. He spoke with a strange accent. Not exactly Middle Eastern, but sort of. Definitely some Irish in there as well.

"It's an Arabic symbol. It means Christian." The room fell silent, everyone absorbing the information. They hadn't had the massive influx of refugees like other parts of Europe, but the culture in Ireland was becoming more diverse. Most saw it as a good thing, but they did notice that the tensions had risen since the country had accepted some of the displaced population. There had been some domestic violence issues that were justified by Sharia Law in the eyes of the abusers, even though Irish Law disagreed. There had also been some assaults in the schools and certain areas of town. Even a few aggravated rapes by refugees who thought it was okay to attack Western women, because they wore shorts and skirts and didn't cover their hair. Those were few and far between, though. And most of the refugees just wanted to make a life here and have a safe place to raise their families.

This is why they didn't want the media getting wind of it. It would be a bad time altogether if this got out. Tadgh was torn, because he understood why they wanted to avoid the inevitable retaliation, but women needed to be warned. But why a task force for just one victim? Then it occurred to him with chilling clarity. He asked. "How many? And are they all American?"

The man's face was sad and angry, but composed. There was also some respect in his eyes that Tadgh had reached the serial killer conclusion. "Three so far. All the same physical type, all American women living abroad, all tortured and marked in the same way. The only thing that varies is where they've gone missing and where they were dumped. It seems to be late night, quiet areas, and the bodies are left on the outskirts of the city where they can do it quickly and get out. We've been in touch with the U.S. FBI. Obviously, they're more than a little concerned. There's talk of sending an agent to oversee the investigation and work with the task force."

"What the hell are you doing letting the Yanks send someone over here to get in our knickers? We can handle this. Since when do they have jurisdiction in Ireland?" The question came from one of the senior detectives. A pudgy, angry looking tosser with overly hairy eyebrows.

The look the commissioner gave the senior detective could have flayed his flesh open. "Watch yer fecking tone with me, Detective

Miller. I can tell you that if this was three of our Irish daughters getting murdered in America, you bet your ass I would send someone from our department to help find the bastard. Secondly, the FBI has a human rights violations crime unit. They can go all the way to Mount Olympus if they've got cause. In cases of torture, which this is, and other circumstances, it is completely appropriate for them to send someone to investigate on foreign soil. I, for one, would rather have him working alongside us, than getting in our way, trying to work alone. So, they haven't assigned anyone, but I think it's inevitable. And you will work with him and treat him as an equal or you will be removed from the task force and will fetch my feckin' coffee and wipe my feckin' ass for the next six months." Laughter rumbled through the room, except for Detective Miller. Sullivan's language was notoriously colorful.

The Commissioner took a cleansing breath and Tadgh decided he liked this guy. "Now, let's continue with the other two cases."

* * *

DEARBORN HEIGHTS, Michigan

Special Agent Ryan slid her keys on the counter as she rolled her neck on her shoulders. After a gratifying crack, she pulled her pistol out of the holster, opened the drawer to her desk that was in her small living area, and keyed the combination for her gun locker. After securing her weapon, she stripped, started the shower, and used the remote to turn on her TV. The hot water in her building was slow moving, so she had to let the shower run for a few minutes.

There was no sofa in her place, so she'd piled her clothes on the bed. She lived in a one-room efficiency with a small bathroom and a galley kitchen. With her salary, she could have probably bought a house in Michigan, given the economy. She had a small student loan to pay off, however. And she had other financial responsibilities that took priority over how much square footage she wanted.

This place was enough, for now. If she needed to get a bigger place down the road, she could. She was on a flexible lease. She fed her fish as she watched the news. After a grim weather report was delivered, she started to head into the shower when a report caught her attention. A young, American co-ed had been killed in Ireland. Cause of death was being withheld, as the case was under investigation. They showed a picture of the girl. She was pretty. Long hair, petite, nice smile. It made Charlie tired. The whole world made her tired. She flipped off the TV and stepped into her tepid shower.

After a quick clean up, she threw on some pajamas and headed for the refrigerator. She pulled out a single, leftover piece of lasagna that her neighbor had brought to her. Her neighbor was a widow that had two kids in California who she rarely saw. She was about seventy-five, as far as Charlie could tell, and a real handful. She also still cooked like she had a full house, even though she was living lean in an identical efficiency. She had a recliner, a circa 1970s coffee table, and a small twin bed in her place with one of those vintage chenille spreads on it. Made good lasagna, even better meatloaf, and smoked Virginia Slims on her balcony every hour on the hour. Aunt Jo, as she insisted Charlie call her, was third generation Michigan and full of opinions and good intentions. Every now and again, she'd pop open a jug of Carlo Rossi Paisano and share with anyone who happened to be on their balcony. The world needed more Aunt Jos.

* * *

TADGH'S HEAD was reeling after the meeting. He got up, gathered his notes, and began walking toward the door. He was stopped by the Deputy Commissioner who was speaking with the man who had translated the Arabic symbol. "Detective O'Brien, is that correct?" Tadgh shook his hand, feeling shaky. "This is Detective Rahim Salib."

The two men shook hands, and Detective Salib said, "It's a bit of a mouthful. You may call me Sal."

Tadgh smiled, nodding. "Sal it is." He led them into an empty office and shut the door, taking command of the desk that didn't belong to anyone, as if he were at home. Then he continued, addressing Tadgh.

"Now that we have introductions out of the way, let me tell you why you need to give a shit who he is. He'll be your partner and your interpreter for the foreseeable future. He's a linguist, speaks several Middle Eastern languages and dialects. You will work the streets in plain clothes. You will keep your ears open, troll the right neighborhoods. You are both military age males. The recruiting has started with a small sect of the Muslim Brotherhood. You keep that to yourself, aye? No one is to know this, and no one is to know what you are doing. Do you understand? You answer directly to me. This bastard is coming into my city and pulling this Jack the Ripper shite on poor, innocent girls. I want him sniffed out. We've secured a flat in the right area of town. You will visit Sal at this location, like you would any other mate. As he has a wife and children at home, he won't live there, but he'll appear as if he does. You will both be armed at all times. That doesn't happen for all Garda officers or even all detectives, but the time for all of us being unarmed is gone. It's just the reality. Go to Jenny on the third floor and she will escort you to the armory where you will be issued your side arms. Then you will clock two hours at the range. Understood?" Both men were completely stunned. Plain clothes, armed, reporting directly to the Deputy Commissioner in charge. *Holy shit.*

"I understand, Sir." Tadgh said. As did his new partner.

"Well, then. One more thing, Detective O'Brien. There will be an exclusion to the gag order where you are concerned. I worked many years with your Uncle Sean. He thinks he's put himself out to pasture, but he's still in the Reserve Garda. So, his ass is mine if I need him. He's got some experience dating back to the eighties with this sort of case. He also did training on politically motivated abductions and assaults, using data he collected on the Ulster forces and the IRA in Northern Ireland. He would be an asset on this case. I will be sending a copy of the case file to him, through you. You will hand carry it to his door. Nothing electronic. As for your cousin Patrick, he's been assigned to the national security forces, and since this is a possible terrorist motivation, he will be brought into the fold, as well as his direct supervisor. He can watch this from his post as well. That said, you are not working together. You are under no circumstances to be seen together when he's in uniform. Low key. Do you understand?" Tadgh nodded and kept his mouth shut, because he could tell the man wasn't finished.

"Now, if you decide to take a trip to your Uncle Sean's at the same time, and let's say, lock yourself in his den and go over the case together, I wouldn't object. Just no street work. Sean will be acting only as a consultant." He took a breath, a sip of coffee, and continued. Both men knew it was a breather, not a time for questions.

"You are also not permitted to try to infiltrate any sort of potential terrorist group. You are to observe, shadow, collect intel, and stay the hell off their radar. Both of you need to stop with the shaving, grow out some facial hair if you think you're old enough to accomplish that, and let your hair shag out a bit. Don't look so much like bloody cops."

Tadgh kept checking to make sure his jaw wasn't hanging open. Uncle Sean was getting reactivated for this case. He was going incognito to gather intelligence. His Aunt Sorcha was going to have this man's balls, if she had anything to say about it. Then again, how much would Sean tell her? Regardless, this was a major assignment. He had to concentrate to keep the grin off his face. Until he thought of those three young women.

Anger did a resurge in his belly. He wanted this case for a lot of reasons. Two of them being his beautiful Branna and Alanna, who were both young, petite, lovely American girls who would officially be staying out of Dublin for the next century. Actually, all of the women would be staying out. To the devil with protocol. He and his uncle Sean would have to figure out how much to share, but he had to have a sit down with Patrick as well. Caitlyn could not be left unattended to roam the city. And what were they going to do about Eve? She was finishing up her last semester. She couldn't just leave. *Damn it to hell.*

TADGH TRIED Eve's cell for the third time, Liam's for the second. As he walked over the Grand Canal on Pearse Street, then over the Quay, he saw the sign for the Lir Academy. Eve taught a class there three nights a week as an internship requirement. She also rehearsed there. So, it would save her some time if she just moved a cot and a small fridge into the main studio. As he approached, he got a ding back from Liam. *We'll be right out.* They must have seen him through the windows of the studio. Liam had asked him to escort her home, as he was in a study group. Obviously there had been a change in plans.

Liam and Eve came out the door a few minutes later. Both blushing from exertion that had nothing to do with dance. Liam had obviously distracted her from her clean up duties. Again. Eve was slender and lovely, her lips kiss flushed, her hair a little disheveled. She looked like a woman who'd been spending some quality time with her O'Brien mate. A pang of longing hit Tadgh. He was older than Liam by a couple of years. Unfortunately, that lucky-in-love gene seemed to have skipped Tadgh's branch of the family tree. Perhaps the tragedy of his mother's loss had tainted his blood. Always desired, never loved. His mother was a looker, but she'd never gotten over losing his father. Never found another man that could accept her and love her. So, now in her late fifties, she'd been alone for twenty years.

"I'm sorry, Tadgh. My phone died and I didn't get to call and cancel the escort," Eve said in an adorable, spritely, Cork accent.

Tadgh sighed. "It's all right, girl. No harm done. It's good to see you. I need to talk with ye both, as it turns out. Let's walk a while, and then I'll be off."

He told them very little. Only that there had been troubles, that he was working a multiple homicide case, and that under no circumstances was Eve to be left alone on the street. If she was at the studio, she should keep the doors secured at all times. If she didn't have a ride, she needed to call a cab. He hoped to God they understood the gravity of the situation, because that's all he could tell them for now.

"I'll be headed for home tomorrow morning. I need to drop some things off for Uncle Sean. Patrick and Caitlyn will be going as well. I need Patrick and Da in the same city for a bit. Any chance of you two joining us?"

Eve sighed. "I am stretched too thin as it is. Graduation is in two months. Opening night is next weekend. Thank you, though. Give everyone my love."

Liam added, "I'll be staying back tomorrow as well. I'm on rotation at the hospital, then I have a meeting with Mother Superior to finalize Brazil. You kiss Mam and all the women for me, and tell Da I'll see them in a week or two."

They all embraced. Tadgh whispered, "Keep an eye on her, dearthái."

Liam's face grew serious, the message finally soaking in. "Aye. Have you talked to the others?" He shook his head. "Tomorrow. It's another reason I'm going home. That's all I can say for now." Liam nodded. "And you, Twinkle Toes, take care and don't work too hard. Make this lout rub your feet and fix you a bit of tea."

Eve giggled, her blue eyes sparkling. "Did you hear that, love? Tea and a foot rub." Liam smiled, pulling her in for a kiss to the top of her head.

"Consider it done."

Something occurred to Tadgh. "Oh, shit! I forgot about Izzy. Is she still in Dublin?" Liam shook his head. "No, she's back home for a final visit. She'll fly back to the states in couple of days, along with Alanna and Aidan heading back to England. They are headed up with Seany, and we'll take them to the airport. Maybe we can all meet out for one more drink before they leave. For now, they're all safe in Doolin."

Tadgh exhaled. "That sounds like a grand idea. I won't be gone more than overnight myself."

CHAPTER 3

The car ride to Doolin was grim. Caitlyn drove, while Tadgh rode shotgun. Patrick was in the back with the case file that they were delivering to Sean. He would periodically mumble curses, rub his face, crack his neck. Tadgh understood. It was tough to look at the pictures, read the details. "Well, what the bloody hell can you tell me?" Caitlyn said testily.

"I've told you all I can. Please darlin'. Don't press me on this and please, just do as I suggest. Take a leave from your substitute teaching and go stay with your parents or Aunt Sorcha. Promise me. I wouldn't ask it if I thought it was unnecessary."

That's when Patrick joined the conversation. "Caitlyn, sweet. Ye must. Jesus Christ…" he choked down what he was going to say and his voice became pleading. "Please mo chroí. Ye must do as he says. I'll drive home every time I have a day off. We won't be parted long. I promise you. We can even spring for a bed and breakfast, or take the ferry to Aunt Katie's sometimes. She's not using the place half the time since she's traveling the fair circuit with her knitting. Just please trust us on this."

Caitlyn searched their faces. Seeing the lines of worry etched around their eyes. "Okay. I'll leave Dublin until this is all sorted."

* * *

Doolin, County Clare, Ireland

"Here are my boys!" Sorcha opened the door to greet Tadgh and Patrick. She kissed them both on the head as they bent to her. She took Caitlyn in a warm, motherly embrace. "Hello, lass. I've missed you."

They came into the house, and Sorcha cocked her head at Tadgh. "No bag?"

"I'm only here for one night, then I have to go back to work. I just need to meet with Uncle Sean, drop something off, and head back tomorrow. I'll sleep at Branna and Michael's. They have a pullout, and you have a full house. My motorcycle should be done at the shop, and I'll ride her back tomorrow."

Sorcha hugged him. "We've always got room for you, a mhic. Always."

Tadgh shut his eyes. Sorcha had taken care of him like her own son, during a very dark part of his childhood. "I love you. And I know you'd put me up. It's just easier for the one night. I'll stay for dinner though, if you're offering." His smile was all teeth and she giggled.

"Don't worry. No tripe. I've made some lamb for Izzy's last night. Everyone will join us." She gave him a sideways glance. "She's pretty, aye?"

Tadgh laughed. "Aye, she's pretty, but she's not got eyes for me, so you'll have to find me another lass. Maybe some feisty distant second cousin on the Mullen side? I'm not doing so well on my own." He blushed as he said it, his dimples making an appearance.

Sorcha's face grew sad. "You are too beautiful for your own good. And it's not many lasses that can see past that, to the heart of you. Your mate is out there, Tadgh. I know it in my bones. Your father loved your mother so dearly and completely. You have his heart and her eyes. This thing will happen for you, lad. I promise you."

He followed her into the kitchen where the smells of home cooking wafted through the room. "Have you seen yer mam? She seems to be doing really well. She's sticking to the no smoking, been doing really well with her business."

Tadgh leaned against the counter, watching his aunt. How many times had he sat in this kitchen, getting a hot meal, sometimes a bath and a bed, having to squeeze in with one of the other boys? "Auntie... thank you."

She had been peeking in the oven, and she closed it and looked up. "For what?"

"For taking care of me all these years, and for never judging my mother."

She smiled sadly. "I'm no saint, love. There were times I wanted to bonk her upside the head. Sisters are like that, even in-laws, but she loved you. She loves you more than anything or anyone, even herself. She dealt with what every policeman's wife fears most. I can't say I would have done so well had I lost your Uncle Sean. But she came out of it. I know she can be...well, clingy I guess is the word. She's afraid of losing you, and depression is a difficult thing."

Tadgh remembered when he was about ten or eleven. He'd been in the kitchen watching his aunt cook like he was now. *Auntie Sorcha, I wish you were my Ma.*

She'd paused over her rolling and put her pin down, wiping her hands on her apron. *Don't ever say that Tadgh. Never. Your mother loves you. It would kill her to hear you talk like that.*

Tadgh had teared up. *You don't want me? She wouldn't miss me. She doesn't love me now that Da is gone. She just drinks and sleeps and cries. I could sleep on the floor. I wouldn't be any bother.* Sorcha had grabbed him, held him as he finally let go. He cried for so long, his eyes were swollen, his head ached. His uncle had come in with his mother to find them on the floor, Sorcha holding him like a small child. That had been the culminating event that had finally snapped his mother out of it. She'd gone to treatment soon after that.

Sorcha watched him as he stared down at the place where he'd sunken to the floor, where she'd held him and let him cry. She went to him, as she had so many times with her own sons. She laid hands on his shoulders as he towered over her. She ran a gentle, motherly hand through his hair. "I think about that day too, sometimes. I love you like my own son, a mhic. I always wanted you. But you were never my own to keep, no matter how much I wanted to. And in the end, it was the right thing to do. She got better because of you. You made her keep living and keep fighting."

CHAPTER 4

*S*ean stood over the case file in his den, silent. Thinking. The ratty sofa he had in the room was threadbare with squeaky springs, but he wouldn't let Sorcha get rid of it. Seated there, his son and nephew watched him. "So, Sullivan wants me to consult on this?" He sighed, "Christ deliver us. This is unbelievable. Three lasses in two weeks? How long has it been since the last?" He looked at the file, answering his own question. "Too long. It's been too long. They've either got another one, or they are getting ready to strike. Jesus wept." He rubbed his palm over his face, then let out a gust of breath. He looked at Patrick. "You tell your mother nothing about this. I'll think of something, but you tell her none of it."

Patrick and Tadgh's brows went up. This was odd. "Da, you tell Mam everything. You told me that, when I married. When I took this job. You told me that you didn't hold back anything from her."

Sean's eyes were intense. He nodded. "I know, son, but this...we can't share all of this. Your mother has a history with political turmoil, religion justified violence...other things. Just trust me. It's better that we don't tell her. Just enough to keep all the women out of the city. Alanna is headed back to England. She needs to stay put until this is over. We can't take any risks. Ye can't tell an Irish girl from an Amer-

ican until they open their mouth, but we don't
desperate and go after a local girl if she fits the de
don't know enough about the motivation yet. The
close to home, and they don't go anywhere alone." I
the pictures. "Tadgh, we need to end this. Whatever
rest until this is over."

* * *

WHEN TADGH FINISHED SPEAKING to all of the fami
pale. Especially Aidan's. He was clutching his wife
over her protectively. Even three years later, Ta
haunting memories of her abduction still swirlin
took his face in her hands, soothed him. Her eyes
together. No one was given the details to any degr
stupid. If the city had formed a task force and acti
be something pretty bad. And it involved dead, yo
all they needed to know. They'd seen the news
beginning to piece things together.

Sorcha was quiet. Too quiet. Then she stood
ready for dinner? Izzy, I think you are really goi
It's a Welsh recipe. Did ye know that Collier is a \
was babbling, trying to change the subject, which
one to shy away from trouble. They all followed
dining room in search of food and distraction.

* * *

SEAN'S BREATH WAS HEAVY, labored. Sorcha was
silent but for her own breathing. He had six gr
woman of his always managed to surprise him.
with a hungry roughness he hadn't experience
years. Not that he was complaining. She'd j
actually.

But he knew his beloved Sorcha. She nee

…en things were boiling up in her mind. As soon as the house had …ared out, and they retired to their bedroom, she'd pulled him by the …irt. They'd almost knocked over the bloody lamp. She'd been all …er him. They'd been married for thirty-eight years, but they never …led to lose themselves in each other when they had the chance. This …d been different, though. Almost desperate.

"It'll be okay, darlin'. Everyone will be fine. Just trust me, and don't … any questions." He felt a shudder roll through her.

"I think Caitlyn looked better, tonight. Don't you? Her color is …od, she was smiling. I'm going to have to take her to tea this week. … be so nice having her close again." Sorcha's tone was light.

Sean stilled, not sure how to respond. She was deflecting. Acting … nothing was amiss. It was not like her at all. It wasn't a good sign. …t a good sign at all.

* * *

…GH UNFOLDED the sofa bed and went about making it. He stood up … watched as the top sheet slowly slid off the mattress. He grinned, …ring footsteps and looking over his shoulder. "Well, now. Have ye …e to help?"

…Brian smiled up at him. "Yes! You need help! Brush your teeth!" He … almost four, and as forceful as any O'Brien man, when he had a …nt to make.

…Michael peeked around the doorway, shaking his head. "Lad, …'re supposed to be in bed. Leave Uncle Tadgh alone."

…Tadgh scooped the boy up and took him to the bathroom. Brian …d on the stool, carefully squeezed half the bottle of toothpaste … Tadgh's brush, and looked expectantly. "Open up!"

…Tadgh opened his mouth and was gagged by a jabbing toothbrush … sickening, bubble gum flavored toothpaste. After some very …sy "help" and a follow-up face wash, Tadgh looked at the boy. …mind me to never let you help me shave, wee Brian." He winked at … and put him out so he could finish getting ready for bed. When

he came out of the bathroom in his t-shirt and shorts, Brian was snuggled into the sofa bed, waiting patiently.

Branna came out, looked at her son, and pointed to his bedroom. "Back to bed, little man. Uncle Tadgh barely fits on that bed alone."

After putting the boy in his own bed in the room he shared with his twin, Branna came out to find Tadgh writing on a notepad. He looked huge on the sleeper sofa, long legs crossed at the ankle. "Is that about the new case?"

Tadgh looked up, setting the pad aside. "More or less. I have a meeting with my new partner tomorrow. I am just collecting my thoughts. I have a lot of questions for him."

Branna sat on the edge of the bed. "I'm proud of you Tadgh. I saw Aunt Katie a few days ago. She's very proud as well. Bragging about her smart son, the detective."

Tadgh blushed. "Aye, she's come around, just as you said she would." He paused. "Listen, Branna. What we said about keeping out of Dublin and not going anywhere alone. It's important. Do you understand?"

Branna nodded. "I do. We all do, I promise. I don't know what you're dealing with, but I trust you."

* * *

MICHAEL CAME out of his bedroom early, headed for work. He had to drive Tadgh to the mechanic's to pick up his motorbike on the way. Tadgh had sold his old car to Seany when he'd moved into the city, and picked up a used BMW motorcycle. Between Patrick, Caitlyn, and Tadgh, they had one shared car. Work and school were walking distance or bus distance and parking was too highly priced to each have a car. So, they figured out a system between two bicycles, one car, and one motorbike.

As Michael walked into view of the sofa bed, he stifled a laugh. Then he grabbed his phone to take a picture.

Tadgh came awake to the sensation of sleeping on the surface of the sun. He was hot, sweaty, and something was over his face and across one leg. The fire in the cottage had long gone out, only the wood smoke scent remaining. Then he heard giggling and a phone camera snapping. He opened one eye. After lights out at around 10pm, he'd heard the bedroom door creak open. Little feet padded over to him. He'd thought it was little Brian, but it had actually been his twin, Halley. *Uncle Tadgh, there's a monster in my room.*

After some negotiating and a sip of water, she'd secured her position for the night right in the crook of his arm. He was such a sap. About twenty minutes later, they'd both begun to drift off when he felt the distinct dip of the crappy sofa bed mattress. Brian had climbed over his face, squeezed in next to him, and had proceeded to kick him in the balls twice, before finally settling upside down with his feet in Tadgh's face. Currently sleeping on his chest was Fergus, a beautiful but willful flame-point Siamese…whose twin, Duncan, was currently living in Tadgh's flat.

As Tadgh took Halley's arm off his forehead, he looked down the mattress where Brian was hugging his shin, foot thrown over his thigh. He looked at Branna and Michael. "Caffeine?"

* * *

TADGH PARKED his motorcycle in the drive of a modest row house in suburban Dublin County. He undid his chin strap as he slid the helmet off. It was strange to feel a few days growth on his chin. He was usually clean shaven. He had to shave every day, in fact, in order to stay within Garda regs. But things were different now. He was approaching the door when Sal opened it.

"Looking as scruffy as I feel, I see." His new partner had thick black hair, cut short, but curling around the edges. His two day growth put Tadgh's to shame.

"Christ, no need to show off. When did you start shaving? When you were still in nappies?" The man laughed and put his hand out. Tadgh shook it. He'd had a partner in his old precinct, but it hadn't been this easy. He felt a brotherly connection to Sal; had felt it almost immediately. It was like that sometimes. A sense of ease and connection that had nothing to do with the amount of time you'd known each other.

"Come inside. My wife has made some lunch for us. She is eager to meet you. I told her you were ugly, and that you weighed twenty-five stone. Try to play along." As they walked in the kitchen, the smell of something spicy and heavenly wafted over the room.

Sal's wife looked to be about thirty. There was a child at her feet, pushing a box of biscuits at her zealously. There was another child in an infant swing to her left. "You must be his fat, ugly partner." She said with a grin. Then she wiped her hands on a towel and extended her hand. She had long dark hair, huge beautiful eyes with silky lashes, and a full set of mauve lips. She gave her husband a look, and he shrugged.

"What would you have me say? He looks like a male model, please don't leave me?" Tadgh coughed and laughed. "Please, you're a legend around the station. You've got the girls panting all over themselves and back biting to get at you." Tadgh bristled, which his partner didn't notice. His wife did, however.

"Don't listen to him. A nice girl will look at those dimples and kind eyes, not the rest of you. My name is Leyla. Please, sit down and let my lying husband pour some tea."

Tadgh smiled. "What does your name mean, Leyla?"

"It means dark haired beauty. It's Arabic, but I'm not of the Gulf people. I am Egyptian."

Sal interrupted, "Yes, I was born here, but she's one of those damn foreigners." His wife swatted him with a wooden spoon as he yelped. Tadgh liked them already. They reminded him of his Aunt Sorcha and Uncle Sean. An easy, teasing way that covered up for genuine love and affection.

"Well, she seems to keep you in line. You don't have any Irish blood mixed in there do you, Leyla?" She shook her head. "No, not a drop. But I do love this country. My father is a businessman. We lived in Cairo most of my life, although we traveled. I moved here almost six years ago, right before they overthrew the government. We were no longer safe."

"Yes, same with my parents. They are from Iraq, originally. We are Kurdish, and they fled Iraq in 1988 during the Anfal attacks. Horrific ethnic cleansing in the Kurdish villages. They were newly married and they got the hell out of there, fled through Turkey and into Europe."

Sal hesitated for a minute, then seemed to decide something. "My parents are Christians. They aren't Chaldeans. They converted about five years after they got to Ireland. I was baptized in a Catholic church when I was a toddler. Leyla is Egyptian Coptic."

Tadgh's brows came up. "Both persecuted in their native lands."

Sal grew serious. "Do you know the Quran's view of apostates? It's punishable by death. This cannot get out while we are undercover. I would be shunned at best, even though it was my father who made the choice. I choose to practice, and they wouldn't give me a pass. Run into the wrong sort of asshole and I'm not going to be well received."

"I understand, Sal. And I can see why you don't spread it around. It won't leave this room. Just don't get spotted coming out of mass."

Sal laughed. "We don't attend mass in the city, and I've got an arrangement for the foreseeable future."

"How on earth did you two meet? Do they have some sort of political refugee dating site or something?"

Sal cracked off a laugh. "No, no. It wasn't that easy. We met because she's a shameless criminal." Another swat. "Ow, darling. You can hardly deny it!"

Tadgh looked at Leyla with her dark, shrewd eyes. "Well, then?"

She rolled her eyes, "He was working foot patrol near the university where I was teaching. He tried to give me a parking ticket." Sal was laughing into the back of his hand at this point.

"You were parking services?" Tadgh asked.

Sal shook his head. "No, just uniformed patrol. I had noticed her before. She liked to play fast and loose with the parking laws. She had this little spot where she would illegally park her little Saab. It was behind a trash bin, so she got away with it for a little while. I borrowed a ticket book from a mate of mine who worked that area. I waited until I saw her coming and made a grand gesture of it. You know, flipping the ticket book, licking the tip of the pen." Swat, swat. He was laughing, his wife smiling as she smacked him.

"I should have turned you in!" she said.

"Anyway, the rest is history. Two hot blooded, non-Irish, looking for a love connection twenty-somethings. I saw that Coptic cross sticking out of her collar and I knew it was fate." He turned a little more serious, "So you can see where this case has gotten under my skin. People who justify cruelty in the name of religion or ethnic supremacy have a tendency to piss me off."

"Sal!" His wife gave him an admonishing look as she motioned to their toddler who was now inspecting Tadgh, staring up at his great height.

"Piss!" he said, as if to put an exclamation mark on his mother's disapproval. Tadgh bent down and patted his dark head. "And, who is this?"

"That is Sal Junior. You may call him Jay." She picked the boy up and placed him in a high chair near the table. "Don't say piss, Jay. Daddy is naughty." She motioned to the sleeping baby in the swing. "The little one is Jasmin. She's sweet like her mother." Once she had the boy settled, she motioned to the doorway. "We will eat in here, and I'll put you two in the dining room. That way you can talk and not be interrupted."

Tadgh wondered how much Sal had told his wife. "Thank you, Leyla. It smells gorgeous altogether." They sat at the table in the adjoining room while Sal's wife brought in a variety of dishes. Rice with dried fruit, mutton, and pine nuts. Stuffed grape leaves, olives, and soft cheeses. Then there was roasted eggplant, a carrot salad, and some sort of spiced chicken.

"This is magnificent! Do you cook like this every day?"

She shrugged, "No, he'll get leftovers tomorrow. You'll have to come when I make my red lentil soup and fresh bread." She filled their water glasses and topped off their cups of tea, absently kissing her husband on the head. He smiled at her, now. All joking gone. A pang of longing hit Tadgh, as it always did. The loneliness always lingering in his mind.

* * *

TADGH OPENED the door to his apartment, only to be bombarded by a white fur ball on four legs. "All right, Duncan. I see you, lad. It was only one day!" He laughed as the cat carried on, wrapping around his ankles and fussing with his little roars. Tadgh picked him up. "Ye didn't shite in my shoes again, did you? No? Good boy. I saw your brother just last night. He's getting fat."

Tadgh put his keys and bag down on the counter so that he could commit both hands to the little fiend. "Cora sends her love, o'course. Now, let's see to that water dish."

Tadgh put the leftovers from Leyla into the refrigerator. Then he bent to the cat's dish, taking it to the sink. Duncan hurried him along from the counter. "Get off the counter, ye wee mongrel." He scooped him up and set him down by his dishes which were now full of fresh water and the remaining food that Tadgh had left for him. He'd stayed at Sal's longer than he'd intended. They had become engrossed in the case file, figuring out a strategy for their intel gathering. In the end, it had been simple. The flat that Sal was assigned was in an area of Dublin that contained the bulk of the Muslim refugees. Tadgh had never worked that area, which was good. The chances of someone recognizing him were slim, especially out of uniform. The same with Sal.

He'd asked the patrol officers in the area what the citizens were like. According to the officer, they were clannish, keeping mostly to themselves, but always polite. They didn't cause any trouble, and every now and again, the older granny-aged women would send him home with pastries. The military-aged males were a little more stand-offish, but there seemed to be a patriarchal vibe to the area. A few older men running the show.

One man in particular, named Zaid, was about forty-five and a good connection in the area. He always tried to cooperate with the first responders when they came into the complex, whether it be police or fire. There had been an apartment fire that was suspicious, a while back. The only person injured was a young woman, about seventeen years old. The fire had started in her bedroom, and they'd suspected some sort of abuse.

Zaid had been cooperative, and it seemed he was more willing to let his family assimilate. His wife and daughters didn't wear the traditional garb other than the head scarf. The plan was to meet at Sal's new apartment building tonight, hang around the common areas, be seen in the hallways, and just pay attention. But first, he was going to meet the family at the pub in Dublin 2. Liam and Eve were taking everyone to the airport in the morning, and he wanted to say goodbye. He pulled his phone from his leather jacket, dialing his cousin. "Liam, I'm home. What time for drinks?"

* * *

EVERYONE WAS LAUGHING. Izzy wadded up a drink napkin and threw it at Aidan. "Enough trying to marry me off, O'Brien. I am very intent on licking my wounds for the next few months."

Eve stuck a bottom lip out. "Poor Izzy. Did some tosser do ye a bad turn, then?"

Izzy exchanged glances with Alanna, whose face was sad. "No, not really. I ended it, actually. He needed more than I could give him." Eve leaned in, wanting the details. Izzy sighed, took a sip of her bourbon, and shook herself. "He was a Lieutenant in the Marines. Went from riding bulls in Texas to joining the Marine Corps."

Tadgh's brows went up. "A rodeo man? Well, that's quite a switch."

She shrugged. "Yes, I haven't given the ring back, so to speak." Tadgh's eyes went to her finger. "No, not a real ring. His buckle. I have to mail it back to him. It's sort of a thing. It's special to him. I just haven't done it. The miles got to us. He was a good man. We just ended up on different coasts. He deployed, saw some action. He needed someone to come home to, and I was in the middle of 24 hour shifts doing trauma rotations. The odds were not in our favor. He got married this past weekend."

Everyone winced. She gave a shrug. "Rebound wife, but I am sure she's gorgeous and ready to have his babies. So…" She put her glass up for a toast. "To better timing, next time. And a few less long distance miles." Everyone clinked glasses. "As for your cousin," she winked at Tadgh, "and your brother. I'm not their type."

It was Liam who laughed. Alanna just smiled, knowing the big analysis was coming. "Oh, really. Enlighten us on how you came to these findings."

Izzy took a sip, and continued. "Well, Tadgh is smart. That pretty face often gets in the way of the ladies actually seeing him, but there is real substance there."

Tadgh grinned, straightening his collar. "Please, do go on."

Izzy giggled. "I'm not his type because he likes a puzzle. I'm too out there. What you see is what you get. There's nothing to figure out. He's had a hard time finding someone who fits the bill. I, however, am not it."

Aidan slapped a hand on the table. "Jesus, that is exactly right. You're good. Really good. What's wrong with Seany, then?"

She smiled, "Not a damn thing. But I'm no cougar. I like a little more patina on my men. Plus, I don't fancy pursuing another woman's man."

They all sat up a little straighter. "He's got no woman." Aidan said with a knowing grin.

She nodded. "I understand, but someone's got a hold on him. I don't know who she was, but she must have been something."

Liam whistled under his teeth. "Wow, you're like some sort of seer. How the hell can you possibly know about Moe?" He looked at Alanna.

She put her hands up. "I didn't say a word."

"You don't have to be psychic to read people. I've always been good at it," Izzy said.

Liam had one arm around Eve, taking a sip of his whiskey. "Well, then. What about me? What's my story?"

She cocked her head, squinting one eye. "You're brilliant, but you hide it behind that smart-ass demeanor. You like to have fun. You don't have any worries. You... Liam, are the charmed O'Brien man." Liam threw his head back and laughed, pulling Eve in for a kiss. "That I am."

CHAPTER 5

FBI FIELD OFFICE-DEARBORN, MICHIGAN

"I'm sorry, sir. Did you just say Dublin? As in Ireland?" Charlie was positive she'd misunderstood him. There was a Dublin in Ohio, if she remembered correctly.

"Yes, Special Agent Ryan. I said Dublin, Ireland. And I am going to be dead frank with you and admit that I'm jealous as hell right now. However, I don't fit the job description, so you are it."

Charlie sat back in her chair, staring at the man across from her. This was un-freaking-believable. There must be some serious shit hitting the fan for them to be sending her, a relatively junior agent, to Ireland. "Tell me everything."

When he was done she exhaled. "Holy hell, boss."

"Yep, that about sums it up, Agent Ryan."

She straightened in her seat. "I'm in. Whatever you need." She looked down at the file he'd shared with her, the photos. All twenty something, pretty young women. Petite, longer hair, fair skinned. All fresh faced American girls. The anger nearly choked her. She also didn't need to look in a mirror to figure out where this was headed. "You want me undercover. That's why you're sending me. As bait." It wasn't a question, but he nodded.

"Any other agents in on this?"

He shook his head. "As you know, we are pulling long l barely spare you. I talked to the head Irishman. He's a strai; totally on board with us working with them. He's not pi: territory. This is bad business for all of us. I trust them to you, Ryan. I wouldn't send you otherwise."

Charlie just nodded. "I will find this prick... or group will find them or I won't come home."

As Charlie walked into her apartment, the case was mind. She remembered the news report of the American died in Ireland. The news channel had not released any d wonder. This was a political nightmare. And it wasn't *girl*

* * *

"OKAY, you've got your agency credentials and passpor traveling under your own name. You're secured in a hot week so that you can get established in a temporary flat. you euro? Plastic?" Charlie nodded. She felt like a kic college. "Yes daddy, you wanna check my tire tread and i

Her boss grunted. "If I was your daddy, I'd be marryi nice Jewish boy and you wouldn't be anywhere near a b;

Charlie laughed. "That is both chauvinistic and ad(Pops." Her boss, Gabe Schroeder, was just about the s; father, but that is where the similarities ended. "Do I h who will be meeting me?"

Assistant Director Schroeder shook his head. "No] he'd be sending someone out of uniform. Now, there' on its way, so be flexible. O'Hare is a shit show wh comes in. Your flight is two days from now, right wh(to hit. If you get grounded, just get a hotel and have a r bureau. Don't sleep at the airport. Get a hotel. T Consider yourself officially on the company dime. don't go overboard, you should not be out any dou adventure. And do not work 24-7, like you do here. Y(the time. I've seen too many agents burn out early an(

careers. And don't be afraid to ask for help. That's why you are hooked up with this task force. You are a team. Don't try to fly solo. You are too far away from your own command. Consider them your adopted family and your backup. Got it?"

"Don't worry about me, sir. This is what I trained for. I'm ready for this. I will make you proud."

* * *

CHARLIE MOANED as she hit the bed of the Chicago hotel. She really hated Chicago, but hot damn... this bed was just what she needed. After doing the hurry up and wait routine for five hours at the airport, they'd finally called it and sent everyone to a hotel. When she got to the hotel in question, it had been a dump. All that was left from a big political rally, a ball game, and downed flights, eating up the availability. Nope. She was not nineteen and on a ramen noodle budget. Realizing that the place was a shit hole with a running toilet, archaic mattress, and what she was positive was a pubic hair on the soap dish, she walked right back out, and told the person at the desk that she needed a cab. She pulled up a four star near the airport, and was now face down on a whole lotta pillow top mattress, minus the pubes. She'd survived on beef jerky and diet coke in the airport, but she knew damn well there was room service at this place. On the bureau dime, she reminded herself. She didn't need Château Lafite. All she needed was some decent chow and a big glass of ice cold lemonade.

Rolling across the wonderfully soft and clean bedding, she grabbed the menu off the desk. Salad, soup, appetizers, no no no. Bingo. She picked up the phone and dialed the *3 for the kitchen. "Yes, I would like the bacon and blue burger, medium rare with extra mushrooms, A-1, mayo, hold the lettuce and tomato. Fries with malt vinegar, no ketchup anywhere on my plate. Do you have lemonade? Fresh? Nope, not out of the fountain, thanks anyway, but forget the lemonade. Do you have root beer? Float? Make that a yes, please, and a pitcher of ice water with some lemon slices." See, she could be healthy. Lemons were fruit.

Truth was, she was nervous as hell. The whole delayed flight had given her a lot of time to dwell on the gravity of this assignment. She needed some comfort food. And comfort food never had lettuce or ketchup involved. Ever.

She had just enough time to take a shower, so she hopped up, bringing her toiletry bag in with her. As she stripped in the bathroom, she caught a glimpse of herself in the mirror. She'd lost some weight. Too much work, too much caffeine, too much chicken shawarma, not enough bacon and blue. She still had a decent body, she figured. Not Barbie proportions, but she had some hips. Her breasts weren't big, but they were round and high. She pulled her hair down and it cascaded in curly waves around her shoulders. Unremarkable brown. Hopefully she could pull this undercover thing off.

She jumped in the shower and made it a quick one, rinsing off the travel bugs. As she emerged from the bathroom with her hotel robe on, the knock came. She looked through the peep hole and let the service person bring in her tray. He was cute, about her age, and he took in the sight of her before he could check himself. "Enjoy your meal, ma'am. And I must tell you that you made a superb selection." He was probably expecting a football player to answer the door, considering the order.

As she dove into the feast, her phone buzzed. The text was from her boss, so she took a picture of the burger and sent it to him. *Atta girl,* was all he replied.

It was the morning following their third night in the North Dublin housing area. Tadgh and Sal had not done much. If they came off too eager, they'd be sniffed out immediately. So, they were content to mill around the common areas, sit on the benches drinking coffee as Sal fingered his prayer beads. He played his part well. His beard was coming in nicely after only a week, and Tadgh could honestly say that he would never have picked him out in the crowd. Tadgh got a few stares at first, but then they just seemed to blend into the scenery after the first two nights.

This morning, they were gathered around the meeting table with their copies of the case file. The task force members all piling in with a cup of tea, digging in the pastry box before taking their seat. They'd discussed the case, with no real developments.

DC Sullivan slapped the file down on the desk, feeling defeated. "I do have one update. The FBI has dispatched their agent as of two days ago. A Special Agent Charlie Ryan. He was hung up due to the weather. Stuck in Chicago, I believe, so our man missed him at the airport. He should be reporting in today. I got a text from him at midnight, saying he finally got in and took a cab to the hotel. So, we'll be meeting him this morning. Everyone will behave professionally." He shot a look at Detective Miller who was chewing his lip, arms crossed over his chest. "Once we decide what roll he's to play in all of this, I'll assign him to work with one of you in an official capacity. We'll call him a consultant. Nothing more. No one is to leak that this man is an FBI agent. I will be receiving more information on him once he arrives, as they didn't want to send any information over unsecured channels."

CHARLIE WAS BUZZING from the three cups of coffee she'd had at breakfast. She'd passed on the full Irish breakfast in lieu of some very grainy oatmeal with berries and a scone. The guest house she was staying in was perfectly inviting. The breakfast room had a fireplace because it was in an old building in Georgian Dublin. She was close enough to hop on a bus this first day and get dropped off right down the street from the Garda headquarters. One of the agents in the travel office had been on vacation in Ireland, and sold the idea that the guest houses were safer, less expensive, and she'd be fed once a day. So, no hotel for her. Which was good. She was posing as a new young American woman, wanting to live abroad. Holiday Inn didn't really fit the profile. She put the Leap card back in her bag and watched as they drove through the city streets. Dublin was modern enough in some areas, but the old world stonework, the traditional looking street lamps, and the painted pub signs reminded her that she was definitely not in Dearborn anymore. This wasn't like any city she'd ever been in. Some of the streets were still stone or brick. She felt a sense of excitement that had nothing to do with her job.

She'd never traveled outside of the US other than one cruise with her ex. Typical of his nature, he hadn't asked her where she'd like to go. He controlled everything, including her cruise itinerary and excursions. She had been younger. He'd been her first serious adult relationship. It took her a while to figure out that he was just a dickhead with a masculine face and alpha facade. Real men didn't need to control everything. Her boss was a good example. Loving husband, good dad, great boss, and gave her freedom to run her cases with little interference. He guided, he didn't try to leash her. She shook herself, looking at the street signs as the bus driver yelled out the next stop. Bingo, she was here.

She dug behind her ear. The wig she was wearing was itchy as hell. She hated wigs. It was short and black, a modern looking bob that was nothing like the unruly mane she'd been born with. She had heels, a black skirt, white silk blouse, and a fashionable, olive colored trench. Also nothing like what she normally wore. The problem was, she had to walk right down the streets of Dublin and into Garda headquarters. If she was going to work undercover in this city, dressed as herself, she needed to go in on the first day not dressed as herself. She slung the carry-on tote over her shoulder like a big purse. A knock off Prada that she'd bought from a refugee on the corner of her neighborhood block. He looked like he needed money, and she was willing to overlook the patent infringement in order to have a faux designer bag for this assignment. Her bag was stuffed with the day's supplies. She was carrying files, her credentials, and a change of clothes with her, as well as her wallet. She pushed the sunglasses up on her nose, even though it was cloudy in Dublin today. When she came to the building on Harcourt, she waltzed through the front door like she had a purpose. The officer at the front desk was a middle aged woman. She cleared her throat and spoke.

"Are ye lost, dear?" the woman asked.

Charlie leaned in, "I'm here to speak with DC Sullivan please." The woman seemed surprised.

"I believe he's in a meeting. Perhaps you could leave a message?"

"I am actually supposed to attend the meeting. I believe you will find me on your list. My name is Charlie Ryan. I'm a consultant, and he's expecting me this morning." She motioned to the visitor list.

Charlie was led down a long hallway filled with different Garda staff both in and out of uniform. Phones buzzed, people were talking, and they all stopped as she walked down the hall. Maybe the wig had been a bit much, but it's what they'd issued her from the office. Incognito until she was in place. She walked into the large conference room and the talking stopped. She took stock of everyone in the room. Most of them looked like your standard issue Irish cops. You could have seen these boys just as easily on the West side of Cleveland. Until they spoke, of course. The Officer Janet Tomblin introduced her. "I believe you are expecting Miss Ryan?"

You could have heard a pin drop. The Deputy Commissioner was visibly taken aback. He recovered quickly. "Yes, thank you Janet." He got up and guided the uniformed officer out of the room, then closed the door. He extended his hand. "Special Agent Charlie Ryan, I am DC Sullivan. Welcome to Ireland."

Everyone relaxed a smidge, and she exchanged pleasantries. She noticed two younger detectives down the table a bit. One was of Middle Eastern descent, which was good. Amazing actually. And by the look of his facial hair and dress, they had him on the street. His partner was a local. He met her eyes. *Holy shit.* He was ridiculous looking. Unbelievably good looking to the point of wondering if this was some sort of joke.

She looked away before the drool started dripping off her chin. That's when she met the eyes of a pudgy, hairy little dickhead. She didn't need for him to even open his mouth. She knew the type. Smug expression hiding a dull wit. His eyes said, *Oh look, they sent a girl.*

What the hell were they thinking? As if he'd read her mind, the idiot actually opened his mouth.

"This is the best the FBI had to spare? A wee lass in her mommy's heels? How the hell is Miss Fashion Plate going to work this investigation with our team if she can't break a nail?"

Charlie was boiling. She'd met this sort of asshole before. They were few and far between, but they were still out there. Like a fatally flawed, useless species that refused to die out.

"Well, fortunately you won't need to deal with me for very long, Detective Hairy Ass, because I will be working in an undercover capacity." Another stunned pause.

DC Sullivan said, "Excuse me, obviously we have some sorting out to do on what exactly your roll will be in this investigation, but I can assure you that Detective Hairy Arse will be shutting his fecking gob right now. He'll also be leaving the room to get me a cup of coffee... as well as one for you, Special Agent. How do you take your coffee?"

Charlie smiled. "Black, two sugars. Now if you'll excuse me, I need to find the locker room to freshen up a bit." Miller was sputtering, incensed that he'd been demoted to coffee bitch.

After Detective Miller had embarrassed the entire group in the space of a minute, no one was going to question her need to hit the privy. She got directions and walked out with her head held high, the head DC mumbling apologies and curses under his breath.

Tadgh was seething. That asshole Miller was a real piece of work. Granted, the elegant young woman that had come into the meeting hardly fit the stereotype for an FBI agent. She also looked nothing like the victims. She looked more like she should be on the runway. Sleek cut hair, fashionable clothes, edgy features. She was on the tall side as well, although, she'd been wearing high heels. He shook his head. When this meeting was over, he was going to have a chat with Detective Miller. Forget seniority. He had no business talking to a colleague like that, and certainly had no manners when it came to speaking with a lady.

The room was buzzing, everyone shocked at the turn of events. Charlie was obviously short for Charlene or Charlotte. He wondered if the masculine name was an attempt to seem masculine in what she perceived as a man's world. *Detective Hairy Ass...*Tadgh chuckled under his breath as he saw the little tosser come in the room with two fresh cups of coffee. Behind him, he noticed a young girl looking around in the various offices. She poked her head in the room and Tadgh realized she was older than she first appeared, but still young and lovely. Probably someone's wife. She had long wavy brown hair with golden highlights. She had it parted to the side, slung over in that casual, youthful way. Loose curls and waves spilling around like she'd just had a man's hands in it. No, she was certainly not a child. He couldn't say what exactly tipped him off. Maybe the hands. She had the same small, un-manicured hands.

"Hello love, are ye looking for yer da? What department is he in?" Sullivan said indulgently.

Charlie had been fast in the locker room. She had to be. She'd quickly washed off all of her make-up, ditched the wig and the entirety of her clothing, and slid into her low slung Levis and Cleveland Indians mini-T. Converse sneakers, a leather belt. no jewelry, and her outfit was complete. With no make up and all that unruly hair down, she looked about twenty. She also lost five inches and about ten pounds when she'd ditched the trench and high heels.

She had a sliver of belly showing just beneath her t-shirt. Now, as she looked around the room, no one seemed the wiser...except for pretty boy. He had his head down, suppressing a grin. *He knows*, she thought. He knew it was her, but he was letting her have this moment. *A gentleman to boot.*

"Well, now. I was just waiting for that black with two sugars. Thanks Detective Hairy Ass." Then she reached over DC Sullivan and plucked her coffee out of Miller's pudgy little fist.

Sal cracked off a laugh, then started the slow clap. The agent winked at him and took her seat. The laughter rumbled through the room, and even hairy assed Detective Miller finally smiled, giving her a bow. She stole a glance at the handsome detective who had wisely kept his own counsel. He was smiling and gave her an appreciative nod as if to say...*Well played.*

Call the priest. Tadgh was in love. The meeting continued as DC Sullivan went around the table, introducing all of the members of the task force.

"And the youngsters down on the end are our men in the field. Detective Rahim Salib, but we call him Sal. The pretty one is Detective Tadgh O'Brien. They are working in plain clothes, combing the neighborhoods with a concentration of Arabic speaking refugees. If you see them out and about, stay clear. They are intelligence gathering only, no infiltration will be attempted."

Charlie nodded at both the men. "Detectives, it's good to know we've got someone planted on the ground. I'll be wanting to meet with you regularly. On the sly, of course." She could have sworn the one named Sal kicked Tadgh under the table. She didn't see it, but Tadgh jerked, then mumbled something.

"Absolutely. The sooner the better." Tadgh said.

Charlie looked at Sullivan. "I'll be securing housing sometime this week, once I've gone over the geography of the city and seen a detailed map of the disappearance and disposal areas. I want to know where these women lived, where they disappeared, and where they were found. Then a list of potential housing areas for me to set up camp. I don't need much, but I should like a mattress and some basic cookware if you can point me in the direction of a home store."

DC Sullivan was rubbing his forehead, the stress evident on his face. "I'm not sure that's a good idea. We can certainly find you accommodations, but undercover? I don't like it. You aren't armed, you've got no back up if you are out on your own. I just can't use you as bait, for Christ sake!" He was starting to get upset.

Charlie put a hand on his arm and looked him in the eyes. "There are a lot of American women milling around this city. It may not even work. The FBI sent surveillance equipment. I have it in my hotel room. GPS trackers for you to keep a location on me, and some extras in case you need them for someone else." Her eyes went to Tadgh and Sal. "They paid the freight so I could bring it on the plane with me. They are willing to back you up with IT support, forensics, anything you need. The US Government has a lot of toys, and they will share.

Anything we use during this case, you get to keep for your department. You just need to play this my way. I need to be on the ground. Not in some patrol car showing up after another girl is already dead. Let me do my job. I promise I will be careful. I will keep in constant contact."

God damn. She was good. Bribery worked on a lot of administrators in any field of work. New toys for the department. Nice touch. But Sullivan was not one of those types of administrators. Tadgh was with him completely with regard to the undercover work. Christ, he didn't even want Tadgh and Sal trying to infiltrate. Sending this small, young female into the lion's den basted in blood? No way. He didn't like it. He hated the whole bloody idea. He needed to talk some sense into this woman. He wouldn't do it in front of the men. She'd had to work for their respect. It sucked, but it was the reality. He wouldn't undermine her progress with them by challenging her at the table. Later though, she was going to hear him out. His mind flashed to those three dead girls. She was perfect for the undercover work. Fit the bill, so to speak. Just another reason to nip this in the bud.

TADGH WAS PACKING up his paperwork after the meeting, when a soft voice spoke. "What tipped you off?" He looked up and his heart jumped in his chest. Those eyes. Like moss and amber, glowing as if lit from behind. She had a smirk and one hand on her hip, the other resting on the back of a chair. He straightened, and had to look down to look at her. Now that she'd lost the high heels and was right next to him, he was aware of how small she really was. The low slung jeans and the tight t-shirt didn't hide her behind the bulky clothing she was wearing before. Her coat had obviously had shoulder pads. He exhaled on a tight laugh.

"I wasn't sure until I looked at your hands. Ye've got wee hands for someone that appeared much taller and broader. And no manicure. The nails are cut to the quick, clean, no polish. Someone with the look of you would be more into their nails, unless I'm being a chauvinist?"

She smiled. "No, not at all. You're right of course. You were the only one who picked up on it. The long nails aren't cohesive to the job or my lifestyle. They get hung up in the trigger guard." She was being a smart ass, and he loved it. "Thank you, though. For not blowing my cover."

Tadgh sighed. "Miller is an ass. A hairy, obnoxious ass. I'm sorry about that, but it seems you've sorted him out on your own." Sal approached them and Tadgh turned to him. "Special Agent Ryan, this is my partner and interpreter. It goes without saying that if you see either of us about, you should just ignore us."

Sal shook her hand and she addressed them both. "Call me Charlie. No one calls me Charlotte and since I'm undercover, you can drop the title as well. I will stay out of your hair. I do have GPS units that will hook into the same software as my tracker. I think it's a good idea to keep it consistent and they are small enough to hide. I wouldn't use your phone, because that can be taken. Maybe some sort of jewelry or belt?" They both nodded. "I also see you are both armed. That's good. I know that isn't as commonplace in Ireland, but it's a good idea. I wish they'd have extended me the same courtesy," she said with a tight brow.

Tadgh said, "I wanted to speak with you in private, away from the others, when you have a minute."

She narrowed her eyes at him. There was nothing seductive in his tone, which only left one explanation. "Detective O'Brien. I have one boss, and it isn't you. I appreciate your discretion today, and I admit I may owe you a beer for that bit of grace, but that's as far as it goes. You aren't going to talk me out of this. Period. I am here to do a job, the same as you. I have my instructions. As much as I would love to say that I was assigned this job strictly due to my investigative genius, we both know differently. All you need to do is look at that file, then look at me. I was chosen for this and I will see it through."

Tadgh tightened his jaw. "Well, maybe in America they have no problem putting your ass on the line unnecessarily, but in Ireland…"

"Any trouble here, lads?" Sullivan was suddenly standing there, looking back and forth between Tadgh and Charlie. "Special Agent

53

Ryan? Or should I call you Charlotte?" Sullivan's Irish was thick, and the side of her mouth turned up as she listened to him.

"It's Charlie, and no. Detective O'Brien was just personally welcoming me to Ireland." Then she walked away, grabbing her bag as she went. She said over her shoulder. "I'll need a rental negotiator. I can't stay in that guesthouse, no matter how good the breakfast was. It's too touristy. I'll be waiting in your office, Sir."

As they watched her walk away, Tadgh turned to his new boss. "You can't let her do this. It's too dangerous." Sal's brows went up and he took a step back. Tadgh didn't give a shit if he was coming on too strong. This was important.

Sullivan crossed his arms over his chest, meeting Tadgh's eye. "I'll excuse the insubordinate tone, for no other reason than I know your uncle. Trying to talk an O'Brien down off the ceiling when there's a woman involved is like pissin' in the wind. Now, as for Charlie. You've got your own job to do. She isn't your problem. Ah..."

He put a finger up as Tadgh started to interrupt. "Shut your gob, O'Brien. I don't like being interrupted. She isn't your problem, but...if you happened to be gathering intel in the same location as she, some of the time, it might be a fortunate coincidence. Seeing how we'll be tracking her, that shouldn't be too hard." His grin was wide and Tadgh exhaled on a laugh. "We're not going to talk the Feds out of this. She wouldn't change her marching orders out of fear anymore than you two would. Just watch her, but be subtle. At the times when you aren't with Sal, that would be a good time. It's going to mean a few more hours on the job, but..."

Tadgh did interrupt this time, "Consider it done."

Sullivan nodded, his black and silver hair a little too long in the front and bobbing into his brows. "She won't like it if she thinks we don't trust her to do her job." He rubbed his eyes, and he looked tired. "Christ, don't let anything happen to the lass. I'd never forgive myself."

* * *

CHARLIE WAS LED out a side exit of the Garda headquart
discretely placed door that was down an adjoining hallway
the two buildings. From the outside, you would never know
been at the police station. "We use it to avoid the press, if w
high profile case. We installed a connecter a few years ago. 1
in handy a time or two. You have a key to the first door, but s
will have to buzz you in after that."

"Thank you Sergeant Tomblin, I appreciate your help t
Charlie smiled at the woman.

"Not at all, dear. And, call me Janet. We women have to s
together, aye? Ye can't be carrying a change o'clothes around with
all the time, now can you? Just make sure yer tail is clear before y
use the doorway."

Charlie liked this woman. Her accent was thicker than some of the
other officers. "You're not from Dublin, are you?"

Janet laughed. "God, no. I came from County Cork ten years back.
Thought I'd find some excitement. I didn't know I'd given up my last
decent parking spot for the rest of my days. I hope your boss is
picking up the parking fees."

It was colder now, but she didn't want to put the big trench coat
on with her jeans and sneakers. It was late fall in Ireland, which meant
the temperatures and weather were still temperamental. She shivered
as she clutched her bag and headed for the bus. Luckily she'd packed
warm clothing.

* * *

TADGH AND SAL watched as the young agent got on the bus. Tadgh's
body was tight, tense. Sal said, "We need to get back to my hovel,
Tadgh. She's fine. She's not going to work today. You heard her. She's
apartment hunting. She'll be fine."

Tadgh looked at his partner. "I didn't say anything."

Sal laughed. "You didn't have to, brother. You were ready to run
after her and put your coat around her shoulders. You're going to
have to cool it, though. She's not going to appreciate you treating her

like an incompetent girl. We'll keep an eye on her, but our job is elsewhere. We need to be subtle."

Tadgh shook off the comment. "Let's head over." He looked at his phone. "I need to break off at seven, tonight. My cousin's girlfriend is in the ballet. It's the only time I'll get to see it."

Sal's brows went up. "Wow, is she the lead dancer?"

"No, she's got a sort of medium sized part, according to her. I know shite about the ballet, but she's a beautiful dancer. I'll just be there for support. Getting my schedule coordinated with Liam's has been a chore. He practically lives at the hospital. We've been taking turns escorting her since this all started."

Sal nodded, shaking himself. "I understand. My wife has agreed to stay out of the city. I know she doesn't fit the profile, but we don't know how many we're dealing with. How deep this goes. It can't just be one guy. Someone has to be driving. You need wheels for this sort of crime. A way to move the girl...and then the body." And didn't that just hang between them.

* * *

"IF I BE WASPISH, *best beware my sting."*
The Taming of the Shrew...William Shakespeare

IT WAS HALF past four when Tadgh and Sal settled at the garden table, between the buildings of the housing complex. They'd made a production of taking a bit of household goods up to the apartment. As they'd hoped, a couple of young men came to their aid as an older man held the door. They'd figured out, relatively soon after, that this was the family that the foot patrol had become familiar with. They talked easily with the two sons, one about nineteen and one a younger, school-aged teenager. They kept the chatter light, building a rapport. Now, as the two men sat facing each other with a cup of tea in their hands, they fell into an easy silence. Until Tadgh watched Sal's

body tense and his face wash with dread. "By all that is holy. You must be joking."

Tadgh turned toward the street and swore under his breath. Special Agent Ryan was walking with an older woman. She was dressed as she had been, but with a cropped pea coat to keep her warm. That's where the good sense ended, however. This woman was obviously helping her find a flat. Right in the worst possible area.

"You can't approach her. You know you can't" Even as Sal spoke, he noticed the different residents turning heads to watch her. Especially the younger men. "I realize that, Sal. Thank you." Tadgh got up and walked around the other side of the building, Sal following him at a hurried pace. When they got into the surveillance flat, Tadgh immediately called Liam.

* * *

"Now, you realize that the rent will be more if you go month to month. Can I convince you to look over a year long lease?"

Charlie was trying to look sufficiently clueless and misguided. "Oh, no. It's okay. My parents will pay the difference. I just never know when I'm going to bug out." She smiled, putting on her best, flaky millennial grin. "I like to keep my options open. I was thinking of doing a trip to Eastern Europe for the summer. Month to month is perfect."

As she talked, the woman glanced at her phone for the third time. "Forgive me, I am going to need to head back to the office. Apparently there's some sort of issue. You said you have a few days left in the guest house, so how about we meet for breakfast tomorrow morning? I can drive you back to the hotel or take you to a car rental place I do business with. It's on the way."

Charlie's brows were furrowed, because her phone was buzzing as well. She picked it up and looked at the screen. *I sent a man to pick you up. Pretend you know him. Look out your south facing window. -DC Sullivan*

Charlie went to the window, and sure enough, a young man was waiting. He gave a little wave. For a moment, she thought it was the officer she'd met before. He was about the same age, but he was broader in the shoulders and there were other differences.

* * *

LIAM WAS GRINNING as an attractive woman came out of the apartment building. Her realtor had been called away, a diversion Tadgh's boss had created by calling the office. "Miss Ryan?" She lifted a brow. "I've been sent to fetch ye to the car hire, and I was to tell you that we've found a flat for you."

She narrowed her eyes at him, ready to argue. Then she remembered where they were. She left without a fuss. Once they were in the car, she turned to Liam. "What is your name, and I want to see some credentials." She knew he must be legit. The text had been from Sullivan and no one else had her burner phone number. But something was off. This guy was off. Liam looked at her, mute but for a grin he was suppressing. "You aren't a cop, are you?" she asked. She went to open the door when a voice came from the back seat.

"No, he's not. He's my cousin. Drive, Liam."

She squeaked before she could help it. She hadn't seen anyone in the backseat, but there was a blanket and a duffel in the back. "Holy shit, O'Brien! You are so lucky I'm not armed! What in the hell were you thinking? And you!" She pointed to Liam. "Pull this car over right now." She said the last while gritting the words between her teeth.

He reared back. "Tadgh, she's scaring me. She looks like Ma when she's in a temper." Tadgh was chuckling in the back.

Charlie flipped around. "Are you laughing? This is not funny. Jesus Christ this is so unprofessional! How dare you send me a message and pretend to be DC Sullivan. You are in deep shit O'Brien. And, I told you pull over!" She said that at Liam who cringed away a little, but kept driving.

They'd cleared the housing area, and Tadgh sat up. "Liam, pull over in that public park and give us a minute, aye?" Liam did, and as soon as he put the car in park, Charlie tried to exit the car. Tadgh put a hand on her shoulder.

"Easy lass. He's going. You're staying." Her look was murderous as Liam hopped out of the car, leaving it running. Before she could start in on him, Tadgh said, "I'm sorry. I didn't know how to get you out of there without an argument. There's no harm done. Your realtor was leaving anyway." Her mouth dropped. "And before you go pitching a fit, Sullivan knows. Who do ye think got your realtor back to the office?"

Charlie shut her eyes. She couldn't concentrate on being pissed at him if she had to stare at those golden colored eyes and those dimples. "What on earth was so important that you had to pull me out of there? I was ready to seal the deal with that apartment." Then her eyes shot open. "Oh, God. It's not another girl is it? Another victim?"

Tadgh's face twisted a bit. "Of course not. Ye think we'd be joking and such, if there was a dead girl found? Ye might not like my methods, Charlie, but I'm not the sort to take a murdered girl lightly. It's about the apartment. You can't live there. That's where we've got Sal set up and where we're doing our own surveillance. Besides, you stick out like a sore thumb. It's not going to have the effect you think." She opened her mouth to argue and he put one finger up. "Christ, woman. This will go faster if ye don't interrupt. I promise I'll be brief."

She closed her mouth and he continued. He was trying not to grin, which was hard. She looked like she was ready to launch her little ass over the seat and start beating on him. He half wished she would.

"They're clannish people. It's too obvious. No American girl studying or working abroad would ever choose that area to live in and no girls have gone missing from there. You'd just be asking for trouble and you'd be a distraction for our mission."

Charlie put an arm up on the back of the seat, meeting his eyes now. "I disagree. I think if I'm going to be bait, it's the perfect location. It's not your call."

Tadgh had been taking a light hand with her up until this point, but she was starting to get his dander up. "It is my call. You put our mission at risk. It's too much activity in one area, for starters. This isn't the only area where there are refugees and resettled Muslims. We had reasons for choosing it, but we don't have any reason to be sure the killer or killers are from that neighborhood. Secondly, the girls were taken from varying parts of town. They had things in common, but they all lived in predominately caucasian neighborhoods. If you hadn't stormed off with your little victory in hand this morning, we could have briefed you more thoroughly. The final point is that this could absolutely be someone that wants us to think it's a refugee, and the Arabic letters in their skin is a way to throw us off the scent of an Irishman. You can't be under our feet, ignoring the other parts of the city."

Charlie was grinding her teeth. Shit. He was right. She hated it, but he was right. She let out a big breath. "Okay. I'll hold off. Show me what you have on the girls and I will reconsider the location." Tadgh's brows went up. "What? I'm not that stubborn." She shrugged one shoulder, then gave him a sideways glance. The corner of her mouth went up. "Well, not always. I just got here, I don't know the area, and I should have asked for some guidance. So, now I'm asking."

Tadgh's body relaxed, the relief palpable. "Okay. You'll come back with me to another area of town once we get your car. You'll have to drive. My cousin has business and I'm on a motorcycle most days. As for the apartment building, it's central, near some churches, not too far from the station. There's a self catering flat that's empty for as long as you need. I know the owner."

LIAM PULLED up to the car rental storefront and Charlie got out. Tadgh exited the back seat, but Liam called him back. "Seven o'clock, don't forget. And don't worry, Patrick took care of what needed done. He just texted me." Tadgh gave him a fist bump and went to leave. "Oh, and Tadgh…are ye sure she's not a Mullen?" Tadgh slammed the door to the sound of Liam's laughter.

The car hiring process was quick, so it was only an hour until they were pulling into the parking garage that serviced the City Center.

Charlie was surprised to see Tadgh use a key to get in the main entrance. "You have a key?"

"Aye," he said. And that was it. Charlie sighed heavily. "D(here?" Tadgh just nodded.

She stopped dead in the hall. It took him a minute to rea wasn't behind him. He turned to look at her. A brow went t folded her arms over her chest. "It's my experience that peopl give inappropriately short answers are deliberately withholding mation. They reveal as little as possible in order to avoid lying."

Tadgh was so surprised that he barked out a laugh before he c help it. "Interrogation Tactics 101?" She said nothing.

"Yes, I live in the building. No, I won't stalk you. Yes, it's a per location for what you're doing. Any other concerns?" She dropped h arms and started walking again. Tadgh agreed with her earlier stat ment. He was certainly lucky she wasn't armed.

Tadgh opened the apartment and led Special Agent Ryan through the door. She looked around, assessing the place. "I hope you're not allergic to cats. The owner has one, but he's not here for the next few months. Not sure if there's any residual cat hair or dander. He keeps it very clean, though." Tadgh walked over to the first bedroom and said, "This is yours. The other will stay locked. He uses it for storage."

Charlie knew something was up. She had the instincts of a mother lioness. "Who do I pay?"

Tadgh waved a hand dismissively. "We'll sort it out later. You can move in tomorrow morning. For now, I can give you directions back to the B&B." He began walking her back to the door, and she almost went. Almost. She stopped and did an about face. Before Tadgh could stop her, she walked into the kitchen and opened the refrigerator. *Busted.*

She closed the well stocked fridge that was full of not only food and beer, but fresh leftovers. She walked over to the second bedroom and said, "Open it." He started to argue but she cut him off. "Open it or I walk. Then, I take the other apartment."

He cursed under his breath, walked to the door, took a small wire key off the top of the frame, and opened it. She walked in without

invitation. She looked around once, then walked right to the dresser, opened the top drawer and he interrupted. "Do ye fancy men's under-wear then?" She ignored him and went to the bottom drawer. That's when she heard him exhale harshly. She pulled out the pictures of Tadgh with his family, one old framed photo of his da in uniform. She placed them back on the dresser, where the dust mark showed that something was missing.

"Well, I guess I should have known better. You are an FBI agent."

She turned around, suppressing a smile. "Where exactly were you going to live, Detective O'Brien? The boiler room?"

Tadgh was scrubbing his face with one hand, the other leaning on the doorjamb of the bedroom. "I only had an hour. Give me a little credit, at least."

She cocked her head. "There is no reason for me to take your apartment. I can find something else. This is completely unnecessary." She laughed a little. "I mean…what were you going to do? Have me do a quick walk through, usher me out the door, and spend all night cleaning out your clothes and the fridge? Where in the hell were you planning on staying?"

Tadgh sighed. "My cousin Patrick lives in the flat above this one with his wife. She's gone to her parents home until this has all blown over. You'll meet him, actually. He's Garda as well."

Charlie couldn't believe this guy. He was big and muscular, too good looking to be real, pushy, and…she hated to admit…kind of adorable. "Why are you doing this? You don't even know me. Why wouldn't you just let me get a realtor and go find some place in another part of town?"

Tadgh could feel his ears turning red. God, she was so pretty. Not in a bombshell type of way, not in a sexy made-up kind of way. She had smart, beautiful eyes and a crooked little grin. She had a temper to battle the women in his family. How could he explain to her that the minute he laid eyes on her, he felt an overwhelming need to protect her?

"You saw the file. You saw the photos. You can't go off half-cocked waving your cute little American ass around hoping some

sick nutter decides to take the bait. You need someone watching your back."

Charlie bristled. "Half-cocked? Excuse me, Detective O'Brien. How long have you been in law enforcement?"

Tadgh shrugged. "Just over three years. Why?"

"Well, because I became a Cleveland PD patrol officer at age twenty-one. I worked nights in the worst part of the city so I could finish my bachelor's degree. I did that for over two years. I was recruited by the FBI and left the department. I finished at Quantico second in my class. I wasn't first because my hands are small and my shooting wasn't as good as the other guy's. Once I graduated, I spent two years in Miami in the fraud division. I transferred to the Human Rights Crime Unit eighteen months ago. I've worked in Dearborn, Michigan which has, arguably, some of the highest terrorist activity in the U.S. So you see Detective, I easily have twice the time you do working in multiple facets of law enforcement. Please do me the courtesy of not treating me like a Girl Scout that needs an escort to go on cookie patrol." She swung her bag on her arm more securely and walked past him, through the doorway.

His voice was soft. "Charlie, please."

She stopped, not facing him. Pausing.

"Just give this a chance. You can tell your field office that the Garda Headquarters has provided you with a flat. It won't be a lie. Ye don't have to deal with me at all. I just want to know you're safe. It's not a matter of competence. It's just plain fear. You look like them. That's why they sent you. You're young and pretty and you've got your whole life ahead of you. Just like they did. You're also used to being armed, and you won't have a side arm with you now. Just... please. Christ, just try it. If it isn't working, ye've lost nothing. You can call your realtor and relocate."

Charlie turned around and looked at him, and her heart skipped a beat at his face. Genuine concern, pleading even. Had anyone ever looked at her with that kind of concern? *Your little brother.* She shut her eyes, the thought of Josh stinging.

She didn't have experience with a lot of selfless men. It was hard for her to trust it. "Does your boss know you're doing this?" Tadgh shook his head.

"He won't be a problem. He's half ready to chain you to a desk."

She walked toward the apartment door and said, "I'd like to see you both try it." Then she flipped around. "We'll take it one week at a time. If I don't make any progress after a while, I might have to relocate. It won't be anything personal."

Tadgh let out a breath. "A week. And I'll stay out of your hair. I swear it." She opened the door and turned to him, a playful smile on her face. "When you take your food out of the fridge, I wouldn't be mad if you left me the bacon." She closed the door and heard his sweet laughter.

* * *

CHARLIE SAT behind the wheel of her car and just stared at nothing. What in the hell had she just agreed to? As endearing as the detective was, this was a bad idea. She paused her thinking...*or is it?* It was a prime location and it was furnished. She needed to be in the neighborhoods. She'd been briefed on the similarities of the victims while she drove to the apartment. She also noticed that Detective O'Brien's operational security was sound. His cousin Liam was not a police officer, even though he had several cops in the family. Tadgh wasn't loose-lipped about the case in front of him.

The similarities between the victims were age, physical description to a point, and they were all on long-term stays in Ireland. No tourists, which was interesting. The truth was that tourists weren't usually alone for long periods of time. Young women traveled with family, lovers, husbands, or friends. You didn't see them travel alone as often. A student or person on a work visa, or even an expatriate might indeed have times where they were walking alone. They lived in residential areas, knew the back streets. Hotel lined areas and big attractions had a lot of people milling around. Pubs were buzzing with activity. They'd also lived in areas with similar people, like Tadgh had said. Predominantly white, European neighbors, middle class houses and apartment complexes.

Charlie started to turn the key in the ignition when she realized she didn't actually need to move her rental car. This parking garage serviced the entire district she was living in. Both the apartment and the B&B she was staying in. She couldn't move in until tomorrow, so she got out, locked the car, and started toward the guesthouse. She needed to check in with Assistant Director Schroeder. He was like a hovering mother when she didn't call.

* * *

"Well, that's very nice of them. Considering the ten thousand dollars worth of equipment we just handed over to them, I guess it's a good trade," said Assistant Director Schroeder. "And you feel safe, like you have support?"

Charlie's mind flashed to the two shaggy, undercover detectives she'd met the previous morning. "Absolutely. They're going above and beyond. I've actually had to tell them to back off a bit. They don't like me in the field."

Gabe grunted. "Well, I don't like it either. You're good at your job, though, Charlie. If you need me to make a call at any point, set them straight on that account, you just say the word. And keep me in the loop."

CHAPTER 6

*T*adgh slid into the seat next to Liam just before the doors were closed and the lights were dimmed. Program in hand and straightening one of two ties he owned, he whispered his apology. Liam smiled sideways. "Aye, well if I hadn't seen her in the flesh, I might be put out. Did ye pull it off?"

Tadgh exhaled, "If ye could call it that. She sniffed me out, literally. She opened the fridge."

Liam chuckled. "Pretty and smart. You should have given Patrick a bit more time." They hushed as the orchestra started, the curtains opening.

The performance was the ballet *Giselle,* a romantic ballet about a young peasant girl who falls in love with a nobleman. He disguises himself as a common man, but is already betrothed. Giselle dies of a broken heart. Eve was not the lead, but played and danced the part of Bathilde, the Duke's betrothed and the daughter of another Duke. She was marvelous. Lovely and delicate, with the flawless strength of a gifted dancer. Tadgh watched as Liam's chest swelled with pride. Eve worked hard and she'd earned this small bit of fame. A sweet, spritely little darlin' that had come to the big city from a village in County Cork. Unlike most O'Brien relationships, this one had begun flawlessly. Liam adored her. Everyone did, even her audience.

* * *

CHARLIE WALKED into a small church located in the heart of Dublin. The bigger cathedrals were on her bucket list during her free time, but this smaller local church seemed more in line with what someone who lived in the area would visit. It was a weekday, and mass had just ended, but she wanted to have a look around and she wanted to be seen walking in.

"Hello, Miss. Can I help you?" Charlie turned around to find an elderly man standing there with a warm smile and wearing a priest frock. She'd been born into a family that was multi-denominational. They argued about which was right, fought over how the kids should be christened, but no one actually went to church or practiced any of it. She'd become disillusioned with the whole idea pretty early on. She didn't have anything against the church. It just wasn't how she lived. Her father had only ever embraced the "spare the rod" bit of scripture, and he'd extended that philosophy to her mother as well.

"Hello Father. I hope I'm not disturbing you. I'm just new to the neighborhood. I wanted to acquaint myself with the church."

"Oh, not at all dear. I'm Father Malichi. Feel free to stay as long as you like. We give a daily mass and two on Sunday. I hope you enjoy our city. American?"

She nodded. "Yes, and thank you. I'll just be a few minutes. I love old churches. The architecture and the art; I just like to sit."

The priest smiled and nodded. "Ah, yes. The Roman Catholic church often wins on aesthetics. I'll leave you to it, Miss?"

She extended her hand. "Charlie Ryan. It's a pleasure, Father."

As Charlie wandered around the beautiful sanctuary, she looked at the icons, the art, and the lovely stained glass and thought about the church she'd gone to only twice as a kid. How coincidental that this priest was named after the same saint. Saint Malichi Parish in Cleveland. It was one of the oldest in the city, full of West side Irish

Catholics who had not abandoned it for the newer suburban parishes. Her family never attended mass. She'd gone for two funerals. Once for a co-worker of her father's, and then once for the funeral of her father's sister. She'd been Charlie's favorite aunt. A small buffer between the rough and angry home environment she lived in, and the occasional trip for ice cream or sleepover at her Aunt Cassie's house. She'd taken the loss hard.

Her mother was German and English, as far as she knew. She was a protestant of some sort, but she'd been too afraid to defy the emperor and sneak her kids to any sort of church. Charlie's heart sank at the thought of her little brother, Josh. So sweet, so beautiful. Bigger than her father, taking his genetics from her mom's side. He was seventeen and trapped. Trapped in a home where his mother wouldn't leave and his father wouldn't love him. He was safe to a point. When Charlie had entered law enforcement, she'd finally had the power to push back. No safety mechanism was absolute, though. And there was more than one way to hurt someone. She closed her eyes. Nine more months...then he would be eighteen.

"This place can make people sad. Would you like to sit?" The voice was deep, but feminine with an Eastern European accent. Charlie jumped a bit, noticing the young woman that had come in behind her. She turned. "I'm sorry, madam. I didn't mean to...be scary to you." The woman was pretty, about twenty. Slim, long dark hair, blue eyes, olive skin, and the beautiful features that you saw in the models of the Eastern block.

"It's okay. I was just thinking of someone. I was distracted." Charlie slid next to the woman, feeling the cool oak and the solid structure of a very old church pew. "It's beautiful here." She put her hand out. "Charlie, it's nice to meet you. Your English is very good and your accent is lovely. Something Eastern?" The girl smiled, a little overlap in her front teeth making her seem a little more human. "Russian. Yes. My name is Tatyana. I'm sorry, I don't tell the difference in American or Canadian."

Charlie smiled, "American. I'm living abroad for a year."

TADGH WAITED OUTSIDE of the church at a safe distance. He'd left his motorcycle in the garage, heading out on foot early this morning. He'd seen the American agent leave her B&B and followed at a safe distance. His ball cap pulled down to shadow his face to a degree, but not so much as to appear to be hiding it. The streets were buzzing with the late morning traffic and tourists, even though this was a slower time for tourism in the grander picture.

Fall in Ireland was beautiful and damp. Color swirling with the textured air, always saturated with the sea. Ireland was, at its simplest, an island. So, the weather and the wind and the latitude meant that it never stayed hot for long. It also didn't snow very often. Cold rain and dim skies just rolled in and out at regular intervals. It was beginning to mist, and Tadgh pulled the collar of his coat up, thumbing the phone in his pocket as he kept his hands out of the damp. He slinked back behind the edge of a building as he saw Charlie walk out of the church.

She was sliding a hat over her wild, wavy hair. She had her head on a swivel, and he liked that. She needed to be attentive, aware of her surroundings. He hated that the Irish government had put their foot down about her bringing a weapon into the country. Stupidity. She was law enforcement and she was within her jurisdiction, as odd as that seemed. She was currently assigned to the International Human Rights Crime Unit. He'd read up on it a bit last night. He checked his phone and realized that he was supposed to meet her in fifteen minutes. She was headed toward the flat on foot. *Shit.* He ducked down an alley, needing to arrive before her.

* * *

TADGH WAS GIVING the counter one last wipe down when he heard a knock. He'd moved many of his everyday belongings upstairs last evening. Clothing for the next few months, toiletries, some kitchen items, books, food, work stuff, and his computer. Caitlyn and Patrick had a two bedroom as well. As he'd put the items away in the spare room, he thought about what the room should have been used for. His heart broke for both of them. They hadn't decorated it, because both of Caitlyn's miscarriages had been in the first trimester, but the room was supposed to be a nursery. Tadgh had a two bedroom because the landlord liked having cops in the building, and he'd negotiated the extra room fairly easily. He had a lot of family, and he wanted them to be able to stay with him when they drove to Dublin.

Charlie walked in rolling a large suitcase with her. She had two bags thrown over her shoulder, and a smaller case stacked on the rolling suitcase. "Christ, I would have helped you," Tadgh said as he tried to take a bag.

"I've got it. Don't mess with the system or I'll topple over." She grunted as she spoke. "That garage is a little bit of a walk, so I tried to get it in one trip." She walked through the living space and dropped the two bags. She carefully took the top bag and propped it on the couch. She cracked her neck and focused on Tadgh. "You sure about this?"

"Absolutely. Let's give ye a tour. A real one this time," he said with a grin. As he took her into the kitchen, she watched as he oriented her to the cabinets and drawers. He explained the cooker and small dishwasher. She noticed all of the appliances were small, and there was actually a combo type washer/dryer in the kitchen.

She looked Tadgh up and down. "That washer probably holds one pair of your socks."

He nodded. "Sorry, it's probably a lot smaller than you're used to. Don't overstuff it or the clothes won't get clean. Maybe about six pieces of clothing and that's it. Now, as for the bedroom. The closet has a few items in it, but the rest of the room is yours. So is the dresser. I've cleaned out the medicine cabinet, so feel free to use that as well. The shower is small, but the pressure is good."

Charlie looked in the closet and saw two items. What looked like a baby pack-n-play and a booster high chair. "Do you have a child? Jesus, I can't kick you out of your apartment if you..."

Tadgh put a hand up. "No, no. I keep that for my family. My

cousins and their families. We're close, you see. More like siblings. Six wee ones and another on the way. If they come to the city, I just keep it on hand. I've got family on the Donoghue side as well. And more family living in England. I don't want them having to... What? Why are you looking at me like that?"

Charlie knew what must be showing on her face. Shock mixed with some sappy female look. "You have juice boxes and animal crackers in your cupboard and you keep baby gear on hand for your cousins' kids?"

Tadgh scrunched a brow. "Yes, and?"

Charlie shook her head, clearing it. "Nothing. It's just...nice. Most single men wouldn't think of that kind of stuff."

Tadgh just shrugged. "I appreciate what I have, and I love my family. Anyway, here in this chest is extra linen and more blankets, although the place stays pretty warm. If it gets too warm, just slide the windows open. Ye get a fair cross breeze. And if you need anything, call, text, or just climb up the fire escape to the flat above."

Tadgh watched the beautiful young woman looking around his apartment and decided he should just drop to his knees and beg to be roommates. That shit had worked out in Michael's favor spectacularly, and Tadgh was way nicer than Michael. Christ, she was a pretty woman. She was tough, no frills, but absolutely lovely. She was also smart. She was currently waging a little battle, deciding whether this had been a mistake.

"You haven't signed a lease. You can bail at anytime if this isn't working for you. I promise, there are no strings attached." She seemed surprised.

"Anyone ever tell you that you're good at reading people?" she asked. "I just feel like this is a bad idea. It's not about strings. It's about taking advantage. We have funds to house me."

Tadgh shook his head. "No, this is not an inconvenience. My cousin Patrick is fine with it. He needs a roommate right now. By himself and crawling around in his own head is not where he needs to be. We've moved his wife out of the city for her safety...and they've had a hard time. They've just lost a baby this past year for the second

71

time. Couple that with the murders, he needs me around. It works for everyone."

She cocked her head. "You take care of people. Is that what you think you're doing with me?"

Tadgh looked away, a blush starting on his cheeks. "This works for everyone. If it starts not working, you've lost nothing. I'll head up and leave you to it," he said, motioning to her luggage.

Charlie sighed, "Look, I didn't mean that..."

He cut her off. "Not at all. Just let me know if you need anything." As he turned toward the window, planning on exiting out the fire escape, his phone went off. Three seconds later, Charlie's started ringing. Dread washed over the room. There was only one reason they'd both be getting a call from headquarters.

* * *

"I NEED to go to the scene. I'll be discreet." As she spoke, Charlie was fixing her wig in place, then a pair of faux spectacles. Janet walked in and handed her a navy blue jacket.

DC Sullivan cursed. "You're a co-conspirator, I see?"

Janet just shrugged. "Sisters before Misters and all that." Then she winked at Charlie.

Charlie slid on the jacket with the Garda insignia on the back. Then she started with the lipstick. Her khakis, sensible leather shoes and white shirt paired with Janet's jacket and the short black wig, no one would recognize her. "I'm not asking permission. You agreed to this. Who do I ride with?"

As she spoke, Tadgh and Sal came into the roll call room. "You two stay clear. Get out on the street. Keep in touch. Continue to use the unmarked entrance." He looked at Charlie then. "Okay, Special Agent. You ride with me. Just remember you are a guest."

Tadgh pulled Charlie aside as she was headed out. "Look around, see if anyone's watching from a distance."

Charlie nodded. She was on the same page. Serial killers often liked to observe the crime scene, see their handiwork go public.

"Take note of the women, too. Not just men."

Charlie frowned, "I thought you were sure the killer was a man?"

He paused. "We are. Just…just don't discount the women at the scene."

Charlie stared him in the eye. "Jesus, you are wondering if there's a woman accomplice. Maybe a wife or something. Have you shared this theory?"

Tadgh grunted frustration, "I'm sharing it now. I have absolutely no reason other than I haven't ruled it out. I may be totally off base. We just can't assume anything, ye understand?"

Charlie nodded. "I do, and you're right. It's just as likely as any other scenario. Some of the attacks in the states involved female accomplices." She turned, ready to leave.

"Charlie!" he called. She turned to him. "Be careful. It's an opportunity for an ambush if there's a bigger agenda at play. My cousin is on the Armed Response Team. They've been running the scenario. You'll have some men nearby, guarding the scene, but if something happens, you move your ass."

Charlie looked at him, and the concern in his eyes was palpable. "I always am…careful I mean. You too, Tadgh. Screw your cover. If something goes sideways, you move your ass."

* * *

GLASNEVIN BURIAL GROUNDS

Charlie knelt down next to the young woman's body, trying like hell to detach from the horror. She'd seen dead bodies before, when she was a police officer. But they'd been natural causes or motor vehicle accidents. The only exception had been one murder and then later, one suicide that she'd responded to in the harder parts of town. Both victims had been grown men. This was different. The victim couldn't have been more than twenty. She was unclothed, but Sullivan had allowed them to put a sterile piece of plastic sheeting over her body. Press could be anywhere, and the last thing they needed was some asshole with a good lens getting this poor girl's brutalized body all over the internet. Charlie steadied herself as she took a gloved hand and lifted her arm, exposing the inner flesh. "Damn." There it was, the same symbol. She closed her eyes against the wave of sadness. This girl had a family, most likely sitting in their home in America, none the wiser that their daughter was dead. She felt a presence behind her just as a shadow came over them.

"I should have known you wouldn't stay in Doolin." Charlie turned to see Sullivan approach the man who had cast a shadow over her. They shook hands briefly, then turned and looked over the girl. "I want this bastard's head on a spike. Do you hear me, O'Brien? This has got to stop."

Charlie's eyes took in the man. Tall, late middle age, salt and pepper hair, and the same facial features of another O'Brien. Not so much Tadgh, although the resemblance was there, but a broader, older version of his cousin Liam. The one that had coaxed her away from her realtor. *Interesting.*

Charlie stood up, slipped the gloves off of her hands, and placed them in a bag for disposal. Then she faced the man and…. he was looking at her so curiously. "Dia duit, Charlie."

CHAPTER 7

Tadgh was coming into the police station's main office area, having come through the back entrance, when he saw his Uncle Sean. His shoulders relaxed as they always did when his Uncle had his back.

"Thanks for calling. I've been to the scene already. I also met your Special Agent Ryan." He gave Tadgh a sly grin.

"Christ Uncle Sean, you're as bad as Auntie. She's just a colleague. Let's head to the flat. I need a shower and some tea." Sal came out of Sullivan's office just then, and Tadgh introduced the men. "Would you like to join us?"

Sal shook his head. "I need to get home, see the wife and kids, but thank you. Oh, and boss is looking for Charlie. Apparently she left the scene to head to the coroner's office, but the parents are flying in as we speak. The victim has been missing for at least three days, but no one called them until last night. They'll be in late, but he wants her there."

"I'll check at the flat, but my suspicion is that she'll head out in the city. She'll call when she's ready." Tadgh tried to sound calm, reasonable even. The thought of her out looking for a serial killer made him mental on the inside, but he couldn't watch her all the time. He ducked into Sullivan's office and asked, "Do you have her on the GPS tracker?"

Sullivan cursed. "Christ, I nearly forgot. It took them a couple of days to set it up, but I'll call our tech boys on the second floor. That reminds me, you and Sal needed trackers as well."

Tadgh said, "We'll go up now, and I'll check on her location."

* * *

AFTER THE TECH department issued them belts with GPS trackers hidden in the buckles, Sal went home and Tadgh and his Uncle Sean headed to Grogan's in Dublin 2 after checking Charlie's last location. It was a traditional pub, not too far from Trinity. She'd either needed a drink after processing the scene, or she had a reason for being in that area. The pub wasn't a sure bet, however. She had no way of knowing that it was a Garda favorite for the City Center officers. "Well, I haven't been in that pub in a while. Probably ten years at least. I'll join you, if you don't mind."

Tadgh smiled as they headed over on foot. "Seeing as your sons provided me my first pint as a lad, and it was most assuredly out of your stash, I suppose I owe you a drink."

Sean laughed heartily. "I suppose you do. I wondered, when Aidan was about sixteen and Michael fourteen, whether they'd been responsible for a missing bottle now and again. What else were you lads up to that slipped by me?"

Tadgh shrugged, "Oh, nothing much. A sip of whiskey, a bit of cider, the lingerie section of the shopping catalogs, the usual." Sean was shaking his head, laughing silently.

"Well, I suppose your da and I did the same. Tis the way of young men. Glad you grew out of it. My boys are good men. Every last one of ye."

Tadgh's chest swelled a bit. "Ye always did include me. You and Auntie. Ye treated me like your own, even though you had your hands full enough. You didn't treat me or Ma like an extra burden. "

Sean stopped and turned. "You've never been a burden, lad. Hands can be full, but hearts...well, they have infinite capacity. You'll find that soon enough, when you've found your own mate. Your children will be everything to you, and yet you'll still look at all your nieces and nephews and realize that nothing has changed. And your mate, whoever the lucky girl is, will be at the center of it all."

Tadgh said nothing, afraid to voice a deep buried fear. *What if I'm the exception? What if I have no mate?* He'd had bad luck with women since he was a school-aged young man. Plenty of attention, attraction, and desire from women, but none willing to love him. None willing to stay past the desired conquest. "I'm sure you're right, Uncle Sean. Patience is a virtue, I suppose."

CHARLIE WAS IRRITATED. She'd come into a central pub, less touristy, thinking that the target age group of early twenty something females would be hanging out this close to the college. She was right, but what she hadn't anticipated were a whole lot of badges. Not crusty old timers like the notorious Detective Hairy Ass Miller, but the younger generation of twenty and thirty something officers with their expensive sunglasses and more modern music tastes. *Flogging Molly* was playing on the sound system and she had to admit to herself that this was just the type of place she would have hung out in. Mahogany bar, clean mirrors, a nice selection on tap, and a digital jukebox when there wasn't a band. Behind the bar was the latest in boutique liquors and top shelf whiskeys.

Rather than do an about face, she decide to sit and have a non-alcoholic drink. Then she'd scout out the Church of Ireland protestant chapel around the corner. The victims had not all been Roman Catholic. Ireland wasn't like America, however. It didn't have a different denomination on every corner. There had been nothing in the case files that would suggest zealous church goers, but they'd all been some brand of Christian, attending church sporadically, and that symbol. Her mind flashed to the symbol carved in flesh and she shivered. As if to make the problem worse, the front door to the pub opened just as she was ordering a drink. She turned to see the gentleman she'd met today while examining the scene, and next to him was her current landlord. His eyes met hers and she was surprised when he approached.

"Charlie, ye've met my Uncle Sean," he said smoothly. He did an involuntary once over on her, and she warmed a bit from the inside. "Don't worry about exposure. No one we're looking for would hang out in here."

She smiled, easing her shoulders a bit. "I noticed. It's like roll call in here for the twenty-something, hipster cops." Sean barked out a short laugh, and Tadgh's smile got bigger.

"Well, Miss Smarty Pants. Can this hipster twenty-something copper buy you a pint?"

Charlie felt herself blush as she was stared down by the two big, beautiful men. Tadgh was good looking to be sure. He was also genuinely sweet and gentlemanly, and he was smart. Probably smarter than most people gave him credit for. Her experience was that a handsome face and great body often made people underestimate a man's other qualities. Just like her gender and age did for her. As if the Tadgh factor wasn't bad enough, his uncle was just stupid gorgeous. Old enough to be her father, probably, but holy shit. He was big, with a nice head of salt and pepper hair and dreamy blue eyes. He was in good shape too. If it hadn't been for the lines around his eyes and the silver fox thing he had going, from the neck down she'd have sworn he was twenty years younger. These beefy Irish boys were downright lovely in every age bracket.

"You checked my GPS coordinates." It wasn't a question.

Tadgh leaned over to the bar man. "Two pints of Creans…and?"

Charlie smiled a bit and turned to the bartender. "Ginger Ale and a cherry." She looked at Tadgh. "Thank you, but I can't really relax yet. I also can't hold my liquor like you local boys. I haven't eaten much today. Just a sandwich from the vending machine, and it wasn't all that compelling."

Tadgh looked at his watch. "Ye've had a rough day, Charlie. Let's

finish our drinks and we'll walk ye home. I can whip up some
and you can climb up and talk over the case, aye?"

She looked at him, one eye cocked. "I had intentions."

Tadgh knew this. "Ye didn't know this was a Garda hang
assume, but you're checking out the local churches. That's go
just have a little chat, go over what we all know, and you
fresh tomorrow. I'd like to hear what ye found today, and
brief you on what Sal and I have been doing."

They took a seat at a high table, resting their drinks
paper coasters. "Is this a regular hang out of yours?" she aske

Tadgh fiddled with his glass, not meeting her eye. "It w
year or so, then I moved on." He seemed to shake somethin
turned to his uncle. "What about you, Uncle Sean? You
worked in Dublin those first several years of your career
move to Clare until ye had Michael and Brigid. And you
lads before ye married. Where did you hang out?"

Sean smiled and took a sip, thinking. "Well, now. W
fashionable as your peer group. We kept mostly to Mulliga
on the piss. If we were playing a session, it was O'Donc
where he met your mother. He had her swooning in her w

Tadgh laughed. "Aye, they did love each other didn
he looked at Charlie who seemed to have a question i
was killed on the job, motorcycle crash. It was a long ti
lad."

Her face was pained. "I'm sorry. That's tough t
especially a good one you can be proud of." She turn
you lost a brother. Was he your only sibling?"

Sean shook his head. "No, I have a sister in Engla
is an estate solicitor. How about you, Charlie? Where

Charlie punched her straw up and down in the
"Cleveland. I left the house when I got the Clevel
once I went into the FBI, I moved around. I don't
keep in contact with my little brother, but that's pr
good kid. The best."

Sean stood up, pushing his chair back on a screech. "I need to go outside and call your Aunt Sorcha. I'll head back after I've seen Patrick." He smiled at Charlie and excused himself.

"He seems like a good man. You're lucky." Tadgh nodded, watching him leave out the door to make his call.

"I am lucky. He's been like a father to me all these years. My mam, she never remarried. Had a bit o'trouble with the drink for a time. Not now, mind you. She's been sober for over fifteen years. She just... she lost herself for a while, when my da died. She couldn't take care of herself all that well, or me. Sean and Sorcha, they filled in the gaps."

Like her Aunt Cassie, Charlie thought. She'd filled in the gaps. In some ways, so had her neighbor in Dearborn, the woman she called Aunt Jo. She noticed Tadgh check his phone, a text buzzing in.

"My uncle is headed to the flat. He says to tell you he's sorry to break off so suddenly, but he wants to see Liam and Patrick before he heads back. I guess you're stuck with me."

His smile was warm, and she noticed again how beautiful it was. Disarming dimples and straight, white teeth. Those eyes, though. He was singly the sexiest man she'd ever had the pleasure of speaking to. It wasn't put on, though. He just dripped a natural sensuality that he neither played up or attempted to hide. Warm eyes, sparkling gold and amber, beautiful skin even with the stubble that was coming in. His hair was light brown with golden highlights like he'd been kissed by the sun God.

She started to speak when she felt Tadgh stiffen next to her. She saw a buxom, tall woman approaching. She disapproved thoroughly the blatant once over the woman was giving Tadgh. She was pretty. She had shoulder length, light hair with expensive highlights. She was dressed professionally, but not enough to hide the prominent breasts. Light makeup, nothing that would scream hussy. She just had that overly familiar look on her face that said, *I had it and wouldn't mind having it again.*

Charlie looked at Tadgh and he seemed to be cringing. He grabbed wallet, ready to drop a tip and leave. "Off so soon? It's been a

while, O'Brien. We don't see much of you anymore now that you've moved upstairs with the detectives."

"Hello, Brittney. We were just stopping for a quick pint. We've got plans." Brittney looked at Charlie like she was a little mosquito.

Despite the chill between the threesome, Charlie put her hand out, "Charlie Ryan. Nice to meet you Brittney."

The woman's brows shot up. "A Yank? Well, now. Sampling the tourists, are you?"

Charlie bristled as the woman sat down. She actually felt the woman's foot cross under the table, rubbing on Tadgh's shin. He jerked, just a bit. "Actually, Tadgh's making me dinner. We can't really stay and chat. Are you ready?" She turned to Tadgh expectantly, giving her best dip-shit girly stare.

Relief flooded his face. "Absolutely."

* * *

"THANK YOU FOR THAT," Tadgh said as they walked. He was scarlet faced and distracted, but Charlie noticed that he stopped her before they crossed. He always kept himself between her and the closest moving car. Instinctual protectiveness. It was strange, because although she could take care of herself, the gesture was better than anything contrived that any other man had ever done for her. Opening doors and pulling out chairs rarely lasted beyond a first date or two. She wondered if Sean's quick departure had more to do with nudging his adopted son toward a couple's night out. It's something her Aunt Cassie would have done. That made her think back to Brittney. She was a piece of work.

"You don't have to talk about it. I don't particularly like talking about my ex," she said. He looked at her, narrowing his eyes as if trying to picture her with a man. "What? Don't look so surprised. I'm not a Fed all the time. I am a girl."

Tadgh chuckled and mumbled under his breath, "As if I could forget it." He shook himself. "She's not exactly an ex. She's more…"

"An indiscretion?" she asked. "Wait, don't answer that. I said you didn't have to talk about it. Now, we're almost to the building. You go ahead. I'll head in after you."

Tadgh stopped, looked around. "I'll go second. Go ahead, darlin'....I mean...Charlie. Sorry, go ahead, Charlie." He emphasized her name, looked her in the eye. She warmed a bit, knowing that he was trying to reassure her. That he didn't see what Detective Hairy Ass had seen. A token honey to keep the gender ratio in order. He saw her as another detective. "Text me when you're ready to come up."

Tadgh looked at her and her expression was unreadable, but there was a small smile. And that was something. It warmed him in a way it shouldn't. He didn't date colleagues anymore, especially ones who were leaving.

"I said the part about you making me dinner to get under her skin. You don't have to cook. I have leftover curry take out. But I do want to discuss the case before I see the parents."

Tadgh's face fell, remembering the case file. The pictures of a young girl robbed of a full life. Someone's daughter. "I'm sorry you have to do that. And, I will make you dinner. It's not often I have someone to eat with, and you'll need more than old take-away in your belly for that meeting. Now go on. I'll see you in a bit." He nudged her forward and she crossed, heading toward the flat.

* * *

CHARLIE OPENED the door to find the apartment a bit stuffy. The night air in Dublin had been early November crisp, the wind whipping her hair around. She went to the window and slid it wide. Just as she did it, a white furball darted past her. She yelped and looked at the beast. He was actually stunning. Long, silky white hair. More ivory, actually. He had a splash of red radiating out from his nose and dappling the tips of his tail. He had the bluest eyes she'd ever seen. He meowed, then hopped up on the counter. She remembered when Tadgh had been trying to convince her about the absentee landlord. He'd asked if she was allergic to cats, because there might be residual evidence. "So, I kicked you out of your apartment. Is that it?" He meowed again and started to purr vigorously when she scratched his head. She looked at his tag and he nipped her hand. "Be nice. Now what's your name?" She picked him up, getting a better hold. "Well, Duncan, I see who's boss around here now. Does your daddy know you're out?"

She got a text just then and it said, *Look out the window. I need the grill skillet. Left bottom cupboard. Tie it to the rope.* She looked out the window and laughed. Well, he had said he wouldn't bother her by showing up unannounced. Apparently he'd meant it. She found the pan, easily. His kitchen was neat and efficient. Then she scooped up Duncan and climbed out the window. She crawled up the fire escape and heard male voices. She hesitated, but she did need to give the cat back. He shouldn't be wandering around the city. She poked her head in the open window. "Sorry to show up early, but I think I found your roommate."

Four men turned around and the breath shot out of her. Just… damn. "Ah, Christ, ye wee mongrel. I was worried sick. Cora would have my hide if something happened to you." Tadgh came over, taking the cat from her. "He walks all over me." He smiled, then put the cat on the ground, helping her in the window as he took the skillet.

"I can come back. I just wanted to drop off His Majesty along with the skillet."

Tadgh grinned wider. "Ye shoulda tied him in the noose."

She knelt down and scratched his ears as he wound around her legs. "Stop flirting, Duncan. She's not here for you," he said. "Come in and meet more of the family."

She backed toward the window. "I don't want to intrude."

Tadgh took her gently by the wrist and her stomach leapt into her throat. "You've met Uncle Sean and Liam the Garda impersonator." She giggled as Liam wiggled his eyebrows at her.

Sean looked between them. "What's this?"

"I'll explain later. We're old friends, she and I." Then he hugged her. "Charlie, love. It's good to see you." Tadgh made a point of getting between them once Liam had let her go, and Charlie noticed the other three grinning to themselves and exchanging glances. She was pretty sure Tadgh wasn't even aware of the behavior, but he probably didn't want her feeling uncomfortable with four huge men and a flirtatious male cat all coming at her at once. "This is Patrick. My roommate and your neighbor for the foreseeable future." Patrick was every bit the stunner that the other three were, but he had a distinct auburn hue to his hair, and his eyes had some green in them.

Charlie became more serious. Tadgh took notice of it when she shifted into professional mode. It was crazy that her being a hard-assed FBI agent should be so arousing, but there it was. She was just so smart, so professional, and the respect that came from that was its own sort of aphrodisiac. O'Brien men liked strong women.

"The Armed Response officer? It's good to meet you. I have questions about your unit. I know it's similar to our Homeland Security and that it's a relatively recent addition. I know you have to leave, but another time? I definitely need to have a sit down with you." She looked at all of them. "All of you, except the doctor of course."

Liam winked at her. "The scrubs gave me away, I suppose. Speaking of which, I'm off. My shift starts in twenty minutes." Charlie watched as he hugged his father, then his brother Patrick. "Be careful, brother," he whispered. Then he hugged Tadgh. "You'll pick up Eve tonight, at the other dance studio? She's teaching across town, not the college. Can ye get her?"

Tadgh looked at his watch. "Nine o'clock. I'll be there, don't worry brother." Then he looked at Patrick. "I'll need the car, can ye take my motorbike?"

Sean interrupted. "I'll drop him off. I need to head back home soon." And it was set.

Liam turned to Charlie and stuck his hand out. "I'll play it safe this time," he said as he gave Tadgh a sideways glance. Charlie laughed and shook his hand. As he blew out the door, she turned to leave.

"Ye keep trying to bugger off. Sit, girl. Dinner won't take long. Talk to Patrick and Uncle Sean while I cook."

It was minutes before Sean had the case files spread out on the dining room table. "It's obviously someone with a grudge against Americans. So, they are hitting us where it hurts."

Sean nodded, "Aye, your daughters. They're taking your daughters." His jaw tightened.

She looked at Patrick. "What about on your end? Any news about Brotherhood activity, recruiting, threats?"

Patrick nodded, "Yes, some. No direct threats, but we are running scenarios for tourist areas. Places like Temple Bar or one of the cathedrals. The train stations and airports as well. The recruiting is happening. We've got intel on that. Not a lot, no names. It's a closed-lip culture and they're afraid of backlash. Like if they admit it's happening, the government will panic and deport them all."

Charlie nodded. "I understand. We've had the same issue. What about Sal? Could he try to infiltrate?"

Tadgh was busy in the kitchen. "No, that's off the table for various reasons. One being we aren't sure he wouldn't be recognized. Dublin isn't that big. And if he's followed, they'll be led back to his family in the suburbs. We need informants, and they are hard-won. I think the gentleman I told you about, Zaid, and his sons could probably be persuaded."

"It could be connected, but this seems like a more personal grudge. Maybe someone off on their own agenda, but part of a bigger organization. Whatever the case, stay sharp. These attacks are one part of a growing problem. There have been other problems. Fights in the schools, assaults on women during celebrations, anytime they can disappear into a crowd. It's nowhere near the issues they're having in Germany, France, and Sweden, or even England. But it's there."

Charlie nodded. "We've been monitoring the European influx. There doesn't seem to be any real vetting going on. Then, once they get into the EU…"

Patrick finished. "They can go anywhere in Europe, aye. It's probably similar to the U.S., most of the families are good people. It's the few bad apples, and they seem to be working the system. Military-aged males, not women and children like before. Ireland is buffered to a degree, but we are seeing it on a small scale. The pity of it is that it causes the good people to be looked on with suspicion. People who just wanted a better life and are following the rules...they don't get any airtime on the tele. "

Charlie shook herself, remembering how fast Dearborn got out of control. "Back to the murders..."

They talked for another fifteen minutes when it was time for Sean and Patrick to leave. "You're a sharp agent, Charlie. They did right to send you. Just be careful. This is not a position anyone is comfortable having you in. You need to use your resources. Stay in contact. This is hard stuff, it gets to you. Keep focused and don't take unnecessary risks, please."

Sean's tone was pleading just a bit, and Charlie met his eyes. She saw the same fatherly concern she'd seen in Assistant Director Schroeder's eyes so many times. The look she'd never seen in her own father's eyes. "I'll be careful."

Once they were gone, things were a little more awkward. Luckily Duncan broke the tension. He jumped up on the kitchen bar stool next to Charlie and began flirting again. "So, what's his story? How does a single man in an apartment end up with a cat?"

Tadgh turned from the stove and Charlie had to bite back a feminine sigh. He had low slung jeans, bare feet, and a University of Limerick t-shirt on that was tight through the shoulders. And he was cooking something for her.

"Well, he's a twin actually. My little niece Cora and I found him in an old shed at the back of my cousin's property. Michael and Branna have a traditional cottage. It's in a more remote area. I think people drop animals off where they think no one will see them. So, there they were. Filthy, brambles in their fur, underfed." He turned something on the skillet and it sizzled. "Well, wee Cora was beside herself. Her da is allergic to cats and they already have a dog. So, she couldn't keep them. We talked about a shelter, but the thought of them getting separated nearly sent her into a seizure. She's eight, almost nine. She's starting to learn about conservation, earthly causes, you know...all that fair trade, recycle, animal cruelty, global citizen shite they scare the devil out of little kids with these days."

Charlie was laughing. "Maybe you aren't as much of a hipster as I thought you were. Go on."

He gave her a sideways grin. "So, being that Cora is adorable and our first niece, Michael and I didn't stand a chance. We each took one. Fergus resides over the O'Brien cottage while having his tail pulled by my twin niece and nephew. I took Duncan."

"Well, sounds like Cora knows how to handle her men." She said with some respect. "But Fergus and Duncan don't sound very Siamese or Irish."

Tadgh motioned to the cat. "Oh, yes. Well, ye see, I was commenting on the filthy state of that little mongrel. He had bodily fluids in his fur, dirt, burrs, and fleas." He stood up straight, a hand on his hip. "She told me, *Don't worry uncle. He just needs a good dunkin' in the bath and he'll be lovely altogether.*" His voice was falsetto and child-ish, with a thick accent for affect. Charlie cracked off a laugh. It was a big, unguarded laugh with all the trimmings. Teeth and dimples and sparkling eyes. He stopped and looked at her, really looked at her.

"What?" she asked.

He shook his head, a little sadness creeping onto his face. "You should laugh more. It's very becoming." He tented foil over a plate and turned the stove off. He quickly set two places at the table and poured two goblets of water. "I figured you'd want to skip the alcohol if you had to go back tonight. I know her parents come in tonight. I do have wine and cider."

She shook her head. "Water is perfect. So, Chef O'Brien, what did you make me?" He plated the food and put it in front of her.

She sighed and closed her eyes before she could guard her reac-tion. Steak. He'd made her steak. He misunderstood her reaction. "Christ, I didn't ask. Do you eat red meat?"

She grinned widely and opened her eyes. "Is there any other kind of meat? Other than bacon, that is."

He seemed to puff up a bit, glad he'd gotten it right. "It's medium, and I fried up some mushrooms and onions and I like a little stilton on mine, but if you don't...."

She slid her plate over. "Cheese me, big guy, and oh my God are those homemade fries?"

He laughed. "Aye, they are. Fresh chips. You don't prefer a salad do you?" She didn't. She'd have certainly eaten it if he'd made one, but less room for steak and potatoes, as far as she was concerned. "It's Irish beef. It may taste a little different than you're used to, but it's good. I think you'll like it. They sell a good ribeye at the Fresh Market. Do you take ketchup?" He laughed as she put her face in a snarl of disgust. "Mustard or vinegar?" He got up and brought both with him to the table. She used the vinegar, which was perfect. Then she cut into the steak.

Charlie took a bite and moaned. "Marry me."

Tadgh grumbled a husky laugh. Then he gave her an admonishing look. "Don't tease me, lass. I'll hold ye to it."

She smiled, still chewing. "Are you some sort of mind reader?"

He looked confused. She was thinking back to that particularly long shift back in the Michigan office. A date, some steak. Maybe a date with a chef who made really good steak. A trip somewhere foreign and exciting with a handsome dance partner. Isn't that what she'd thought? This was pretty damn close.

"Never mind, it's a joke in my head that probably wouldn't make sense to anyone else. Thank you, though. I haven't had a home-cooked meal in a while. My elderly neighbor in Michigan makes a good lasagna, but this…this is art. Who taught you to cook? "

"My Aunt Sorcha, Uncle Sean's wife. She taught us all to cook. Said we needed to marry for love and not for a housekeeper and cook. I'm glad you like it. I don't get to cook for people other than Patrick and Caitlyn very often. We take turns with dinner. I don't have a varied repertoire, but learning to cook a good steak is crucial to manly survival. Caitlyn's forever stuffing vegetables down our gullets."

She nodded. "And, Eve? Who is she? Is she Liam's wife?"

Tadgh shook his head. "No, they're both still in school. It'll happen eventually, but her parents would never go for it while she's still at Uni. She still lives in a dormitory, since she's on scholarship. They'd have a seizure if she moved in with Liam before they were wed." He read her face. "Ye probably think that's a bit archaic. They're just protective, and very Catholic."

"I think it's nice. I can't imagine having doting parents like that. Or like your uncle, for that matter. I think you are all very lucky. Not judging at all. So, what about you? You're 29 and unmarried. I can't figure that out. You're adorable and you cook. The dimples and the brains should have gotten you a slew of women suitors."

Tadgh blushed, took a sip of water. "Aye, well. Slew of women maybe, but none who want to stick around." She noticed he played with his stubble, not used to the feel of it. "And what about you? Too ambitious to bother with a husband?"

She cringed. *Touché.* "Too much self respect to deal with a cheating boyfriend. Number one on the long list of reasons you shouldn't date within the department. You get to see him, and the chick he was banging behind your back, every day at work."

Tadgh hissed. "Ouch. Sorry I brought it up." He raised his glass. "A toast. To steak and spuds and not talking about your ex."

They clinked glasses. "Amen, O'Brien."

* * *

SEAN CAME into the house well past sundown. The house was dark, with a few sporadic lights on here and there. He called for Sorcha, but there was no answer. Her car was in the garage, so he walked through the house in search of her. Then he saw it. He cursed under his breath, knowing why she was in his den.

He cracked the door open as he said her name. He didn't want to startle her. She was sitting, the copy of the case files exposed. He'd locked the door, always, to avoid this very thing. He'd pinned the different incidents on a cork board. Not the photos, of course. It was too gruesome and seemed like an invasion of the women's privacy. Just the names, ages, and a map and details. Where the crimes and victims intersected, where they differed. Then he looked down. "Dammit, Sorcha. Ye shouldn't be looking at my case files."

For once, she didn't argue. She didn't even bristle. "I know." Her sigh was soft, sad.

Sean got on his knees in front of her, taking a photo out of her hand. "Sorcha, love. Let's leave this. Come out of here and let's talk, aye?"

She went, almost as if she was sleepwalking. He sat her on the couch, took a seat next to her. He'd locked the office door behind her. "I'm sorry, darling. It's why I kept you out of there. I know this must bring up bad feelings. You lost a lot of friends and neighbors in the troubles. And I know about the attempted kidnapping, when you were nineteen. Your brother told me. Do you remember?"

Sorcha looked at him, a single tear coming down. "Barbara Leary."

Sean was confused, he cocked his head. "Who?"

"That was the name of the young woman who died in my place. When my brother came to my aid on the street, I was walking home alone. I knew I shouldn't, but he was late and I was so tired. He was just a lad, but he saw them try to grab me and pull me into the van."

Sean was shaking. She'd never told him the full story. "Oh, my love. I'm so sorry." He tried to hold her but she stiffened.

"Let me finish." She spread her pajama bottoms tight against her legs, collecting herself. "He interfered, ye see. He came around the corner, started screaming. I was fighting like hell, like my life depended on it. And, it did. The man cut me in the struggle." She turned her arm over and the long healed scar across her forearm was barely visible.

"You told me that was from..."

She cut him off. "I know what I told you. It was a lie. Probably the only lie I've ever told you in thirty-eight years. Anyway, my brother pulled me away from him. Beat him with the torch he kept on his belt. They sped off." She swallowed. "They didn't get me. So they went to another area of town, grabbed another woman off the street. They beat her, then they cut her throat." Sean clapped his hand over his mouth and stifled an indescribable sound.

She had tears in her eyes. "She took my place. Died in my place. They never officially charged them with her death because their

victims were usually men. There were so many. Some shot, most stabbed, or had their throat cut. The Shankhill Butchers were busy men, and if it wasn't them, it was a couple of men that were inspired by them. Copycats, that's the word, isn't it?" Sean just nodded. Sorcha snorted in disgust, waving a hand. "Who the hell knows. They couldn't prove all of the crimes, but we all knew about Lenny and his band of psychopaths. But, they didn't get me. I'm still here, and Barbara Leary isn't. She was twenty-five, and she had two children. She had an evening cooking job, didn't have a car. I didn't know her, but I found out about her in the paper."

Sean pulled her to him now. His trembling was intense, more noticeable because she wasn't trembling. There was an ache in her voice. "You have to get this bastard. Whoever he is. You have to get him or them or however many there are. It's the same horrible butchery. Different names, faces, different religion, but they're the same."

They sat there in silence for a time, then Sean picked up his wife and took her to bed. Her still body melting into him. "I'll do my best, Sorcha. The boys and I, we'll do everything we can to end this."

"Just be careful, Sean. You and the lads. I don't think I could survive it."

* * *

"So, tell me. When Brittney was being...Brittney, why did you ₁ her think we were on a date? Not that I wouldn't jump at the cʰ but you said you were trying to get under her skin."

"And you want to know why I wanted to get under big Brittnaaaay's skin?" She drug out the A which made Tadgh she'd meant it to. "Because I didn't like how she was lookⁱ Like you weren't there. Like you were a piece of meat person. I know what that's like. It's got no place on the good guy and a better officer, and whatever went dow boobed jerk."

Tadgh was smiling so big his face was going to cocked a brow, rubbing his chin. "Aye, they were pre'

Charlie's jaw dropped and she threw her napkin at him. "Shut it, O'Brien. I'll take my steak and your cat and go home to my new apartment."

As she helped him clean up, he dug in the cabinet. He came out with some cookies. "Dessert. My Aunt Sorcha bakes every week and sends them home with everyone. Sometimes it's scones or bread or some hand pies. These are her lemon cookies. They're gorgeous altogether. Would ye care for some tea?" Charlie nodded, but then her phone buzzed. She pulled it out and checked the text messages. "Crap. It's Sullivan. He wants to meet up before the parents touch down."

Tadgh's face grew serious. "Christ, Charlie. I'm sorry it has to be you."

She straightened her spine. "So am I, but I'm more sorry that their daughter is dead. The least I can do is assure them that the U.S. is involved in the investigation. They need to hear that I won't go home until this is over, and we've caught the person responsible."

He looked in her eyes, those lovely sparkling eyes that were like shards of amber pressed into deep, green moss. Earthy and otherworldly all at once. She was fierce when he looked there. Not fragile like she appeared with a passing glance. She was small, but she was fit. He could tell that she had power in her little frame. Fit and disciplined, except for her taste in food. Another thing to admire about her. She could wolf down chips and red meat like a rugby player. Her face shifted, questioning. He realized he was probably staring.

Tadgh handed her two cookies. "For the road."

She smiled. "Thanks for dinner. I owe you one."

As she left out the window, Duncan tried to follow her. Tadgh grabbed him. "Et tu, Brute?" The cat meowed loudly and Tadgh scratched behind his ears. "Don't get attached, wee Duncan. She's not staying," he whispered. As he closed the window and put the cat down on the floor, he wondered who he was trying to warn. Himself or the cat?

CHAPTER 8

*T*adgh pulled in front of Eve's door just as his phone went off. It was a quarter past nine. "Sal, aye. I'm headed over. Hold a minute." Then he covered the phone speaker. "Eve, darlin'. You need to call if Liam is at the hospital. Call me or Patrick, or take a cab in a pinch. Liam will pay for it. Don't go trying to walk to the bus stop, especially at that local studio across town. You understand?"

Eve blew him a playful kiss. "Don't worry so much, Tadgh. Just go catch your bad guys with your stubble and your shaggy hair."

Tadgh smiled and said, "I'll have you know this shaggy look is a magnet for the lasses."

She cutely curtsied to him and ran toward her dorm to escape the cold.

"Girlfriend?" Sal said.

"No, God no. My cousin's girl. We just take turns picking her up. We don't want her out at night."

"Well, I certainly get that. Now, how about you get your ass over to the government housing and play my sidekick."

Tadgh blustered. "Oh, no. 'Tis you that is the sidekick," and they bantered on as he pulled out of the student housing complex. He drove to the parking garage, parked Patrick's car, and grabbed his motorcycle helmet from the back seat. Within fifteen minutes, he was pulling into the North Dublin housing area. It was tired, impoverished, and highly populated. He often wondered why they didn't spread out. Dublin was singly the craziest housing market in Ireland. The only reason he and Patrick had the nicely located flats was because the building owner came from an old Dublin family. Civic minded and supportive of the city workers. He gave preferential renters packages in a third of the units. He liked his building full of fireman, cops, and city workers.

Tadgh had lived with Patrick and Caitlyn until the lease for the flat below them had come up for grabs. So, he understood how hard it must be for these people to afford housing. Many of them were illegal with regard to occupancy. Apartments for a family of four were often topping out at eight people. But the city turned a blind eye, because they had nowhere else to put them and the people didn't want to leave. They were indeed a clannish lot. He noticed, however, some divisions. Certain groups stayed together. Jordanians, Yemeni, and Lebanese stuck together to a degree. Kurds and Turks as well. Then the Eastern European, the Stans… they seemed to section off as well. Zaid had explained the dynamic when Sal, as a new resident, had explained that he didn't know where he fit in. He kept as much to the truth as he could, so they couldn't catch him in a lie. He was first generation Irish. Parents were Kurds, from Northern Iraq. Zaid was from Bagdhad, so they'd fallen into a comfortable acquaintance.

Sal was better at distinguishing the different languages and dialects, and he'd taken a particular interest in a group of males who always seemed to be together. They weren't as social, didn't seem to have families, and they were watchful, on the defense. They were constantly pulling out their smartphones. "Zaid said they're worth watching."

The night was chilly, and Tadgh was glad he'd layered. He pulled up his collar.

"I can't believe you ride a motorbike at this temperature. You're off your nut, O'Brien," Sal said in jest.

Just as Tadgh was ready to give him a pithy comeback, Zaid's middle son came out of the building. He turned down an alley, which seemed odd. It was late and Zaid usually kept a tight rein on his kids. "What's his name again?"

"Abdul. Pretty late for a seventeen year old to be running the streets." Tadgh nodded in agreement. "Maybe we should follow him," Sal said.

As they walked toward the same alley, Zaid's eldest came outside. "Hello, Malik. Are you looking for Abdul?" It was obvious he was, head on a swivel.

Malik shook himself, "No, for you sirs. My mother has made some tea. My father asks if you would like to meet him. I mean, to join him. To come join him for tea."

They went into the building. All three men stealing glances down the alley where the other son had gone. As they entered the apartment, it was small but surprisingly clean for the number of people living there. Zaid and Sharis had five children total. The kids were all smiling, taking coats and offering biscuits. They had a couch, but Zaid led them to a group of pillows with triangular back rests, and a low table. "I still like the old way. Someday I'll be old and prefer the couch." Tadgh smiled, liking the floor seating and the way the cushion propped his back.

His wife, Sharis, served them tea and left the room after introductions. He looked at them apologetically. "I promise, I don't treat her like a servant. She's shy and wary of strangers. The adjustment has been most difficult on her."

"How long have you been in Ireland?" Sal asked.

"Four years. I was interpreter for British forces. I knew some Englishman, some Fusiliers, a Scot or two. I met a friend with the Royal Irish Regiment as well. When he leave Iraq, he apply with Britain to get our family asylum." His English wasn't perfect, but it was very good. Tadgh liked this man, he decided.

Tadgh spoke up at this. "My cousin is RIR. He was mostly in Afghanistan, but it's good to know one of his comrades repaid your service."

Zaid smiled. "Oh, yes. We go to Belfast at first, but we were having troubles with housing. I found work here in Dublin two years ago, and now here we are. It doesn't pay much, but the schools are good for the kids. And you have…what's the word? Ah, yes. Craic. Your craic is very good." The men all laughed.

"Now, I brought you here to talk to you. I want to help you."

They looked at each other dumbly, then him. "With your investigation. Don't worry, no one else knows."

Now Tadgh understood why he sent the kids away. "I was intelligence officer in the Iraqi Army. I also saw a weapon on your waist, Rahim. You need to wear a longer shirt than the one you wore yesterday. Don't worry. I'm the only one who saw this."

Sal cursed. "We're not undercover, we're just observing. I'm sorry if you felt you were deceived."

"No, no. We only have one TV, but I can guess the reason. Why do you think it's a Muslim man responsible? Can you tell me?"

Both men said it at once. "No."

"I understand. I will keep my eyes open. If I hear any talk about this, or if we see any problems arising, I will call the police station and ask for one of you. I'm assuming I know your real names?"

Tadgh didn't know why, but he really did trust this man down to his guts and bones. "Yes, you do. You ask for either of us and we'll be here."

* * *

CHARLIE WAS DESTROYED. Absolutely destroyed. She'd met the parents in a private interview room, away from the buzz of the headquarters. Deputy Commissioner Sullivan had been there as well. The parents had watched on a video screen as the coroner lifted the sheet from their daughter's face. The crime report results were not in, so she was given a small reprieve with regard to the sexual assault. The death was hard enough, and they would eventually find out the details, but no report meant no confirmation. She would not share a detail like that unless she was positive of the information. They knew, though. She'd seen it in their eyes when the mother had asked, *"Where are her clothes?"*

She'd been attending the Irish American University branch in Dublin. She was a liberal arts student, played tennis. She also had a little brother three years younger than her. They'd left him with his grandparents in Buffalo. The parents had run the spectrum of emotion tonight. Anger, guilt, disbelief, denial, but under it all was a deep chasm of sorrow. The father's face was ruination incarnate. The mother's face was the pale, anguished look of a woman whose soul was eating itself alive.

She walked into the apartment at three o'clock in the morning and didn't even turn the lights on. The light over the stove had been left on, and she slid her keys on the counter. She looked around at the modest, neat apartment and wondered fleetingly whether Tadgh was out on the street or home in his cousin's apartment. Had he made any progress tonight? Was he sleeping? Reading in bed? He'd told her, earlier, that he'd left his bedroom door unlocked. After she'd found him out, he had nothing to hide. His books were in there, and he'd invited her to borrow anything she liked.

She walked across the dim apartment to his room and opened the door. It was clean, but she could smell him faintly. Manly, musky, and clean. Her belly stirred, and it occurred to her that maybe this hadn't been a good detour. She was too tired for one more ounce of guilt, however, so she came further into the room and turned on the light.

She combed through the books, surprised at the selection. He had everything from dog eared paperbacks of Tolkien to poetry collections of Dylan Thomas and Lord Alfred Tennyson. Yeats, too, of course. Some modern fiction authors like Vince Flynn, Bernard Cornwell, and Stephen King. He also had an entire hardback collection of Hemingway. She pulled out *A Moveable Feast* and opened the cover. There was a book plate. *The Library of William O'Brien.* The collection had been published in 1982, before Tadgh was born. *How sad*, she thought. Tadgh had obviously had a good dad. Not everyone did. And he'd died on the job. She put the book back, feeling a bit like she was invading his privacy.

She moved on, seeing something that interested her. He had a small collection of art books. Rossetti, Waterhouse, and Edward Burne-Jones. Beautiful women with feminine curves and long, cascading hair. She slipped the book on Waterhouse off the shelf. He was one of her favorites. Mythical nymphs and sirens, knights, and Shakespearean scenes. She found her favorite, *Miranda-The Tempest-1916.* Whipping hair, fair skin, the roaring sea. Rocky cliffs and stormy hues. Art didn't get much better. She started to retreat from the room when she saw it. An old turntable.

She inspected it, nestled on the second shelf of one of his bookshelves. It was plugged in, which meant it worked. There was a small collection of vinyl albums next to it that looked about the same age as the Hemingway collection or older. She knelt down, sliding out the stack. Janice Joplin, Rolling Stones, a really early Clash album, Muddy Waters. Obviously, Pops had some taste, or Tadgh's mother. She slid out a Zeppelin album, flipped on the turntable, and set up the record. Her Aunt Cassie had loved her old stereo, refused to transition to tapes or CDs. When she was sick, Charlie would stay with her a day or two and help out. She'd change the albums for her, and when the crackling sound gave way to the music, she'd watch the memories flicker over her aunt's face.

She put it on the track she was looking for, and the smooth voice of Robert Plant and acoustics of Jimmy Page washed over her. *Ramble On*, perfect accompaniment to his ragged Tolkien collection. She felt a little indulgent, and a bit like she was stealing something, by sitting here in Tadgh's room, getting a feel for him during his absence. She felt her phone buzz in her back pocket. She checked the text.

One of my favorites.

Her head popped up, immediately looking at the window. She stood up, pulling the curtain aside. Nope, not at the window. Then she looked at the ceiling. No vents. Interesting. Did he have it bugged? Then she saw the radiator. It had a pipe that went up into the ceiling.

The seal around the pipe wasn't great. It was an old building. The music must be radiating up the pipe, into his room. Christ, it was three o'clock. She turned the record off, and thought about just slinking away, but she changed her mind. She stood on top of the warm radiator, put her mouth to the ceiling and said. "Get your ass in bed, young man. Do you know what time it is?"

She heard a distinct male rumble of laughter. Then she heard shifting and movement. Then a sweet, baritone voice. "I was sleeping. Some daft, little Yank started singing along to Led Zeppelin and woke me."

She giggled, getting off the radiator. As she turned the light off, book in hand, another text came through.

Rough night. Glad you're home. Sweet dreams to you, Charlie.

CHARLIE SLEPT A FEW HOURS, waking with the art book across her chest and the nightstand light still ablaze. It was about eight o'clock and it was her stomach that woke her. She still hadn't gone to the grocer. Tadgh had left her some basics. Bread, butter, condiments, a token beer, and some apples and oranges. She started the coffee and leaned against the counter, peeling an orange. She had to get some supplies, because an orange wasn't going to cut it for breakfast. She'd get dressed, have some coffee, and head to a local bakery. She banged in a search on her laptop. Lots of artisan bakeries, but the one that jumped out was The Rolling Donut. *Bingo!* Just across the river in Dublin 1. Better to walk than to try parking and re-parking. She put some warm clothes on, her hiking boots, and a coat and hat. The morning was chilly.

Forty minutes later, Charlie was coming in the door. A container with two fresh coffees in one hand, bag of six donuts in the other. She wasn't sure if the boys were home, but she'd brought extra donuts home in case. Hardly a payback for a grass-fed ribeye, but it was a start. She unlocked her window and slid it open. She climbed out, reached back in to grab the goodies, and headed up the fire escape. As she came to the window of the apartment, she was expecting the blinds to be shut. She'd been distracted, trying to text. She was poised with the drink holder and bag of donuts in one hand while she thumbed in a message. *Coffee and breakfast is at the window.* She hit send and looked up, right into the clear view of the apartment.

It only took her a second to realize that Tadgh was very, very detained. Her view was partially obscured by half open blinds, but what she saw was vivid as hell. A well muscled back and firm ass working overtime, standing in the kitchen. The sleek, feminine legs were wrapped around his waist with one heel pressing into his ass, pulling him tightly into her. Female moans and husky groans and *oh shit!* She dropped the coffee and it splashed everywhere. Her pants soaked from the knee down and one streak shot all the way up to her chest. She snatched the bag up because she'd be damned if she was leaving those amazing donuts. She scurried down the stairs like a mad woman, hopped in the window, and slid the window closed. She sprung the lock, dropped the donuts on the counter and leaned on her hands. What in the hell had she just seen? Dammit. She should have called first. She should never have assumed that someone who looked like Tadgh O'Brien was going to be sleeping alone every night.

But, what the hell had that been about last night? Was he actually flirting with her through the radiator pipe while sleeping next to another woman? She shook her whole upper body, trying to jar the thought of his beautiful ass out of her mind. The noises the woman was making told her that he definitely knew how to give a girl a work out. On the counter, no less. She'd only had two lovers, but she couldn't ever remember getting hiked up on the counter for a go. A wave of irrational hatred for the unknown female rolled through her. Charlie had spent the evening dealing with a dead girl's parents. This woman, whomever she was, spent the evening with her legs wrapped around Detective O'Brien's waist.

She pushed herself off of the counter, looking down at her jeans. She hadn't packed a lot of clothes, needing to make room for equipment. She needed to wash these in that little, sorry excuse for a washer.

* * *

PATRICK WAS GROANING, pulling Caitlyn back and forth as she dug her heel into his lower back. He took the hint, having her nice and deep. "Oh God, darlin'. I missed you. I need this." His big body drove into her as she lay her head back, eyes glossy, breasts swaying as she took all of him. "Give me your mouth," he growled as he cupped her ass and picked up his pace. She came hard as he swallowed her cries. Then he heard something behind him.

She heard it too, and asked. "What was that?" She was breathless and it came out like a whimper.

"The feckin earth moving. Ignore it!" Then he joined her, growling as he spilled inside her.

* * *

TADGH WAS WALKING BACK to the flat when he finally had the chance to read his texts. One from Cora on Brigid's phone, sending him a picture of Fergus. One from Uncle Sean, telling him to call about the case. The last text made his heart jump. Damn. He'd probably missed her. Right in the middle of his brief with Sullivan, she'd texted that she was bringing breakfast to the window. He picked up the pace, wondering if there was any chance she was still around.

He took the stairs two at a time until he got to the third floor. When he opened the door, he immediately knew something was up. The place smelled different. Like perfume. He looked in the dining room and clothes were scattered around the floor. He froze in place, because obviously Caitlyn had disobeyed orders and come to see Patrick. "Hello, everyone decent?" he yelled.

Patrick came out with a towel around his waist, looking like a cat who'd gorged on cream. And then came Caitlyn. She was in a shirt of Patrick's and leggings, freshly showered as well. Her cheeks had the distinct flush of a woman who'd been enjoying her husband's morning off. Tadgh blushed, running his hand through his hair. "Sorry, didn't know you were coming home. I can head out."

Caitlyn waved a hand dismissively. "Not at all, brother. I've already had my way with him. Come in and have some breakfast."

Tadgh barked out a laugh and looked at Patrick. "That she did," Patrick said as he smiled.

"Don't go rubbing it in, for God's sake. It's not polite to brag to some poor sod who's got no prospects," Tadgh said. "Speaking of breakfast, when did Charlie come by? Did she leave anything?"

Both of them looked at him strangely, then realization came over Patrick's face. He walked to the window, blinds half open, and slid the glass aside. He cursed, then reached down to retrieve some trash from the fire escape landing. Two spilled cups and a carrier. He stood up and looked at Caitlyn. She had a hand over her mouth, a look of horror on her face. Then they both looked at Tadgh.

"So, can I take it you missed her, too busy in the bedroom?"

"Not exactly," Patrick said, suppressing a grin. Tadgh looked at the window, at the cups, then at Caitlyn's guilty face.

"Really guys? With the blinds open? Do ye think she could see? Where the hell, wait...don't answer that. Too much bloody information."

Caitlyn was laughing now. "Well now, it depends on the time frame. See, there was the counter, then the table." At this point Tadgh had been leaning, palms on the table. He yanked them off, hands in the air. He put a palm over his face and rubbed his jaw. "It's all right. I'll explain. You're married, for God's sake. I'm the one that got us in this mess. I shouldn't have you two in the middle of this."

Caitlyn walked over to him, looked him in the face, and gave his bicep a squeeze. "You're taking good care of him, and I'm safer to the West for now. We should have told you I was here for a visit. Do ye want me to talk to the lass?"

Tadgh shook his head. "She'll understand. She knows Patrick has a wife. Just keep the blinds closed next time, aye?" He walked toward

the window. "See you two later. I've got to go see how traumatized she is."

* * *

CHARLIE WAS SITTING on a public bench, eating her fourth donut and watching the students walk by as they changed classes. The Irish American University was right in downtown Dublin, and she knew that with a backpack and casual clothing, she looked like any othe college student. She was in a green space, and she looked over at large flower bed that had a concrete ledge walling it in. It made like bench of sorts and a familiar person was seated. She got up, stash the remaining two donuts in her bag, and approached the you woman.

"Tatyana, right?" The woman smiled.

"Yes, it is good to see you, Charlie." They fell into an easy con sation, as women often did. Her English was a bit broken, but good. When they got to the part where Tatyana answered why come to Dublin, Charlie was surprised by her answer. "I've looking for my sister for four months. I lost my trace of [London, but I came here based on the number of Russian imm in Dublin. We were from a small village, but she was studying city. Not one of the big universities, but at a small business She wanted to clerk? Like assistant of businessman." The face was sad.

"I'm so sorry, Tatyana. Do you think it was human traffic] said you tracked her through Europe."

Tatyana was fighting tears. "Yes. She'd sent me emails. man. He was older. I told her not to be so trusting, but..." off, not wanting to seem like she was blaming her sister. looking. I will never stop looking. There's nothing for me East. I can't go home without her."

Charlie's stomach sank. She had brushed up against ficking in her current job. The FBI had a unit specifically the huge, global problem. She wished she could help,

supposed to be a young woman living abroad. She couldn't probe this woman or go poking around. It wasn't her mission. "What was your sister's name? I'll light a candle for her at church."

Tatyana seemed to take comfort in this. "Nika. She is nineteen. We were close in age. She was smart and beautiful and she was a good girl. You can tell God, during your prayers, that she was a good girl."

CHAPTER 9

*C*harlie was ignoring his texts. That was the only explanation. Sullivan kept a close eye on her. If she'd gone dark, he would have sounded the alarm. It had been seven hours since her morning text. He finally broke down and decided to call his boss.

He'd made a day of it at Sal's fake apartment. There had been a birthday, Zaid's youngest. They'd invited the men last night at tea. Zaid had a nineteen year old daughter, just eleven months younger than Malik. Her name was Yakira. Tadgh was pretty sure that he was eyeing Sal as a potential marriage for his daughter. Sal didn't wear his wedding ring when he was undercover, knowing that it would raise eyebrows that he was living alone. So Zaid had incorrectly assumed he was single.

Today, it had been the youngest lad's sixth birthday. So Tadgh had stopped at a department store in Dublin to get him a Star Wars light saber. He'd received three footballs, an Ireland Rugby team shirt, and Legos, but Tadgh's present had hit the mark. He'd run around for hours, challenging his envious mates to a duel. They'd been forced to use sticks, and little Karim had felt like King Shit of the Universe with that light saber.

Tadgh genuinely liked many of the people who lived in the complex. They were family oriented, kind, and the women loved to stuff him to bursting with their regional dishes. He felt slightly guilty about deceiving them, and was actually relieved that Zaid was now an ally. He'd been cooperative with the patrol in this area in the past. He hoped that they would be friends, even after this ugly business was done.

Now that he was at Sal's, having been invited to a light dinner, he was starting to worry about Charlie. She was either pissed, embarrassed, or something was really wrong. He couldn't assume Sullivan had been in contact.

Leyla's rich, cultured voice invaded his thoughts. "What's bothering you, big man? Is it this awful case you and Sal are working on?" Tadgh looked up from his phone, his brow creased.

"It's nothing. Something happened this morning with...a colleague. Now I can't get a hold of her. She's in the field, but it's making me nervous."

Leyla smiled. "Is it this new female officer you have your eye on?"

Sal broke in before the conversation traveled in the wrong direction. "The new Garda officer, she means. Charlie. She's transferred into the unit. Right?" He gave Tadgh a look that said, *I'm not so stupid as to tell her about the undercover FBI Agent.*

"I don't have my eye on her at all. He's mistaken. I just don't like officers out in the field alone."

Leyla gave him a doubting look, but let it drop. "Call and check on her. We've got five minutes to let this rest." She pointed to the lamb skewers that were hot off the grill.

He got up off the kitchen chair and left the kitchen, "Thanks, Leyla. I won't be but a moment."

When Sullivan answered, he was obviously at home. Tadgh heard kids running around in the background. "I spoke with her an hour ago. She's checked in via text every two hours, then called at the end of the day. She's probably home, but I think her intention is to go out again tonight."

Tadgh didn't like the sound of that, and he said as much. "For the love of Christ, O'Brien. While you were having tea in some warm flat and going to bed early, she was dealing with that young woman's parents. She wants to find these psychopaths as much as any of us. She's not here on holiday; this is her job. If you're worried, go see her, plan to monitor the situation from a distance."

Tadgh was exhausted and he needed a nap. He couldn't imagine what Charlie was going through. She couldn't have had more than four hours of sleep. He went back into the kitchen and the smell of the grilled lamb and exotic spices made his stomach scream for mercy.

"At least take some food with you, before you run off like Prince Charming." Leyla's no nonsense tone put him in mind of Brigid or his Aunt.

"Leyla." His tone was chiding, but she was undeterred.

"So can I assume that my husband's description of an old sea hag with browning teeth and a saggy bum was inaccurate?" Tadgh looked at Sal who was slashing across the air.

"I've got no comment. You can decide for yourself if you meet her."

"A perfect idea. You can help this lazy Kurd move the holiday boxes from the attic, and she and I will get to know each other."

"Damn, woman. You are a mastermind. He walked right into that," Sal said, not hiding his respect.

"Yes, dear. And when she shows up young, pretty, and perky, I'm going to box your ears."

CHARLIE WAS EXHAUSTED, but too wired to sleep. She'd hit the pavement early, wanting to get as far away from this apartment building as possible. She knew, realistically, that she needed to go back and get some rest, a shower, and a snack. She wouldn't be any use to this case if she ran herself into the ground. She let the water pour over her, washing some of the tension in her body away with the powerful jets. The shower was, indeed, small. Not really for her, but she had a hard time picturing a man the size of Detective O'Brien in here. She'd decided, during her long day of wandering the city, drinking coffee in local cafes, stopping in churches, and strolling campuses, that she'd let herself get too familiar with the Detective. She probably needed to move. As if on cue, the mere fact that she was showering in his shower made flashes of his smooth naked back, bunched, powerful shoulders, and...nope, she was not going to go there again. She turned the shower off, realizing that having herself all wet and soaped up wasn't helping the situation either. It had been so long since she'd been with someone. Ted, her ex, had been four years ago. She'd gutted it out six more months on the department, having to see him every day, then she'd left when the FBI had recruited her.

She'd thought her sex life with him had been okay. Granted, she didn't have a lot to compare it to. Her first boyfriend had been in college and he'd been kind of a dickhead. He certainly hadn't been a tornado between the sheets. He wanted a regular hook-up, and she'd read more into the relationship than there was. She'd given him her virginity, they'd seen each other off and on, and it had fizzled out because he wasn't ready to have a real relationship. She was too serious and too self-respecting to be demoted to friend with benefits. She'd rather have no one.

After that, she'd started working at the Cleveland police department. Her last year of school, she worked nights at the PD, attended classes during the day, and survived on four hours of sleep a day. Ted had been one of her training officers. Bad move, but he was older and charming. She was in awe of him, and she'd been lonely.

In hindsight, she'd missed a lot of warning signs that he was bored with her and straying. Her doe-eyed innocence and hero worship had been a power trip for him. She was pretty inexperienced with men, and he'd enjoyed teaching her the ropes, so to speak. Once she'd learned them, though, and become more comfortable with him, her own body, her own needs, he'd cooled. No more power trip. Men could be like that. They liked control.

Charlie toweled herself, skipping the body lotion because she really didn't need the sensory input of rubbing something all over her skin. Her two previous lovers may have lost interest in her, but she liked sex as much as the next person. And, she was way overdue. She didn't do casual hook-ups, though. And that little scene in the kitchen, as sickened as it made her, had sparked a dormant horny trigger in her. Perfect timing.

She looked over at the dresser and her phone was glowing. She had been ignoring Tadgh's texts today. She was working. She didn't have time for idle chat and if he had information to give her, he could do it at their meeting, two days from now, or pass it on to Sullivan. It buzzed again.

I know you're home. I'm coming down.

She growled. He was a pushy son of a bitch. She heard the tapping on the living room window. *Dammit.*

"We need to talk. Please let me in." He spoke through the glass and blinds, but she could tell he was trying to sound calm and keep the irritation out of his voice. She heard it though. He didn't like being ignored. Who the hell did he think he was?

Tadgh was squatted on the fire escape landing when the blinds went up. The breath shot out of him at the sight of her. Hair in a wet tangle, and wearing a terry cloth bathrobe. Her cheeks were pink, flushed from the shower and what looked like a hint of irritation. Her face was placid, but the eyes were sparking. Holy shit, she was absolutely breathtaking. Then he remembered the fact that she'd been ignoring him all day, deliberately, and his temper flared again. At her and at himself. She slid the glass open. "I checked in with Sullivan. Did you need something?"

He gave her a look, not answering, and she finally stepped aside. He stepped in, remembering the real reason he was here. The dropped coffees, the open blinds. She was obviously keeping her distance because she'd regretted that walk up the fire escape. She was second guessing any growing friendship with him and Patrick.

"Why have you been avoiding me?" he asked. He'd start there and see what she said.

"I have a job to do, Detective O'Brien. I don't know why you think

I need to be in contact with you. Did something happen with the case?"

His brows went up. This prickly little fireball was not the same woman who'd joked with him over steaks and chips last night. She was putting up defenses, but he couldn't figure out why the hell the accidental peep show had her so upset. Patrick was a married man having sex in his own kitchen with his wife. It wasn't the scandal of the century.

"Listen Special Agent Ryan..." She bristled, not liking the *two can play at that game* poke he took, using her full title. "About this morning."

She folded her arms over her chest. "I don't know what you mean."

Tadgh let out a short laugh. "Ye dropped the coffees by the window, so it's obvious you know what I mean. Look, I'm sorry you got an eye full, but it's not as if..."

She threw a hand up, cutting him off. *Shit shit shit!* He knew. The smug bastard knew. Why hadn't she gone back for the coffee cups? "Listen, Detective. It was my mistake. I should have given you more notice before coming up the stairs. What you do on your own time is none of my business. Let's just forget it. This obviously isn't working. You need your apartment back. I'll start looking..."

Tadgh barely heard her after the first couple of sentences. "Wait, stop." She closed her mouth, but she was irritated at the interruption. He narrowed his eyes at her. "You thought it was me." It wasn't a question. More a realization verbalized. "In the kitchen. You thought it was me with...well, I don't know who you thought it was. What exactly did you see?"

"It doesn't matter. I don't want to..."

"Well I do want to talk about it. You've gone radio silent and your dander is up. So, you thought what, exactly? In between dinner with you, my work, a midnight serenade of Led Zeppelin, and a few hours of sleep, I managed to sneak some random woman into my schedule for a quick breakfast shag?" He was half smiling, half scowling, if that was possible.

"Apparently, because I looked up right into your naked ass

working some woman out on the countertop. As much as she was obviously enjoying it, and as spectacular as your ass looks in the flesh, I wasn't expecting a porn show that early in the morning. Try shutting the blinds at least, if we aren't going to use front doors."

Tadgh's cock was hard as a rock. He might not have been able to keep a woman for long, but he'd been around enough women to know when one of them was jealous. She was pissed, despite her best efforts to the contrary, because she thought she'd seen him with another woman. He closed the distance slowly, because if he descended on her too fast, she might actually hit him, or he might kiss her. Neither was advisable.

He looked down at her. To her credit, she met his eyes and didn't back up. Her face was still, unreadable except for those eyes. She couldn't control those, although she tried. "I'll be sure to tell my cousin Patrick that you find his ass spectacular. I'm sure his wife would agree, since she came into Dublin early this morning for the specific purpose of getting a piece of it."

Charlie was looking up at Tadgh O'Brien, and this was the first time she'd seen a genuine spark of anger. What he said sunk in slowly, her brain addled from being so close to him, and half naked in only a bathrobe. The heat was rolling off of him. His eyes sparked, daring her to pop one more word of shit at him. He looked like he was ready to turn her over his knee. The flush hit her cheeks. *It was Patrick. Jesus, Joseph, and Mary.* She hadn't seen the whole length of him or she would have known him by his hair. Why in the hell hadn't that occurred to her?

Because you were so jealous, you were ready to spit nails. You weren't thinking, you were feeling. Too much. Way too much. She backed off, looking away. "I'm sorry. It was…shit. I'm sorry. I didn't see the hair. It was so fast and I just assumed. It doesn't matter, anyway. It was a mistake. This whole thing is a mistake. I need to move."

Tadgh knew what the problem was. She was over tired, stressed, fighting the jet lag, the overwhelming responsibility, and she was also fighting sexual attraction. She'd had a relationship at her previous job that had gone sour. Like him, she probably tried to keep dating out of the workplace. But there was an underlying current between them. An undeniable energy and it was making them both nuts.

He looked her over, flushed, half dry, and probably naked under that robe. He instinctively measured the distance to the bed. He could have her under him, and what had she called it? Oh yeah, working her out. Pushing inside her. Or maybe delay that, and have his mouth parting her thighs beforehand. He jerked as the image shot through his brain. Her hands in his hair as she came against his mouth. He backed up, running his fingers through his hair. His cock was throbbing.

"Get dressed, Charlie. I want to take you somewhere." His voice was rough, edgy. She bristled, not liking the command. He cleared his throat, took a breath, and said a little more civilly, "Please, Charlie. I need to get out of this apartment." *Away from you in that robe and that bed.* "I'll show you a part of the city you haven't seen, and I've got some food from Sal's wife. Will you come with me, steal away for a bit?" He'd found his tender tone again. He just wanted her with him. Safe. And he wanted to pretend, just for a minute, that their lives were simple.

Her shoulders relaxed, her eyes less guarded. "I'd like that. I'm tired, but I won't be able to sleep. I just need some…"

"Peace. You want peace, and I'll give it to you. And Charlie, wear your jeans and boots and some warm clothes. We're taking the motorbike."

CHARLIE LOOKED at the motorcycle and then at Tadgh. "These things are dangerous."

His eyes shifted. "I know that more than most."

She winced. "Oh, God. I'm sorry. That was a stupid thing to say."

He smiled, sadly. "It's all right. It was a long time ago. And I won't be chasing a drunk driver. We'll go slow at first, until you get used to her." He handed her a helmet. She took it in her palms and stared at it. "If you really want to take the car, then we can."

There was no judgment in his tone. He waited patiently for her to decide. She slid the helmet on and began fumbling with the chin strap. Her hair was getting tangled in it.

"Here, let me help. Take it off a second."

She did, and he came behind her. He scooped her hair back with both hands to the back of her neck, like a ponytail. His voice was strained, husky. "Okay, put it back on." When she did, he turned her around, fixing her chin strap. His soft breath was on her face and his eyes fixed downward on his task. Every nerve ending in her body was lighting up. Then he looked at her. And just for a minute, she thought she saw a little bit of the flash she'd seen in the apartment. Heat. Then he took one hand and pulled her hair back over one shoulder. It was a silly gesture. The wind would have it behind her again in another minute. But it was sweet and intimate, and he fingered it just for a moment. "You're hair is beautiful."

She raised a brow. "It's brown." He shook his head.

"It's waves of chestnut, caramel, and light. It's like the sun has come up."

Wow. Not an ounce of calculation, and singly the best thing anyone had ever said to her. This was no street cop. This was a glimpse of the man who liked Tennyson and Waterhouse. This was the man who kept a playpen for his little cousins to sleep over. She was so screwed. She shut her eyes and breathed. *You don't get sappy over colleagues. You do not.*

Tadgh needed to stop. Now. If he didn't, he was going to kiss her and neither of them was going to benefit long term from that. He didn't want to be her convenient, Irish piece of ass while she was on assignment. She didn't seem the sort, anyway. She was a forever girl. Whoever that sod of an ex was, he was completely insane for letting her go.

He stepped away and mounted the bike. "Hang on around my waist or put your hands on my hips. Not the arms. It'll hinder my steering. Now, one foot on that pedal. That's right, and swing the leg. Keep your feet fixed. The pipe gets hot. Really hot. When I turn, don't lean with me, aye? Just stay upright and let me steer the bike with my body." Then he roared the bike to life.

He turned his head, a leather half helmet on and clear glasses. He'd given her the same. "Are ye ready, Charlie love?"

Nope. Not at all. His hips were between her thighs and the damn bike was vibrating. A woman could only take so much. Flashes of Patrick pounding into his wife took on a whole new meaning now. There was no jealousy with Patrick.

It was unseemly, now that she knew it wasn't Tadgh, it was sort of a turn on that she'd seen some beautiful man inside a beautiful woman, hearing her orgasm as he took her deep and hard. She was going to have a hard time looking Patrick in the eye again. She didn't have any impulse toward married men, and she wasn't attracted to him, but damn. Caitlyn was a lucky woman. And he did resemble Tadgh in build and size. So did Liam. That was some potent DNA. She was wondering just what it would be like to be the focus of all that power and sexuality, when Tadgh revved the engine, causing a burst of vibration. Her hands squeezed involuntarily, where they were holding his hips. He took one hand off the bars and drew her arm around his waist.

"Relax, Charlie. Just let yourself go a bit, and enjoy the ride. I promise you're safe." He'd misunderstood her lust for fear, thank God. It's not like she could say, *I'm not scared, I'm completely sexed up. How about you rev the engine a few more times, because I'm close to orgasm.*

She leaned in and put her other arm around him. She could barely circle his waist, even though he was lean. He had layers on, and a thick leather jacket. But she eventually got comfortable, and released herself to the wind and streets and the swirling city lights that were starting to disappear behind them. She started to laugh, a little at first, then shaking with it. She felt his body smile, if that was possible. "I told you," he yelled over the engine. "Much better than a car."

* * *

THE LOT near the water was empty this time of evening. The wind had picked up, the closer they got to the sea. Tadgh parked as close as he dared to the beach. They dismounted and he took off his helmet, then helped her with hers. She was shivering. "It's colder here. I'm sorry." He dug into his saddlebag and pulled out a large blue fleece.

"I'm fine, I'm used to the cold," she said.

"Ye'd be a little more convincing without the teeth chattering, lass. Now be cooperative and take that coat off." She eyed the warm looking fleece and shrugged off her coat. Then she put his half zip fleece on over her sweater, then back on with her coat. He pulled her lapels together.

"Better?"

She nodded. "Downright toasty. Thanks."

"I tried to get us as far down the island as I could. The beach we rode along is called The Strand. It takes you to North Bull Island, which is where we are. Now, if you look that way, down the water you'll see the North Bull Wall and the lighthouse. It's harder to see at night because it's green, and along the opposite side is the South Bull Wall. More prominent and with the red lighthouse."

Charlie was paying close attention. He noticed with a chuckle that she got on her tiptoes when she was looking hard and far. She wasn't actually trying to see over anything, but he imagined it was one of those short girl things, done without knowing. They walked along the path, through seagrass and fierce blowing wind. "The Poolbeg Lighthouse, I've seen on the map. What made you choose this side?" She was grinning, but she genuinely seemed to want an answer.

"I suppose because it's a bit wilder on this side, isn't it?" As they approached the watery coast of the island, he paused and pointed. "Ye see how the tide is low? There's a rocky wall leading out to the lighthouse. It's slippery, a bit treacherous in the wrong weather. When the tide is high, it disappears almost completely under the water. Then the lighthouse is unreachable unless you've got a mind to swim or row out in a small boat. It's beautiful, though. I wish ye could see it when the fog has settled on the shore. If ye catch it perfectly, the rocks are poking up out of the water and the path is clear, but the fog spills over them like liquid, in the crags and around the base of the lighthouse. It gives it a spookiness that the other lighthouse doesn't quite manage." He stopped, realizing that Charlie had gone silent.

"What?"

She was smiling. Just a small smile. "You have an artist's eye, O'Brien."

He snorted. "Not really. An appreciative eye, perhaps, but I can't put it into practice."

She loved her sketching. She'd never shared it with anyone but her Aunt Cassie. Well, Ted had seen her do it. Called it her doodling, which was beyond condescending. And her father had resented anything that brought anyone any joy. He called them her scribbles. The two significant male figures in her life had made sure to knock her down to size when she tried to forge her own path or express herself.

"What are ye thinking about in that brain of yours, Miss Ryan? Ye've scrunched your brow up quite fiercely."

She shook herself. "Sorry, just remembering something." She looked out across the water, relating to that lighthouse on a lot of levels. Even with low tide, she'd made herself hard to get at. "Do you come here very often?"

Tadgh pulled the pita and lamb out of a bag he was carrying and sat, motioning for her to do the same. He handed her a sandwich and began to talk again as they ate. The wind blew his hair. It grew fast, and it was already out of regulation if he were wearing a proper uniform. He pushed it off his face.

"I come here when I need to get out of the city. It chokes me a bit, sometimes. So much activity and so many people. You probably don't understand. It sounds like you've been in the city all of your life. I haven't, though. I'm from the West coast. I spent some time in Clare, near my uncle. When my da was alive and sometimes after, when my ma was poorly and I had to stay with them. When he died, we moved back to the island where my mother was born. So, I've lived a simple life. Worked in a pub and at the ferry. I knew all of my neighbors, mowed the lawn for the local parish. Performed in the local pubs. Not so fast as all that." He gestured to the city lights. "So I come here, and I pretend I'm home. The rocky shores of Doolin or on my island. The wind and the sea air, it gives me some peace."

"So I was right. You are an artist. You're a musician," she said softly.

He shrugged, "I suppose. And, what about you? When do I get to see your sketches?"

He actually felt her jerk. "Do you have that apartment bugged or something?" He was laughing at her. She smacked his arm. "Answer me. How do you know that I sketch?"

He stopped laughing, just looking at her face. Then he took her hand in his. In between her fingertips was pencil staining. And on the outside of her pinky where she'd used it to smudge her lines. He rubbed her fingers in his. "I am a detective, Charlie."

She retracted her hand. "It's just scribbling. It's nothing of note." Then she took a bite, so she didn't have to talk.

He tilted his head and narrowed his eyes. "When someone says something like that about their own work, it's usually a result of hearing it from someone else. Someone who is trying to make you feel less than what you should."

She looked away, her hair blowing around. "Don't, Tadgh. Don't profile me."

"Sorry. It was out of line. It's not my business." He took a bite as he looked around the edge of the island.

"These are good. Sal's wife can cook," she said.

More to break the silence than anything. That reminded him, however. "She's invited you to dinner this coming weekend."

"That sounds nice. I'll pick up some tea or something for them this week." Tadgh thought that was thoughtful. They didn't drink, so tea was perfect. When they polished off their small sandwiches, he helped her up onto a rock that looked out over the water. The wind was roaring around them and she noticed he was looking her up and down, smiling.

"What are you thinking in that brain of yours, Detective?" He laughed that she'd thrown his words back at him.

"Well, I'm watching your profile. Wild hair in the wind, my long blue shirt tail billowing out like skirts. Ye look like Miranda. It's a piece of artwork by Waterhouse. Miranda, The Tempest. Do ye know the painting?"

The warmth in her spread from her chest to her limbs. She tilted her head and answered, "Yes, I know it. It's a favorite of mine." Then, she whipped the hair around one shoulder, fluffed out the shirt tail to catch the wind, and struck a pose.

"Perfect." Tadgh's smile was warm and genuine. She dropped her arms, feeling a little silly. She hadn't had such a fun night in a long time.

"We lived near Lake Erie. It wasn't like this, but it was nice. There are islands there too. I remember going, once. My father was..." She paused. She remembered Tadgh admitting that his mother had been a drinker for a time. Fair was fair. "...well, he was having one of his sober periods." *And, less violent.* "He took us to one of the islands to go fishing and camping. It was a good weekend. One of the only good ones. My little brother actually got his attention for a little bit, learned to fish. It was nice. This reminds me a little of that. I wandered to the edge, in the dark. My mother almost had a heart attack, but not my dad...he had the same kind of risk taking personality. It was probably just turned in the wrong direction. Not used for good, you know what I mean?" Tadgh nodded, not wanting her to stop. She shrugged. "Anyway, thank you for bringing me here." She turned to him. "I should get back. I have some work to do. Some areas I want to walk through, check out."

"Aye, I need to pick up Eve again. I need to head back as well." He looked at his phone. "Plenty of time to get back. It should only take about fifteen minutes once we get on the road."

* * *

IT WAS ABOUT ten minutes into the drive when Charlie's phone buzzed in her pocket for the third time. She let go of Tadgh's waist with one arm to slip her phone out and check. Jesus, something was wrong. She tapped on Tadgh's shoulder. "Pull over! Now!"

He didn't question. He barely had the bike stopped when she was dismounting. She fumbled with her helmet frantically. "Easy, lass. Let me get it." He loosened the strap and she whipped it off. She clicked on her phone and dialed. Tadgh had never seen her so undone. "Pick up, pick up. Jesus, he called three times!"

"Who, darlin'? Who is it?"

She didn't answer because the person obviously answered. "Josh, what's wrong? Are you okay?" She was silent for a moment. "Did mom call the police? What am I saying, of course she didn't. Where are you?" She closed her eyes tight. "Can you go to a neighbor's house? What! What do you mean you moved?" She was pacing around, grasping her hair with her free hand. "Okay, honey. Listen to me. You're going to call Ted. He will come and get you."

Tadgh could hear mumbling on the other end. "I don't care about that. Just because he was a jerk to me doesn't mean he won't help you. None of that matters. Call him, right now. Use the other phone I gave you, the prepaid that dad doesn't know about. Call him while you have me on the line."

Charlie couldn't figure out why her hand was getting wet. Was it raining? Then she realized she was crying. Silent tears, but she couldn't stop them right now. It would take too much effort. She heard her brother talking to Ted. Cheating manwhore he might be, but relief washed over her regardless. *I don't think he has any weapons. No, my door is locked. I think he went into the bedroom with my mom. I'm worried. Should I go check?...Okay. Okay, I won't. I can get out if I'm quiet. I will.*

He was whispering, hidden near his closet as far away from the adjoining wall as he could get. "Josh, tell Ted thank you. I want you both to call me when he has you. Do you understand? And, stay on the phone with him until he has you." She choked on a sob. "I love you, too. I love you, buddy. You did a brave thing."

Tadgh's heart was splitting in two. *Oh, God. Charlie. He did more than drink, didn't he?* He stood by, not too close but close enough for her to feel his presence. If she'd been worried about privacy, she would have walked away. She wasn't worried about anything but her brother. Christ, to be this far away and have to call on your ex? Well, he was a cop and it sounded like the guy was handling it. He was suddenly sad for her. They obviously didn't have any family to help them. She hung up and just breathed. She was staring at her phone, clutching it tight with both hands as if she could will herself into it. Will herself to her brother. He moved slowly, put a hand on her arm. She jolted, looked up at him. Then like a switch was flipped, she backed up, wiped frantically at her tears, and started putting her helmet on.

"Charlie." She cut him off.

"Let's go. I need to be able to answer again. I shouldn't have been out of contact."

He sighed. "Charlie, stop." He took the helmet from her.

"I can do it! I don't need you to dress me!"

She was lashing out, so he just stayed still, holding the helmet.

Charlie was ready to snap. Like full apeshit if he didn't get that understanding look off his face. "Don't pity me. I got this."

"Your father. Did he hurt your brother tonight?" he asked, an edge to his voice. She snapped her eyes to his. Edgy she could handle.

"No, he didn't. He's been warned, but I don't know how long that will hold. Josh said my mother told him I was out of the country. Typical. He didn't hurt him. He shoved him when he got in between my mother and him. Jesus Christ! Nine more months. That's all I need. Nine more months and he's eighteen."

Tadgh understood. Someone with those types of anger issues liked to control the family. He'd never let Charlie take the boy out of the home. And obviously the mother wasn't going anywhere.

"Did he ever hurt you?" She started back with the helmet, not answering him. "Charlie, look at me."

"No." She didn't look at him.

"I don't believe you."

Anger flared in her eyes. "I don't give a shit what you believe. It's none of your concern. Now, are you going to start that thing or do I need a cab?"

* * *

CHARLIE HAD BEEN UNFORGIVABLY rude to Tadgh. She knew it, but maybe that was better. He needed to stay clear of her. She was not what he needed. Josh, on the other hand, did need her. She hated that he'd had to call her ex, but Ted wasn't all bad. He'd always liked Josh and always hated her father.

"Ted, is he okay?" He sounded tired, and a pang of guilt hit her. The time change on top of shift work, God only knows what time Josh had called him.

"He's okay, Charlie. I went up and checked on your mother, too. She managed to get him in bed. She had some red marks around her wrist and arms and a scratch on her neck. Josh said he'd had her by the hair at one point and must have scratched her. It's not as bad as it has been, but it was getting there. I'm glad he called."

"Can you call our old neighbor? Josh has the number. I didn't know they moved. She'll take him. His best friend lives there and his mom takes him in sometimes."

"He called them already. Apparently your dad lost his license. He needed a cheaper apartment that was on the bus route. It's in a real crap neighborhood. Josh has that same neighbor pick him up every day so he doesn't have to change schools. I think the school is turning a blind eye since it's his senior year. I'll take him there after I get some dinner in him. I would keep him, but I'm on nights."

No, no, no. "I don't want you to do that. Thank you for helping, but the emergency is over. I don't want to…" She paused.

"You don't want to deal with me anymore than you have to, right?"

"That's not what I meant. Thank you for helping him. He didn't have anyone to call that would feel safe walking into that situation, but he's not your problem long term. I don't want to put you out anymore."

"Charlie, please. Can't we just talk?"

"No, Ted. If you mean about you and me, then no. It's been four years. I've moved on. You need to talk to the nineteen year old you got pregnant. She needs you. Your kid needs you. You should be hanging up the phone and calling her. Having a good dad matters. The kid must be what, three now?"

He sighed. "She's married. Has been for a year. She doesn't need me. He's a good guy. On the force, actually. I stepped back. I'm just a child support check now."

Stepped back my ass. You never stepped up. And you were forced to pay the child support. What a dick. "Good for her. Now, do you need the address? For the neighbor, that is? My dad won't look for him until after school. So he needs to go home. You're sure my dad didn't hurt him?"

"Charlie, this is not a long term solution. He shouldn't be living there."

"No shit? Really, Ted? You think this is my choice? I called CPS once. It didn't go well. We have nine months. I'm saving for a retainer for a lawyer for him. I need another couple of weeks and he can start proceedings to get emancipated."

"Okay, we'll play it your way. He says your dad hasn't come after him since you threatened him. Do you need money? I can..."

"No. I don't want your money. We can do this. I'm living lean. I can swing it right before Christmas."

"Okay, I'll call and check on him. Tell him to keep that other phone on him and don't use up the minutes." She heard him go into the other room and give the phone to her brother.

"Hi, buddy. How are you?" she asked.

"I shouldn't have called. I'm sorry. I just came home from school and he was really drunk. He was swinging mom around, she was crying."

"It's okay. You did the right thing."

"I hate him, Charlie. I wish he was dead." She understood that. She couldn't tell him that though.

"Don't say that, honey. Just keep doing what you're doing. I have almost enough money. That lawyer will be calling you on your secret phone in a couple weeks. I just need another thousand for the retainer. Can you hang on that long?"

"Yes, I can. I swear I can. I've been getting good grades, I don't get in any trouble. I got a job on the weekends. I look super responsible on paper," he laughed.

"You are super responsible. You are the best man I know, Josh. This is going to happen. Are you kidding? Some little shit sued her parents for college money. This is going to be a piece of cake. All you want is out, and to be safe and happy. We'll make this happen. Then you and I can be roommates. No strippers after ten, though. I have standards."

Her brother barked out a laugh. "You are twisted, sis. You know that?" She loved hearing him laugh.

"You call me again if you get scared, okay? Night or day."

"I will. How's Ireland?" So, she told him. She told him about the art and the city and the lighthouse that was hard to get to.

"I'd like to see it," he said. "If I was there, we'd swim to the lighthouse. We'd race."

"Yes, we would. And you'd beat me because you have those long monkey arms and I'm the runt with the short arms." He laughed, as she'd meant him to. "Maybe we'll come back when you graduate. We'll save for it, okay?" The thought of it was almost too good to tolerate. Them together, leaving their screwed up parents behind.

"I love you, sis. This call must be costing Ted a fortune. I gotta go." It was a fed phone, so probably not. "Don't worry about that. Uncle Sam is paying for this phone. Just call if you need me. You got it?"

"WHAT TIME DOES Liam get off tonight?" Tadgh asked. Eve was riding shotgun, her dance bag in her lap. "About two. I won't see him until tomorrow. How is work going? Any progress on the big case? It's the women on the news, isn't it? It was all over the tele today. Apparently, they think the government hasn't been doing enough to warn everyone. The parents of this last girl went public with it."

Tadgh had heard the reports. He could hardly blame them. "Aye, that's it. It's why we're being so careful with ye, love. Until this is over, ye must follow what I told ye. No walking alone at night. You get a ride or a taxi."

"I understand now, and I'll be careful."

* * *

TADGH PICKED up the phone just as he watched Eve go into her building. "Sal, what's the news?" As Sal talked, Tadgh did a U-turn in the shared O'Brien car.

CHAPTER 10

DOOLIN, CO. CLARE, IRELAND

Sean ended the call with Alanna, sitting at his desk for a few minutes in the aftermath of the conversation. According to her, Sorcha was showing signs of PTSD, and she should know. She was going to call Sorcha tomorrow, try to get her to go with her to Belfast, to her old flat where Edith and Michael, Sorcha's parents, were living.

He needed to get Sorcha away from the distractions of kids and grandkids and her work. And, he needed to get her away from this investigation. The locked office door was a constant reminder of the case he was working on, of the danger that she perceived for the family. She also needed to talk this out with someone, and she wouldn't see a family counselor. Alanna was the most logical choice, and if Alanna thought that Sorcha needed to walk the streets of Belfast and tell her story, then so be it. The hard part was going to be getting Sorcha out of here. He picked up the phone and called Edith next.***

Dublin, Ireland

Tadgh parked his motorcycle in a narrow motorbike spot near the housing complex. He'd had to drop the car off first, because he didn't want to struggle trying to find a safe place to park it. Sal was in the garden of the complex, sitting alone and pretending to look at his phone.

"Where is she?" he asked.

"Last Sullivan called in, she was about three blocks northwest. She's walking around alone in the worst possible spot for her to be. What the hell is she thinking? Sullivan said she's not picking up her phone."

"She's not. She had a rough night and she's not thinking. Let's go."

It took them about ten minutes to find her. She obviously thought Tadgh had gone home, and she was trying to wave a red flag in front of a bull by walking around alone in this area. He spotted her near a bus stop and the infernal woman was wearing headphones. It was like she wanted to get jumped. They kept hidden, observing her. A van went by her, and Tadgh tensed until he saw it was a Taxi. She looked up briefly, then went back to bobbing her head to the music. Then he saw them. A group of young men coming out of the alley, whispering to each other. One pushed the other toward her, daring some interaction. "Hey beautiful lady."

The accents were distinct. Some sort of Middle Eastern. "Hey, turn around so we can see that pretty face, girl." Charlie turned around and looked at them, then took a step back. She was pretending to be scared, he could tell. There were four of them, and she sure as hell should be scared, but she wasn't. Then, it happened. One of them touched her. She slapped his hand away and the mood shifted. He got angry, his buddies chuckling. This time when he grabbed for her she was ready, and she bashed him a good one right in the nose.

Tadgh was headed for her before he made the conscious decision. Sal was yelling something. *Stay back? Like hell I will.* Then Sal was with him. He grabbed one of the guys who was closing in aggressively and yelling at Charlie, punched him in the face, and threw him down on the ground. The other two had run off. Charlie had her foot on the other one's neck, his arm twisted up and back as the man squealed.

Tadgh leaned down, took the wallet out of the man's pocket. Took a picture of his ID, and dropped it back on him as he lay there on the sidewalk. Then he did the same to the other little asshole with the busted nose. He pulled him up by the shirt and got in his face. He had a split lip and frantic eyes. "You keep your hands off her or you will be using your guts for a jump rope, got it ye little bastard?" He pulled him up and shoved him toward the alley.

Sal came running back. "The other two went into an apartment building. It's locked unless you have a code."

Tadgh looked at Charlie like she was next for a spanking. She stuck her chin up. "I had this under control."

He narrowed his eyes. "I wouldn't take on four men at once. You had nothing under control. Now, where's the car?" She said nothing. "So help me God, woman. I will throw you over my shoulder. How did you get here?"

"What the hell is your girlfriend doing here, Tadgh? Can't you control her? She should be at home at this hour!" Sal was talking with an extra thick accent and extra loud. They both looked at him like he was nuts, then his eyes went up to the windows. Apartments with people looking out. He mumbled. "Unless you want to blow all of our covers, you act like you're together, you idiots." Then he got loud again. "Take her home. This is why women shouldn't live on their own!" Charlie snarled at him, but kept her mouth shut.

She started walking away when Tadgh took her arm. Gently, because he wasn't a brut, but he was barely keeping his shit together. He whispered, "Sullivan wants us all at headquarters in twenty minutes. It's not a request."

She snapped back at him. "He's not my boss," she hissed on a whisper.

"For now, he is. If you don't want to be sent home on the next plane to Detroit, you will start remembering that." She pulled and he didn't let go. He leaned in. "Charlie, please. Ye need to calm down. You're not thinking." Then he did something unexpected. As mad as he was at her, he didn't try to bully her. He leaned his forehead down to her temple, closing his eyes. "Ye scared me, Charlie."

She stood for a minute, not sure how to respond to the gesture. "Twenty minutes."

* * *

SULLIVAN LOOKED LIKE HELL. "I should be asleep in bed next to my lovely wife right now. Instead, I get called in because you've gone off on your own again. Are you actually trying to get attacked, Special Agent Ryan? Because let me remind you that you aren't armed. Four men in a dark alley. Have ye lost your bloody mind?"

"I was handling it until your officers interfered and almost blew my cover! I don't need a shadow!" She looked at Tadgh. "How long have you been tracking and following me? No wonder I can't get a break!"

Tadgh threw his hands up in the air. "Listen Feisty Pants, those four assholes will be dealt with. We have them on harassment, and one on assault. We will have uniforms pick up the two I identified in the morning. They are not our guys, though. Surely you know that. That was a crime of opportunity. They saw some eejit out alone at night and took an opportunity that was dangled in front of them like a bloody carrot!"

"Idiot? You listen to me, buddy!" The whistle was piercing. They all three looked at Sal.

"Would you two shut your bloody holes a minute. This may have been an opportunity." He looked at Sullivan. "We made it look like they were together. Like she was out looking for him and he came to her defense. We can use this or we can let our covers get blown. The best thing to do now is go with it."

Charlie was shaking her head. Tadgh was smiling, starting to wrap his head around it. Sullivan said, "He's right. You don't need to work together constantly, but at this point ye've been seen together. You need to play things out as a couple. And you can stop with the head shaking, Miss Ryan, because the other option is to call and tell your boss that you're a loose cannon and a liability and that you need to be replaced."

Tadgh was trying to keep the grin off his face, but just watching her, ready to boil over, was amusing him. She'd trapped herself and she knew it.

As Charlie began walking out the back passageway and through the unmarked door, Tadgh came up behind her and took her hand. She stopped and looked at him. He shrugged. "Now, come hen. Ye can't stay mad at me forever. Let's head back home and make up properly." Her teeth were going to fracture, she was clenching them so hard.

He scooped the back of her neck with his palm and leaned in close. "Will it really be so bad, Agent Feisty Pants, pretending to like me?" His face had lost all of its mocking. "We want the same thing, but I don't want it at the cost of your safety, darlin'. Let's just try it, aye? If it doesn't work, then we'll have a big public break-up. Maybe get Brittney and her big boobs to play along?"

She tried not to laugh. She really did, but the tension in her body couldn't be maintained and she lost it. "You are such a jerk," she said through her laughter.

He nuzzled her a bit, and she didn't know if that was role playing or genuine, but it melted her. It completely melted her. "You are so beautiful when you laugh."

THEY MET BACK UP in the garage, she parking the rental and he his motorcycle. He waited for her, taking her hand again. She looked down at their hands, then up at him. "Strictly business," he said. But his smile was sweet and flirty. They started walking to the flat which was a mile or so away.

Tadgh was a sap. An utterly, pathetic sap. He should be angry with her. He should be serious. This was a serious situation. But all he could do was quell the feeling of giddiness at getting to hold Charlie's hand. They walked along the windy streets and a drizzle began, misting over the brick building and stone streets of Dublin 2. Tadgh wriggled out of his leather jacket and draped it over Charlie's shoulders. "It's too cold. You should wear it," she said, trying to take it off.

He stopped and pulled the lapels tighter. "I'll do. Just let me take care of you, aye. You're no good to anyone if ye catch a chill." He put an arm around her shoulders, pulling her near as they began to walk again.

Charlie looked around the lantern lined streets, the misting rain, the lights by the river in the distance. His arm around her made it all perfect, even if it wasn't real. She relaxed a bit, accepting his touch.

"Did ye talk to your brother again? How are things?" She looked ahead. Having a hard time with the shift in dynamic. "You can talk to me Charlie. I want to help."

She exhaled. "He called just to tell me he was at his friend's house. I'm glad. Ted doesn't need to be overly involved."

"He's your ex? The one you told me about when you were a police officer?" She just nodded.

"Listen, if I could redo that phone call I would have done it in private. It's completely unprofessional that I aired my dirty family laundry in front of you." She stopped walking. "I don't want you to think that I'm distracted, despite what you saw tonight. It was a momentary slip. I just want this over. I want to stop having to notify parents that their daughter is dead. I want my brother to have my support. I don't want to seem ungrateful for what Ted did, but he's a very controlling man. He'll use this to try to…" She stopped.

Tadgh filled in the blanks. "He wants you back. Well, I can hardly blame him. I guess the woman he cheated on you with didn't last?"

"He got her pregnant," she said.

Tadgh winced. "So he's got a wife and child and he's still trying to get back in your knickers? What a piece of shite."

"He didn't marry her. She was nineteen, alone and pregnant. She was starting to show when I left the department. I actually just felt bad for her. He was a lot older than her and she got all moony over him just like I did. It shocked the hell out of me, because he wasn't the careless type if you get my meaning." She shook her head. "Anyway, he's not the devil, and he did do me a favor, but I don't really want him around my brother for very long. It's bad enough the way he has seen my dad treat women, he doesn't need an education from a manipulative man-whore either. Josh is a wonderful kid. The best. All

I want is to get him away from that household and to start fresh with him. I don't think we can wait nine months."

"So what's the plan?" They'd entered the building by now, and Tadgh instinctively opened the apartment door. Then he realized what he was doing. "Sorry, I'll just…"

She opened the door and swept her arm inward. "Come in, it's okay. We are dating, right?" He came in and turned the lights on, looking around out of instinct. "The plan is that we get a lawyer. I've almost saved enough for the retainer. Then, he tries to get emancipated by the court, meaning he's legally an adult. He's got a lot of people willing to vouch for him. Teachers, a swim coach, his boss at a dry cleaning place he makes deliveries for. The bottom line is that he's not safe. When my father finds out what we have planned, he will need somewhere to go. He is a very controlling man, and a violent drunk."

"I'm so sorry, Charlie. It seems like this was a bad time for you to leave."

She shrugged. "This is the job. I can't pick my own assignments. And if it wasn't for this job, we'd never get a fresh start. The income, the moving, it's all good for us. If we stayed in Cleveland, we would never truly be free of him."

Tadgh reached his hand out before he thought about it. He smoothed her hair down the back of her scalp to her shoulders. It was damp and curling and held little droplets from the misty rain. *If you were mine, you'd never be hurt again. You'd never feel unsafe again.* But she wasn't his. She had the weight of the world on her, and she would leave at the end of this case and manage her life.

"I'll see you at the meeting tomorrow? Everyone will be there, including my Uncle Sean." He walked toward the window, sliding it open. He stopped and turned to her. "Tonight, I wasn't trying to control you. I just wanted you safe. I think about those girls, their lifeless bodies. I couldn't bear it if something happened to you." Then he went up the stairs without waiting for a response.

CHAPTER 11

$\mathcal{T}$he conference table was full at headquarters. As Charlie looked around, she noticed that in addition to the task force, Tadgh's uncle and the Assistant to the Lord Mayor of Dublin were there as well. There was also a trusted representative of the Prime Minister in attendance. They were all arguing.

"We agreed to let the bloody Americans come in here with the understanding that they'd actually help. Yet we've got one more victim, and now the press is all up in our knickers wanting answers. What exactly has the lass accomplished?" The occupants of the table stiffened and looked at the Mayor's assistant. Tadgh was ready to throw his career under the bus, when Sullivan took his place.

"Her name is Special Agent Ryan, and you'll do well to remember that or you will be shut out of these meetings. You have no investigative expertise to contribute, and you are here on invitation." The table rumbled with approval as the Mayor's assistant sputtered.

An unlikely ally spoke up. "Oh, and wouldn't we love to be seeing you out on the street at night. Alone with your arse hung out as bait and the Lord Mayor of Dublin and Prime Minister making sure ye can't arm yourself. Best mind yer manners, Assistant." Miller put an emphasis on Ass- which was as schoolyard as you could get, but it warmed Charlie to her core. The men were sticking up for her, but she needed to reel this in.

"He's right. It's okay." She shrugged. "You're right. I haven't made a lot of progress. We need the crime scene notes. They should be ready," she nodded to the CSI officer and coroner in attendance. "I've been wandering the city aimlessly, guessing at potential target areas. We need to narrow it down."

"And she needs a weapon." She looked across the table at Tadgh and his face was serious. "This is a load of shite that you'd put two grown men that are twice her size and working as a team on the street with a weapon, and you're leaving her defenseless. The FBI would never send one of their agents in the field without protection. We should do no less!" The group nodded, gave a few supportive comments.

Sal stood up, unholstered his issued weapon, took the magazine out, and laid it in the middle of the table. "She almost got jumped by four Middle Eastern men last night. They weren't our suspects, but they had bad intentions. If she doesn't carry a weapon, I don't carry a weapon."

Charlie's voice was seized up. She was seriously ready to break down and cry like a girl in front of this whole group of male cops. Nope. Screw that. She bit her cheek. Then she watched as Tadgh stood up, unloaded his weapon and put it on the table. One by one, all of the armed men in the room did it, including throwing a couple of tasers, impact weapons, and knives in the mix for the men who didn't get issued a weapon. Most Garda weren't armed with guns. Even Detective Hairy Ass tossed his expandable baton and pepper spray in the pile.

"You don't arm her, you don't arm us. Hopefully the need doesn't arise where we need these," Tadgh said.

Sullivan looked at Sean. "Just like his bloody da. You O'Briens are a pain in the ass." Sean was grinning ear to ear.

"Aye," he nodded at Tadgh.

Tadgh replied back, "Aye."

Patrick was standing in a side door, having shown up late due to another meeting with his unit. "Aye, indeed. Stubborn as the day is long." He winked at Charlie. "But I'm not throwing my rifle on that table, I haven't brought it with me for a start." The men rumbled with suppressed laughter.

Sullivan answered, "It's not my call. This came from the chief and the mayor." A collective brow was raised.

"It's okay, sir. We realize it wouldn't be politically savvy of you to use your own judgment." This was one of the older Sergeant detectives that could get away with a little more insubordination. The man folded his arms, challenging DC Sullivan to nut up or shut up.

Sullivan looked at the two bureaucrats from the Mayor and Prime Minister's offices. "Can you excuse us?" Both were tilting their heads, incredulous that they were being dismissed. "I'm assuming you want to have the option of denying culpability or knowledge of what's about to be decided?"

Tadgh didn't know that soft bellied politicians could move so fast. When they shut the door behind them, Sullivan looked at Tadgh. "Take her to the armory. Something small, easily concealed, make her put fifty rounds through it at the range." The shoulders around the whole table loosened a bit, the men letting their hackles down.

"Good for you, boss." One of the men said.

Charlie was looking down at the pile of weapons, willing the lump out of her throat. She looked at all of the men in the room. "Thanks, guys." That was all she could manage.

They all got up, some blushing, some suppressing a smile. They gathered their weapons and resettled as the crime scene investigation officer started his brief.

"We got a good set of tire tracks in the cemetery where the body of Danielle Cooper was found. She's the most recent victim. Large tires with good tread, common brand, a distinct difference in the wear on the right, front tire. Seems to fit a large SUV or most likely a van of some sort." Tadgh was looking at his copy of the report and he circled the word *van*.

"There was also some debris transferred into the mud. Metal filings, some sort of steel. There were trace amounts in the hair of the victim as well, as if she'd been dragged through the area where the tires had been. The steel could be from tool and die areas, a warehouse, an old mill, a body shop. There were also traces of copper found in her hair, bits of wire. We've sent the samples to the team in America. The FBI will try to narrow down a more definitive source but it might take a while." The officer flipped the page as did everyone else. "The grey carpet fibers found in different areas of the body seem to indicate she was transported nude, post-mortem in a vehicle that was carpeted where they placed the body. Consistent with Toyotas, Hondas, and a few other Asian car manufacturers, a model between the years of 2008 and 2012. These fibers are consistent with each murder, so they are using the same vehicle or identical makes and models."

Tadgh circled the years, then looked up at Charlie. She was taking notes and rubbing the bridge of her nose. No doubt picturing these poor broken girls being tossed into a grungy vehicle, nude, ready for disposal.

The officer continued. "The carving on the inner arm seems to have been done with a small blade, something precise like an X-Acto style tool or a scalpel. It's too cleanly executed to be a big knife or box cutter. It's precise, like they wanted to get it right." The officer shook himself. "Semen, hair and skin have been collected. Nothing on file for those, but they are all good solid samples. Again, consistent with all of the victims. One male is doing the rapes. The bruising on the arms and legs, for restraining purposes most likely, indicating three people. One with significantly smaller hands than the other two. We weren't able to lift a print off of the skin." He flipped to the final page. "Cause of death was strangulation. One set of hands matched all four victims. Most likely the one who raped them. Restraints used seemed to be a combination of tape and latex covered steel roping, maybe bicycle chains."

The officer was sweating, completely uncomfortable. She could hear curses throughout the table, under their breath. It was hard to listen to, but they needed this. This information was crucial for narrowing down the areas where the crimes took place, what was used, how many were involved. According to these findings, there were two helpers and one psychotic, serial rapist and murderer.

* * *

CHARLIE LOOKED at the two handguns, shook her head. "Where in the hell am I suppose to hide these? I need concealable, not a cannon."

The officer looked at Tadgh. "She's right, and I know you have some smaller guns. This is per the Deputy Commissioner in charge. Don't dick with me, O'Deens. Let's see them."

The armory officer sighed. "These are for special assignments. I don't have many, so don't lose the bloody thing." He brought out two boxes. Opened the first.

"A Walther PPK/S? How very Hollywood of you. James Bond never mentioned that they jam constantly. Next."

Tadgh was laughing, the armory officer scowling. He had a grudging smile tipping up the side of his mouth, however. "Ye know your guns, lass. How about this one, then? Will this satisfy Her Majesty?" He cracked open the box and the Sig Sauer P320 Sub-compact.

"Now you're talking. You were playing hard to get, Officer O'Deens. .40 cal?"

He shook his head. "It's a nine millimeter. Easy to hide, light weight, and I've got a holster."

"That's the one. I'll need fifty practice rounds and enough to fill it and two extra magazines. And a cleaning kit."

As the officer collected everything, he stole a glance at Tadgh, then back at her. "What time do ye get off, Miss Ryan? Maybe you'd like to…" Before he could finish, Tadgh interrupted.

"She's got plans." Then he grabbed the bag he'd prepared for her and turned her in the other direction. Away from O'Deens.

"Wait, you need to sign for this," he said, miffed at the cock-block.

Charlie walked back, signed the paper, and he winked at her. "Territorial, isn't he?" Charlie crinkled her brow in confusion, and the officer laughed. "You may know a lot about guns, love. But ye've got a lot to learn about men."

After fifty practice shots, Tadgh had a whole other level of respect for Special Agent Ryan. "You're impressive with a pistol, woman. Remind me not to sneak up on you."

Charlie smiled, "Yeah, well. You're good back up. I think I'll keep you." She looked down as she packed up her supplies, a cleaning kit, and the pistol and ammo. "I never thanked you. You or Sal. I put myself in a bad situation. If you hadn't been there, I could have really gotten hurt. I'm not Superwoman, as much as I like to wish I were." She looked up at him and his eyes were intense.

"Would you come somewhere with me today, Charlie? Out of the city. I have a commitment with my family, and I'd like to show you a bit more of the island."

"If it is a family commitment, maybe I shouldn't intrude," she said hesitantly. Deep down, though, she really wanted to go.

Tadgh waved a dismissive hand. "My family will be fine with it. It's sort of my decision. It's an anniversary of sorts. They do it for me. Come on, girl. Ye haven't had even a few hours off since ye set foot in Ireland last week." He slung her bag over his shoulder. "Just come with me, Charlie. You're supposed to be playing my sweetheart. Will ye leave me without a partner for this?"

Her stomach did a leap. "Well, when you put it that way. I guess O'Deens will have to go out tonight without me." She was teasing, of course, but he stopped. Then he leaned in, looking at her mouth.

"Did I interfere? Do ye welcome his attentions?"

She swayed, just a bit, but he saw it. He looped his arm around her waist, never breaking eye contact. "Answer me, darlin'. Is he who ye want?"

She answered him, and her voice was hoarse. "No."

Someone pounded on the security door. "Are you almost done in there? I need to run quals with another officer."

"Feckin' O'Deens." Tadgh's voice was harsh. He backed away, collecting himself. *What the hell are you doing, O'Brien?* "I'm sorry. We should head home. I need to change and shave."

Charlie did a little mental shake, trying to get her brain to work again. That's what happened when all of the blood in your body rushed to one area. Damn, but that man was potent. Barely restrained heat and sexuality. She was completely aroused and he hadn't even kissed her. He'd wanted to, though. *Feckin' O'Deens is right.*

* * *

CHARLIE OPENED the door to her apartment and the breath shot out of her lungs. Tadgh and Patrick stood in the doorway. Tadgh was freshly shaved, hair combed back tidily. She looked down at herself. He'd told her to dress warmly, that they would be outside. She was wearing black trousers, brown riding boots, and a caramel colored cashmere sweater. She was also wearing her pea coat with a plaid scarf. "Is this okay? I think I should change. What exactly is this event? I should change." She turned and Tadgh caught her wrist gently in his hand.

The electricity shot up her arm, as it always did when he touched her. Her eyes flared, and she noticed that Patrick was looking back and forth between them. "You're fine. You look beautiful."

She extracted her hand. "Come in, please. I just need to shut and lock the windows. Hi, Patrick."

She was blushing. The woman was actually blushing. Tough, FBI agent Charlie Ryan was turning scarlet. Then Tadgh remembered. *Spectacular ass. Working some woman out on the counter.* He looked at Patrick who was grinning. The cocky bastard was glowing. He shrugged. "Sorry brother. I'm something to see when I get down to it. The poor lass is starstruck."

He knew Patrick was just having a bit of fun, but it chaffed. He didn't like that she'd seen his cousin naked. He looked up as she yelped, Duncan popping in the window. "Jaysus, Duncan!" The cat yelled at him with a little roar, going directly to Charlie and winding around her legs.

She picked him up, scratching behind his ears. She took him to the kitchen and pulled out a small can of cat food. Opening the cupboard under the sink, she took out a disposable cat litter box, and set it out on the kitchen floor. Tadgh laughed. "You have stolen my cat, and yer bribing him!"

She looked up and smiled. "What can I say? He's a lady's man. He keeps coming to the window." The damn cat was purring so loud in between bites, it practically shook the floor. She washed her hands and dried them, then she looked at Patrick. He was trying to keep a straight face, but she was no dummy. "You know, don't you? He told you!" Then she smacked Tadgh on the arm.

"Aye, he did." The voice was feminine and came from behind the men. Charlie saw a woman emerge from behind them, through the doorway. She was stunning. Long blonde hair, pretty eyes, and a light dusting of freckles all over her face. "And, I'll have to agree. It is a spectacular ass." Then she smacked Patrick on the bum.

Caitlyn walked into the apartment and went straight to Charlie. "My name is Caitlyn, and I'll have to apologize for our little performance. I'll admit that when I laid eyes on him, the state of the blinds was furthest from my mind." She winked and shook hands with Charlie. "Now then. Are we ready? Will ye both be joining us back home?"

"No, love. Sorry. I've got to be back here for work." Tadgh looked at Charlie. "Could we take your car? I'd take the bike, but it might upset my mam today."

Charlie nodded, "Of course." Then she walked by Caitlyn, leaning in and winking. "You were pretty hot too."

Caitlyn laughed loudly. "I like her."

As they drove out of the city, headed West, Charlie looked over from the passenger seat. Poor Tadgh was crammed into the seat of her rental car. Economy sized cars didn't do well with extra large drivers. "So, why would the motorcycle upset your mother, and why more so today?" Even as she said it, it dawned on her. A family commitment that was outside. "Oh, Tadgh. It's the anniversary of his death, isn't it?" She took him in, so handsome in his dress blues. They had pulled over to a cafe just outside the city, and the two men had changed into their Garda dress uniform. They weren't supposed to be seen together with either of them in uniform, since Tadgh was under cover. So, they'd left the city and changed their clothing. He was breathtaking in his uniform. His rapidly growing hair tidied up, his face clean shaven. He'd worn his Garda blues for his father. Suddenly, her throat was tight.

Tadgh looked at Charlie and she looked like she was about to tear up. "It's all right. I should've told you. It's a hard day for all of us."

"I can drop you off and go busy myself. I don't want to intrude. Your family probably doesn't need an audience for today."

"Yer not an audience, Charlie. You're my friend. I know we work together, but I didn't just ask ye for a ride. I'd like you there. You can meet the rest of the family. Though, I will warn ye up front, they'll try to marry you off by tea time."

Charlie laughed, "I don't think I'm a dream daughter-in-law. You won't have to worry. I'm sorry, though. Losing your father so young, it must have been hard. On you and your mother. I don't have a good dad. You were lucky to have him and I'm so sorry you lost him."

Tadgh was taken aback as Charlie put a palm over his hand that lay still on the seat. She gave it a squeeze and he smiled at her. It was a sad, sweet smile. So incongruous with the size of him and the masculinity he exuded. "Thank you, darlin. I'm glad you're here."

That simple phrase warmed her all over, spreading out from her chest and into her whole body.

* * *

Drumcliffe Cemetery, **Ennis, County Clare**

Tadgh pulled into the old cemetery that stretched across the rolling green hills of County Clare. It was large, containing some very old, weathered and moss covered graves as well as more current ones. There were also ruins on the property, and Charlie thought to herself that she'd never realized cemeteries could be beautiful. The thought of this being a final resting place seemed kind of soothing. This was an old civilization, the ruins proving that point as they watched over the dead.

"Are ye Catholic? I didn't think to ask."

Charlie shook her head. "No. We weren't really taken to church.

My father's people are Catholics, but he didn't practice. My mom was some sort of Protestant, Lutheran I think, but she never took us to church. I'm sorry, will that be an issue? I can stay in the car."

"Of course not. I'll tell ye what. I spent more time in a church than most, since I volunteered to keep the grounds. I'll let you count some of my hours."

She snorted a little. "I don't think it works that way, but thanks. I'm a quick learner. I'll stand in the back and watch everyone. It works in yoga class."

Tadgh laughed. "All right. Let's go meet everyone. I'll need to tend to my mother, see. So I'll have you settled with one of my cousins' wives or Brigid. Just be warned, you'll probably end up holding someone's baby. They breed like rabbits, the lot of them."

"That must be hard on Caitlyn. Maybe I should stand with her."

The surprise on Tadgh's face gave way to gratitude. "I think that would be perfect. She's pretty good friends with Eve, but Eve has a dress rehearsal and a test today, so she couldn't come. Just don't be ogling her husband's ass from behind."

Although he must be joking, his tone was less light. She narrowed her eyes at him. She thought about the way he'd reacted when O'Deens had hit on her. Was he jealous? She could barely fathom it. He was too beautiful for words, and he could have any woman he wanted. Before she could respond, he opened the car door, came around as she was putting her gloves on, and opened her door. She was taken aback. She tried to think back to the last time anyone had opened her car door for her. Probably never.

They approached the other vehicles where there were several people standing. Another car had parked near them, and a priest got out to join them. Tadgh started making introductions, but all she could do was gape. The men were all cut from the same gorgeous cloth. From the grandfather David, Sean Sr., all through the younger men Aidan, Michael, Patrick, Liam, and Sean Jr.

The women were equally beautiful. Granny Aoife, as they all called her, had that thick gorgeous silver hair that had no hint of yellowing. She had smooth, lovely skin like some British actress who'd aged into a gorgeous older woman like Helen Mirren or Vanessa Redgrave. Tadgh's Aunt Sorcha had lovely auburn hair, sprinkled with just a touch of silver. She was a stunner with green eyes and a beautiful smile. Brigid was equally as stunning and looked a lot like Sorcha. She had some of her father in there as well, though. The smart eyes that took shades from both parents as Michael's did.

There was a middle aged woman, clearly an O'Brien, with a tall, dark-haired husband and two dark haired younger men. Tadgh introduced her as his Aunt Maeve. Her husband Nolan and her handsome sons, Cian and Cormac, were living in England. She'd guessed the sons in their mid to late twenties. *Both single if she really is just a friend.* She'd nudged Tadgh, made the two sons blush, and her husband roll his eyes. Tadgh smiled tightly and shot a look at the two cousins. "She's not making plans for England, Auntie. Sorry."

Alanna, Aidan's wife, was carrying a baby and wheeling a toddler. She was absolutely lovely. Long blonde hair braided down her back and glowing skin and green eyes. She watched as Tadgh picked up the last woman and swung her around. Michael's wife, Branna. She was a dark beauty. Ivory skin, deep blue eyes, and long, silky black hair. Tadgh's face lit up as he spoke with her, and a pang of irrational jealousy hit Charlie right in the gut.

"They're close, Tadgh and Branna. He was her first friend in Ireland." Charlie turned to see a woman with the most beautiful whiskey colored eyes she'd ever seen. They glowed golden. She had short, fair hair with a touch of silver. She was taller than the O'Brien women. There was no doubt who she was. She had her son's eyes. "I'm Katie O'Brien. Tadgh's mam. And you are?"

"I'm Charlie Ryan. A colleague of Tadgh's."

"Well, now. You must be more than a colleague if he brought ye here today. We've been doing this for twenty one years, and he's never brought anyone."

Charlie thought maybe she was teasing, but her face was tired, not mischievous. She said it matter of factly. "I think he was just trying to get me out of the city. We've been working a lot. I'm so sorry, Mrs. O'Brien. About your husband, I mean."

Tadgh approached them at that moment and Katie turned her attention. She hugged her son. "How's my lad?" As they began to catch up, Charlie started to back away. Tadgh put a hand out, taking her gently by the wrist. "Have ye met my friend Charlie?"

* * *

CHARLIE MET SO MANY O'BRIENS, she was having trouble keeping everyone straight. The family was huge. She'd settled near the back of the group, overwhelmed by the greeting she'd received. They were all so kind. All smiling at her like she was the only one that was not in on some big secret. She, at one point, indeed had a baby shoved in her arms. Alanna was busy tending to a dirty diaper, from her toddler Davey, back at their car. The little girl was lovely. Clear blue eyes and a tuft of fair hair. The child flapped her arms, grabbing fists full of hair. Tadgh had to detangle her now spit covered hair from the baby's fist as he smiled down at her. His eyes sweet and a little sad. He put the baby in the crook of his arm and brushed Charlie's hair back with his free hand. "She likes you, I think."

Charlie had experience with babies, being eight years older than her brother. She loved taking care of him when she was a little girl. But, she was rusty. When she said as much, Tadgh smiled and said, "I'd imagine it's a bit like riding a bike. The body remembers." Then he took the child over to his mother. He looked way too good and way too natural holding that baby in his arms, and Charlie had to shake herself.

"Did ye hear that explosion?" Charlie turned, and it was Brigid who spoke to her.

"I'm sorry?"

"It was your ovaries exploding. A beautiful man holding a baby will do that to a lass." Finn burst out laughing and nudged her.

"Jaysus woman, do ye have no filter at all?"

Charlie coughed on a laugh as her face colored. Just then, Alanna came back with Davey. "What's so funny? Where is Isla?"

Brigid pointed, "She's over there charming Tadgh."

They all looked over and Tadgh had the baby up, arms raised so he could blow raspberries under her chin. The women all let out a collective sigh. Finn groaned. "There is way too much estrogen on this side of the lot. I'm out." He walked over to Seany, leaving the women to themselves.

Branna approached. "They're ready."

Charlie watched as all of the women gathered up the children so that the men could collect together. Three O'Brien men were in police dress blues. The eldest O'Brien brother was in what appeared to be a tailored military uniform. It was dark green with a beret style hat. The hat brooch was a feather and a harp. Michael was in his Coast Guard dress blues. The other men were in matching fisherman crews and slacks. "It's the O'Brien clan weave. They all have them. Tadgh's mother made them for everyone. She's a weaver on the island." Caitlyn had settled next to her, and had promised to fill in the blanks when it came to tradition or ceremony, and to translate the Gaelic if need be.

The priest started. He gave a beautiful prayer, and as little church as she'd had, it stirred Charlie as she looked around at the beautiful family, the old cemetery, the stone and moss and tangible loss that hung renewed in the air between them. She thought of the young woman's body, ruined in that Dublin cemetery, then she pushed the thought away with a shiver. She was not going to work today. Even in her mind. She felt someone on the other side take her hand. It was Sorcha, Tadgh's aunt. She looked at the woman, and she saw a mother's wise eyes, survivor's eyes. She smiled weakly. Sorcha squeezed and let go.

Charlie watched as the little girl Cora approached the middle and read a poem she'd written for her Uncle. The one she'd never met, but would someday meet in Heaven. The tears were rolling throughout the crowd. Then, Tadgh addressed the crowd, clearing his throat that was thick with emotion.

"Thank you, leanbh mo chroí. That was lovely."

Child of my heart. Caitlyn had whispered the translation in Charlie's ear and a wave of emotion rolled through her as well. She thought about the children's snacks and baby gear he had in his apartment. What kind of man was he? She couldn't fathom him, any of them. What would it have been like if she and Josh had been surrounded with this type of family? Or her mother? Her mother had no one to turn to, no alternative in her mind other than staying with an abusive husband and father. Tears pricked her eyes and she blinked rapidly, the echoes of a burning sensation returning, just at her left shoulder blade. That scar that was forever. Had she ever been the child of someone's heart? She thought of her brother. She would make sure things changed for him. He was the child of her heart. The moment he'd come home from the hospital. She'd been eight, but she'd been allowed to hold him. *My baby. He's my baby.* He'd always been her baby.

As if to rattle her from her inner thoughts, the crowd shifted. The men all lined triangulating out. The only one that stood to the side was Finn, Brigid's husband. He held a large, flat, round thing that kind of looked like a drum. A piece of wood in the other hand. Tadgh was at the front and everyone fell dead silent as he opened his mouth and began to sing. Caitlyn whispered. "Mo Ghile Mear, my gallant hero." Then she fell silent, as if knowing that Charlie wouldn't want to miss a second of it. As he sang, each of the men joined him, all taking their part as the voices blended in deep, rich, lovely tones. The song picked up as Finn began to beat the drum with the wooden piece. Charlie had a knot in her throat, hot tears threatening at the corners of her eyes. Tadgh's voice was so beautiful. They all were beautiful.

Tadgh's face was stoic as he concentrated on the music. He looked ahead, unable to look at his mother, his family, even the name on the grave before him. When he finished the old Gaelic tune, and the drum came to a halt, his eyes fell on Charlie. She met his eyes and didn't look away. He wasn't sure what he saw there, in those green and amber depths, but it was what he needed. It filled him up, soothed him. He stepped back then, and turned.

Charlie thought about the small woman next to her. Those warrior eyes offering her strength, and that's what she tried to muster as she looked into Tadgh's eyes. *I'm here. That's all I can do for you, but I'm here.*

She looked over to see the American wife of Michael, Branna. She was silently sobbing. She thought the response odd, since she'd never known Tadgh's father. She wondered again just how close she was to Tadgh.

"She lost her father as well. In the war. That's why she weeps for him." Charlie turned to look at Sorcha's knowing eyes and flushed. Obviously, Sorcha was tracking her thoughts. She was ashamed. Her jealousy had no place here.

"That's terrible. I'm so sorry for both of them. Good fathers make all the difference. They should have had a full life with them."

There was a question in Sorcha's eyes, but she didn't pry. Charlie watched as the men lined up, filling small glasses that were set on a stump next to a bottle of whiskey. All of the women did the same, and finally the old priest at the end of the line. The only one who didn't was Katie, because she was a recovering alcoholic. Charlie stared at the glass in her hand, smelling the strong fumes. Just a sip for each person, and it was obvious that it had a purpose.

She looked around and felt, for the first time in a long time, true connection with a group of people. This time Sean Sr. took the front. The men gathered around the grave, holding their glasses. The women moved in behind them until there were layers of them circled around this man, *William O'Brien: Loving Husband and Father. Beloved Son. Loyal Brother.* She remembered the priest's words, and realized that they weren't platitudes. To have this gathering every year for the last twenty years? He must have been quite a man.

She watched as the men all looked at Sean. He took a half step forward, as if to prepare everyone. Then another song began, and Charlie was happy to know that it was in English. He sang alone at first, but then the entire O'Brien clan and extended family joined him. It was so beautiful that the hair stood up all over her body.

Of all the comrades that e'er I had
They are sorry for my going away
And all the sweethearts that e'er I had

146

They would wish me one more day to stay

CHARLIE LOOKED at Katie O'Brien and that's when the tears started. Sean's beautiful, baritone voice was comforting, but it was also opening old wounds. That was what remembering was, though. You took the good with the bad. Katie was the only one of the group who wasn't singing. Even Caitlyn, who swore she couldn't carry a tune, had joined them.

But, since it falls unto my lot
That I should rise and you should not
I'll gently rise and I'll softly call

SHE WATCHED AS SEAN CONTINUED, and she saw him break, his voice trembling. Liam came beside him and put an arm around him for strength. Taking the lead, Liam raised his voice.

A man may drink and not be drunk
A man may fight and not be slain
A man may court a pretty girl
And perhaps be welcomed home again
But since it has so ought to be
By a time to rise and a time to fall
Come fill to me the parting glass
Good night and joy be with you all
So, good night and joy be with you all.

SEAN HAD RECOVERED HIMSELF, and he turned to Tadgh and raised his glass, the parting glass. Everyone did the same, and Charlie joined them, swept up in this beautiful display of family loyalty. "Til we meet again, mo dheartháir." Then everyone tipped their glass and drank.

* * *

THE GROUP WALKED BACK to their cars slowly. There was a lot of talking, some laughing through tear-stained faces. Brigid had her husband on one arm and her little brother, Seany, on the other. He wasn't so little, and he was devilishly handsome. She thought of her own brother, not for the first time today. She looked at Sean the elder, hugging his sister who lived in England. "You're thinking about Josh." Tadgh said softly as he appeared next to her.

She looked at him, startled, then let out a nervous laugh. "You are mind reading again, O'Brien."

He took her arm and hooked it in his. "It's not that hard to see. And besides, Cora's the psychic, not me. I'm just observant." She laughed until she realized he wasn't kidding. She looked over at the lovely child with long, chestnut curls. She was holding the hands of her younger cousins, the twins Halley and Brian.

"You're serious."

"Don't give me that look. You bloody Yanks have no old magic left. Ye've choked it to death with cheeseburgers and bad music." He was teasing her, smiling as she feigned offense.

"Cheeseburgers have been perfected by us bloody Yanks. You haven't lived until you've had my bacon and blue burger."

He looked into her eyes, then to her mouth. "It's a date then. Tell me when to come to you, and I'll be at the window." *Damn, but doesn't that have a potential for two meanings.*

Warm tingling spread out from her belly. "Thank you for including me. It was...something...being a part of this today. Your father was very loved. I don't have to tell you that." She saw Tadgh's mother being led to her car. "This was hard for her. I'm sure it's hard for everyone, but she lost her..."

"Mate. She lost her mate," he said simply.

On impulse, she broke away from him and came beside Katie. "It was nice to meet you, Mrs. O'Brien." She put her hand out and Katie enveloped it in both of hers.

"Call me Katie, dear. Thank you for coming today. And watch out for this one." she motioned to Tadgh. "He's got an adventurous streak like his da."

"Well, he's a wonderful detective but he's also a gentleman. That tells me he had a good mother. Your William would have been proud of both of you."

Katie's eyes lit up and she raised her chin a bit. "Thank you." Then she awkwardly put her arms out and Charlie hugged her. She hugged her son next, whispering endearments that Charlie didn't understand. She got in her car and drove away.

Tadgh was so quiet, she'd forgotten he was there. She turned around and not only was he looking at her, but the bulk of the O'Briens. Granny Aofie approached her. "She's had a hard life without him. Thank you, Charlie." Then Aofie pushed her hair back and smiled like she was looking at her own grandchild. "You are a beauty. And not a stitch of make-up. My William would have liked you." Then she looked at Tadgh, and held her arms out for a hug. "My sweet boy. He'd be so very proud." Then one by one, all of the O'Briens lined up to say their goodbyes.

It took the ever blunt Brigid to break up the goodbye party. "Surely you two don't think yer buggering off back to work? You are thirty minutes from home, Tadgh O'Brien. You're going to get in that little Yank mobile and join yer family for a pint at the pub. Show the lass a proper night out, O'Brien style." Her grin was sweet, but the eyes were unbending. She was not going to be denied.

CHAPTER 12

"We won't stay long. I'm sorry. I should have known we wouldn't get out of here easily." Tadgh was driving now, headed northwest toward the coast.

"You don't seem too upset about it. I can drive back to Dublin. Go ahead and enjoy yourself."

Tadgh smiled. "Thanks. My cousins have a way of getting me in the drink with little effort. I may need to take you up on that. Now, what's our plan for work? I think public displays of affection should start immediately. In fact we should start practicing."

Charlie was shaking her head, smiling, and Tadgh had to admit he was pretty pathetic. "I'm glad you're so committed, O'Brien. I hope it isn't too much of a strain on your acting skills."

"Oh, I'll muster. It'll be tough, but..." She smacked him hard in the chest. "Ow! Ye daft harpy! You're going to make me crash!" he was laughing now.

"Well, after seeing the brides your cousins have brought home, you don't have to remind me I'm the ugly stepsister." She was giggling, but there seemed to be a note of truth to her words that stopped Tadgh cold. He slowed to a stop.

Charlie looked around. "What's wrong? Did we miss a turn?" She looked at him and was baffled by the look on his face. She crinkled her brow in question.

"You're beautiful, Charlie. Beautiful to the point of distraction. If I didn't need another reason to hate that ex of yours, the fact that you haven't been told that enough is at the top of the long list of reasons why you are better off without that dickhead." Then he pushed the gas pedal and carried on.

Not willing to dig that nerve ending any more raw, she changed the subject. "The cemetery where your dad is buried is really old. It's lovely, if that doesn't sound too weird."

"Not at all. It's a lovely spot to be laid to rest and not too far from home. I wish it wasn't so dark. You'd love Doolin. It's where Brigid and Michael settled to be close to Aunt Sorcha and Uncle Sean and Granny and Grandda. Caitlyn's parents are about twenty minutes north, toward Galway. She and Patrick lived in Ballyvaughan, in a little condo. Then, they moved when he finished his training. We both did. And Liam's been at Trinity for eight years, so it's nice when we can all get together in one place. Especially with Aunt Maeve and Aidan visiting from England. We'll likely fill the pub."

* * *

GUS O'CONNOR's Pub
Fisher Street, Doolin
County Clare, Ireland

AND, fill it they did. Gus O'Connor's was usually slow in the off season, especially during the week. However, it was currently filled to bursting with O'Briens, Murphys, Kellys, and Carringtons, which was the family that Aunt Maeve had married into. Even Doc Mary and Hans were there. Tadgh was sad to see his mother go back to Galway to her mother's house, but he understood. She stayed sober because she stayed out of pubs when she was feeling vulnerable.

He looked down at Charlie and had to smile. Her face was lit up with excitement. She'd been so busy working, she hadn't really left the city except for the night he'd taken her to the lighthouse. She'd been fascinated at the landscape change when they'd driven from Dublin in the daylight. Then she'd spent the entire drive from Ennis trying to see through the escaping light. She'd asked a lot of questions. She was very intelligent, which he already knew, but she also had the eye of an artist. She noticed things like shadows, old trees, shifting light. He'd inquired again when she was going to show him her sketches, but she'd been non-committal.

Now she was looking at the crowded pub, amazed at the size of his tribe. He sneaked around the bar and squeezed Jenny from behind. She squeaked and then gave him a big hug. "I'd heard you came into town a couple of weeks ago and didn't stop to see me!"

He kissed her on the cheek, brotherly, and returned to the right side of the bar. Then, he put his arm around Charlie's shoulders and Jenny gave a knowing look. *This is what has been keeping you in Dublin.* "Jenny, this is Charlie." Jenny smiled as she wiped down the bar. "What can I get you, love? He's buying."

Tadgh nodded. "Absolutely. A cider? A pint of lager?"

"I'm going to have a coke. I told you, relax and let me drive back. I mean it. I'm not going to drink, so you may as well."

"Thank you, lass. Jenny, I'll have a pint of Creans and get this lovely woman a Coke."

"Put a club soda on that tab! He just got a promotion." Tadgh and Charlie turned in unison to see Branna grinning behind them. Tadgh leaned over and kissed her forehead.

"Well, now. Club soda is it?" He looked down and patted her tummy. "Anything you want to tell me?"

She gave her own tummy a pat. "Nope, too soon to tell. You'll be the second to know after the baby-daddy." Tadgh handed Charlie her coke and Branna her drink. "To more O'Briens. Sláinte."

"Charlie, why don't you come sit with us. I think the men on stage want to borrow Tadgh."

She cleared her throat. "I think I'll go find the ladies room first, then I'll join you."

Tadgh took her hand. "I'll show ye where it is. Branna, tell them I'll be a minute."

Charlie's heart jumped at the contact, but she was starting to realize that Tadgh was just an affectionate person. She'd started to read into it until she'd seen him with his family.

She didn't have a lot of experience with affectionate people, other than her little brother. Her mother was a walking ad for domestic violence induced PTSD. She tried. She really did try to offer them tenderness and love, but none of them had ever had it from her father. They'd had indifference, anger, and violence. There had been small periods where he'd given the normal dad and husband thing a try and stopped drinking. It had never lasted. As she watched this big family, all the hugs and kisses, the easy teasing, she realized that Tadgh was as much a product of his environment as she was. He was a loving man. "She's nice, Branna is. You two seem close."

Tadgh hesitated, narrowing his eyes. "I suppose we are. Michael's my best friend. More like a brother, really. I like to think I played a big part in getting them together. He deserved some happiness and so did she."

Charlie relaxed a bit, which didn't go unnoticed. "Branna has always been just a friend. You didn't think otherwise?"

She shook her head. "No, of course not. Why would you think that?"

Tadgh sighed. "I'm sorry. It's just, Michael had a hard time with jealousy at first. He thought I had an eye on her. After his first wife, I understood the underlying issue, but it still hurt me. I love Michael. I would never hurt him like that, no matter how beautiful Branna is."

"What happened with his first wife? Wait...that's none of my business. Jesus, I'm sorry. I shouldn't be prying. It's un..."

"For feck sake, Charlie. If you say it's unprofessional, I am going to break something."

Charlie's eyes shot to his, defiant. But his eyes held an urgency, confusion. She shut her eyes, overwhelmed. Someone yelled from the stage area. "Hold on a minute, Robby!" he yelled back. Then he said softly, "Open yer eyes, Charlie."

Tadgh watched Charlie battling with herself, and he took her by the elbows. She opened her eyes, looking up at him. Her eyes were torn, unsure. "I'm sorry, Tadgh. I don't know what I'm saying. I'm trying to stay focused. This case, this job, my brother, everything is pulling at me and I don't know what I'm doing."

He understood. She had a lot going on, a lot of important, heavy things weighing on her. And he was letting his libido...no, that wasn't right. He was letting his heart interfere with his judgement. He shouldn't be adding more stress. She was leaving and she wasn't the type of girl who gave her heart easily, or her body. No matter how much he wanted her, he had to deny himself.

Still, he wanted to be her friend. He wanted to tell her things. He trusted her, more than he'd ever trusted any woman. He stepped away. "It's okay, darlin'. Go ahead. The water closet is just there," he said as he pointed. Her look was sad, pleading. "It's okay. You've got a lot going on, more than anyone should have to deal with. I'm not going to add to that burden. You and I, we're going to solve this case. You'll go home and fight for Josh. Anything you need, Charlie. I'm here."

She turned and he went to the stage to meet his cousins and Robby.

Charlie used the bathroom less out of necessity and more to rein in the emotional hurricane that was brewing in her mind. She could hardly face the big, happy family on the other side of the door. She was such an asshole. This was the anniversary of Tadgh's father being killed on the job. She shouldn't be feeling the way she was feeling. She was having some nutty territorial response over him. Then, she switched to the cold retreat of *strictly business*. Tadgh probably thought she was a lunatic. Especially now that he knew about her shady family life.

He was so sweet. God, he'd actually been trying to support her, today of all days. She splashed water on her face and dried it off. She looked at herself in the mirror. Her wild, unruly mane was everywhere, splayed over her back and shoulders. No make-up, either. She smoothed the only nice sweater she owned down over her undersized chest and flat stomach. The cashmere had been a gift from Ted on their first Christmas together. She certainly would never have bought herself such a costly piece of clothing unless it was a suit for work. She may not have kept Ted, but she'd definitely kept the soft sweater.

The O'Brien women were so beautiful. All of them. Granny Aofie with her timeless beauty. Sorcha and Brigid with their auburn hair and beautiful skin. Aidan and Michael's wives were both stunners. And, no wonder. All of the men were absolutely gorgeous. Even Finn, who wasn't blood, was dark and handsome, with his black hair going past his shoulders and dark arching brows. No wonder Cora was so adorable.

When she looked at herself, she knew she wasn't ugly. She was more like the cute tomboy at the princess ball. She shook herself, stiffening her spine. It didn't matter. She wasn't involved with Tadgh. This had been a day trip, to get out of the city. She was going to buck up and enjoy the distraction before she headed back to work.

Before going to the women, she stopped by the bar again and ordered dinner. She hadn't eaten since breakfast. "I'll have the mussels, the ploughman's platter, and the burger with chips and onion rings. Send it to the table of women and put it on my tab, not Tadgh's. Oh, and an assortment of desserts." Jenny smirked. "I'll send over extra plates."

* * *

SEAN O'BRIEN WATCHED his wife with some amusement. She seemed like her old self tonight. Head on a swivel watching all her children and grandchildren, ever the diligent mother hen. "That young detective or consultant or whatever she is….she's quite something, isn't she? Tadgh seems to fancy her." Sorcha said as she watched Special Agent Ryan exit the ladies room. Sean hadn't told anyone about her true identity. Only he, Patrick, and Tadgh knew she was FBI.

"Aye, they work well enough together. She's been a big help, actually. She's sharp, intuitive."

Sorcha gave Sean a dry look. "That's not what I meant. Ye see the way they are dancing around each other. He seems quite smitten, though. And she watches him with the other women. I don't even think she means to do it, really. Must be those law enforcement types. Mistrustful." She gave Sean a sideways glance. He pinched her under the table. She jumped and let out a squeak. "Watch your manners, love. I play dirty."

He leaned over and whispered in her ear. "I'm counting on it."

"Da, would ye stop with the smoochy talk in front of your children." Liam plopped down with Brigid on his tail, taking the other seat.

Brigid leaned in. "Have ye been watching Tadgh with the new Yank?"

"Would you two hens knock it off. You're shameless. She's a colleague." Brigid looked at her father like he was daft.

"Oh, aye. And how many colleagues has he brought home to meet the family? Sell it to the tourists, Da. I'm not buyin'." Liam was shaking his head laughing. Then Aidan slid in next to Brigid.

"What's with the Yank? Tadgh's like a tea kettle ready to boil over. She's a beauty, too."

Sean stood up, giving up his seat for Alanna. "You are all incorrigible. I'm ready to play some music. Liam, off your arse. I need ye for this session."

THE REST of the evening was spent with a revolving stage of O'Briens and Murphys. Charlie loved the music. She didn't have much experience with Irish music. Her father was half Irish, but he didn't seem to have any interest in the music or that part of his DNA other than favoring the drink. He wasn't a Jameson guy, though. A handle of Canadian rot gut or Evan Williams on rare occasion was all he would go for. These people? They went quality over quantity. Moderation in their alcohol consumption while they enjoyed the music, conversation, hugs, lots of hugs...and they laughed. Not just an occasional snicker or giggle. They were full of easy laughter and smiles, even considering how the day together had started. Whoever William

O'Brien was, and wherever he was, he was probably looking down and smiling.

"You're smiling." Branna slid in the seat across from her. "You feel like sharing?" Charlie blushed a bit at being caught. After her initial hesitance toward Branna, she'd come to like her a lot. The fact that she was so obviously completely in love with her husband didn't hurt.

"I was just thinking that this is a happy family."

Branna cocked her head, an unasked question lingering in her eyes. *And your family isn't?*

"They are something. It's like a throw back from the old ways. Large clans sticking together. I thank God every day that I found them. What about you? Do you come from a big family?"

"Not really, and the extended family isn't really around. It's nothing like this. You were a lucky woman indeed, to find them. Sorcha told me you lost your father in the war. I'm so sorry."

"Thank you. Yes, and I lost my mother four years ago. Breast Cancer. This family saved me. More from myself than anything. I had resigned myself to spending my life alone. And I am so glad that the big Irishman over there with the pretty face and prettier ass decided to derail my plans."

Charlie barked out a laugh. "Yes, there are some fine genetics in the rear-end department."

Branna's back shot up, eyes wide. "And you know this how, exactly? You and Tadgh?" She was starting to spin like a top. She was actually starting to bop up and down in her seat, so Charlie had to stop that incorrect line of thinking before it got any gas.

"No! Jeez, not what I meant. Not Tadgh. I mean yes, Tadgh, but there was this morning and donuts...ah shit." She was covering her face now.

A sparkling feminine voice came from behind. "What she meant to say is that she got a primo shot of Patrick's spectacular...that was the word wasn't it? Aye, spectacular ass shagging my brains out on the kitchen counter."

Charlie groaned and looked behind her. Caitlyn was unrepentant, grinning ear to ear. Then she looked again at Branna who was shocked and delighted. All three women burst into laughter. Caitlyn plopped in the seat beside Charlie giggling hysterically as she slung an arm around her.

"This, I have to hear. Don't leave a thing out," Branna said through her laughter.

"Are you three sharing stories and having a laugh without me! Have ye no loyalty at all? I want to hear!" They all turned to see Brigid, looking alarmingly like Cora with her hands on her hips.

Charlie rolled her eyes. "Have a seat. You'll all hear it soon enough." That's when Jenny showed up with a truck load of food, and the women looked stunned at the spread.

Alanna pulled up a seat, coming from nowhere. "Oh, ladies. We are definitely keeping her."

* * *

TADGH SAT with his cousins at the bar, enjoying the round that Michael had just purchased. Branna slid between the two men with some effort. Their shoulders side by side made a wall of sorts. "Club soda?" Jenny asked. She slid one with a lime in front of Branna.

Branna clinked glasses with the men and said casually, "So, Charlie's amazing. Remind me again why you're not trying to get in her knickers?"

Michael barked out a laugh. "Nice, Hellcat. Do tell, Tadgh. Why indeed?"

Tadgh was stifling a begrudging, husky laugh. How many times had he said that to her when they first met? "You are a nosy peahen, lass. She's a colleague. And she's leaving as soon as this case is done. We're working on a homicide investigation, for God's sake. This isn't social. She's not here for some big, complicated romance. She's got a life back home."

From behind him, a sweet southern drawl interrupted. "Oh, that old chestnut? Yeah, we've heard it all before. Just ask my darling husband." Alanna came along side him. He rolled his eyes. He looked at Michael for reinforcement.

"Don't look at me, brother. You're outnumbered. And Brigid's over there, undoubtedly doing the hard sell."

Tadgh looked over at Charlie, surrounded by Caitlyn, Brigid, Sorcha, and his Gran. They were all laughing and chatting and stuffing their gobs with pub food. His heart squeezed painfully. He turned away before anyone caught the emotion on his face, then took another sip of his pint.

CHAPTER 13

*C*harlie drove, the quiet of the night washing over her. She was wired from the good company, three cups of strong tea, lots of food, and a spectacular clear sky. The night was chilly, but she'd bundled herself in her coat and put a fleece over Tadgh as she cracked the window and let the night air sharpen her senses. It was a little over two hours to Dublin, and Tadgh had drifted off dreamily about five minutes after they left. She had GPS, so she let him sleep. He'd been more than a little buzzed when they'd left. They'd sung all night, drank, and shared stories about his father. Katie had been absent, but considering she was a recovering alcoholic, Charlie thought it was a good thing she hadn't shown up.

Tadgh didn't have a problem with the drink, which is why he was pleasantly buzzed right now. Alcoholics didn't get drunk from four drinks, especially at his size. He was adorable, curled up against the window. He'd been humming the song from the funeral, the one in which he'd sung the lead. She reached over and ran a hand through his hair. He was breathing softly, but he turned his face to her. "You were beautiful tonight, Charlie. You're beautiful when you laugh." He was mumbling, half asleep. Then he drifted back off and slept soundly the entire ride.

She eventually found her way back to the city, maneuvering her way to Dublin 2 where she could park the vehicle and make the short walk to their building. Tadgh instinctively woke as she entered the parking space. He looked around, disoriented, then at her. "Ah, Christ lass. I'm sorry. I didn't mean to leave you to find your own way back!"

She laughed. "I have GPS and you needed a nap."

He blushed. "I told ye, my cousins have a way of getting me pissed. By the time each one buys a round, yer done for. I had to start turning them away after the fourth pint."

She shrugged. "Lesser men don't have the restraint to turn down a drink no matter how many they've had. You were a good boy, Tadgh O'Brien. Everyone was. And the women in your family are either nursing, pregnant, or too wise to overindulge."

He laughed. "They're a breeding lot. Wee Brigid's five months along. Alanna has a new babe and a toddler, and Branna's goin' for a third." He looked at Charlie and she was covering a giggle, because third came out sounding like tird. "What are ye on about?"

"Your accent gets thicker when you've been drinking."

He furrowed his brow, but one side of his mouth was turned up. "I don't have an accent. Do ye mock me, woman?"

"Never. Now let's get you to bed, big man."

"Are ye offering to tuck me in, Charlotte?"

She narrowed her eyes. "Charlie, and no. You're a big boy who can tuck himself in," she grinned. "And, I don't take advantage of intoxicated young men." She heard him mumble, but she could have imagined that she'd heard him say, *more is the pity.*

"I'll miss you, a ghrá mo chroí. Be safe and don't work too much at your mam's. Just enjoy the break."

Sorcha knew her husband better than anyone. She also knew her mother didn't need her in Belfast. It was the nightmares, the confession about the night she'd almost been abducted, and it was about this new case. He was worried about her. Why else would Alanna leave

Davey with her father and stepmother, taking only the nursing child? Why come with her?

"I don't have PTSD."

Sean sighed. "I don't know about all that, Sorcha. I'm no expert. But I know you have some demons resurfacing. Demons you need to confront for good. I never took ye for a coward."

A burst of aggression went through Sorcha's body, like a lightning strike. As he'd meant it to. "I'm no coward, Sean O'Brien. Are ye sure you want to rattle my cage? You've been bitten more than once over the years." Her jaw was tight, chin lifted, eyes sparking.

"Sorry, love. As appealing as that sounds, no time for it." Then he pulled her close. "But when you return, you can sink those sharp little teeth in as hard as you like." He whispered it, just for her.

She tried to hold that fighter stance, but damn the man. She could never stay mad at him. He knew all of her weak spots. She turned to him, lips barely touching. "It's a date." When she turned to pick up her bag, he swatted her on the bum.

"That's my girl."

"Da, please! Not in front of the grandkids!"

Sean turned to his son, Aidan, smiling mischievously. Then, he winked at Alanna, who was giggling. Davey said, "Granny naughty? Ye spanked her bum, Grandda."

Sean took the boy out of Aidan's hands. "Aye, she was. But we're O'Brien men. We like our girls with a bit of fire. You'll see." The toddler furrowed his brow, not really understanding. Sean looked at his wife, who was grinning with her hands on her hips. *You will, lad. Someday you will.*

* * *

Charlie looked at her brother through the laptop screen. "How is school going? Still getting a four point?" Josh nodded as he looked around the public library. "Yep, which is probably one of the only reasons they're letting me skirt the residency rule. The call from your boss didn't hurt either. I don't know how long I'll be able to keep doing this, though. When dad finds out..."

"Don't worry about that. I talked to the lawyer's secretary last night. He's just waiting for the retainer. Once it's in the court system, he'd be crazy to do anything stupid."

"But he is crazy. I feel like he knows. Jesse's mom will keep driving me as long as there's no danger to them, but if he pulls something, she won't put them in danger. She's a single mom."

"Don't worry, okay buddy? You let me do that. I love you and I'm proud of you."

"I'm proud of you too, sis. It sounds like you're on a cool assignment." She'd lied a bit, of course. No way was she going to tell him she was bait for some serial murderer-rapist. "What about the lighthouse? Did you go again?"

She shook her head. "No, I went to a little village. It was so cool. There's this one family there, friends. They take over the whole place when they get together. They sing and dance and they are really nice. I didn't get to see it in the daylight, but you can Google it." She told him about the tower, the cliffs, the castles. He was completely enthralled.

"If I was there, I would have found the prettiest girl and danced with her. I never go to the dances at our school. I work on Fridays. It sounds nice. They all sound nice. It doesn't sound like the bars Dad goes to. What about lighthouses? Are there lighthouses?"

She smiled, knowing he was still imagining swimming out to the green lighthouse. "There's a couple more near me here in Dublin. A big red one, some more along the coast. They're all automatic now, no lighthouse keeper, but they are still cool. The red one looks like some kind of boss watching over the harbor." She giggled at his face, like he was picturing it.

"I'd like to see the ocean."

"You will, Buddy. I promise you." Her heart was breaking. He'd never been out of Northeast Ohio. She'd tried to get him to Florida, but their father had forbidden it. Her mother had tried to smooth the way, but he wouldn't bend. Charlie had spent a lot of money on car rides and airfare to get some face time with her brother, and to remind her father that she wasn't going away. That she was still watching him.

It was one of the reasons she hadn't managed to get the tail end of her student loans paid off, or the retainer in full. The efficiency hovel in Michigan had helped a lot. She'd chipped away at all of the debt by living lean and pocketing her cost of living and housing money from the FBI. When she left for Ireland, she'd sublet her apartment to another agent and sold her car. She liquidated as much as she could.

"When you live with me, you'll have a lot more opportunities. We won't be rich or anything, but..."

"We'll be free. We'll make it work."

She smiled sadly at him. He was repeating the words that she'd said to him so many times. "Exactly. Now, it must be late, you probably need to go home."

"Yes, the library is closing. What time is it there?"

Charlie checked the corner of the screen. "It's almost two. I need to get to bed. I have an early morning mission to find a bakery. You know how I love my pastry."

"I wish I was with you."

"Me too, buddy. Me too."

* * *

CHARLIE WALKED THE DUBLIN STREETS, checking her phone's GPS for the bakery. Tatyana, the Russian girl she'd met at the church, had mentioned a good bakery in Dublin 4 in Ballsbridge. The area was less touristy, kind of run down and lower income in the area where the bakery was. But she'd grown up in Cleveland, not in the posh suburbs. She'd worked in big cities. The dodgy end of the city rarely intimidated her.

She looked toward the water and could see the stacks jutting out like guardians of the city. It was cold and a misty fog had settled over the harbor. She wondered what the jagged rocks and lighthouses looked like with the fog coming over them. She thought of that wonderful night with Tadgh, when he'd shown her one of his thoughtful spots, where he went when he was feeling homesick. Nope, she was not going to dwell on that sweet, dimpled face sleeping in the car. Or what he must look like when he was home alone in her temporary apartment, using that chin-up bar attached in his bedroom doorway…shirtless and sweaty. "Staaahp!" She'd said it out loud and some man coming out of a shop had looked at her strangely. *Stop thinking about him. Shirtless. No, bad Charlie.*

She reached her destination and opened the door, a bell ringing. She looked up to see a stout man with an apron arranging bread and assorted baked goods. She peered around the counter and saw Tatynana coming out of the kitchen with a mop. She stopped. "Hello, Charlie." She turned to the man and spoke in Russian. He shrugged and went back to his work. "I will just clean this and be right to you for some ordering."

Charlie watched as Tatyana cleaned up some spilled milk under a cafe table, then stowed the mop in the kitchen and returned. "How are you? I've been thinking about you and I thought I would stop and try these tea cakes you were so proud of."

Tatyana smiled. "Yes, fresh this morning. We have ones with walnuts, but these…" she pointed to the white powdered balls behind the glass, "these are pistachio. They are very good. We also have the gingerbread and some apple cakes."

After settling down with some pistachio tea cakes and a pot of Irish breakfast tea that was served in Russian style tea cups, Charlie invited her to take a break and sit. She was their only customer in the place, so Tatyana sat with her own cup of tea. "How have you really been? Any news?"

"No, nothing. Rumors, really. And, how about you? Are you enjoying this city?"

Charlie kept the conversation light, general. She couldn't afford to compromise her cover by linking herself to the Garda in any way. As they chatted, a man came in, ringing the bell over the door as he brought in a brisk morning breeze. His face was dark and harsh. His eyes holding nothing warm.

"Excuse me." Tatyana got up, returning to her duties. She noticed that the man spoke in Arabic. She waited, wondering if Tatyana would understand him. She spoke in English. "I'm sorry, could you point?" The man looked over his shoulder briefly, taking in Charlie. Then turning back to Tatyana he pointed to what looked like the Russian version of Turkish delight. He would have been surprised to know that Charlie had understood part of what he said. Not all of it, but it had been rude. Something about doing her job instead of sitting. What an insufferable jerk. She wiped the crumbs onto her plate, took her empty teacup and dish, and walked to the counter. She slid next to the man.

"Thank you, Tatyana. I'll be off." Then she slid twenty euro, an exorbitant tip for two tea cakes and a cup of tea, but God knew this dickweed wasn't going to tip her. Tatyana insisted she take a few cookies with her. She smiled gratefully. Then she turned to him. "As-Salaam-Alaikum."

The man's brows jumped at the Arabic greeting. Her tone had been cold, not rude, but not friendly. Then she walked out.

As Charlie walked the several miles to her apartment, a text came in from Assistant Director Schroeder. *Call me. I need a brief.* She dreaded it. He was a great boss, but she was sickened by how little progress she'd made. As she climbed the stairs to her building, she hit the video call on her phone.

"I understand. It's a bit like looking for a needle in a haystack. It was overly ambitious to think that you could be bait with no target area, given the size of the city. Keep at it. In the meantime, change your appearance and insert yourself in the investigation. You can't let them push you out. You need your feet on the ground."

"Absolutely. I told you I went to the last scene." She was a little miffed at the comment. "They know they can't push me aside."

Schroeder cocked his head. "Then, why aren't you checking warehouses with the detectives unit today?"

* * *

DC SULLIVAN WAS GRITTING his jaw. "I thought we were taking a new approach? You'd work the streets with Sal and O'Brien."

"That doesn't mean you are ditching me for the investigation. I need to be with you. No one will recognize me. I'm going." She was fastening the bullet proof vest over her t-shirt, and then sliding a sweater on over it, careful not to dislodge the most recent wig selection. A dark blonde, unremarkable hairstyle that looked real enough because it was boring. Then, she added the final touch and slid on the glasses. Behind her Patrick and Sean were gearing up as well. They were all out of uniform. Patrick smirked at her hair. "How many of those do you have?"

"Only two. Two is enough. You ready, boys?" They were breaking up into teams of three. The O'Briens had immediately insisted she come with them. Tadgh was leaned up against a desk next to Sal. He was pouting. He was visibly pouting like a kid sitting on the bench during a baseball game. He couldn't be seen with them, he knew it. It still chaffed.

Tadgh was watching Charlie suit up to clear buildings. They weren't going in guns drawn. It was more a snooping excursion. Abandoned warehouses around the city. There were teams spread out all over the city. All incognito, but searching.

He had other things to do. He and Sal were headed over to the housing complex they'd been working. He'd been keeping an eye on some military-aged males that seemed to disappear periodically, always tapping on their phones. He wanted to check in with Zaid as well. He'd been monitoring the comings and goings and was also struggling with his teenage son, who seemed more and more to be associating with what Zaid thought were bad influences. No wrong doing, but Zaid knew how recruiting worked, and his sons were as young and impressionable as any boys their age.

Still, the thought of going off with Sal and leaving Charlie to do her work without him was difficult. His only two comforts were that she was now armed, and that Patrick and his Uncle Sean didn't like it any more than he did. He grinned as his uncle had inserted himself like he was Sullivan's boss, which he had been ten years earlier, and assigned himself and Patrick to team up with Charlie. Tadgh felt his phone go off. It was late morning, and he didn't know who could be calling.

"Liam, what's up?" Liam sounded tired. He was doing internal medicine rotations at the Catholic hospital, plus clocking hours in the ER when they needed him, for the experience. The pay was a joke, but that was the life of a medical resident. "Ye sound knackered, brother."

"Aye, I'm just about to take a nap. I've got five hours before my next shift. What are you doing tonight? Eve's performing tomorrow, again, but she's got something late across town."

Tadgh sighed. "I'm working. Things are getting crazy around here. They're worried about another attempt. It's been long enough. Da and Patrick are working too. What about Seany?"

"Didn't ye hear? They're doing building inspections alongside your group of officers, on the south end. They pulled the trainees in for extra manpower." Tadgh groaned. Now, even Seany was in on the search. "It's all right, Tadgh. I understand the urgency. Stay focused. The sooner they're caught, the safer she'll be. I'll arrange a cab. They are working on the filing system at the studio, computerizing it all. It's extra internship hours and extra money. She'll be late. She'll rehearse, then work, and it could be past midnight."

"I'm sorry. I just won't have a car. I'll be on the bike and working. Maybe she should stay home, take a night off."

"I'll try. You know the lass almost as well as I do. She won't slow down until she graduates. Maybe not even then."

Tadgh put his phone away and walked over to the large table where a map of the city was unfolded. They had these searches planned during down times in the city. Some around tea time and some late for two days straight. He noticed that Charlie was watching him and his family, looking between them. "You only have two beds. Where are you all sleeping?" Tadgh shrugged. "We're working late. Don't worry, lass. I'll crash on the sofa."

"I'll book a hotel. I'm funded. You should sleep in a bed. You need your rest in between all of this." She motioned around the map. "I'll book something." She took her phone out.

Tadgh put a hand over hers, stopping the thumbing she was starting to do on the internet. "I'll do. You're settled." She started to argue. "I said I'll do. I don't want you off somewhere in the city alone when you're already settled in my place. This isn't a problem."

She shook her head. "You don't have to take care of me, O'Brien." His face was firm. God, had anyone ever tried to take care of her like this? She loved it and hated it in equal measure.

"We'd like you to come to dinner. We're breaking at seven. Are ye busy?"

She smiled at that. "Psh. Yes. I have dates lined up for months. They're beating down the door. And,friends…tons of them."

His smile was wide. "No, ye don't ye big loser. Be at the window at seven. And bring my cat."

Charlie feigned offense, but Tadgh moved in close. "We're supposed to be a couple, mo ghrá. You don't want to be accused of layin' down on the job?"

Tadgh knew she could take care of herself, but he wanted to do it. The instinct was so overwhelming that it was a force all its own. She made him feel so many things. Her beautiful, smart eyes. Bits of amber mixed with the mossy green that you only found in the dense, rich depths of the forest. Golden skin and lovely, wavy hair. It was wild, untamable although she tried. It was full of those natural streaks of golden sunlight that brunettes often had after a long, hot summer. He wanted that damn wig off. He wanted to bury his hands in it and touch her sweet, rosy mouth. Whatever she saw in his eyes, he knew it wasn't colleague to colleague. Her eyes betrayed her as they glossed over a bit.

The connection was broken as Sal slapped him on the back. He looked at him, a little irritation creeping into the exchange. "Sorry, brother. Duty calls."

He looked at Charlie. "Seven, or I'm coming for you and Duncan. The little traitor." The corner of his mouth was turned up, and she internally sighed as those infernal dimples made an appearance. She looked away from those golden eyes, afraid Sal would see how absolutely pathetic she was for his partner.

CHAPTER 14

*S*orcha walked along Springfield, headed toward the center of the city. Alanna was beside her, having left little Isla in Granny Aoife's care. "You shouldn't be here dealing with this, Alanna. Isn't this one of your American holidays?"

Alanna shrugged. "It will hold. One thing about being a Marine brat. You learn to postpone and be flexible on holidays. Besides, I'm thankful every day. Today, I'm thankful I can be here for you." She put her arm around her mother-in-law. "And, you know my daddy. He's frying up a turkey, as we speak, for Mary and Davey. He'll undoubtedly have Branna and Michael and the twins over as well."

Sorcha laughed. "I didn't know ye could fry a turkey."

"He's from the South. You can fry just about anything, if you try hard enough."

They were quiet for a while as they meandered through the streets. "It was right about this time of year that there were a mass number of bombings. Mostly IRA thinking they were proving some sort of point. Taking out as many Ulster targets as possible." She shook her head. "I'm a Catholic and an Irish woman. I understand the outrage. I remember the conditions we lived under during the troubles. The occupation was wrong, the segregation based on religion, being treated like less. I understood all of that. I especially worried for my brother, John. He was young and passionate. My father managed to keep a tight rein on him, though, when it came to the political activity. We just wanted to live in peace, go to school, be a family. It was hard. My whole childhood and early adulthood was colored with violence."

She looked up at an old building, but not really seeing it now. She was in the past, and Alanna knew better than to interrupt. "But, the bombing of civilians. I can't sit well with that on either side. November 14th started a particularly big series of them. Fifty bombings by the IRA in at least a half dozen cities. It wasn't just in the North. They bombed parts of Dublin and London as well and other parts of England. Not that the Ulster side didn't do the same and worse. The IRA loved their bombs, though. And they started taking money from other terrorist groups in other countries. The Libyans mostly. They taught the PLO how to make car bombs. Did you know that? Then the PLO taught the Iraqis. My son is over there fighting, dodging IEDs and..." her voice broke. "I don't want you to think I don't stand behind the cause. We were mistreated for almost a century. I just can't justify the methods of either side. Killing women, children, fathers and sons. Blowing up a pub full of people. Blowing up shops and cars on crowded streets. Blowing up British soldiers not older than my Seany. Young boys that had nothing to do with politics. It was so awful, so much suffering." She put her head in her hands, overcome.

Alanna was fighting the tears, but she needed to stay in as much of a professional mode as she could muster. She put an arm on Sorcha's back and rubbed. "I'm so sorry, Sorcha. I can't even imagine."

Sorcha straightened. "I'm okay, love. Really. I just haven't thought about it in a while. I thought I'd put it to rest. I really did. It's just, some stuff has come up with Sean's case. The one they brought him in as a consultant. The kidnappings and murders? It just stirred up some old feelings."

Alanna spoke softly. "About your attempted abduction."

Sorcha looked at her, realization flickering across her face. "Christ, ye shouldn't be talking me through this. Ye've got your own demons."

171

"That's not here with us. I can separate the incidents. I did a year of counseling after the fact. I'm okay, Sorcha. This isn't about me. Please, I want to help."

Sorcha sighed. "Well, back to that week in November." Alanna knew that mass bombings were somehow safer to talk about right now. Safer than the brush with the Shankill Butchers. So, she let her talk.

"I went to the University. I started out in a Catholic school, but I needed some classes at Queens University, where the big midwife program was. I fought hard to get in the program. I needed the training. So, I crossed the lines to go to school, ye see."

Alanna's hand was over her mouth. "Oh, God. You were on the Protestant side for the bombings?" She watched a tremble go through Sorcha.

"I'd seen it before. Dead Catholics during the conflicts. My brother lost his best friend when he was fourteen. Wrong place sort of thing. I lost a classmate as well. But, I had never seen the true carnage that our side inflicted. I was a nurse, for God's sake. The retaliations started, and soon the entire city was a mess. I made it back across the border, but there were people hurt everywhere. I wasn't the only one that got caught in the middle. We set up a clinic in one of the areas that bled the two together. Where the lines were a bit blurry going from Catholic to Protestant. We took in wounded. Any wounded. The one doctor that was there and I made that clear. We wouldn't turn anyone away. Gun shots, stabbings, burns. The military took care of their own, so we didn't get any soldiers, which was probably best. We started using a civilian station wagon to transport them to the closest hospital, if it was more than we could treat. That's the day Sean came over the border to get me." She smiled then. "A rather insistent hero, I might add."

She took Alanna by the arm, walked through the streets of Belfast, and continued to talk.

* * *

CHARLIE WAS EXHAUSTED. It had been a productive day with regard to ruling out locations, but no luck miraculously finding an active crime scene. She needed a shower, but she wasn't going to take one. She had to do it all again in four hours. Then she was headed over to Sal's satellite home-away-from-home for a little face time as Tadgh's girlfriend. He didn't know this, of course. He'd give her shit about it. So, she was just going to show up. For now, she had a date with four gorgeous O'Brien men. Apparently Liam was going to scarf down a quick dinner before his eight o'clock shift at the hospital.

She knocked on the window, and when Tadgh looked over, she waved Duncan's paw at him. He slid the door open with a big smile, and took the feline. "It smells amazing! What did you make?"

Tadgh took her hand and brought her to the table. The other three men were lined up like a wall, blocking the kitchen. "Close your eyes, darlin'. We've got a treat for you." She cocked her head, but the men looked genuinely excited, so she played along. "Okay, they are closed. Feed me, boys." She heard the laughter grumble as they shuffled around. Someone set something heavy on the table.

"Open up."

She opened her eyes, and it took her a minute to put it all together. A huge, beautifully browned and roasted turkey lay in the middle of the table. "Happy Thanksgiving!" they all said in unison. Her mouth was open, she knew it. She had completely forgotten about Thanksgiving. It was an American holiday, so there were no ads or turkey sales or pyramids of pumpkin-everything here to remind her, not that she went to the store often. She was living on coffee, fruit, and takeout...and lots of bakery items if she was being honest. She'd put back the missing weight she'd been worrying about. Her jeans fit perfectly within a couple of weeks of leaving Michigan.

Her brother hadn't mentioned it either, too wrapped up in talking about other things. She looked up at the men who had separated, revealing the other dishes on the breakfast bar. Potatoes, yams, stuffing, pie, cranberry sauce. They'd done their research. That's when the unexpected tears started to blur her vision.

"You did this for me?" Her voice was hoarse.

"Aye, it's not steak or burgers, but..." She launched herself at Tadgh before he could finish.

The hug had been a surprise. Charlie hadn't ever touched him affectionately other than for show. The tears that she was fighting were just as unexpected. He took full advantage. He scooped her off the ground, returning the hug. He laughed, feeling giddy at the contact. "I really need to cook for you more often."

She leaned her head back and looked at him. "I haven't had a full Thanksgiving meal in years. It's a thing of beauty."

He put her down and she went down the line, hugging the other men. Liam scooped her off her feet again. "I just showed up to eat, but you're not getting away now."

She giggled and he put her down. She wiped her hands on her pants, suddenly nervous and a little embarrassed. "I'm sorry. I got a little carried away. I'm not used to men cooking for me."

Sean spoke then. "Well, we can't take all of the credit. Branna made up some of these dishes yesterday and we just reheated them. Tadgh put the turkey in this morning, though. We had to take turns running home to check on it. Now, let's eat while it's still hot."

They filled their plates as Sean carved and handed out juicy slices of turkey breast with crispy skin. Patrick took a leg, then they all piled the sides and gravy on their plates. They sat around the table and Charlie felt such warmth go through her. These men were like nothing she'd ever experienced. These are the type of men she wished her little brother had been raised around.

"Did you have a big meal like this when you lived at home?" Tadgh asked.

"Yes, my mom likes to cook. We weren't what you would call a happy home, but we could eat." Her tone was light, and Tadgh's face softened.

"Uncle Sean, would ye do the honors?" They all crossed themselves and Charlie bowed her head. He said a quick blessing and they dug into the feast.

Charlie took a bite of turkey dipped in gravy. She groaned. "Marry me."

"I told you not to tease me, lass. I'll hold you to it." Tadgh's tone was teasing, but Liam elbowed him.

"And, how do ye know she was talking to you?"

She smiled warmly at Sean. "Boys will be boys," he said.

After a nice meal and lively conversation, Charlie said. "Let me clean up. It's the least I can do. We've got a long night ahead."

Liam was headed out, his shift starting soon. "I can't be late. Sorry to eat and run." Charlie watched as his family hugged him. They showed their love so easily. She couldn't ever remember her father hugging Josh.

Tadgh turned to Sean and Patrick. "Get some rest. I'll help her with this." He motioned to the table.

"Take some back to the flat with you, love. It's going to be a busy few days. You'll need the leftovers." Sean gave her a fatherly look. "And get some rest, aye?"

They worked in companionable silence for a while, but Tadgh finally broke the quiet. "How's Josh? Have ye spoken with him?"

Charlie looked up, surprised. "You're mind reading again, O'Brien."

He laughed. "You know, if you're going to hang with the family, you might have to start calling me by my first name, lass." He put the dish down, and motioned her along. "Go ahead, practice. Unless that's too personal for you?"

She narrowed her eyes, then the corner of her mouth turned up. "Should I say it like Brittnaaay?" Then she batted her eyes. She opened her mouth to say it, stopped, fluffed her chest, and gave a breathy *Taaaaadgh*. He snapped her with the drying towel that he'd slung over his shoulder.

She giggled and squeaked. Not at all the sounds you'd expect out of a Special Agent in the FBI. She was playful, though, and he loved that. She was loosening up a bit. He moved in, pinning her with his presence against the counter. "You, mo ghrá, are nothing like Brittney."

Her face grew more serious. "I'm not, and I shouldn't tease you about her. I don't know what went on, but it probably wasn't funny at the time."

He smiled tightly, backing away. "No, it wasn't. It was rather piti-ful, to be honest." He started continuing the clean up as he talked. "She paid a lot of attention to me. I'd been in Dublin about a year. She'd always approach me at the pub. But the thing was, she'd always been drinking. She was fun and flirty and well...you've seen the boobs." Charlie smacked him and he laughed. "Anyway, I'm not a fiend. I don't start relationships off by getting a lass drunk and taking advantage of her. So I'd either put her off or put her in a cab. I always told her to call me. That I'd like to take her out when we weren't both in our cups. She finally did." He shrugged. "I was going to take her to break-fast one morning, but she said she'd like to just sit and talk and that I could just...you know...make her some toast at my apartment or something. Well, ye can imagine how that went." His face blushed.

"You had Brittney for breakfast?" He barked out a laugh, because she was grinning. Teasing him.

He rubbed the spot between his eyebrows. "You're blushing, Tadgh. You're actually blushing. Brittney the man-eater didn't know a good thing when she had it."

He smiled wryly. "Well, I wasn't blameless. I didn't turn her down, now did I? We had fun. I thought it was the start of something. She didn't tell me that she was engaged to a parking services officer. She never wore her ring at the pub. I didn't know."

Charlie hissed. "What a bitch. That poor man."

Tadgh nodded. "Aye. I felt awful. I called her several times, she'd always let it go to voice mail and then text me later. She said she had fun, but that she was in a relationship. I was shocked. I shouldn't have been. It's not like I don't know that women do that shit, but I don't know. I guess I was lonely and I missed the warning signs. Anyway, it was Janet who set me straight. She likes me, like a big sister. She told me that Brittney and a few other women in the neighboring stations had a betting pool who would get into bed with me first. It was all some big game to them. They liked this. They saw this." He motioned up and down his body and around his face. "They didn't see me."

"I'm so sorry, Tadgh. I do understand. I worked with mostly men at Cleveland P.D. I get it more than you know. I'd like to think that women wouldn't act like that, since they get treated so shitty on the job sometimes. I guess I overestimated the species."

"Yeah, so like I said. You are nothing like Brittney. You don't appear to notice any of this." He motioned to his body and face again. "You see me as a professional and as a person. It doesn't happen often, so I notice when it does." She smirked. "What?"

She shook her head. "You think I'm immune to all this?" she mimicked his motion up and down his frame. "I'm not. I'm just able to separate the job from everything else. I've learned the hard way how to do that."

His eyes flared. He loved that little confession so much he was ready to shove the dish dryer off the counter and hike her up on there. She must have read his mind, because her eyes went to the counter and her cheeks reddened. Maybe this was the spot she'd seen Patrick working out Caitlyn. She shook herself. Then he got back to what she'd actually said. "Learned the hard way? From Ted the ex?"

She nodded. "Yeah. I was a rookie. He was my training officer. The affair started when I was almost done with my training period. Grossly inappropriate on his part, I might add. We were together for two years. I'd only had one other boyfriend before him. Remember, I was twenty-one when I started on the force. I finished my last semester of college while working nights."

"He was older, almost thirty. I was infatuated, not so much in love. Do you know what I mean? Anyway, it worked for a while, but things changed. He was controlling, and I outgrew wanting to be controlled. He tried to steer my career, although I didn't need his help. I was a great cop. He knew it. I think he was a little jealous, actually. I got some major arrests, broke up a human trafficking ring that was starting up in Cleveland. That's how the FBI noticed me."

"You're smart Charlie. Smart and ambitious and beautiful. It's an intoxicating combination for some men, and an intimidating combination for others. I, for one, am glad you outgrew him. The last thing you need is some aging, jealous wanker tarnishing your fecking shine. You've got the world by the ass, Charlie. You're doing great things."

She smiled and closed her eyes. "God, O'Brien. When you say it like that, I almost believe it."

He bent in, speaking softly. "Believe it. And you'll get your brother out of Cleveland and he'll have the same opportunities."

She looked at him, almost pleading. Then, her eyes filled. He took her in his arms, and there was nothing sexual about it. He didn't press into her. He just held her. "Oh, God. I'm sorry. My brother is my kryptonite. He's everything." Tadgh felt her tears soak his shirt.

Tadgh reflected on the fact that if you very vehemently ordered your cock to stay down, by threat of disembodiment, that it actually stayed down. Being this close to Charlie would have normally stirred him instantly to arousal. He'd been at half mast ever since Patrick and his uncle had left them alone. However, it wasn't what she needed right now. So, the *down boy* order was obeyed. For now.

Charlie pulled back and looked up at him. "Brittney was a fool, O'Brien." Then she kissed him on the cheek. He swayed. He actually swooned like a bloody woman. Then he tightened his grip, looking down at her mouth. "Say my name. Please." Any good intentions he had were gone, and there was no way she didn't feel his instant arousal.

When she said his name, soft and sweet, he dipped his head down just before he heard the bedroom door come open. Patrick looked at them both as they shot apart. He grinned, pointing to the only bathroom. "Sorry, duty calls." Then he walked into the bathroom.

They both burst out laughing, the tension broken. Tadgh's eyes sparkled with mischief. Charlie picked up the container of leftovers. "I better head down and take a nap, too." As she headed for the window, Duncan darted across the room from some hidden spot. "No, stay and visit. Daddy's starting to get jealous." The cat meowed at her. "Go now. He's got turkey." Tadgh made a little whistling sound between his teeth and Duncan turned and scurried to the kitchen. "I'll see you tomorrow, Charlie. Be careful tonight."

She motioned her head toward the bedrooms. "Did you put them up to partnering with me?"

"Not at all. They did that on their own. They respect you, Charlie.

And they're O'Brien men. We take care of..." *What is ours*, he thought. "We take care of our fellow officers. You're in good hands."

"So are they, Tadgh. I'll take care of them too. We will end this. I promise. Then your women will be safe."

* * *

CHARLIE KEPT her hand on her pistol as she maneuvered through the old warehouse, following behind Patrick. He was armed as well. Sean, a reservist, was not. Not that she doubted his ability to kick some ass. Ireland wasn't America, though. They didn't arm most of their police. Once they'd determined the building was not occupied, she began searching with her flashlight for any signs of activity. There was trash. Someone had taken shelter in here at some point, but nothing recent. She took samples from the ground. The place had been an old flour mill. Sean inspected other rooms, doing the same. There were old machines, conveyers. The wiring and metal shavings that were found on the bodies needed to be matched. They'd done two other buildings prior to this. It didn't feel like the place, though. No recent disturbances.

Patrick was near her, always. She suspected that was on Sullivan's orders. "Can I ask you something without you asking why I am asking?"

Patrick looked up, smiling from his own search. "Well, now I have to know. I'll likely beat it out of you if you clam up now."

She gave him a dry look. "I'm serious." He just stood up straight, hand over his heart.

"Ask away, love."

"What does mow grah mean? I Googled it, but I don't think I'm spelling it right."

Patrick's eyes softened. It was uncharacteristic. "A ghrá or mo ghrá...it means *my love.*"

Charlie swallowed, hard. Then she remembered that Patrick had just called her Love. *Ask away, love.* It was like a friendly endearment.

179

Not necessarily a pledge. It was like how some southern people called everyone honey. She'd heard that a lot in the South.

"Oh, so it's just an endearment, like honey or darling or something. I got it." She started looking around again, moving on from the discussion, but he spoke again. "No. Not really. It's not like 'Hey, pass me the remote, love. It's Gaelic, and it's a more personal endearment. My love. There's a sense of belonging when you say it. Ye belong to someone or they to you. Do you understand the difference?"

Charlie just stood, looking down at nothing. "Yes, I think so."

Patrick was quiet for a moment, then he said. "Ye know he cares for you? He's had a hard time with women. He's afraid of getting attached or of sending the wrong signal or something. I don't know exactly. He gets a lot of attention. He just never seems to find one who wants to keep him. He's such a good man. The best. Please, Charlie. Be careful with him."

She turned to him. "I'm not Brittney. I wouldn't just use him. I'm not made that way. I just need to do this job and get home. I think you're wrong, though. He respects me, maybe even finds me attractive, but Tadgh could have any woman he wants. He won't spend too much time thinking of me. I'll keep it professional. I promise you."

"He told you about Brittney?" She nodded. "Did he tell you about Fiona?"

She cocked her head. Then she remembered. "Is it something to do with Michael? He didn't tell me, but I know something happened."

"Nothing happened. Do ye hear? Nothing. Tadgh would never. She tried though. It made things hard, because of course he told Michael. He had to. It's just, I think Tadgh blames himself a bit. Like maybe he had something about him that made her think he would do something like that. It wasn't him though. It was her. It was never him."

"Did anyone ever tell him that? Did Michael?"

He shrugged. "I don't know, but maybe someone should. He's shy around our women. Michael was suspicious of him with Branna. No other reason than bad memories. There was never anything but brotherly affection. I think Tadgh just thinks he's got something to prove. He loves Branna and Alanna, and Eve and Caitlyn. All of them, like sisters. He just keeps a bit more distance now. It's sad, really. I'd trust him with Caitlyn's life. We all would. He's making himself pay for something that wasn't his fault."

Sean walked in and interrupted whatever Charlie was going to say. "Thank you. It's none of my business, but it explains some things. Thank you for telling me." She was quiet as Sean approached.

"I think we're done here. This isn't it, but we'll have them take a look at the samples just in case." He stopped, looking at his two younger companions. "Is something amiss?"

"No, of course not. We were discussing the lack of progress. That's all."

Sean looked at Charlie indulgently. "We'll get there. This saturating the city, checking the empty buildings, it'll bear fruit. Patience, lass."

"I know. I know. You sound like my boss back home. I'm just worried. It's been too long between women. Let's do the next one. Where to?"

TADGH LOOKED AT HIS PHONE. He'd texted Liam to see if Eve had found a ride. He couldn't leave. He knew that. Zaid's middle son, Abdul had just come in. Time to press the kid with dad's help. He was sneaking out, starting to mingle with some questionable men in the neighborhood. Men who were a few years older. The desire to be a man was a problem with kids his age. They were easy to lure into idealism. Liam texted back and he let out a sigh of relief. He'd arranged a cab for Eve. He rubbed the back of his neck, stress tingling his nerves. He wondered where Charlie was right now. He shook himself. Sal looked at him. "Everything all right?"

"Yes, sorry." He smiled as Zaid's eldest daughter brought in tea service and pastry. Tadgh had never seen the appeal of Turkish delight, but he loved the flakey pastry with nuts and honey. He bowed his head. "Shukraan, it looks lovely."

Sal translated and the girl blushed. He noticed that she seemed less and less interested in Sal and more so in him. Maybe she knew Sal was married. Or maybe, like so many young girls, she liked the unknown and exotic. He gave his attention to Zaid instead, as was proper. Zaid was surrounded by his sons and Sal and Tadgh, like he was heading a council meeting. It was the right approach. His house, his meeting. He began to question his son, the boy fidgeting. They had spoken with Zaid before the boy came home. They were light on the details. Only wanting information on empty buildings, abandoned areas, warehouses, etc., where he may have seen the men gathering. Zaid started out amicable, but the father tone creeped in and the lads shoulders slumped in defeat. Once he started talking, the older brother shook his head, then said something short to him in Iraqi. I guess calling your brother an eejit worked in several languages. The boy motioning to himself, talking with his hands.

Sal translated. "Apparently they've been trying to recruit him. Trying to get him to convince his family to go to a more zealous mosque. They've been feeding him some anti-Western propaganda. Telling him that this country will ruin his sisters if they don't all stick together. He said they go in and out of a certain area of town, but he doesn't know it well. He also said he never did anything bad other than sneaking out. They treat him with respect. Like a man."

Sal cursed under his breath. "This is exactly the age group they target. Thirteen to twenty. Sometimes younger." Tadgh knew he was thinking of his own son at home. It was something that Tadgh, as a native born Irishman, would likely never have to deal with. Although, Sal was born here as well. Some people didn't understand that. "We'll raise your son as a proper Irishman. Don't worry. We've got his back." Tadgh spoke quietly as the two eldest in Zaid's family handed an ass chewing to the middle child. Sal gave him a fist bump. "Amen to that, brother."

Luckily, no damage was done, and they had some new information on places to check out. Ballsridge, Sandymount, Ringsend, that whole area to the south of the harbor. It was a big area, but it narrowed down some shitbird activity, even if they didn't have anything to do with the murders. This was progress.

* * *

EVE STOOD at the doorway of the studio, checking her phone. It was cold. She should have worn an extra jumper. The cab was supposed to be here ten minutes ago. It was almost quarter past midnight. She jumped when her phone rang.

"Hello, Love. How's the hospital?"

Liam sighed. "You're outside. I can tell. Where the bloody hell is the cab?"

"He's late. This place is a pain in the arse to find. Ye know that yourself, well enough. Maybe I should walk to the corner. It's only a couple blocks to a main road."

"No, Eve. Stay put. I'll call him. Go back inside and I'll call the taxi service."

"All right, ye pushy brute. I'm goin' inside."

Before they hung up, she said. "Liam. I love you, mo shíorghrá."

"I love you too, darlin'. Always."

Eve dug for the keys as she disconnected the phone. That's when she heard it. A woman screaming for help. She didn't think, she just ran as she hit the command button on her phone.

"Siri, call the Garda!" *I'm sorry. I don't understand call done guard at.* "Bloody hell! Siri call the Police! Call the police!" *Calling police.* Eve came around the corner as she saw the scene unfolding. An older taxi van was sitting idle, the side door open. There was a person at the wheel, and two men were dragging a woman into the van.

"Dublin Garda, what is your emergency?"

"Help, there's a kidnapping! They've almost got her. By O'Reilly's Cleaners in Finglas! Oh, God. STOP! HELP!"

Eve ran at the van, screaming! Lights started to come on in the building windows. "Someone help!" Eve was screaming her head off. The girl screamed as she went wild, instinctively knowing that she had one shot at getting away. Eve took the phone from her ear. "Siri, open camera!" She knew the Garda would never get here in time. She hit video, and she knew that would disconnect the call. She started screaming again, but she had the van and the men on camera. They had ball caps pulled low over their faces, and neck gators covering their chin and mouths, but she got them and the driver, who looked to be female, on camera. The woman had long brown hair. She couldn't see her face clearly either. They all looked at her, then someone yelled from above in one of the buildings.

The one man said in a thick accent. "You fucking bitch!" That's when the girl got loose. She bashed the other one in the face and ran like hell, screaming. The men jumped in the van, knowing they had to get out of there, that they'd drawn too much attention. As they pulled away she watched, almost in slow motion, as the man grabbed the steering wheel from the woman, wrenched the wheel to turn the van toward Eve, and hit the gas. The last thing she heard as she tried to dive out of the way was the scream of the girl she'd saved.

CHAPTER 15

Charlie cracked her neck as she checked the time. It was late. Almost one-thirty. "I think it's time to call it a night. That's four places we've checked. Let's call the station and head in. Maybe someone else found something."

Sean and Patrick took out their phones, unsilencing them. That's when the texts started dinging. All three of the phones blew up with texts and missed calls. Then Sean's started ringing.

"It's Sullivan." He answered it. "Aye, what's going on? Another one? Shit! Where? Oh, wait. Attempted. She's alive?"

He furrowed his brow. "I understand. We'll be there in fifteen." He hung up and looked at Charlie and Patrick. "There was an attempt tonight. He's being cryptic. Doesn't want to talk on the phone. They need us there now. They called everyone in, including Tadgh and Sal. I don't know any more than that."

* * *

TADGH WALKED into the police station through the back entrance. Sal was beside him. He'd received a message as they'd been leaving the housing area. As he walked into the detectives' headquarters, he stopped cold. Patrick and his Uncle Sean looked at him, and the looks on their faces sent a wave of panic through him. Ruined. They were ruined.

"Charlie? Jesus, is it Charlie?" Before they could answer, Charlie came out of Sullivan's office. Her face was tight. When she looked at him, she was utterly devastated. "Who? For fuck sake, who?"

Sullivan walked over with an evidence bag. "A young woman was killed trying to stop the abduction. They ran her over with their vehicle. She had your card in her wallet, and Patrick's as well."

Tadgh started to breathe heavy as he looked down at the two cards they'd given Eve. "Oh God, no. Jesus, no. Ah, God!" He was holding his head, in full melt down when Patrick and Sean were surrounding him, arms linking together to cling to one another. "Oh, God. Uncle Sean. Not Eve. How are we going to tell him?"

Charlie watched the three men as Sal came next to her and put an arm around her. "Did you know her?" he asked. She realized she had tears coming down her face.

She wiped them and cleared her face. "No, but I know Liam. They were in love. He wanted to marry her. Oh, God. She saved that girl." She put her head down, willing back the emotion. They'd been screwing around for hours checking warehouses and this had happened with cops combing the city. It made her crazy. She wanted those bastards dead.

She wiped angrily at her face and excused herself. But as she started down the hall, she was tackled from behind. She knew who it was. She knew his smell, felt his presence. She'd also heard the panic when he'd thought she'd been hurt. He pulled her into him, her back to his chest. His face was in her hair. Her breath stuttered as the tears started again. She twisted in his arms and then he held her so close, it almost cut off her air. He kissed her forehead, up and down her hairline. "I'm glad you're safe, darlin'. I'm sorry. I know this is unprofessional, but you're going to have to cut me a bit of leeway." His voice was tight, aching with emotion.

She pulled his neck, bringing him closer so she could hug him back. "I'm so sorry. Oh, God, poor Liam. Her parents. I'm so sorry, Tadgh. I wish I could take this away."

They stayed that way for another moment, then collected themselves, straightening their clothes and taking deep breaths. But their eyes never left each other's. They walked back to the area where the other detectives were gathered. They'd discreetly busied themselves, giving Tadgh and Charlie a bit of needed privacy, but now it was back to business. Sullivan spoke. "I know you will tell me no, but we can do the notifications…"

"No, I'll do it. I'm his da. I'll do it."

"We'll all do it." Patrick was standing, arms folded. There was no argument. "We do it together."

Tadgh came next to him. "We need to do it now, before something leaks. He's at the hospital. It's why he couldn't pick her up. We were all working. She was supposed to be in a cab." He choked down the emotion.

Sullivan cleared his throat. "She was waiting for the cab when she heard the girl screaming. She called 999, but they couldn't get there fast enough. It was happening as she called. We know this because her cab driver came on the scene only minutes afterward and he called an ambulance. The other victim had run a couple of blocks until she flagged someone down. She called emergency services as well. The operator is coming in for an interview and we've pulled the recordings. Sal and Detective Miller will handle those two things. Charlie and I will head to the hospital to see the victim. The other victim, I mean. She's banged up, a sprained wrist, but she's okay. Lucid. She'll be our first real witness. We need to get to her while it's still fresh."

"We can't release Miss Doherty's things. They're evidence. Just…if it helps…it was fast. The initial findings say that she most likely died on impact. She didn't suffer."

Sullivan's face was composed, but briefing them was taking a toll. It was different when you weren't just talking to officers, but to friends of the victim. Practically family. He addressed Sean directly.

"One of you will need to identify the body, to make it official. I hate to have your son or the family do it if we can avoid it. If you can do that before you go to Liam, it would be best. It'll only take a minute."

"I'll do it," Tadgh said simply. "She's not at his hospital is she? That could be bad. We'd have trouble keeping him away."

"No, Mater was the closest hospital to the scene. That's where they took them both. He's at St. Vincents?"

Tadgh shook his head. "St. James. We need to go do this. Now. Are you all ready?" Then he turned to his uncle and cousin. "I'll go in alone, then we'll head to St. James. You'll need to call Michael. He can tell everyone in person or decide who to call. Michael's the best choice. I hate to put it on him, but he'll know how to go about it."

Both Patrick and Sean grumbled an agreement. "Okay, I'll call him in the car while you're in the hospital. In the meantime, DC Sullivan should go with us. I want as many facts as possible before I call. Then we can decide what to tell everyone."

* * *

TADGH TOOK A DEEP BREATH, realizing of course that no amount of breathing was going to prepare him. Normally he would have been behind glass if he were a civilian. The doctor at the morgue had not stood on formality, since he was also an investigating officer. He nodded at the doctor as he felt Sullivan's hand rest on his shoulder. When he pulled the cloth back to reveal her face, Tadgh's breath stuttered, a tremor quaking through his body.

"We cleaned her up a bit after the initial photos. Nothing to compromise the exam of course." The doctor's demeanor was awkward.

Tadgh cleared his throat. "Thank you, doctor. For taking care of her, I mean. It's her. It's Eve Doherty." They'd known it of course. She'd had ID on her, but this needed to happen. Tadgh took in her features for what could be the last time. She was so still and pale. A head injury at her left temple. "Oh, God. I'm so sorry. I'm so very sorry, Twinkle Toes." *Find my da. He'll watch over you until ye see us again.*

* * *

MICHAEL HUNG up the phone and just stared for a while. The tears fell in silence. That's when Branna came in with the twins. He felt Halley's little hands reach out to him. "Daddy hurt?"

He took a hand and kissed it, then he looked at his wife. Branna's hand was over her mouth, fear evident in her eyes and body. "Who? Oh, God. Who is it? Is it Tadgh or Patrick?"

"No, mo chroí. Put the twins in their room and come sit with me."

* * *

BRIGID SAT ON THE COUCH, holding Caitlyn as she sobbed. Caitlyn had been closest to Eve. They'd all spent a small amount of time with Eve over the last three years, but that was because she was from Cork. She'd only come to Doolin a couple of times a year since she'd started seeing Liam. They'd seen her in Dublin from time to time as well. They all adored her, of course, but she was closest to Patrick and Caitlyn due to proximity. They all mourned for Liam, knowing that he'd loved her. That she'd made him happy and that they were just waiting for school to be done to marry. Caitlyn, though. Caitlyn had lost a dear friend. One of her first friends in Dublin.

"I'm so sorry, love. I know she was a close friend." Michael rubbed her back as Brigid soothed her. Granny Aofie was there as well, holding Cora who was also very upset. She barely knew Eve, but she was very sensitive. She'd grown up with tales of the O'Brien's finding their mates. She wept for her uncle, no doubt. Knowing that when an O'Brien man lost his mate, it was catastrophic. He looked at Branna, and a new spike of fear struck him. She'd had so much trouble with the twins. She'd hemorrhaged, had them prematurely. Maybe they shouldn't be trying to get pregnant again. As if she could sense his fear, she looked up at him, cradling their sleeping son in her arms. She mouthed, *I love you.*

* * *

CHARLIE WALKED down the hospital ward with DC Sullivan and her heart was in her throat. Tadgh had come out of that morgue like a wounded animal that was trying to stay upright. And as bad as that was, now he had to go tell Liam. She'd been picturing the smiling younger O'Brien for hours. He was more lighthearted than the other men. A hopeless flirt, but never in an inappropriate way. He was smart and funny and loved to tease. Eve Doherty had been a lucky woman. She wasn't sure if she was upset or glad that she'd never met the woman. One thing she knew for sure is that she admired her. She had sacrificed her own safety in order to intervene. Some people would have simply called the police, some may have not even done that.

Charlie walked into the victim's room, and the young woman was sipping some water, propped up in her hospital bed. Her wrist was wrapped and her eyes flared with panic before she settled again. Post trauma stress, most likely. She had visible bruises on her arms and on her cheek. "Are you the detectives that they said would come?"

"Yes, dear. This is Charlie Ryan. She's an American consultant here to assist us and you. My name is Detective Sullivan. How are you feeling?"

Tears welled in the girls eyes. "I'm alive. I got away, and that's more than the other girls did. It's the same people, isn't it? From the news. The dead girls?"

Sullivan said, "Aye, most likely. That is what we're here to talk to you about. You're our first witness, Miss Hathaway. Anything you can tell us would help."

She started talking and it was all Charlie could do not to rub her arms where the goosebumps had come up. "I thought it was a taxi at first. It looked like one. It had one of those lights on top. The woman asked me if I knew where Temple Bar was. She had an accent, but it wasn't Irish. I didn't think anything of it, because it was a woman. Then the two men jumped out of the sliding door. I fought like hell. My dad was in the Army. He taught me to fight. That's when I heard the woman screaming for help."

Then the girl stopped and put her face in her hands. "I've never been so grateful to hear or see someone. I saw her. She had her phone to her ear. I kept fighting them. She ran toward me and held her phone out like she was taking a picture. The men got distracted just enough for me to get an arm out and bash the one in the face. Then I ran. She saved me. I need to thank her. She never stopped yelling. People heard her! She saved me!" The girl was starting to get louder. "Do you know her name? I want to see her."

The girl was looking between Charlie and Sullivan and neither could find their tongue. "What's wrong? Oh, God. They didn't take her did they?"

Charlie closed her eyes and took a breath. "No, they didn't take her. I'm sorry, Miss Hathaway. When they fled, they hit her with their van. On purpose. There was a witness that looked out the window just as the van swerved to hit her. She tried to jump out of the way, but they ran her down. She died on impact."

The horror on the girl's face was something Charlie was never going to forget. "She's dead? No! No! She can't be dead! She saved me. Oh, God. It's my fault!" The girl was coming completely undone.

"No, no Shannon. This is not your fault. She made the choice to get involved. It is their fault. They are animals. She saved you and she wouldn't want you to blame yourself. Do you hear me?" The girl was crying so hard that Charlie broke protocol and put her arm around her. "I'm so sorry this happened to you. If you help us, I promise you that those bastards will pay for her death, and the deaths of those other women. I will not leave Ireland until they're found."

She looked at Sullivan. "Please tell me they have her phone in evidence."

Sullivan nodded once, then left to make a call.

* * *

TADGH, Sean, and Patrick paced nervously in the meeting room of the hospital as the admin on duty went to retrieve Liam. How in the hell were they going to tell him? The thought of it made Tadgh's stomach roll, like he was being eaten alive from the inside.

Sean had done this type of thing before, when he was Garda. He'd actually been the one to tell Katie and Tadgh when his brother had been killed. This was different, though. They were preparing to break his son in half.

Liam walked through the door and froze. "What's happened? Jesus, look at you three. What is it?"

Sean walked over and shut the door. "Is it Gran? God, I told her to slow down."

"It isn't Gran."

He looked at them all hard, then like something occurred to him, he looked at his phone.

"Liam."

He threw a hand up as he made a call. "Eve, love. I haven't heard from you since I called the cab again. Call me when you get in." He hung up and stared at the phone. He'd called her repeatedly, and the phone kept going to voicemail. He'd assumed that she'd forgotten to charge it, as she often did. The silence was deafening. He pointed at his father. "No. I called. They were two minutes away. No!" He knew, though. He'd felt something deep in his gut and had continued to call. He knew. He just couldn't absorb the reality. He wouldn't.

Tadgh walked forward. "Liam, please listen."

"No! She was going back inside. When we hung up, she was going back inside to wait. No!" The three men closed in, feeling the escalation coming. "What the fuck are you trying to tell me?" He grabbed Tadgh by the shirt. "What are you telling me!"

Sean spoke softly. "She's gone, son. Oh, God. I'm sorry. She's gone. She interrupted another kidnapping. She tried to help the girl."

Liam was shaking his head back and forth. He was shaking, tearing up. Then it registered what Sean had said and his eyes shot to his father's. "They took her? Then she might still be alive! What the hell are you doing here? We need to look for her!"

"No, son." Sean put his hand up, as if he could soothe him before he spoke the truth. His eyes were filled with tears. "They didn't take her. She died when they fled. They hit her with the car. Deliberately. They hit her because she was screaming for help for the girl."

"No! No! I need to see her. Maybe she's just hurt. Where is she?" He started going for the door, completely out of his head. Sean grabbed him around the shoulders and he went ape shit. The three men restrained him as he lost control. He screamed like he was being tortured. He cursed, he screamed her name. It took the full strength of three of them to keep him from hurting himself and them. "I don't believe you! I need to see her!" Tadgh looked across his struggling figure as Sean held his son, his face pressed into Liam's hair. He was sobbing. They all were. Everything they'd done, all the precautions they'd taken, and still...death had come for one of their women.

Tadgh wasn't sure when the struggle had shifted, but he came to the realization slowly that Liam was no longer fighting and they were no longer restraining. They were huddled on the floor, completely ruined. The four of them holding on to each other like their lives depended on it.

* * *

SORCHA SAT STARING at her father, not completely sure she wasn't dreaming. "I'm sorry, Da. I just..." She looked at Alanna who was crying silently.

"Edith, darlin'. Maybe some tea for the girls? This is all a bit much." He'd told his wife about thirty minutes ago. They'd had their moments of disbelief and tears, then collected themselves in order to tell the story to his daughter and Alanna.

"I don't understand. You say it was the case Sean was working on. But she was in a car accident?"

So he told her again. Slowly. And he could tell that she was fully absorbing the horror this time. The tears spilled down her cheeks. Her jaw tight. "Oh, Eve. Such a pretty, sweet girl. Her poor parents." Then the sobs started. "My Liam. Oh, God. My poor Liam. This wasn't supposed to happen!" She clenched her fists. "They were so careful!"

Then Alanna was next to her and the women held each other, crying. "I knew it. I knew somehow this would all come back to me. I felt it." She wiped her face with a tissue that her father had given her. She looked at them. "I escaped, ye see. And then I put it all behind me. But, when I saw that case file. I saw what was happening in Dublin. It descended on me like a dangerous, thick fog. I knew the evil had come back." She was trembling now.

"No, Sorcha. This isn't..."

"It is! I felt it! I knew. I'd escaped, but it was coming for me. It was owed a life. It took from my son instead of me!"

"Sorcha, that doesn't make sense. Surely you understand that this is all unrelated. You can't take this burden on yourself." Her father's voice was soft.

She looked at him simply, explaining it as if he were slow or a child. "I'm his mother. It's always my burden to take. Now, I have three deaths on my hands."

They all looked at each other, confused. "I'm sorry darlin'. I am trying to understand, but you are losing me. How could you think you have one death on your hands, let alone three? Ye've spent your life doing for others. You've saved lives."

"Well now, there was Barbara Leary." Sorcha wiped her eyes. "She was taken that night, in my place. Then, my brother John, and now Eve."

They all exchanged looks, baffled and torn. She was talking with perfect clarity, but she wasn't making a lick of sense. "My darling. Why would you think that you had anything to do with John's death? He had cancer, Sweet. Ye know that."

Edith was sitting now, having brought the tea tray into the living room. Her face was stricken. "No, sweetheart. John was sick. Ye had naught to do with it."

"I did. He went to work in the mill when I was starting Uni. He could have gone to school, but he knew you couldn't afford both of us going. He was a smart lad. He could have done anything, but he went to work in that bloody mill instead. He helped pay the bills. I know he did. He left his books out on the desk and I saw that he'd started paying the power bill and he helped with other things. He became a man at seventeen and I went to school. That mill killed him, and he was there because of me."

"Jesus, Sorcha. Is that what you think? You're wrong, darling. He made his choice to work in the mill. He could have gone to school. He had high marks like you. He could have gone on scholarship. And you didn't stress the family finances that much. You got scholarships as well. Your mother and I tried to get him to quit the mill. He'd come home covered in dust and coughing. But there was a girl there that he fancied. We never met her, but he was head over heels. He stayed so he could see her, I think. Even when she left, he stayed. I think he was waiting for her to come back."

Sorcha's brows were furrowed. "No, he would have told me. That can't be right."

"He didn't tell us either, love. It's just, I did his washing, you remember. He'd come help your da at the house and I'd do his washing. There were letters. I found them in his pockets. I never read them. He was a man after all. He'd been at the mill for two years. But it was a woman's handwriting, and they smelled of perfume."

She smiled at that. "It was our little exchange of respect. I would clean his clothes and put them back in the pocket. After two times he started catching on. He changed while he was at the house and put his fresh pants on. He patted the pocket, pulled the dry letter out, sort of looked at me and blushed. Ye know how easily he blushed."

Sorcha let out an unexpected laugh and the women exchanged glances. Sorcha was crying now, a silent, lighter sort of crying. "Aye, I do. Those redhead genes. He blushed something fierce. It made him nuts that he couldn't control it." Then, something occurred to her. "I remember one night when I was visiting from down south. I was already married, actually I was pregnant with Aidan. I came to see him and stay in the flat, had made him a nice dinner. But he'd been on the piss with his mates after work and forgotten about me. They brought him back to the flat. I'd never seen him so drunk. You know, he didn't drink all that much. Just the occasional pint. The lads...they told me not to give him too much of a bad time about it. Said he'd lost someone today. I pried, o'course. You know me. But they just said he had to tell me. He didn't. I remember him mumbling. He said, *Don't go, darlin'.* I thought he wanted to sit with me a while, but then he said *Molly.* I didn't know a Molly. I asked him about it later and he just said it was some woman at the pub the night before. I didn't really believe him, though. His voice had been so...sorrowful. Could that be when she left?"

Edith shrugged. "So you see, love. It was never you. He had his own reasons for making the choices he did. Perhaps that girl is why he never married. I don't know," her father said. "You can't keep making yourself pay for things that have happened to other people, my sweet girl. Bad things happen, even evil ones, but those deeds lay at the hands of the evil doers. You can no more stop these twists of fate as you can stop the wind. Right now Liam needs his mam. He doesn't need your misplaced guilt. He'll have enough of that on his own. Ye must put these things to rest, for his sake. Do you understand?"

"It's not that easy."

Alanna put her arm around Sorcha. "But you have us, and we'll help you. And besides, Sorcha O'Brien, unless you are some sort of demi-god, you must realize that you don't affect the state of the world and everyone in it?" She was looking at Sorcha with a little smile and a little challenge in her eyes.

"Are ye saying I've got an ego problem?" Sorcha said, smiling through her tears.

"Maybe. Maybe you need to realize that you can't shield everyone from the world. All you can do is love them and let them love you. You also need to understand that this isn't about forgiving yourself. You haven't done anything that needs forgiving. You just have to let it all go. Then you can be the mother, daughter, and wife we all need."

* * *

SEANY KNOCKED and Tadgh let him in the apartment. They were all at Liam's. He was living alone now, having outgrown the need for a roommate, but they'd planned for Seany to move in the second bedroom once he'd graduated from the fire academy.

Seany's eyes were puffy, but he was solid. "How is he?"

"He's been sleeping. They gave him a valium at the hospital. It was either that or they were going to admit him for a psych eval. Once he heard that, he submitted to the meds. They should be wearing off, though. It wasn't a high dose."

Seany put his bag on the floor by the couch. "I can stay all weekend. Are ye sure we can't get him home? I could take him."

"He isn't ready. I know when this all sinks in, he's going to have more questions. I don't know how much to tell him."

Behind them, Sean Sr. spoke. "We tell him everything he wants to know. It's already hit the press. He should know everything. It's his right. She was his, and he hers. It's his right." Sean's eyes were bright. He'd been talking to his wife on the phone. It had taken a toll on him. This whole thing had. Telling his son that his first real love was dead, that she'd been murdered, had ripped him open, broken his heart.

"You need to sleep, Da. Take the bed. I'll be fine on the sofa." Then he looked at Tadgh. "You need to go home and sleep as well. Do ye need me to take you?"

"No, I've got the bike. I've just had some coffee. I'll be okay to drive."

Then he grabbed Seany with no warning. "I love you, brother. Thank you for coming."

Seany's voice was hoarse. "I love you, too. Oh God, Tadgh. I don't know what to say to him."

They turned as they heard Liam's groggy, dim voice. "If ye can't tell me I've been dreaming, then nothing you say will matter."

They were quiet for a bit. He walked into the kitchen, poured a glass of water, and drank. "I won't take those pills again. And if you want to admit me into the hospital, you're going to have to shoot me. Are we clear?"

His voice was tight. It was like it was someone else. Liam was the lighthearted one. The one who always found something to laugh at. It was like that part of him was dead. It was in his eyes.

"Da, do you have the case file with you? I want to see it. All of it." Sean just nodded.

He walked past Tadgh and didn't look at him. He actually hadn't made eye contact since he'd come out of the bedroom.

"Liam, do you need me to stay?" His voice was pleading.

Then Liam looked at him. "No. Take a feckin' nap or whatever else you need. Then you get out there and do your goddamn job. If ye'd been working at this a little more and chasing after Charlie less, maybe they'd already be in jail instead of running Eve down."

Tadgh's head snapped back like he'd been struck. Sean hissed. "Jesus Christ, Liam. I know you're hurting, but how could you say such a thing? He's been out every night. Every single night putting his ass on the line. He's been undercover, trolling the refugee neighborhoods. The only night he took off was for William's memorial!"

A hint of contrition flickered across Liam's face, but he stifled it. "Aye, well obviously he's barking up the wrong tree. My mistake, though. You've been doing a bang up job." His voice was toxic. Tadgh was looking at him, and Sean watched the transformation. Complete shutdown. His face turned to stone.

"I'll head out now. Uncle Sean, I'll call you when I talk to the team."

Seany walked out with Tadgh, trying to stop him. "Wait, Tadgh. He didn't mean it. Please, stay. Have another cup of coffee. Please."

Tadgh moved past him. "I've had enough. Take care of him, Seany."

* * *

CHARLIE WAITED for Tadgh for an hour. After talking to Sean, she'd been ready. Liam had taken a particularly brutal hunk out of him. Insinuating he hadn't been doing enough to find the killers. She understood, to a degree. Tadgh was an easy target. He was a nice guy. The best. He wouldn't retaliate. He'd take the blows and walk away because he knew that Liam was hurting. Not that he was some sort of pussy. He was smart and sharp and tough. He was as strong as they came, both physically and in his character. But his family was his weak spot, his kryptonite. She'd never known such a close family. He would give Liam his pound of flesh, even if it was not his responsibility to give it.

He'd undoubtedly convinced himself that somehow Liam was right. She'd thought the same thing. Not about Tadgh's work, but her own. They'd been running in circles, half in the dark. This witness, however. This was the break they needed. And that phone. It was smashed, but that could be worked around depending on how bad the damage was. She needed to access a tech savvy person. Someone who wouldn't screw up this crucial piece of evidence collection.

She checked the time. She'd called her boss, giving him an update. He had been taken aback by the turn of events, but glad, as they all were, that the woman had survived. And that Eve had been heard on recording and seen by the victim taking video of the assailants. If that video survived, it could be a game changer. She hadn't heard from Tadgh. He was off somewhere, coming to terms with everything. He wasn't with Sal. She'd checked. Everyone had needed sleep. Sal was at home. As if on cue, he called her.

"Think, Charlie. Where would he go? I don't want to bother the family. I don't want to worry them. Where would he go to clear his head?"

She was rubbing her brows, exhausted. Then it hit her. "I know where he is."

* * *

CHARLIE FOUND his bike near the South side of Bull Island, near the wall. She'd gone to the other side first, but he hadn't been there. She parked and walked down the long paved wall to the big red lighthouse that stood guardian over the Dublin Port. He had a thing for lighthouses, obviously, and that made her think of Josh. She shook herself. Her personal baggage had no place here. She was here for Tadgh. She found him perched on a stone, at the edge of the wall that circled the lighthouse. He stared out at the water, not acknowledging her for a moment. Which was odd. His instincts were good. He'd surely heard her approach.

"I'm fine Charlie. Go home. Get some sleep."

She exhaled. "I didn't say you weren't. I'm just here to see the light-house, clear my head. It's been a long night." The sun was coming up over the water and it shined a golden halo around Tadgh's hair. It was getting longer and his stubble was in full force after he'd stopped shaving again. He had beautiful hair, she thought. Almost as beautiful as his eyes. He turned around, a grin struggling to rise.

"Right, and you just happened to pick the spot I was sitting, even though you've never been here?"

She laughed. "And how do you know that? I might be up to all sorts of things when you aren't around. I have flying lessons planned for four o'clock, and I'm going to this swinging singles orgy at midnight."

The smile got bigger. "You're lying. You came to check on me. It was nice, but unnecessary."

"Let's go home, Tadgh."

Tadgh was close to cracking right now. When he heard those words come out of Charlie's mouth, he shut his eyes as a wave of emotion rolled through him. She'd meant it in a more general way, but the thought of sharing a home with her, of coming home to her, filled him with such longing.

He'd struggled with loneliness before. This was different. This was about her. He was falling in love with her. Despite his best intentions, he'd been doomed almost immediately. He'd had a hard time with the whole "love at first sight" thing. Supposedly it had been like that for his father and his uncle. Aidan as well. O'Brien men sometimes fell hard and fast. Usually, as a matter of fact, even though it took them a while to realize it. He loved her, though. That was not a doubt. She was one of the few women, other than the women that had married into his family, who had not immediately tried to seduce him. She was attracted to him, by her own admission, but she saw past the attrac-tion. She was trying to be his friend. And that made him love her all the more.

He stood up, dusting off his pants as he climbed off the rocks. He took her hand without asking, and she let him. They walked in silence to his bike. "Are you okay to drive? Can we lock it up and leave it?"

He threw a leg over and she grunted. She took his helmet off the back and handed it to him, as if she instinctively knew he was feeling reckless. "I'll meet you in the garage. I have a lot to tell you when you're ready."

* * *

"Do they have someone working on the phone yet?"

She shook her head. "No, it's cracked and wet. They have it in some sort of demoisturization vacuum seal. They're afraid to try turning it on while it's wet. It could fry everything. Honestly, I don't know who to use for this. It's about as crucial a piece of evidence as you can get. We have to have the best."

Tadgh picked up his phone. "I know who to use." He called and Finn immediately picked up. The Garda in Shannon had used Finn to crack a phone in a fraud case. He didn't look the part, but Finn was a super-geek. He'd do this right or he'd find someone who would.

"So, is there anything Michael would like to do on this case? It seems the gang is all here. You are a talented bunch." Charlie was shaking her head in amazement. "If the zombie apocalypse ever happens, I'm hanging with you guys...although, I'll bring the weapons. You Irish are sorely lacking in that department."

Tadgh smiled. "Well, that's one way to earn yourself a spot on the island."

He stared off then, distracted by dark thoughts that kept coming to him off and on. "You're exhausted. Come and lay down before you fall over." Charlie took his hand and led him to the outstretched sofa bed. He obeyed, because he was too tired to argue. He sat and the bed squeaked under him.

"Come on, big guy. Swing those legs up and I'll tuck you in." She was teasing him, but he took her hand. She stilled, and then she stepped into him, standing between his legs. She cradled his head against her abdomen and she felt a shudder go through him. She ran her fingers through his hair. "It's okay. I'll stay a while." She put a foot on the arm of the couch, climbed around him and he turned and settled against her. Her back was to the sofa, her legs stretched out, and he lay next to her, putting his head back on her stomach. She played with his hair for a bit, then said, "I'm sorry Liam hurt you. I don't know exactly what happened, but I know you've done more than anyone to solve this case. I know you watched out for Eve like she was your own sister. He didn't mean it, sweetie. I promise you. I know all about lashing out when you're hurting. He didn't mean it and what he said isn't true."

He looked up at her and she saw the tight face, so contained, but a tear escaped and ran into his hair at the temple. "She was a good, sweet girl." She kissed him on the forehead, smoothing his shaggy hair back. "I'm so sorry you lost your friend." He put his head back down, absorbing the comfort she offered.

That's when he started to talk. He told her all about his family. It started with Liam of course, but as the minutes and then hours went by, she learned all about the O'Briens. From the grandparents to baby Isla. She heard it all. Sometimes he was serious, sometimes he was laughing as he talked about being one of a band of naughty boys terrorizing the small streets of Doolin and Inisheer. She envied him such a childhood, but also was glad for it. Even with the loss of his father, he'd been loved as a boy. He'd had magic in his childhood. It was times like this that he needed those memories. She'd spent her childhood in survival mode. Maybe some of her adulthood as well. So had her brother. She had never really thought about having kids. Even after two years with Ted. But Tadgh O'Brien would make a wonderful father. He'd had some great examples.

He told her about the family lore. The history of the O'Brien clan, and finally of the legends and stories surrounding the O'Brien mates. She thought about the women she'd met. Branna, Alanna, Sorcha, Caitlyn, even Granny Aoife. She understood. They were amazing women. All extraordinary in their own way. Brigid, who was O'Brien by blood, was feisty and strong. She ran around like a mother hen, pecking at all of her brothers. They were quite a family.

He also opened up to her about what had gone on with Michael's ex-wife, Fiona. He'd carried a lot of guilt over it. "I always thought maybe I'd invited the attention in some way. We were all friends, and I can be a bit of a flirt, or at least I was back then. It wasn't inappropriate. I don't know. I just thought, why me? Why not one of his brothers? Why did she decide that I might be open to her advances? I felt terrible."

"She sounds like a piece of work."

"She was. She got better though. She was bi-polar. She started therapy, some medications. She really was doing better."

"So where is she now? Still in Doolin?"

Tadgh shook his head. "No, actually. It was the strangest thing. She'd had a fling with an American man who had come to Alanna and Aidan's wedding. He was a good sort. We thought they'd started a relationship, but he went back to the states and she went abroad. She was a photographer. She wanted to travel and get out of that small town. Start fresh without the reputation dogging her. But, no one's seen her since. She may have had a falling out with her parents because it's been three years and nothing. They act like they don't even have a daughter. Her older brother lives in Shannon, no one really talks to the family much anymore except for the B&B they run. She's just gone."

"That is strange, but sometimes a fresh start is best. It sounds like your family was willing to bury the hatchet with her. That's good. But you have to know, Tadgh, people with her kind of problems don't need a reason. You can't blame yourself for her choices, and you told Michael right away. That had to be really hard on you. As hard as it was on him. I'm glad you're close with him again. He seems like a good guy and his wife too. Your whole family is amazing. You're a lucky man, Tadgh. I don't have to tell you that."

He was drifting off to sleep, despite his efforts. He mumbled something along the lines of, *Yes I am.* Then he was asleep.

* * *

CHARLIE DIDN'T REMEMBER FALLING asleep. They'd been talking, then nothing. She slowly came to with the realization that she was sprawled on Tadgh's chest. He was stirring too. That's when the mood shifted and she felt his hips roll. His hand smoothed its way up her spine, nestling in her hair. The other was at her tailbone. Heat lanced through her body, settling between her legs. He rolled his hips against her and God help her, she returned in kind. He moaned in her hair, his breath against her neck. He was hard, his erection thick and big. She burned as she felt it rub against her stomach. Her mind was in that delirious place between wakefulness and sleep, but her body was right on board with his. He lowered his hand and cupped her ass and she let out a little gasp. That's when she realized how unawake he really was. His whole body jerked as he rolled her to the side, pulling his pelvis away from her.

"Jaysus Christ, I'm sorry Charlie! I thought I was dreaming."

Heat flushed her face. Oh, God. She'd been all over him. She tried to jump up. "No, I'm sorry. I didn't come here for this. I'm sorry, Tadgh." He had a hold on her wrist, not letting her flee. He took in her face, her breathing.

"Wait, don't go." She was still trying to get up when he pulled her closer. "I said I thought I was dreaming, but I was hoping I wasn't." Her face was conflicted, caught between complete sexual frustration and embarrassment and horror at herself for God only knew what.

"You're not in a good place. I should go. I'm so sorry. I would never use you, Tadgh."

Suddenly, he was aware of just how bad his cock was throbbing. He needed her. Not just for sex. Falling asleep with her, feeling her under him as he talked and then drifted off. He needed her. Even if it was just for a little while. He'd kept his distance and it hadn't done a bit of good. He'd fallen in love with her anyway. Now, as he looked at her warring with her own desire, he couldn't figure out why in the hell he'd been holding back. Better to have a few weeks with her, loving her, than to never have anything. "Charlie." He heard the ache in his voice. Saw it in her eyes. She cared for him, despite her best efforts to keep him at a distance. She also wanted him. This beautiful, smart, successful, tough woman could have anyone she wanted, but she wanted him. More than she was comfortable with.

She touched his face as she hovered over him, their breath mingling. His hand was gentle as it threaded into the hair behind her ear. Then slowly, he stretched his neck, bridging the distance. Then he kissed her. Soft and sweet, taking his time. She whimpered as he teased her mouth. He tangled his hands in her hair and reclined back on the bed, pulling her with him. Then he got serious. He moaned and pressed his arousal into her as he deepened the kiss. Then he rolled and she instinctively cradled him between her legs. He propped himself on his elbows and moaned again as she scraped his scalp with her fingernails. He rocked his cock right where he wanted to be, despite the clothing between them, as he deepened the kiss. Then he broke the seal on their mouths and their eyes met. "Charlie, I've wanted this for so long. Oh God. You're so beautiful."

She ran her hands up his shirt to feel his broad, muscled chest and he pumped his hips against her. She put her head back and bit her lip, stifling the noise that was trying to come out of her. He got up on his knees and took his shirt off, then he was on her again, rolling until she was straddling him. He needed skin on skin. He wanted to feel her. He took her hips in his hands. Her jeans were loose and low on her waist. He thumbed the skin and she jerked against him. "Give me your mouth, mo ghrá. I need your mouth."

His voice was husky, demanding. His golden eyes sparked with arousal. When he kissed her, he felt her let go a bit, starting a slow grind with her hips. He ran his hand up her shirt and she knew right where he was headed. She straightened as he cupped her breasts over her bra, thumbing her nipples.

Charlie was out of her head. She'd never been this turned on. He was so beautiful beneath her. Completely at her mercy. When he touched her hard nipples through her bra, he'd been staring into her eyes and his hips reared up as he cursed. "Ah, Charlie. You feel perfect." She remembered, in a flash, the size of Brittany's boobs and wondered how he could think that about her unremarkable chest. Doubt must have shown on her face, because he pulled her ribs as he reared up and met her face with his. "Perfect."

He started to lift her shirt over her head when a cold reality struck her. Before she could think about how he would react, she was off him and then off the mattress like a jack rabbit.

His face was shocked, then softened. He put a hand out, as if to soothe her without touching her. "I'm sorry. Charlie, I pushed you too fast. I'm sorry. I won't..." She was shaking her head. He didn't understand.

"Please darlin'. I'm sorry. I won't push. Jesus, one kiss and I'm all over you. It's unforgivable. Please, sweetheart. Just don't run off. I won't do anything you don't want."

"Shut up!" She screamed it and couldn't take it back. He was shocked stupid by the outburst. "You didn't do anything wrong. I want this. Jesus, I'm ready to explode right now I want this so badly."

He cocked his head. "Then what is it, Charlie? Talk to me."

She wrapped her arms around herself and shut her eyes. "It's not you, Tadgh. You're perfect. This was perfect. I just...I have to tell you something. I don't know how to tell you without wrecking the moment, but it can't be helped. If this goes any further, it'll be inevitable."

He was baffled. It showed on his face. Then something occurred to him. "Charlie, you said you were single, that you had no one." She shook herself again, obviously that wasn't it and she was frustrated. "What then? Lass, talk to me. Please. I won't touch you. You can trust me."

She opened her eyes and lifted her chin. "I lied to you. I lied to you about something. It's not another lover. I haven't been with anyone since I broke it off with Ted four years ago. I just..."

"Whatever it is, you had your reasons. But it's time now, love. It's time to trust me. What did you lie about?

She stared at him for a long time, and he let her get comfortable with the idea of confiding in him. He didn't push.

"When I told you he never hurt me. It wasn't true."

Tadgh stiffened, trying to remember the conversation. "Your father." It wasn't a question. Then he watched as she slowly pulled her shirt up, pulled her arms out of the sleeves, and left it hanging around her neck. He got up and walked to her and she hesitated briefly. Then she turned around.

Tadgh knew that whatever she was going to show him was going to make him mental. He also knew that he couldn't react with anger. That emotion had no place here between them. He thought that she might show him an old cut, from having taken a fall. Maybe a surgical scar from having broken a bone. Nothing prepared him for what he saw.

The burn was about six inches on each side. A strange mark, almost triangular, but for the curves as the lines descended. Then he saw the small circles and realized what he was looking at. A groan escaped him as he lay his head on her shoulder. "Oh Charlie, love. My sweet darlin'." She started to shake.

No matter how much time passed, the perfectly shaped burn from the iron never got any less impressive. Charlie hated the weakness, the fact that she felt shame about it. She'd done nothing but try to protect her brother. She hated the imperfection, though, because it represented the long line of broken and screwed up memories that was otherwise known as her childhood. It was like he'd branded her as some Cleveland white trash kid, with an alcoholic father and an abusive home life. Tadgh's silence spoke volumes. He was undoubtedly sickened by the scarring. She was ready to turn around and put the shirt back on when he did something so unexpected, it stole her breath. He leaned down and kissed the scar.

"It was the worst thing he ever did. He didn't want me going to the hospital. He knew there would be questions. But the shirt I was wearing, it melted to my skin." Tadgh hissed. She kept going though, needing to get the story over and done with. "My mother never stood up to him, but that time she did. She took me to the hospital and the police came, and a social worker." As she talked, Tadgh finished slipping the shirt off of her, then he held her to him, hugging her from behind. She melted into his bare chest, so warm and solid.

"I don't think he'd planned it at all, to hurt me, I mean. He went after my brother, you see. He was eight, and he'd been playing with my dad's shaving cream." Her voice was strained. "He's a good boy. So good. He just wanted to be like my dad. He'd seen him shave. He didn't mean to..."

"Charlie, you don't have to explain. Every little boy gets in his da's shaving kit."

She just nodded, continuing. "My mother was ironing. She just kept her head down like a coward and my father was starting to get really worked up. He grabbed Josh by the shirt, I knew he was going to start hitting him. I got between them. My father let go of his shirt, and I turned to Josh and told him to go into his room, to lock the door and not come out. My father turned his anger toward me then, which was exactly why I did it."

She felt Tadgh pull her closer, but he didn't interrupt her. "I told him I'd clean it up and go get him some more. That I'd use my birthday money and ride my bike to the store, so he didn't have to be mad." She shuddered at the memories. "When I turned to walk away, that's when he did it. *Don't you turn your back on me you little bitch. Who the hell do you think you are?* She hadn't seen it coming, just the white hot flash of pain and the smell of melting fabric, cooking flesh. Then the sound of her own screams mixed with her mother's. It flashed in her mind like a sensory overload.

She felt the tremble start in Tadgh, small at first, then shaking. "What are you thinking? That you don't want someone with such a screwed up family?"

"No, Charlie. I'm thinking that your father is lucky there's an ocean between himself and me. Because if I could, I'd drive over there and kill that son of a bitch with my bare hands. We've got to get him out of there." Josh. She knew who he meant.

"I know. I lied to the social worker that day. My mother begged me to lie and say I was ironing on the bed and forgot it was plugged in. That I rolled over on it. The fracture in my shoulder blade went untreated because of the lie. They never x-rayed it. I told the truth in the FBI screening, so they had me sent for X-rays and found the old fracture. They wanted to make sure I was fit for duty. Anyway," she shook her head, "I went home after the hospital. I told my father that if he ever touched me or Josh again, that I would tell them what really happened. That he'd go to jail. I couldn't help my mother. She was never going to leave him, but I could protect Josh. He laughed at me and said no one would believe me now that I had lied once. So, I leaned in very calmly and told him that if the police didn't help me, that I would wait until he drank himself to black-out and I'd put that iron on his face. That I'd burn him like he did me. He didn't touch me again."

"When I became a police officer, the first thing I did after graduation was go to the house in my uniform. I'd moved out several months before. He was sitting in his chair with a handle of cheap whiskey next to him. I told him that if he laid a hand on Josh, I'd make sure he went to jail and that I'd take Josh to live with me. I also told him that if he tried to keep me from seeing Josh, that I would have him charged with the original assault. Because he'd permanently maimed me, the statute of limitations was twenty years. He had a few mocking remarks, but I made my point. He hasn't hurt Josh. The closest he has come to it was this last time, when Josh called me. He is older now. He won't sit by and let my father beat my mother in front of him. I have to get him out of there. My father doesn't exercise a lot of judgment or control when he's drunk, no matter how good my threats are."

"Why don't you just do as you threatened? Put him in jail?"

She sighed. "Because my mother would have nowhere to go. She hasn't had a job in twenty-five years. She has no money. She's completely estranged from her family. Josh would have nowhere to go. My dad is a douchebag, but he's the only breadwinner. My mother would never leave Cleveland and I have tried to get her to go to a safe house, but she won't. God only knows where she and Josh would end up. I don't want him in the foster care system. In nine months he's eighteen. I just need to help him get emancipated."

"I'll help you, Charlie. Those aren't empty words. We'll put our heads together and we'll get him free. If you need money for the lawyer, I'll sell the bike." His voice was soft but sure. He was completely serious. That's when she knew for certain that she was in love with him.

She turned in his arms and he knew what she needed. He kissed her deep. Then the bad memories were gone and all she knew was him. All she felt was Tadgh. Their skin mingled and it was intoxicating. He ran his hands all over her, moaning against her mouth. He lifted her and she wrapped her jean clad legs around his waist. He was hard and ready, and he walked her back over to the sofa bed and lay her out before him. Then he reached down and unclasped her bra where it hooked in the front.

"I need to see you." He spread the two halves of her bra apart and dipped his head to taste her. She coiled her fingers in his hair as she bowed off the mattress. "Christ, you taste like heaven," he said. Then he took her other nipple in his mouth, cupping her with his hand. He had a rhythm going below the waist as well. He was back, cradled between her thighs and she was so wet that she was afraid she was going to climax just from the little bump and grind he was doing, and what he was doing with his mouth. He broke the contact and started to kiss down her abdomen and she bit back a moan as he licked her lower belly. That's when she heard the key in the lock. He heard it too, because he shot up just as the door opened. The chain prevented any entry, thankfully.

"Tadgh, are you awake? Bloody hell, why'dya have the bloody chain on?"

Charlie looked at him, stifling a giggle as she fumbled with her bra. His eyes got stuck there for a minute, watching her stuff her perfect little breasts back into her bra. "What bloody timing," he hissed. Then he tossed her shirt at her as he slid his back over his head. "Just a minute, Brigid! I was just letting Charlie in the window."

"Did you just say you made her come in through the window?"

He smoothed his hair back and pulled her in for one more kiss. Then he answered the door.

Charlie watched Tadgh's mood shift yet again when he saw his cousin. Brigid's face was pale. She was a lively woman. Charlie had immediately liked her. The strain of Eve's death had taken a toll, however. She took in Brigid's handsome husband, the technically talented Finn, and still felt a little spark of amazement at how good looking he was. Longish black hair, dark eyes, large build. Dark Irish is the term she'd heard. He was carrying Cora who was asleep on his chest.

"I'm sorry we had to bring her. She's been out of sorts. Nightmares, crying. I think it's her way of grieving for Liam."

Finn went to the sofa bed and laid her down. She stirred and began to drift off again when Duncan jumped on the bed with a spurt of energy. He started smelling her eyelids, tickling her with his whiskers, and she woke. It took her a moment to realize where she was, then she smiled. "Duncan Doodlebug!" Then she scooped up the cat and hugged him. "Your brother misses you something fierce. Yes, Mr. Fergus Fancypants misses you."

Tadgh plopped down next to her laughing. "Duncan Doodlebug and Fergus Fancypants? Christ, girl. Couldn't ye think of something more masculine….like Duncan the Destroyer or Fergus the Fierce? They've got their male pride!"

Cora gave him an indulgent look, like he was a child being schooled. "No, Uncle. They like their names. Look at this pretty boy with his fancy petticoats and blue eyes. He should be in the movies." She nuzzled the cat, smoothing his long feathery tail. Tadgh rolled his eyes, because apparently his cat valued female attention more than his male pride.

"How are you, Tadgh?" Brigid's voice was uncommonly soft. Tadgh looked at her and shrugged. "It was a rough night and day. The Garda sent an officer and a chaplain to Eve's parents. They know now. Da said Liam spoke to them. They were out of their heads." He shook his head. "She was twenty-three years old. How do ye come to terms with such a thing?"

Brigid motioned for him to come into the kitchen, and she started making tea for everyone. "I'm so sorry, Tadgh. I know you were closer to Eve. You and Patrick and Caitlyn. Da said you identified the body, and you three had to tell Liam. So, I'm going to ask you again. How are you, really?"

Tadgh just stared at her, not sure how to put it into words. *I feel like I've been gutted. I feel like I just killed my cousin, only he's still walking around. Liam hates me. I feel to blame.* He didn't say any of that, though. "I'll do, deirfiúr."

Brigid let out a grunt of frustration and looked at Charlie. "I'm sorry, love. I didn't greet you properly." She stopped what she was doing and hugged Charlie. She whispered, "Thank you for taking care of him." She pulled away, then decided to lean in again. She whispered, "And your shirt is inside out, dear." Then she pulled back and winked, settling into her task again.

Nothing could deflate an erection, Tadgh lamented, like your cousins and an eight year old showing up to your apartment. He'd had to look away from Charlie more than once. Her hair looked beautiful, but it was a little more disheveled than normal. Because he'd had his hands in it. And her shirt, for a while, had been inside out. He'd guessed that was what the whispering had been about, because she'd very discretely went into the bathroom and righted it. *Leave it to Brigid.*

But the thought of why it was inside out was another distraction. His lips and nose still had the essence of her. Her warm skin, rosy nipples, her arching hips. He'd kissed a lot of women in twenty-nine years…well, to be fair only the last nineteen counted. He wasn't proud of that fact, it just was. However, he knew that with all of those lovely lasses he'd locked lips with, they didn't hold a candle to Charlie. Her mouth was sweet and she gave to kissing like she gave to everything. She gave it all she had. For a short time, he hadn't thought about anything but her. Which was remarkable, given the last fifteen hours. She'd been heaven. He looked over at her now, talking to Finn and filling him in on the details of the tech job he'd be consulting on. Her eyes met his for a brief second and she looked away, not wanting him to distract her. His look was clear, however. Next time he got her alone, they were definitely picking up where they left off.

* * *

THE CONFERENCE ROOM WAS FULL. Full of cops, and surprisingly, the Lord Mayor and the Prime Minister had not sent representatives. They were there in the flesh, and they were pissed. The Prime Minister wore his in a more dignified manner. The Lord Mayor, however, looked like he was ready to hear the bell ring and come out fighting.

"What the hell is going on in my city? How can ye have this bloody task force working the hours it's been working and we have another murder on our hands! And a local girl, no less. Mowed down like a stray dog by some soulless bastard on one of our Dublin streets!"

Tadgh liked this guy. He disliked the implication that they weren't doing their jobs, but he understood the outrage. He had no patience for politicians. They were usually full of shit. This man, however, matched an O'Brien when he was in a temper.

The Prime Minister put a hand on his colleague's shoulder to calm him. "Now, now. Let's not lose our heads. I am sure they've been relentless in their investigation." The mayor exhaled, a look of contrition flickering on his face. He looked at Sullivan and Sean who were shoulder to shoulder, arms crossed. They were silent, eyes forward. He cleared his throat. "Yes, I know. I'm sorry. It's just a bit much to keep getting these calls in the middle of the night. Dead girls. Jaysus. I'm afraid to let my wife leave the bloody house."

At this, Sean's eyes darted to his. Cold anger spiking his words. "Aye, we understand. I just told my son his girlfriend was dead. I just ripped my son's soul out and threw it down on that street next to her broken body. So you'll pardon my shortness considering your family has security 24-7."

The man's face blanched and he crossed himself. "Christ defend us. I had no idea. I'm sorry. She was…she is, a hero. I just want these bastards caught. And between you and me, I don't give a shite if they are caught dead or alive."

Sean weighed the sincerity of the man's words and then nodded. The group moved on.

Finn was an impressive man. Tadgh watched as he briefly discussed accessing the contents on Eve's phone. Because the phone had been not only cracked, but it was immersed in a puddle. It had to stay in the air tight container with dry rice for a solid 72 hours before they could attempt to power it up.

"Rice? There isn't some high tech product you can use? You have the phone in rice?" It was Detective Miller aka Hairy Ass who asked.

"Aye, but rice will do the job just as well and that's what they had on hand. At this point, it's better not to break the seal or move the evidence in any way. It needs time. It's already been twelve hours. That gives us sixty hours until it hits the safe zone. Then I go to work. Even if some of the mechanics are damaged, I feel confident I can retrieve the data. I will retrieve it." His jaw tightened. "She died to get this information. We can't cut corners with the process."

After Finn was done, he left, not authorized to be in there for the case briefing. Sal was up next. "We spoke to the operator. She talked briefly with Miss Doherty, but the situation was coming to a bad end fast. She feels that the call disconnected because the phone can't use the video microphone and the phone microphone at the same time. She gave the command to open video and then the call went out. It's likely the officers would have been too late to intervene, so Miss Doherty had to choose. She chose to try to stop them herself." After that he briefed them on the information they'd found out from Zaid's son. "It could be unrelated, but it could focus the search for a bit."

Then the coroner's assistant gave an update. The autopsy was not complete, but likely cause of death was blunt force trauma to the head.

Finally, Charlie briefed them on what they'd discovered from the victim of the attempted abduction. Two Middle Eastern or Eastern European sounding males. They were speaking Arabic, but the accent was distorted a bit. Dark clothes, neck gators pulled over the bottom half of their faces, and ball caps covering their hair. But, it was dark. The driver was female, brown hair mid shoulder, thin face. She didn't get a good look at her either. She had glasses on and the streetlight glare hid her eyes. She had a ball cap shadowing her face as well. The van was older, probably ten years old. A Japanese model, but she couldn't remember which one. White with a taxi sign on the top. They all watched her, so smart, so insightful as she expanded on her theo-ries that had developed from the new information. And what they could do to work the information to their advantage.

"Jesus. A taxi cab? A white cab in this city?" Detective Miller said.

Patrick said, "A cab with the right front bumper and headlight damaged and a young, female driver. It's not nothing. Charlie's right. We need to start the searches again, and start checking out cab companies. It's likely this isn't a real cab, but it can't hurt. Uniformed patrol can help. I like the angle of stolen cabs as well. We can have the people in the Records Department look for old reports involving possible stolen taxis or shuttles."

Sean's pride in his son was evident. Tadgh thought about what it would be like to have been able to be on the job with his father. He returned Sean's smile. As the meeting came to an end, Sullivan spoke up.

"Every O'Brien in the room, stand by. Charlie, you too." They waited as the room emptied. Then they all looked at Sullivan, waiting for their marching orders. "You are all taking the next sixty hours off. Go home. I don't want you out on the street. As a matter of fact, I'd prefer it if you left the city altogether. Take Liam home."

The protests started in earnest and he threw a hand up. "NO! Jesus Christ! Your family needs you. You need to rest and to grieve. If she'd been Liam's wife, I'd be taking you off the case altogether. We won't have any new news until that phone is up and downloaded. The foot patrol and the other detectives can take care of the rest. You need to step back or so help me God, I will take you off this case."

"Excuse me sir, but I am not your..."

"Shut your gob, Special Agent Ryan." His voice was tight, and he'd used her title. The men in the room lifted their brows in unison. If they were betting men, they weren't sure who to back. "I called your boss. I told him that you have had one day off in the entire time you've been in Ireland. You are on leave for the next sixty hours. That's an order from your Assistant Director if you need his number."

The group stared at Sullivan, considering mutiny, but eventually submitted. "Her body won't be released for another three days. Then it will go to Cork. I spoke with St. James Hospital and to the dean at the medical school to verify what's happened. Just enough to get Liam a pass on his residency hours for the next two weeks. Apparently your boy is a straight-A student.

Sean softened, then his eyes misted. He embraced his old buddy like a brother. "Thank you, mo cara."

Sullivan patted him on the back. "I remember that little lad running around in a nappy at the precinct picnics. Take him home Sean. Take him home to Sorcha." Then he whipped an arm out and grabbed Patrick. "And you too, ye little scrapper. The O'Brien boys were always fun at a picnic. At least one up a tree, one in the lake, and one running around with a stick clubbing people. Come to think of it, that was usually the lass. Brigid, wasn't it?" The men laughed.

Then Sullivan walked over to Tadgh. "I wish your Da was here. We'd likely be unstoppable with Sean and William on the team. Your Da loved to clear a building. He was a big fecker, like the lot of you. He was o'er fond of ramming doors." He turned to Sean who was smiling. "Go home. And take this trouble-making lass with you. She'll find nothing but trouble here in Dublin."

* * *

FINN WAS WAITING for them when they came out. "Brigid called. She and Seany are having a hell of a time with Liam. He wants to go out on his own, check the streets. Apparently Eve's family told him not to come down until the funeral. They can't deal with anyone else's grief right now. He's like a caged tiger in that apartment. He's keeping his cool because Cora is there, but Brigid needs help. Now."

"I'll take Cora. I'll follow you over and take her if that's okay? You need a woman there to keep you all calm. I promise I'll take care of her if you think she'll go with me."

They all looked at Charlie and the relief was palpable. "Maybe I shouldn't go," Tadgh said.

Sean palmed the back of his head. "You're as much a brother to him as any." Tadgh's jaw tightened. "He doesn't blame you. You were an easy target and he lashed out. Please, come. You don't have to say a word. Just be there with us. Your family needs you, mo mhac." Tadgh's breath stuttered. *My son.* Sean pulled Tadgh to him, his mouth against Tadgh's hair. "You're my own. As much as the others. William would feel the same. You're ours. You're ours!"

CHAPTER 16

$\int$ orcha walked along the cold street with Alanna next to her. She was pushing a pram as Isla slept. They'd had dinner out, a sort of goodbye to the city they'd both lived in for a time. They were headed home tomorrow. Liam needed her, even if he didn't know it. She stopped at a storefront. An old building that had been remodeled. "This was it, I think. This was where we treated everyone. It's a lot different now, but I remember the location."

Alanna squeezed her arm. "Quite a start to a career as a nurse."

Sorcha snorted. "Ye don't know the half of it. The streets were blocked. The hospitals were so busy. I'd just tended to a stabbing, my frock covered in blood. My brother gave me a clean shirt. No bloody idea where he got it from." She was smiling, like she was picturing her brother's face. "Then I came out of the water closet to find a woman in the doorway. The men who had been helping me, including Sean, had looks of horror on their faces. She was breathing hard, standing with her legs far apart. There was a puddle beneath her and she had her hands on a very round, very pregnant belly."

Alanna put her hand over her mouth. "No."

"Yes. Talk about an audition. I was a year out from graduation, I

218

wasn't certified, and the doctor had gone in our makeshift ambulance. So, it was me or no one. She was past ready."

As she spoked, Alanna watched her face take notice of someone behind them. Then she paled, like she'd seen a ghost. Alanna looked behind her. There was a good looking man standing there, equally dumbstruck. "Sorcha O'Brien?" That's all he said. His accent was somewhere between English and Scottish. A Lowlander, perhaps. She looked at her mother-in-law and realized something was wrong.

"John?" Sorcha said weakly, and then she started to go over. Alanna tried to put the break on the pram so she could help her, but the man beat her to it. He caught Sorcha right before she hit the pavement. He lowered her to the ground, not letting her go. Alanna was completely shocked.

"I think she's just fainted. Should we call the medics?" His voice was a bit alarmed. She kept looking at him. Something was so familiar.

"Who are you?"

"My name is Daniel. Daniel Jonathon MacPherson." Then he looked at Sorcha. "I'm her nephew. I'm her brother John's son."

Alanna's mouth dropped. "I'm sorry Mr. MacPherson, but there's been a mistake. John died without any children." But even as she said it, she was distracted by the auburn tint to his brown hair, so much like Patrick's. And the green eyes. He looked a little like Sorcha. He looked a little like Edith as well. She remembered the photos of John Mullen that were still on the mantel in Edith and Michael's home, and in albums at Sorcha and Sean's house. He was the spitting image of his father.

"No children he knew about." His face was passive, there was no bitterness in his tone. He struck her as a man who had put things in perspective. "I never knew about him, and when I did find out, he was gone. I'm sorry I frightened her. I just…wanted to meet her. To meet his family. Should I call an ambulance?" His face was pleading for something. Forgiveness, guidance?

Alanna began to speak, but Sorcha did instead. "Ye've got your grandfather's nose." He looked down, surprised. Sorcha sat up slowly.

"And your grandmother's eyes." The man stood, helping her to her feet. She just kept staring at him, taking him in. "Christ, you are the perfect image of him. But you're a bit taller than he was and a little more brown in your hair, like my Patrick."

He was, in her estimation, in his mid-thirties. About Aidan's age. Her brother must have been about twenty-one or twenty two when he was born. Not much older than Seany was now. He seemed unsure at how to proceed, so he stuck his hand out to her. "Daniel MacPherson, ma'am. It's a pleasure to meet you."

* * *

"Come away, O human child: To the waters and the wild with a fairy, hand in hand, For the world's more full of weeping than you can understand"
William Butler Yeats

CHARLIE ARRIVED at the garage and helped Cora out of her seatbelt. When they walked a short distance to the flat, she got the child comfortable and settled. Cora started rifling through the drawers of the entertainment center. "Uncle Tadgh keeps videos and a Wii in here for us to play when we sleep over. I got a new game. Do you want to play?"

"Why don't we eat first, and you can show me how to play later? I'm going to need some big time lessons."

Cora helped her set two places and heat up some of the Thanksgiving leftovers from the fridge. She leaned over her plate and said, "When you finish that, I have a stash of ice cream sandwiches in the freezer."

Cora giggled. "Thanks for taking care of me, Charlie. I like you. I needed some girl time." Charlie tried to keep the grin off her face. This kid was something else.

"Me too. Your mom said you've been upset, not sleeping. Do you have something on your mind? That's what girls do when they're having girl time. They talk about their problems." Charlie sighed dramatically. "You know, boy drama, friend drama, secrets you don't want to tell your parents. So, if you can't talk to your mom, maybe you could talk to me since we're just two girls hanging out."

Cora stared at her food for a minute. "If I tell you something, do you promise not to tell Uncle Liam. If he knew, he'd hate me. He'd never forgive me."

Wow. Of all the things she was expecting, that didn't come close. "Honey, nothing you could tell me would ever make your Uncle Liam hate you. He loves you. Everyone does."

She noticed Cora wouldn't raise her eyes. She got up from her seat and knelt in front of the little girl. "I promise you. Whatever is on your mind, you have nothing to apologize for. We'll sort this out, make you feel better. You have to trust me, though."

"I had a dream. It was about Eve."

"It's normal to have nightmares, honey. Your family is grieving."

She shook her head. "No! That's not it. It was before. It was before and I didn't tell anyone! It's my fault because I didn't tell anyone!"

Charlie remembered what Tadgh had told her about Cora's gifts. "What was your dream about, Cora? If you tell someone, it doesn't have any power over you anymore."

Cora wiped tears from her cheeks. "She was in the street screaming. There were wolves. Three wolves. They were big and mean. They wanted to hurt her. One had green eyes. Glowing green eyes." Cora was trembling now. "The other red. The last one had white eyes. Oh, Charlie. They were going to kill her. I should have told!"

Charlie took the child in her arms and let her cry. "It's okay. Get it out, Cora. You've got nothing to feel guilty about, do you understand? I know you have gifts." Cora raised her head and looked at Charlie.

"You know about me?"

Charlie nodded. "Yes, your Uncle Tadgh told me. But Cora, do you dream a lot?"

Cora shrugged. "I suppose I do."

"And does every dream come true? Do you have psychic dreams every night or are some of them just dreams?"

Cora thought about that. "No, o'course not. Only every once in a while. Maybe two or three times a year I might get a real one, the kind ye heed."

The hair on Charlie's neck and arms stood up on end. She kept her voice level, though. She didn't want Cora to think she was freaked out by her. "Well, then. How in the heck could you have known, Cora? Some dreams are just dreams. I've had terrible dreams. Sometimes weird ones. Sometimes romantic ones. None of them came true. Especially the romantic ones." She nudged with an eye roll.

"Do ye ever dream about Uncle Tadgh, then?" Cora was grinning now.

"My point is," she continued, not answering her. "You can't blame yourself. There aren't any wolves in Dublin, right? How could you have possibly known it was a warning? You have to let this go and let yourself take comfort from your family. Do you understand?"

Cora just nodded. "Can I call you Auntie Charlie?"

Charlie smiled. "Well, I'm not really your aunt, but I don't mind a bit."

Cora shrugged. "Uncle Tadgh's not really my uncle. He's a cousin. A second cousin is what Granny told me, but it's okay for me to call him uncle because he and my mam are more like brother and sister. My da said she pecks at him just the same as the others, so I can call him Uncle. I think he likes it."

"I think I'd like it too. Auntie Charlie it is. Now, let's eat up and get to the ice cream and video games." She gave Cora a final squeeze and then she stood up to take her seat at the table again.

* * *

TADGH OPENED the door to his flat and heard music. Brigid and Finn came in behind him. As they entered the living room, Brigid stifled a laugh behind her hand. Tadgh leaned against the doorway and just watched with unhidden joy. They were playing the dance game he'd bought Cora for her birthday. Meghan Trainor's *Better When I'm Dancing* was playing this round, with Snoopy and other Peanuts showing the dance moves. He looked at Finn and a look of horror was across his face. He'd been watching Charlie shake her ass, but he turned his attention to Cora and barked out a laugh. She was really shaking her little eight year old bombom and apparently Finn didn't appreciate the moves.

They both turned around and Cora waved the controller at them. "Hi, Mam! I'm just teaching Auntie Charlie how to play!"

Finn's voice was strangled. "Cora, pet. Where in God's name did you learn those dance moves?"

Charlie was laughing, "Exactly what I asked. This kid is crushing me!"

Brigid and Tadgh were trying to stay composed and failing. Cora just flipped her head around mid jiggle and Finn actually covered his eyes. "Don't worry Da! Auntie Izzy taught me. She told me to shake it like I ain't afraid to break it!" She was trying to sound American, shouting over the music and then Brigid and Tadgh really lost it, holding on to each other as they laughed. It was a relief of sorts, after all of the tears of the day.

"Izzy. I shoulda bloody known." Finn's voice was grim.

Brigid just kissed him on the cheek. "Come on, Da. Have ye lost all of your moves?" She pulled him through the doorway and made him dance with her. Tadgh smiled as Charlie looked over her shoulder at him. Then he was across the living room as well, scooping her into an embrace, swaying to the music. Cora turned around in disgust. "Yer messing up the game. Have mercy, yer like a bunch o'teenagers." They laughed as Cora continued to dance, a smile on her face despite the protest.

Charlie warmed when she saw Brigid pull Finn into an embrace. Finn's protests ceased as soon as he got a feel for his wife. He looked at her like they were the only two in the universe. She envied them that. Then Tadgh pulled her away from the TV, eyes inviting, slow moving as he wrapped his arms around her. Damn. She really shouldn't get used to this. But it was so nice. She hadn't felt like this in a long time. Probably never. She'd had crushes. Been in relationships. But this was different. It was consuming, being the object of a man like Tadgh O'Brien's affections. He smiled as they swayed. Playful and sexy.

He whispered in her ear. "Ye feel perfect, Charlie. When I get you alone again, I may just decide to kiss every single inch of you."

She cocked a brow, head back to look at him. "Surely not every inch?"

"Aye, every single inch. It may take me hours. I'm a thorough man."

He tossed her over his shoulder before she knew what was happening and Cora laughed. "Uncle Tadgh, she's not a sack o'spuds!" He bit Charlie's hip and she yelped.

"No, much sweeter."

* * *

BRIGID BEGAN COLLECTING HER THINGS. Cora, tired from the stress of the day and her exertions on the video game, had drifted off in Tadgh's bed. "We've got to get on the road. Da and Patrick have Liam. Seany's following behind them. It wasn't easy, but we convinced Liam that there was no reason to ramble around that bloody flat alone all weekend. He'll come back, most likely, when you all are done with your liberty."

Charlie was finishing cleaning up from her girl time with Cora, listening as Brigid prattled on to Tadgh. She interrupted their chat, now that Cora was out of ear shot. "Brigid, could I speak to you and Finn? Tadgh can stay too. I just have something to tell you about Cora and she told me I could talk to you. We had some girl time and she opened up a bit about why she's been out of sorts. I think you all should hear it."

The three stopped what they were doing, circling the breakfast bar to give Charlie their full attention. She told them everything.

Brigid's eyes were teary as she interrupted. "The poor lass. She actually thought Liam would blame her?"

Tadgh fidgeted and Charlie remembered the anger that Liam had directed at him. She continued. "People feel a lot of guilt when tragic things happen. Even if it's not their fault. Cora gave me a pretty descriptive account of the street where it happened, though. It was uncanny. I know you said she's had some experience with seeing people who have passed on. Has she ever experienced pre-cognition before? Where do you think this comes from? The FBI has used this type of help before, believe it or not. They don't advertise it, but it happens. Are there any other people in the O'Brien family with this gift?"

Brigid shook her head. "No, we haven't found any familial connection. To answer your other question, yes, she has had precognitive visions before, but they are not clear cut warnings. They come in a dreamscape and they can be just flashes. It's hard for her to make out what they mean sometimes." Charlie noticed Finn was not making eye contact. He seemed nervous. She could imagine this whole thing was unsettling for a father. He couldn't protect Cora from her abilities and the toll they took on her. "What about the Murphy side?"

Brigid answered, not Finn. "Nothing. It's the damnedest thing. We just accepted that the Almighty had his reasons for giving this ability to Cora. We try not to dwell on it, but we respect it. When she does have an episode, we take it seriously."

"Well, anyway. I wanted you to know. She's a beautiful little girl. It was a nice evening with her. I'm glad you are getting her out of the city, though. This is no place for any of you right now."

Tadgh tensed beside her and then she saw his head turn. "Charlie." She ignored him. "Charlie, you heard Sullivan."

She snapped her eyes to his. "He's not my boss. I can take a night off and still stay in the city."

He narrowed his eyes. "Ye know he'll check the GPS?" Then he thought about it. "You weren't going to use it. You were going to leave it here and he'd think you were home."

She didn't say anything, to her credit. He could tolerate insubordination better than lying. "You are coming home with me, love." She glared at him. He leaned in. "If I have to tie you up, throw you in that rental car like a sack of spuds, and drive there with you in the boot."

"Well, we should be going. Finn darlin', can you wake Cora?" Brigid could tell when an O'Brien was getting ready to go nose to nose with his woman. It was a sight to see, actually, but she didn't think Charlie would appreciate an audience. That's when they all jumped out of their skin from the scream that came out of the bedroom.

Finn was to her first, the rest piling in behind him. He scooped up his sobbing daughter. "What is it, love? Ye can tell your daddy." Cora didn't look at him. She looked at Tadgh.

He knelt down beside her. "Tell me, sweetheart."

"I was in the dark, in some sort of old place. I could hear someone screaming. It was dark, I couldn't see where!" Finn hugged her closer. She wiped her tears. "But then there was a man. There was light around him, like an angel. He was your Da, Uncle Tadgh. I saw your Da. I knew him from the photos, but he told me he was my Uncle William. He said to tell you to follow the pigeons. The pigeons will show you the way to the wolves."

After getting her calmed they got her ready for travel. The Murphy family said their goodbyes, and Brigid hugged Charlie. "It's good to see you again, Charlie. You're good for him. He was always such a tease, so playful. He's had a hard time, though. Been a bit distant. It's good to see him so playful again."

* * *

"I DIDN'T MEAN to get high handed with you, Charlie. I just...I want you with me. Please. I need ye with me. Just take the rest you've been given and come with me, away from this city and this case."

He came behind her as she leaned on the counter in his small kitchen. He put a hand on her hip and his nose in her hair. "Just come with me. I don't want to be alone."

She turned and he was so close. So deliciously close that it was hard to concentrate. "You'll have your family." He backed up, not speaking. "You are headed to Doolin with the rest of them, right?"

He shook his head. "No, I'm headed to Galway. I was going to take the ferry to the island. It doesn't run from Doolin in the winter. My mam and her parents are there. She stays with them in Galway, once the weather turns for the season. But I can still get there if the ferries are running. I checked the schedule. It leaves at eight. We could be to Galway in a couple of hours, stay the night at my Gran's house, and get the boat in the morning. Just for a couple of nights. It's quiet in the winter, and I could use the quiet. I just…I wanted to show you my home. To get away with you." His eyes were shy, vulnerable. Then she thought about his promise to kiss every single inch of her. If that wasn't a good travel ad, nothing was.

"Okay. I could use a night or two off. Getting away sounds nice. What should I pack?" She laughed at the surprise on his face. "What? I'm not that difficult."

He smiled. "We'll agree to disagree, Feisty Pants. As for packing, make it warm. The temperatures and wind on the island are rather fierce. You'll want to bundle up. We'll be on foot a lot. If ye've got hiking boots, that would be best." Charlie nodded. "I don't have a lot of super warm clothes. Mostly business and my ditsy American-girl wardrobe. I can layer, though. And I do have boots." She started to leave the kitchen on a mission.

He trapped her with his arms on the counter. "Not so fast, mo ghrá." His kiss was soft at first, then he leaned into it, deepening it until she could barely stand up. Every nerve in her body was firing off. She wrapped her arms around his neck and slid her tongue in his mouth. He moaned and within a flash, her legs were spread and she was on the counter. He was pressing into her, hard and aroused and kissing the hell out of her. Her phone texts started binging and so did his. "Dammit, woman. We cannot start down this road or I won't make it to Galway." His voice was rough, almost a growl. Then his hands were in her hair and he was kissing her again. *Bing bing bing.* He broke off, cursing and backing away from her. He grabbed his phone out of his pocket as she leaned over and picked hers off the counter. They laughed in unison. It was from Sullivan. *Get out of my city. That's an order.*

* * *

"Da, why do you keep checking your phone?"

Sean looked up into Michael's eyes. "I'm sorry. I don't mean to be rude. I just haven't heard from Tadgh. Brigid's been home for two hours. Patrick, too. He's not..."

Liam approached just then. Sean smiled tensely at him. "Can I get you something to eat? Yer Mam left some cookies and scones in the freezer. I could thaw them and put the kettle on."

Liam just stared at him, brow crinkled. Then he looked at Michael. He looked like death warmed over. "What were you saying about Tadgh?"

Sean rubbed his upper lip nervously. "It's nothing. He's just a bit later than I expected. He's not in the flat. I called both his and Charlie's phones. He's got her with him. I'm sure it's nothing." But it wasn't nothing. He knew it deep down.

"He's not coming home, is he? Because of me." Liam ran his hand through his hair. "For fuck sake. I told him I shouldn't have said what I said. Why would he stay away?"

Sean kept silent. Michael spoke, then. "What are you two talking about? Did you have it out with Tadgh or something?" Neither man said anything. That's when Patrick spoke behind them.

"If you want to call it that. More like him blaming Tadgh for letting Eve get killed, and Tadgh standing there like a human punching bag letting him do it."

Liam glared at him and Patrick's face softened. "I'm sorry for it. All of it, brother. I know you were just lashing out. Any man would be capable of it under the circumstances. If something happened to Caitlyn, none of you'd be safe. It's just..."

"What?"

"It was awkward this last meeting. You barely spoke to him. Yes, you told him you shouldn't have said the things you said, but you didn't take the words back. You never said you didn't mean it. You never said it wasn't his fault. And you brought Charlie into it. They're not together. He's been struggling with that. He cares for her and he's protective of her, even if he won't let himself love her." Patrick cleared his throat and lifted his chin. "He'd never have brought her here if he thought you'd say something like that to her. The both of them have done more than anyone. Christ, they're using her as bait. We didn't tell you that, I know, but that's why she's here. She's FBI, Liam. They're using her as bait. She walks the streets, visits the local churches, cafes, puts herself in view every single day. She looks like the victims. Same age and physical description. It's why she was chosen. She's out there every day and night daring some murderer to grab her. Alone except for a GPS tracker. Tadgh is undercover with a Middle Eastern officer, working the military age male angle and gathering intel among the refugees. They don't know the suspect is a refugee, but some details of this case suggest it's some sort of terrorist activity."

He looked at Liam, pinning him with his eyes. "No one has done more or risked more than those two. I know you didn't have all the facts, but you know Tadgh at least. He doesn't do anything half way. And he's sick at the thought of something happening to Charlie. He's also full of guilt, because until this last attempt, we've had no witnesses. Eve saved her and now she's a witness. It's our first break, but at such an unspeakable cost. He went and identified her body so that you didn't have to do it. So her parents didn't have to do it. So, no. He's not coming. He's taking her home."

Sean interrupted. "This is his home."

"Aye, well maybe he didn't feel like it was just now. He's taking her to the island. He sent me a text. He knew I'd understand."

Liam was quiet. So quiet. He hadn't interrupted once. He just stood there, half dead, listening to Patrick lay it all out. "I didn't mean it." Then his eyes misted, his breath stuttering. He fought the tears, not letting that flood gate open, but his voice held such remorse and sadness. "Oh, God. I didn't mean it. I wanted to hurt him because he was there and I knew he wouldn't fight back. Patrick." His voice broke, choking on his words. "What have I done?"

Michael put an arm on his shoulder. "You can make it right. I know from which I speak. I've taken a chunk out of him myself, when he didn't deserve it. He forgave me and he'll forgive you. He loves you, brother. And he loved Eve. He'll forgive you. Mam will be here early, so we can't leave. We'll go to him though, in a couple of days. Just let him...let him have this time alone with her. It may be all they get."

* * *

"WHAT IS *the price of a thousand horses against a son where there is one son only?*"

Riders to the Sea, Act I... J. M. Synge

KATIE EMBRACED HER SON, smelling his hair and kissing his head like she'd done when he was a newborn. He was a foot taller than her, but he was still her little boy. She'd tried so hard to get pregnant, and he'd been their only success. Then William had died and she knew that her sweet Tadgh would be the only man in her life until she was in her grave. She smoothed her hand over his cheek. "You look tired, mo chroí. Did you eat?" Tadgh blushed, giving Charlie a sideways glance. His mother caught it though, and her eyes warmed as she looked at the girl who'd caught her son's eye. "Come, lass. He won't eat without you. Even if you've eaten, come sit and I'll make us a pot of chamomile tea."

Charlie came farther into the house, feeling awkward. "That would be nice. I'm afraid I put away a good amount of food and dessert with Cora earlier."

Katie put the kettle on and smiled at that. "She's a rare beauty, our Cora. She has an old soul. The old ones speak to her."

Charlie looked at Tadgh. "Yes, I saw it firsthand. I never really believed in that sort of thing. I didn't dismiss it outright, but I was never quite on board with the whole idea of psychics. She's the real thing, though. It's a blessing and a curse, it seems."

Tadgh cleared his throat. He had to tell her. She'd hear it eventually. "Um, Ma." She turned expectantly. "She had one of her dreams tonight. She said Da came to her." Katie almost dropped the tea cup she was holding. He came around to her. "It's okay. He gave her a message. It was about this case." Katie looked visibly rattled. She looked hard at Tadgh, then nodded.

"He was a good man, your da. And oh, how he loved you. He was beside himself when he found out you were a boy. We got the sonogram done. They weren't as clear back then, but apparently you were a showman." She winked at Charlie and they were both giggling.

"All right you two. Enough talk about my amazing baby man-parts."

"Are ye sure, love? I've got some adorable photographs in the closet of you in the bath. Then there was the time you pulled your nappy off on the ferry." She looked at Charlie. "He was potty training, ye see."

"Mam!"

"They figure out they've got this little wand and they can pee anywhere they like. He stood on the bench and pissed right off the starboard side."

Charlie was really laughing now. Tadgh turned her around. "I'll show you where to put your bag! Mam, Charlie needs a warm jumper. Do ye have something that will do?"

He knew that would distract her. His mother loved to show off her creations. He brought her into the main room of the old house. The Galway city had rows of multicolored houses that ran along the river. His grandparents had a modest house, but the view was nice from the second floor. It wasn't right on the water, but it was close enough that you could hear and smell it. They walked up a narrow staircase that led to the second floor, Tadgh carrying her bag.

"You aren't going to pee off the ferry tomorrow, are you?"

"Shut your gob, woman. I was three. I was trying to hit a dolphin!"

Charlie had relaxed a little now, falling into easy teasing and laughter. He walked in the bedroom and before she could turn the light on, he'd closed the door. He pressed her up against it and took her mouth, demanding. She gasped as he nibbled down her neck. "Tadgh! Your mother is right downstairs!"

"I just need a kiss. It's been making me crazy, the whole drive I was thinking about it." Then he was on her again. He nibbled her chin, gave tiny sipping kisses as he cupped her face. Her hands were on his chest but she brought her fingers to his face, touching his stubble and soft skin. He pulled away and looked at her. The street lamp was coming through the window mixed with moonlight.

"What are we doing, Tadgh?'

His face grew sad. Then he kissed her eyelids. "We're taking a shot at a little bit of wonderful instead of having nothing." Then he kissed her one more time and flipped the light on. "This will be your bed. I'll be down the hall. Don't go getting any ideas about sneaking down to compromise me. My mother's got superhuman hearing."

She launched a pillow at him. "Don't be so cocky, O'Brien. I plan on sleeping. I've had three hours of sleep in as many days." He slid a hand around her waist.

"I know, darlin. You need your rest. Let's go see what Ma has for a bedtime snack."

Chamomile tea turned into a spread of epic proportions. "You're looking thin, Tadgh. You need to eat more. You and Patrick. How's poor Caitlyn handling all of this?"

Tadgh wiped his mouth, swallowing the steak and potato pie he'd been devouring. "She's had a rough time of it. She and Eve were close."

Katie nodded. "Yes, and she's had enough sadness in her young life." She pushed the hair off his forehead. "I know the pain of fertility problems. I was blessed to finally get you. It's hard, watching all the women around you popping children out left and right. Although, I'm sure Brigid and the other girls are a bit more sensitive than my sisters were. Everyone with their bloody opinions and advice and criticisms. Your Da never made me feel less, though. Patrick is a good lad. He'll manage to make her happy no matter the outcome."

Tadgh reached over the counter and squeezed his mother's hand. "You're doing really well, aren't ye Mam? I'm glad we could visit."

Charlie swore she wasn't going to eat. Not after leftover turkey and ice cream. But Katie O'Brien was a genius in the kitchen, and she'd been sucked in. The Irish version of a pot pie, steak and potatoes and peas, just enough salt, stilton cooked into the crust. She actually moaned while she ate which seemed to amuse Tadgh and please his mother. Then she'd brought out the pastries. Little hand pies with apples and raisins and cinnamon, some sort of tarts with Nutella in the center. Nutella for God's sake! And a sponge cake with dark syrup soaked into it. "Mrs. O'Brien, I think I'm going to have to steal you and bring you home with me. This is literally the most exquisite spread of leftovers I've ever seen in my life."

Katie preened and it warmed Tadgh's heart. "Ma's a good cook. O'Brien's like to eat, so it was a good match. The Donoghues on the island have a tea house, but they're closed for the season. I thought you'd meet my grandparents, but apparently they've taken a weekender to Cornwall. My Gran is half Cornish. Hardy coastal people like the O'Briens and Donoghues."

Katie started rummaging around in the cabinets. She brought out a small cooler and a reusable grocery bag. "Ye'll need to take some food with you tomorrow. I've got nothing but tin beans and some frozen dinners at the island cottage. I'll pack enough for a couple of days. You won't find much open in the winter."

Tadgh kissed her on the cheek. "Thanks Ma. I love you."

After packing enough for an army to survive on the island, Katie took out some tubs from a storage area under the stairs. "Well, now. I've got the perfect jumper for you. That wild hair and your hazel eyes, navy blue is just the thing. I just happen to have one in the O'Brien weave I think will fit ye."

"Oh, wow. These are amazing. I can't take this. You have to let me pay you."

"You have paid me, sweet lass. You've put a smile on my son's face at one of the most difficult times he's ever had. I see the toll this has taken on him. In his eyes and the set of his shoulders. But when he looks at you, his soul gets lighter. So, it's thanking you I am. Now here." She handed her the sweater. "This will keep you nice and warm on the boat and while you explore my island. There's magic on Inis Oírr. It's the small island. Lots of old tales, a shipwreck, a castle. No other place like it in the world. Now try it on."

Charlie pulled off the thin sweater she was wearing over a tank top. She heard Katie gasp, and thought she'd gotten a glimpse of her scar, but Katie was looking at her pistol. "I'm sorry. It's habit. I can take it off."

"You won't need that on my island, sweet. But I'm glad you have it. Poor girls. It's hard being a woman. We can be strong, yes. But the men, they're just bigger. Stronger. And when there's more than one, a woman doesn't stand a chance. You keep that with you in Dublin. You keep it and you use it if you have to. I won't have my boy losing one more person in his life."

"It seems as though Tadgh had a wonderful life and a good set of parents. I'm so sorry about his father."

"Aye, it was a dark time. Made worse by a mother who crawled in the bottle." Katie smiled sadly.

"Katie, I don't know if Tadgh told you, but my father is an alcoholic."

Katie's brows lifted. "No, he didn't. He wouldn't have. He's not one to share a confidence."

"Yes, well I guess I'm telling you because I know how alcohol can get its talons around a person. You beat it every day, Katie. You had a hard time, lost your way. Things like tobacco and alcohol, well... they are legal...accepted. Even fun. And for someone in pain, they can be a brief escape. It's not like some major drug that's illegal and hard to get. It starts out slow, as you know. It begins with a drink here and there for courage or a bit of oblivion. But it's seductive and sneaky. It lies and it steals. Sometimes they are small thefts. Productivity, time, some money. But then the thefts get bigger. It steals judgment, relationships, happiness, and even your health. And it amplifies. If you already have anger issues, or a violent nature, it makes it a lot worse. Self control being replaced by uncontrollable rage and violence. It makes a home a prison."

Katie's eyes were knowing and she took Charlie's hand in hers. "Oh, love. Oh, my dear girl."

Charlie continued. "I just wanted you to know that you have nothing to be ashamed of Katie. You managed to quit drinking and quit smoking. I've known full fledged junkies who have managed to kick a heroine addiction and never kicked smoking. You are doing wonderfully. Tadgh is so proud of you. I'm envious, quite honestly. I wish my father had even a fraction of your strength. And my mother, for that matter. Her co-dependency has trapped her and us. I still have an underage brother at home."

Tadgh stood out of sight and listened to the exchange between his mother and Charlie. He was surprised, because Charlie didn't share her family issues readily. But she did it because she knew that her story would help his mother realize just how far she'd come. If he hadn't already been in love with her, the way she treated his mother would have put him over the edge.

* * *

"O'BRIEN, you're supposed to be resting. Where the hell are you calling from?" Sal's tone was light, but chiding.

"I'm at my grandparents' house in Galway. I will be on the island tomorrow for at least a night."

Sal spoke to his wife in the background. "Hold on, honey. This is business." Then he sighed. "She wants to know if Charlie is with you. I told her probably not, but she's…" Tadgh heard his wife giving him an earful in the background, but then Sal noticed he hadn't answered. "Holy shit. She is with you! You took her to meet your family? That's both sides of the family now, right? Well, well, well."

Tadgh cut him off. "Don't start. I practically had to drag her. I did have to threaten her. She doesn't want to leave the case. None of us do."

Sal decided to let it lie, even though he absolutely needed briefing on the Charlie situation. How in the hell was that even going to work? Because, the Irishman was head over heels. This was no fling.

"Okay, this is what's been going on. Foot patrol has been hitting the taxi companies. We did find something. Oval Taxi Company sold some older vehicles from the fleet, about the same age and possible make of the suspects' van. The next step is for Miller and his partner to go to the wrecking yards and speak to whoever bought them. I have been monitoring the housing areas. I had some inquiries about where my buddy was, from Zaid and his family. I told him about the latest attack. He's really upset. Zaid is taking a more active role. He's using his sons as well, although they don't know who I am or the real reason. We'll see what they can shake loose."

"I'm sorry you're alone, Sal. I wish...Well, I wish I would have picked Eve up and left work, if I want to be honest. But I also wish I was there with you. I don't like you working alone."

"Don't worry about me, brother. I am a hairy Iraqi, not a little white girl. No one's going to bother with me."

Then there was light knocking on the door. He heard Charlie whispering. "Is that Sal? I want in! Tadgh!" If you could yell and whisper at the same time, she was doing it. She opened the door, finally.

"I gotta go, Sal!"

"Don't you dare!" whisper yelling again. She went for the phone and he put it out of her reach. Then he looked at her with mischief and hit *end call.* "Oops. I butt dialed him. We weren't discussing the case. I'm on leave, remember?"

She had come across the bed to try to grab the phone, but instead she gut punched him. Not hard, just enough to get his attention. He grabbed his belly, laughing. She narrowed her eyes. "I can make it harder if you didn't get my meaning. Now spill."

He pulled her all the way down, rolling on top of her. "It'll cost you, ye nosy little peahen."

She pushed hard, and despite her size she reversed their positions. She was straddled right over his cock in her thin pajamas. He hissed as he arched his hips. She leaned down, and instead of kissing him she spoke softly, right above his lips. "Spill your guts, O'Brien. Like a good lad."

"Charlie, darlin'. Do ye need another blanket? That room has a nice view, but it's a bit drafty!" The voice came from across the hall, but Katie's door was still shut.

Her voice was strangled, "No, thank you Katie. I'm plenty warm!" Her voice rose at the end because Tadgh thrusted his hips up. She smacked him on the chest and dismounted. Completely aroused and stupidly embarrassed, like a teenager who'd been busted making out, she looked at Tadgh. "You will brief me at six. Be up!" He was lying down, looking every inch the sex God he undoubtedly was. He only had bottoms on and his arousal was loud and proud.

"Any chance of a debrief right now?" He wiggled his eyebrows.

She stifled a giggle. "You are shameless."

"And you, Charlie Ryan, are absolutely stunning straight out of bed." He sat up, his smile turning reflective.

Her face softened. *Nope. You are not swooning. No you are not.* She shrugged, playing it off. "You're just sucking up because you got caught working. Unless you think unkempt hair and raggedy pajamas are actually hot." She turned to walk out and he rose, taking her wrist. She turned around and his whiskey-colored eyes were afire.

"Christ, look at you. Your hair is all tousled like I've just had my hands in it. You're flushed and your eyes are sparkling. Like bits of amber in the forest moss. You near stop my heart, Charlie. You're beautiful. You don't know how beautiful, but I see you. I see everything." Then he leaned down, doing as he'd imagined. He put his hands in her hair. Then he rubbed his lips so softly against hers. Just a light back and forth, a caress more than a kiss. She softened in his arms, which was new for her. She was a tense person, showing the stress in the lines of her body. "Get some sleep, mo ghrá. I'm sorry I woke you."

CHAPTER 17

*S*orcha held Liam for a long time. He'd been in his old room when she arrived. He didn't cry, which was not a good sign. She just felt him loosen, his whole body shuddering as he took the embrace. She'd loved Eve. She didn't get to see her often, but she made Liam happy. It was the easiest O'Brien relationship she'd ever witnessed. Eve was sweet and attentive to Liam. She was talented and had a quiet, frail beauty that was perfect for the life and career path she'd chosen. She was graceful and elegant, and she'd been his first and only true love.

"I don't know how to comfort you, Liam. I feel completely inadequate as a mother right now."

Liam pulled away from her. He sat on his bed and she took a seat in the upholstered chair that she'd moved in there for visitors. "Ye can't help me, Ma. No one can. I've been emptied. Everything is gone but anger and sorrow. I'm sorry, Ma. I know that's not what you want to hear. All you can do is wait to bury me." He leaned on his knees, his hands in his hair.

Sorcha went to him, kneeling on the floor as she took his hands. "Don't say that, love. You'll survive this. I promise you, you will survive it."

"I don't want to. I don't want to survive her."

Sorcha's tears started again. "I know, darling. I do. Your Da said something similar to me when I was diagnosed. He didn't have to find out, though. I'm so sorry that you did. I'm so very sorry, my sweet boy." He looked up at her, ruined.

"You were always the most lighthearted of my sons. The one who liked to have fun and never took your talents too seriously. But I've watched you succeed at everything you've ever done. You don't know how to give up, Liam. You don't know how to fail. That is the only reason I know that you will indeed survive. You don't know how to do otherwise. Your thirst for life is too great."

She left him then, as he went back to his bed. Sean, Alanna, Michael, and Patrick were all portioning out the baked goods that Gran had sent down from the North. "How is he?" Sean asked.

Her face was telling, she didn't have to answer. He pushed a plate in front of her. "Eat, love. Alanna said you left this morning and didn't eat anything." She smiled at Alanna.

"Sorry, Momma. He asked. Eat up. This barmbrack is spectacular with Granny's lemon curd. Y'all have some baking talent in this family."

Sorcha nibbled nervously, then took a cup of tea. "You're quiet, Sorcha. Too quiet. Did your time in Belfast go poorly?" Sean looked back and forth between Alanna and his wife. Then he looked at Michael and Patrick.

"They're hiding something. I know you can smell it." Michael said, then he looked at Patrick. "You're the cop, interrogate."

"You should tell them, Sorcha. You saw Liam. Now it's time to tell them."

Sorcha sighed, nodding at her daughter-in-law. "I wanted the whole family together, but that's not possible right now." Behind her, Liam spoke.

"Together for what? What's amiss?" They all looked at him, Sorcha smiling nervously.

"It's not important just now, love. Come in and have some breakfast. Couldn't fall back to sleep?"

Liam gave her a pointed stare. "I'm not a lad. I'll eat in my own time. Right now, I believe you were going to tell the family something."

Alanna broke the tension. "Why don't we take our tea into the dining room where we can all sit? I need to nurse Isla, and it would be better for me if we could sit." That was of course, the perfect excuse. Michael jumped to pull out her chair as Sean set her tea and plate of goodies at the table. O'Brien men didn't like their women to be uncomfortable. Patrick followed behind his mother, pulling her chair out. When they were all seated, she told them.

"Of all the things I could have imagined you telling me, this never even occurred to me." Sean said. The kids were equally shocked. "A son. Jesus, Sorcha. I can't even wrap my head around it. He died and never knew he had a son."

Sean put his arms around her. She was a strong woman, but the tears came in silent willfulness. "The boy never knew until it was too late. Daniel said he turned thirty and his stepfather died suddenly, within a month. His mother's name was Molly. Molly Price. She was twenty years old when she'd fallen in love with John. Her parents owned the steel mill where John worked. They were English. Are, I mean, even though he and his mother don't speak to them anymore. He's not sure they're even alive. When they learned of her entanglement with one of the workers, they forced her back to England. They found correspondence." Sorcha's face was sad. "That's why he stayed at the mill. He was waiting for her."

"I'm surprised they kept him on." Sean said.

"According to Daniel, they didn't know John's name and she never told them. All they knew was that he was a Catholic and a laborer. When they found out she was pregnant, she was already relocated to England. They tried to make her have an abortion."

"Holy God, she told her son that?" Michael said.

"No, not that part of it. He found out from his governess. She's long retired, but he still keeps in touch with her. When Molly finally told him the truth, he went to the other woman. She told him the rest.

Apparently when his stepfather died, that's when Molly decided to tell him. He never knew that his stepfather hadn't sired him. She married a childhood friend, someone who wanted to take care of her and get her away from her parents. His name was McPherson. She wasn't far along and he had an estate in the lowlands. He took her away and raised Daniel in Scotland. No one ever questioned his parentage."

"So why did he decide to come to Belfast now? It's been five years."

"He looked for John, did some research on his own through the family records and then through the website that helps adopted children find parents. It took him awhile, but he finally found a death certificate for John. He let it lie for a while. But he said it just nagged at him. He felt cheated. They'd cheated him and John. He wanted to know him, to see if he had family. When he found my parents and me in the database, he came to Belfast." Sorcha swallowed a sip of tea, fortifying herself. "He looks just like him, Sean. I thought he was a ghost. I was a bit inside my head, talking and walking through the past." She nodded toward Alanna. "You know, about the bombings and such. I looked up and saw him, and I went into a dead faint. Scared the poor lad half to death."

"She wasn't hurt. He caught her and we made sure she was okay."

Liam had kept silent during the entire reveal, but he finally spoke. "I want to get a blood pressure on you, Ma. And you need to keep hydrated and keep something in your stomach. And I want blood work. You may be anemic." After shifting into doctor mode, he digressed. "Where is he now?"

Sorcha smiled. "I took him right to the flat. Mam and Da had a right to meet him. I didn't want to wait. As you can imagine, it was quite a shock. He is staying the night. They insisted he cancel his hotel. He wants to meet everyone. I told him about my family in the South. He'll come in time. It's just...well, we have a lot going on right now and he had to go back home. Alanna made arrangements for him to meet Aidan this week. He'll come back, though. John's son will come back and you'll all get to meet him."

* * *

CHARLIE COULDN'T HELP but show her excitement as Tadgh drove her around Galway City. She looked out over the bay, then took pictures with her phone. "I just want to send them to Josh. He would have loved this."

"You'll have to bring him back. Once he's with you, you can show him everything, Charlie. He has a whole world waiting for him."

She stared out the window, too overcome to meet his eyes. The depth of feelings he stirred in her were too much. He didn't just attract her because he was beautiful and smart and strong. He understood her. He understood how much was at stake, and how seriously she took her responsibilities. He didn't give her any lectures about living her own life, enjoying her twenties, or any equally vapid platitudes. He understood her. That alone was enough to break her heart, because she couldn't have him. Not really.

She knew what was ahead. This trip to the island was their one chance to shut out this case, their separate lives, everything that would inevitably cause them to part. These two days were all they were going to get. And by God, she was going to take it. Whatever part of himself he offered, she was going to take it and savor it. She'd been alone so long, this was an opportunity to make memories that she could feed off for a lifetime.

Watching Tadgh say goodbye to his mother had been sweet. She was a bit more fragile than the other O'Brien women. Then again, that's the result, undoubtedly, of losing her husband. It had to pain her to be around his brother and all their children. From the pictures she'd seen in Katie's home away from home, and the picture at the gravesite, William was O'Brien through and through. Sandy hair, although a little curlier than Sean's. Aoife's hair had a bit of wave, which is probably where it had come from. Maeve's as well. Other than that, he and Sean and the other men were all cut from the same cloth.

Tadgh was the wild card, of course. He had Katie's lighter hair and whiskey-colored eyes that glowed golden in the light. The rest was O'Brien. The bone structure, the build, the beautiful mouth. His kisses were mind bending because he knew just how to use his mouth. He explored, tasted, even nipped a bit, like he was savoring her. Like she was the only person in the world. Utterly focused. He held nothing back when he kissed her. His sounds of pleasure, his body's arousal, he revealed it freely. Even his slips in self-control. She could only imagine that he was the same when he made love. She shook herself at the thought and Tadgh looked at her.

"Are ye cold?" He went to adjust the temperature and she stopped him.

"I'm perfect. Just lost in my thoughts."

"Care to share?"

"Nope. Not going to happen."

He didn't tense up or get irritated. He laughed. It was a beautiful, spontaneous laugh.

"Someone once told me that my problem with women was that I liked a puzzle. I think you may give me a bit of a challenge, Special Agent Ryan." She gave a small smile, not meeting his eyes. He turned onto the ferry pier, finding a place to park. Within twenty minutes, they were seated on the ferry, headed over the water.

"Once we get on the island, a cousin of mine will be waiting. He'll drive us to the cottage to drop off our bags."

Drop off? "What's the itinerary after that?" Her voice was casual, but the look he gave her wasn't. It was unreadable. Something between pleading and impatience. He closed his eyes.

"Whatever you have planned, Tadgh, I'll like it. Love it, in fact. I've seen pictures of this area, but I never dreamed I'd get to see it. I'd never even left the county I grew up in until I was eighteen. Don't feel any pressure to entertain me."

His smile was wry. "It's not that. I just…" He looked at her again, those beautiful eyes softer now. "I don't want you to think I brought you here to get in your knickers. I want you Charlie. So badly I think I might actually die from it sometimes. But I just wanted to bring you here, to my home. Well…one of them at least. I love this island in the winter."

He looked out over the water, as if picturing the island from his front door. "The tourists pour in as soon as it's warm, but it kind of goes to sleep in the winter. It's peaceful, and starkly beautiful, and it's harsh. It's the reason a lot of people close up and go ashore in November. But there's a beauty in that harsh, unforgiving climate. The blue-gray sea and the wild wind. The punishing surf."

His eyes met hers again, and he smiled. "It's why I told my mother to give you an island sweater. The sheep here make the finest wool. It's something to do with the oils they excrete. It protects them from the island weather, makes them tougher." He put his finger on the edge of her collar, fingering the knit. "And the O'Brien weave. It's a good one. It's lovely on you. The blue sets off the green in your eyes. I like seeing you in my clan weave."

Charlie loved the warmth in his eyes. Combined with the warmth of his finger touching her neck, it was intoxicating. He was so close, huddled with her on the deck of the ferry. He'd offered her a seat inside, out of the wind, but she declined. She didn't want to miss anything. Suddenly he jerked his finger away and pointed. "Look just there!"

She turned around just as the whale started to submerge again. She gasped, then looked at him. "A whale! I just saw a whale! Josh isn't going to believe it!" Then she grabbed her phone. "Shit! I think it's too late." Tadgh shook his head and called back to the captain, whom he knew well. "Can ye bring it alongside her?"

"Aye, I can. She's got a calf with her. Look! There it is! And the Da off to the East." The man positioned the boat alongside the family and Charlie started to notice the other bodies surfacing and disappearing. She held the phone as she video-recorded them.

"They stick together. Just as family should." Tadgh's voice was gentle. This was another reason he'd loved his job at the ferry. It certainly wasn't for the pay, but for the sea and all its inhabitants. It was the lifeblood of an island boy.

They moved on and Charlie's grin was so wide, Tadgh thought her cheeks might crack. This. This is why he'd brought her. To see that grin. To help her forget the carnage and darkness that waited for them in Dublin. "Whales. I just saw a pod of wild whales."

He put his arm around her and pulled her to his side. "Yes, you did. And when we get to the house tonight, you can download that video and show it to your brother."

She looked up at him, and without thinking, she cupped his face and brought his mouth down on hers. When she broke the kiss, they were both breathless. "Thank you. Thank you for doing this. And for understanding me."

"Tá mé i ngrá leat, Charlie." She furrowed her brow, about to ask for a translation. "Don't ask, love. Just let me say it, and keep it close for now."

* * *

As they docked and exited the ship, alongside a few stray passengers, Tadgh waved to a handsome man in the adjoining lot. He had a boxy, older model Isuzu Trooper with two bikes on a rack. It was rusty, but the engine was running, so it was obviously serviceable. "Mac! How are ye, cousin? Left the horses at home, I see." Tadgh embraced the man. Charlie took in the sight of the two. Mac vaguely resembled Tadgh, but his hair was longer and back in a ponytail. "Charlie, my cousin Mac Donoghue. Mac, this is Charlie." Charlie gave a solid handshake and greeting, one bag thrown over her shoulder.

The man was shaking his head, laughing. "Christ almighty, Tadgh. Where are you O'Brien men finding all of these beautiful Yanks? Do ye have some sort of mail order bride website I don't know about? If ye do, could ye share the wealth?"

Charlie interrupted. "Oh, I'm not his...I mean, we're not..." She cleared her throat. "We work together. He was nice enough to bring me out here for a break. That's all."

Mac gave her a doubting look, then a sideways glance at Tadgh. "Aye, purest intentions I'm sure. In that case, if you're single..."

Tadgh shoved a bag at him, thumping him in the chest. "You can load that and I'll unload the bikes. Just drop them off under the carpark and we'll get them later."

Mac wasn't fazed by the aggressive treatment. In fact, he seemed amused by it. "No problem. And Ma will want to see you. Stop by at teatime. We're closed for the season, but she'll be open for you. She's been baking today."

That perked Charlie up immediately. "Baking? Like pastries, bread, scones?"

He laughed, nodding. "The finest cream tea in the West. The Brits have nothing on my Ma's tea time spread. Just stop in around four, lass. We'll feed you to bursting."

* * *

"WAIT! That's cheating! You're legs are twice as long!" Charlie was pumping her legs but it was no use. The infernal man was fast on a bike, and his tires were larger and his legs longer. She finally reached him at the top of the hill and he was smiling smugly. She swung a leg over and engaged the kick stand, ready to give him an earful, when she stopped dead in her tracks.

"Jesus. Is that it? Castle O'Brien?"

"A fort, really, but..." Tadgh was cut off as Charlie ran. As winded as she'd been by the ride, she ran to the ruins. He caught her easily. Like she said, his legs were longer and he'd always been a runner. She stood at the foot of the castle, dumbstruck by the slowly decaying, eroded beauty of the place. She slowly approached, and he took the lead as he enveloped her hand, taking her around the exterior wall.

"It's beautiful. I've never seen something so old. God. I can't even take it all in."

Tadgh was undone by the reaction. This was such a personal place to him. This island, this ruin, it was as ancient as his two blood lines. And there she stood, gazing up as she donned his family weave. It was just enough, too much in fact, and it tossed him right over the edge of reason.

Charlie had just maneuvered through a tricky stone notch in the ruin and into the inner most part of the castle, when she felt an arm come round her waist. Then there was stone against her back and Tadgh was against her. Her surrender was instant.

"Charlie." He moaned as his mouth came down on hers. He pressed himself against her and she arched. He traveled down her neck and she could feel his warm mouth on her skin. It was cold and windy, but he'd nestled her between the walls of the castle, and he was so very warm. So alive.

Tadgh broke the kiss, needing to back off before he tore her trousers off and pushed inside her right here in the open. He bunched her hair in his hands and forced her eyes to his. "Oh, God. I tried. I tried to wait." Then his mouth was down again, his tongue in her mouth, his cock pressed into her as she whimpered. He couldn't do this here, though. He knew that. When he took her...really took her, it would be in a bed. He would take his time. He would love her like no other. But, now...now, he needed her. He needed something.

"Please, mo ghrá." He said it against her lips. Her eyes were glossy, senseless. "Just let me feel you. You are so beautiful with your hair so wild in the wind." He put his nose to her neck and smelled. "You smell like home."

He read it in her body, not her words. She raised her mouth to his and kissed him softly, her hips rising to his touch. "Look at me, Charlie."

Charlie was out of her head. He was everywhere, his hands, his legs, his mouth. She felt him undo the top button of her jeans and her hips jerked.

He undid another button and she could feel her heart racing. His mouth hovered over hers as his eyes locked with her own. His fingers were cold as he slid his hand in. "I want inside you, Charlie. I want everything. I want my mouth right here." She gasped as she felt him slide the back of his middle finger along her sex, right to that perfect spot. Just a graze of the nail, and he stopped, suspended right there.

He groaned. "You're wet. You're ready for me." He moved the edge of his finger so slightly, he almost hadn't done anything, but she was raw and he knew just how to send a bolt of electricity through her with little effort. His voice was hoarse, rough. His big hand was slipped into her jeans, and she felt him move it again. "Tadgh!"

The torture was unbelievably pleasurable. He kept her hovering on the edge of orgasm, moving just enough to have her wild and aching. "Will ye have me, Charlie? Will you take me inside you, just for a little while?"

She nodded, knowing that if she tried to form a coherent sentence she would just end up sounding like a wounded animal. That's when he kissed her again, and he turned his palm to face her. He slid the pad of his finger deep, stroking her as he moaned at the feel of her. She came so violently that she took his sweater in her mouth and bit, stifling the screams as she bucked against his hand. She hadn't even noticed his other hand that he'd slipped upward. He was cupping her wet sex with one palm, and her breast with the other and she screamed again, the orgasm dragging her along. He was whispering to her. It was beautiful against her neck, her hair, her mouth. She couldn't understand him, but it was beautiful. She'd disengaged from his sweater, confident her screaming was over, and he was kissing her. Softly. So very softly and thoroughly.

She opened her eyes to see the sun and stone and green moss that covered the castle. She looked at him and his eyes were bright, his face flushed. She felt his hard cock on her thigh. She reached for him and he grabbed her wrists, hissing. "No, darlin'. Not yet." She'd begun to come back to herself then. She laughed. "How are you going to ride a bike like that?" He smiled, leaning down for a languorous kiss. "We'll walk the bikes. It's not far."

He buttoned her jeans for her as she leaned against the stone, completely spent. "That was..." Her breath was ragged and words were failing her.

"I liked watching you. You're gorgeous when you're aroused. Come now, see the view from the castle."

They weaved out of the structure and low stone walls until Charlie could see the view from the ruins. Strategic, no doubt, because you could see for miles in every direction. She pointed. "So, is that the coast, where the cliffs are?"

Tadgh wrapped his arms around her. "Aye, it's rough this time of year, but I'll see how close we can get when we take the boat back. You may be able to see the O'Brien Tower."

"So, Lord O'Brien. Where else do they have your name?"

He squeezed. "It's not like that, so much. The name will be common around Clare, just like certain names are even on this island. I'm sure the Donoghues living here are all related if you go back far enough, but if I run into one in Galway, the relation is so distant it barely signifies. Ireland isn't like the states. Your history is young, in the scheme of things. If you went back far enough, you'd find some of your Ryans here, no doubt, or in England. We've got structures in this country that are older than the Egyptian Pyramids. It's an old land and the blood lines are the same. Now, that said, I'm not getting a cut of the tour fees when you visit the tower." He was smiling against her cheek.

She was staring over the island. The stone walls and rolling land, stark in the winter. The cottages and winding roads held a quiet beauty. She wondered what the place looked like in the lushness of late spring, when everything was full of life. "This is quite a place to grow up, Tadgh. When you said you were an island boy, I didn't really understand it. But this is so small. And in the pub with your family, everyone knew each other. It's hard for me to imagine. I lived in Cleveland. The dodgy part of the West side. It was nothing like this. Then Miami, which is another sprawling city in Florida. Hot and full of violence or the uber rich. Nightclubs and hotels and restaurants. Florida is at the very bottom..."

He interrupted her with a giggle against her ear. "I know where Florida is."

"Sorry. It's not that I think you're ignorant. It's just, I didn't know where Inisheer was until I got off the ferry."

"I understand. And the only reason I know all about Florida is that Disney World is on the top of the Cora Murphy bucket list. She's campaigning hard, but Brigid's pregnant again so it will have to wait."

Charlie smiled at that, and turned in his arms. "She's an amazing kid. If she ended up giving us any clues on this case, we need to make that happen."

Tadgh laughed. "For what Finn charges hourly, we'll let him handle that."

"He's not charging them."

Tadgh looked at her to see if it was true. He knew it was, though. "Aye, because it's Eve's phone. He'd never profit from that." He looked out over the water, toward Clare. She moved alongside him, shoulder to shoulder as they stood at the stone wall and watched the gray sea churn toward home.

"Why aren't you with them? You should go be with them. I can find somewhere else to go."

He leaned over to the side and kissed her, slow and deep. Then he put his forehead to hers. "Because, I need you, Charlie. And, I can't be there right now. Liam is hurting and I can't even imagine what he's going through. I just can't help him with it. He won't let me." He picked his head up and looked out across the water again. "And because, if I take you there, everyone is going to see it. Plain as day."

"See what?"

"That I'm in love with you," he said simply.

"Tadgh."

He turned at his name and saw her eyes, so beautiful and lushly colored. She was tearing up as much from emotion as the sea air. "It's okay, darlin'. I know this is not forever. This time together isn't forever."

"I'm sorry. I'm not like the other women in your family. I'm not in transition like Alanna or Branna. I'm smack in the middle of a really hard part of my life. I have a job. It has to be about stability for Josh. I can't be like them. Even for you. I'm needed."

Her voice was strained and he put his arms around her. "I know, Charlie. I do. I knew it when I brought you here."

"This isn't me using you. I'm not made that way. I want so many things that are pulling me in different directions, but this isn't an empty fling. I wish I could give you more. I wish we could have more!" Her voice was raising.

"Shhh, love. It's enough. It'll have to be enough. Just be here with me, Charlie. This weekend and however long we have. It's better, I think, than having nothing." He kissed her eyes, then, softly kissing away the salty tears. "I'm okay to ride. Let's just go to the cottage. It's early. We can go to tea in a few hours. I just want to take ye home, to my home. I want to love you, Charlie. Will ye let me love you?"

She kissed him in answer, raising up on her toes.

* * *

THE COTTAGE WAS MODEST, but neat. It wasn't as old as some she'd seen on the ride around the island. Probably thirty or forty years old. But it was built in the same style. It was charming, like a cottage should look. Tadgh was quiet, she noticed. And he was standing still. She moved around him and saw it. A *For Sale* sign. "Your mother is selling?"

It took him a while to answer. "No. She's not the owner. It's a local idiot who owns a few houses in the area. He's getting older though, and these houses need a lot of maintenance. Honestly, he hasn't been maintaining this one. I have. He gets the materials and I do the work. He can't get a lot of rent for this area. No view and the houses are close together. Not much of a garden. He's just enough of an arsehole to do this before telling my Ma. He knows she can't afford it and he'd not want her to move out early. He wants her rent right up until the end. She'll never find a place this cheap, though."

He ran his hand through his hair. "It's okay. I'll talk to our family on the island. Maybe someone will buy it or has somewhere for her to go. She can live in Galway, but…" He shook himself. "It will hurt her to leave the island altogether. It's where she goes to work. Her quiet spot. It helped keep her sober, the work. She's even quit smoking. Two years now." He rubbed his palm over his face. "It's ours for now, though. She's paid up through March. It's ours today, and that's what I want to focus on right now."

Tadgh took a key from his coat pocket and opened the door. He led Charlie into the main living area. He smiled. "Mac started a fire.

Good man." He'd also left their bags inside the cottage near the front door.

Charlie looked around, taking in the cottage interior. It was simple but clean, and it was nicely decorated. There were mismatched pieces of artwork around the rooms. Tadgh saw where her eyes were looking. "She's traded with a few local artists. Sweaters for pictures. You should sketch something while you're here. She told me you tried to pay her for the sweater. Leave her a picture."

"How do you know I brought my stuff?" She said with a grin.

"It's not likely you would have gone somewhere new without it. Just let me know what you like to draw, and I'll try to find a spot." He was busy putting the food away in the kitchen. "Are you hungry?"

Charlie shook her head. "Those Irish breakfasts are no joke. I'm still full from this morning. Do I get a tour?"

He took her through the small cottage, showing the one bathroom and his mother's room. He noticed with a tight smile that Mac had started the burner in his room as well. He walked her through the door and the warmth enveloped them both. "I can take the couch or my mother's room. You don't need to feel like you have to share."

"Did you come here to sleep on the couch, O'Brien?"

Then he was on her, his mouth warm and firm as he cupped her head and slid his tongue in her mouth. He broke off with a hiss, his cock up to full salute. He left without saying a word, then brought his ruck sack into the room and set it by the bed. "Sorry." That was all he said before he was taking her down to the bed. She wondered if it was the fact that his gun was in the bag. Then, she didn't care.

Tadgh stretched Charlie across his bed and kissed her thoroughly. His erection was throbbing, painful from being denied for so long. But he wasn't going to rush this. He propped up on one elbow and just stared up and down her body. The navy blue sweater was loose, her jeans unremarkable, her little feet covered in plain white socks. But she was lovely. Her eyes were sexy and drowsy, and they held a question. "I just want to look at you, darlin'. I like you in my bed. Can I kiss you?"

She smiled. "Weren't you already kissing me?"

He took a hand and lifted her sweater and shirt, showing the sliver where her tummy disappeared into her jeans. "This spot. I like this spot right here. It was peeking out that first day, when you changed your clothes and tricked everyone."

"Everyone but you."

He lifted a brow. "Aye, well. I am pretty smart." She smacked him and he grinned, resting his head right on her pelvis. She burned where his cheek pressed into her. He was looking up with those beautiful, boyish eyes. "You're smart, too. You're good at what you do."

She reached down and ran her fingers through his hair. She saw and felt the motion on the bed. He was pressing his hips into the mattress, trying to control himself, to take this slow for her. God, she wanted him. It had been so long, and it had never been like this. All he had to do was touch her.

Then his mouth was on her skin, just below her navel and she arched, pressing her lips together to keep the moan from escaping. His ascent was slow. He slowly kissed her abdomen, her ribs, and under her breasts as he continued lifting her clothing. Then he slid it all off. "Where do you want me Charlie? Anything you want of me, ask."

She wasn't a virgin. He had to know that. She was twenty seven years old, for God's sake. But honestly, her sex life had been pretty unfulfilling up until this point. First the tipsy, fumbling first time encounter with her college two-pump-chump. Then, there had been Ted. She'd been with Ted over and over again, but sex was more of a power play for him. The more he taught her and the more comfortable she became with the whole thing, the less he'd seemed aroused by her. If she moaned or tried to guide him, he backed off. His terms. Always his terms.

Now she had this beautiful man asking her what she wanted and she was robbed of speech. She felt him open the clasp of her bra and draw her nipple in his mouth. She put her hand on his head, then pulled it back, not wanting to show her eagerness. She was whimpering through closed lips when he stopped. *No no no.*

"Charlie, sweet." She met his eyes and he came up to her face, cupping the back of her head with his hand. Then he ran his hand along her denim clad leg, then up between her legs. He watched as she arched, head back as she held in her pleasure. "Look at me, mo ghrá."

When she did, his hips jerked. She was completely sexed up. He took his hand away, bringing it up to her lips. "You don't have to stay quiet. I don't want to control you, Charlie. I want you out of control." His voice was tight with lust. "I want you to scream as loud as you like, moan, order me around, scratch me, sink your teeth into my skin. Nothing you do will be wrong or too much, because I trust you. I don't have to hold anything back and neither do you." Then he rolled on top of her and kissed her as he pressed into her. The steel in her eyes was clear. She wanted everything he'd just said. She wanted to be free. That prick she'd been with before obviously liked to have control of the wheel at all times, but not him. She could throw him down and tear him to ribbons if she wanted.

He moaned as he arched into her, throwing his head back. Then he felt her nails in his shoulders, through his jumper. He whipped it over his head and pulled her up to him, their chests meeting. He barked out a groan at the hot contact.

She smoothed her hands over his back. It was strong and the skin was perfect. His chest had a dusting of hair across his pecs and abs, just enough to add that delicious masculinity without being hairy. It was golden and his muscles were lean and beautiful. She ran her hands over him and arched, kissing him where his shoulder met his neck.

He started fumbling with her jeans and she was right there with him, lifting herself so he could take them off. He was standing, now, at the edge of the bed right between her legs. "White cotton. I like them."

Her face flushed. "Are you mocking my practical panties? I'm sorry, Tadgh. I'm not going to wear a thong while riding a bike, even for you."

He threw his head back and laughed, then shook his head. "No, I'm serious. I like them. They fit you just right. They show me this spot I love so much." He ran his knuckles over her lower belly. "And they accent your hips and thighs. Just the right amount of curve." His eyes worshipped her, and suddenly she knew he wasn't teasing.

"The way you look at me," she whispered.

"I look at you like a man looks at his woman when he finds her absolutely gorgeous. I look at you like I love you, Charlie." Then he slid his hands down her thighs, parting them. "Like I know just where you need me, and I can't wait to get there."

Tadgh slid her panties off slowly. Her skin was golden, not as fair as a lot of women he knew. But the panties hid some faint tan lines. Funny, he'd never pictured her in a bikini. He could tell she was ready for him. She'd climaxed so hard in the castle, been so wet. She was wet now. He looked at her, drawing her in with his eyes as he knelt down between her thighs. "I want to taste you. I want to watch you come again." Then he put his palms on her thighs, spreading them as she was bared to him. Then he covered her with his mouth.

She threw her head back and moaned loudly. "That's it. I love the sounds you make. I want them, darlin'." Then he rubbed his lips over her, kissing her. He let out his own moan as she put her hand in his hair and arched up to meet his mouth. She opened her eyes and watched as his pink tongue emerged from her center, and that's when he felt the start of it. He teased her with slow, exquisite glides as her breaths grew shorter, her hips rolling. Then she shuddered and still he watched her as he drank and tasted her until she fell off the edge, a new flood of moisture as she came for him. He drew her into his mouth, and cupped her ass with his hands, holding her to his mouth, making her ride it out to completion. She screamed as the peak crested, her hips jerking as she shut her eyes and felt her body fly apart.

Charlie was coming down to earth when she felt Tadgh kissing her inner thighs, nibbling the backs of her knees, and then leaning to get something out of his bag. Now she understood why he'd grabbed it, the condom emerging. She wanted to tell him she was on birth control, but it seemed awkward. He had the condom ready. And would he really believe that she'd been with no one for four years and was still on the pill? Honestly, it made her cycles almost non-existent, so she'd been hesitant to give them up. Then he was standing and taking his jeans off, ripping the wrapper with his teeth. She'd never seen Ted put one on. He always turned away. She swallowed hard as she watched him roll the condom onto his erection. The breath shot out of her. "Wow."

He looked at her, up from his task, and grinned. "You see something you like, Charlie?"

"You're beautiful. Jesus, O'Brien. Look at you. And that..." She dipped her eyes below his waist. "If I'd known that was hiding in there, I may have come around sooner."

He laughed and shrugged, because what the hell do you say to that? He stretched next to her. "I know it's been a while. I won't hurt you. We'll fit together beautifully." He kissed her then and she cupped his heavy erection. He groaned. "I want you, Charlie. I want to fill you up."

He put himself between her legs, sliding against her. She raised her knees as he started to part her flesh. He went slow but persistent as he pushed. She gasped as her nerve endings fired off. He was so big and thick, and he was kissing her so deeply, mimicking the slow glide that was helping him get into her. She wondered, fleetingly, what this would be like without a condom. Then all thought escaped her with that final push. She moaned as her body jerked around him. He was in her completely. A stinging, sweet invasion.

"Don't hold back, Tadgh. I'm okay. This is..." she arched and moaned as he pushed. "Don't stop!"

Tadgh started the grind of his hips as he filled her. He looked down and she was arched, lips glossy and pink, nipples hard. Then he looked between them. Their hips were fused. He drew back and watched as his thickness filled her again. She was small, but she was tough and she loved it. She was taking all of him, moaning softly. He couldn't wait to have her ride him, throw her head back as she came. That hair flying everywhere. But, right now, this was just too damn good. Her hair was splayed out all over the pillow and she whimpered under him, submissive. Her eyes begged him to go deeper, harder as she dug her nails in his chest.

He'd always used condoms. That was the prudent path of a man who had never been able to keep a woman for long, but liked sex too much to give it up. He knew, though, that she was telling the truth. She didn't casually sleep around. She respected herself enough to wait for the emotion that went along with the act. As if she read his mind, she brought a hand up to his chin, her thumb running over his bottom lip. "I love you, too. I love you, Tadgh."

That's when he lost it. He kissed her hard and dove into her as she started to orgasm again. He went with her this time, breaking the kiss and shouting her name as he jerked inside her. She was right there with him, her heel pressed into his hips pulling him in tight. And she was most assuredly not quiet.

* * *

THE PHONE on the nightstand started to ping, and Charlie opened her eyes to look at the cause of the disturbance. She felt Tadgh's eyes on her. "I fell asleep."

"I wore you out." His grin was teasing.

"Is it scone time? Please tell me I didn't sleep through the scones." He giggled against her mouth.

"Have I mentioned that I love how much you like to eat?"

She rolled into him. "Because, when I'm fat and old and on choles-terol medicine, you'll be here married to some little Irish honey?"

He grinned, but it didn't reach his eyes. There would be no marriage for him. He'd found his mate, and that was all there was to say. He'd never marry another woman, now that he'd bound himself to Charlie. He couldn't. He and Liam may very well be two old men, living in a cottage somewhere with cats and goats. Liam a retired doctor, him a broken down old copper. O'Brien men never got over losing their mate.

"I like that you aren't afraid to enjoy good food. You don't nibble on a stalk of celery and pretend you're not hungry. Besides, you don't have the genes for obesity. You're one of those little shits who doesn't have to work at it."

"Oh, and you do?"

He laughed. "I had a chubby period, when I was about ten. That's when I started the running. It stuck. I ran in school, all the way through college."

She ran her hand over his six pack. "Well, I appreciate the effort. I actually have a gym at the field office. I try to get in there a couple of times a week at least. I'm afraid work has been busy, though. Dearborn is up and hopping, and I was working almost around the clock. I'm weird. I lose weight when I'm stressed instead of gaining it. And I was under a lot of stress, working long hours."

"Just like here."

She shrugged. "Yes, I suppose. There's no help for it, though. Someone has to do it. I'm getting extra money for this job. I am living lean. As of Wednesday, I have the money. I'll wire it to the lawyer when I get to Dublin."

Tadgh straightened up. "Good for you, lass. You did it."

She nodded. "I did, and I'll pay off the last of my student loan at the first of December. It wasn't big, but it was there. I hate worrying about money. I wanted to start my life with Josh debt free."

Tadgh kissed her. "We'll celebrate. Tea instead of champagne, but we'll get the full tea setting. You can gorge yourself."

"Okay, do I have time for a shower?"

He rolled her on top of him. "We have time if we share."

* * *

TADGH SOAPED up his woman nice and thoroughly. Her hips, her legs, her breasts. Then he turned her around to get her back. He bit back a response as he saw the burn marks. He soaped her back, kissing her shoulder blade lightly. He needed a condom. She was pressing her hips back, begging him to take her from behind. He went to slide the glass door. "I need a condom." She turned around and sank to her knees and he hissed. "Charlie, I can get it. You don't need...Ah!" She ran her tongue from his balls to his tip. He flipped the water off and watched her go to work. He cradled her head with his hands as she took him deep. "Charlie, I want you. You can't keep doing that!" But he moaned as she palmed his testicles. He slid the door open and reached to the edge of the sink where he'd left a condom. After this, he only had one left, but there was no way he could stop now. Then he had her up, kissing her. He pulled her out of the shower, tripping as he spilled out of the tiny stall. His back was on the rug and he pulled her astride him. "Take me hard. Ride me, Charlie!"

He didn't have to ask her twice. Charlie stood his big erection up and slid herself down on it. She felt herself taking him in and he was watching her, so close to the edge. She put her palms on his chest and started arching and straining her hips. He palmed her breasts, thumbing the tips as she rubbed herself just at the right angle, his rough skin and hair teasing her right at her most sensitive part. She was sore from the first time, but it didn't matter. She looked down at him and he was so beautiful. He was pure male sexuality. His eyes were glossy, looking up at her with complete abandon. Completely at her mercy and loving it. "Come with me Tadgh." She was so close, rubbing him against her as he filled her so deeply.

"No, not yet. I want to watch you. I don't want to miss it," he whispered. She moaned. She wanted to let go, but she wanted him on top. She was wild, swinging her hips, but she wanted him to pin her to the floor and have her hard and deep while she came. "Tadgh, I need you."

"Say it. What, mo ghrá? Say it."

"On top!" He knew what she needed. He flipped her on her back and pinned her hands to the floor. She liked his dominance, wanted him to dive deep, take her hard. He gave no quarter as he pumped his hips over and over again. Her legs were spread wide and he felt something give inside her. Then her muscles seized up and the moan that came out of her raised like a cry for help. He watched her, senseless and overrun with so much pleasure that it took her somewhere else. She was watching him like she was far away… and in that moment, he saw her own, complete surrender.

* * *

"TADGH! It's been months, lad! I thought Dublin ate you up and spit you out!" Tadgh's cousin Beverly came out of the doorway and grabbed him for a hug. "Mac said you were coming to tea." Charlie hung back a bit, watching the older woman hug Tadgh and welcome him. "And this must be the wee Yank he was telling me about. My my, girl. Aren't you a pretty thing? You certainly don't look like a copper."

Charlie put her hand out and the woman dismissed it, hugging her. "Now, I heard you might need some home cooked food. Your mam doesn't get here that often in the winter. I'll bet it's tins of beans and crackers and canned milk."

Tadgh smiled. "She sent some food with us, but I was telling Charlie here about your famous high tea. Can you be open?"

"Tadgh, you're family. You're not a customer. Bring your lass in and see everyone. Everything is ready but the kettle."

Charlie looked around the stone house she'd been invited into and just had to smile. Big kids, little kids, women, men. Apparently the Donoghue extended family had caught wind of Tadgh's arrival. The spread was a thing of beauty. Chicken curry salad sandwiches, smoked mackerel and some sort of herbed goat cheese from the neighbor's goat. Homemade brown bread. Then there were the sweets. Victoria sponge, scones with clotted cream, jams, honey, butter, more bread with raisins, tarts with rhubarb and strawberries that she'd cooked up and frozen for winter baking. The tea was dark and strong and poured freely out of pottery pots. She noticed Tadgh look at his cousin, and she knew what was coming. He'd waited a polite amount of time to ask.

"Did you know that he was selling the cottage?"

She sighed. "No. Mac just saw the sign today. Surely he called your mother and told her?" He shook his head, and she snorted with disgust. "That little chancer. He's inland counting his pennies, no doubt. I'll call his son." She took a sip and put down the cup. "The truth is that it was inevitable. It's not an earner and he won't pay for improvements because of the location. He wants to make the coin, but he doesn't want to spend it. It's better for a long term tenant. No doubt some investor will grab it up."

Mac spoke then. "I'd buy it if I could. It's too much of a strain on my wages. The private flights are less profitable with the fuel expenses, and my coachman duties are too seasonal. I've got a lot tied up in horses and the plane and they raised the hangar fees." His cousin was a carriage driver for the tours on the island, but he also recently bought his own small plane that was used for tourists, charters, and to bring in supplies.

"We lose more family to the mainland every year. They won't lose me, though. I'll keep the schools full of children and the bellies full of these." Beverly raised the scone as if to toast and bit into it.

"I'll talk to Jack McCain. He probably knows the realtor. I'll see what he's asking, then see if I can pull off a miracle. I want Ma to be able to come back and forth. She needs the island. You know that."

* * *

TADGH WATCHED the sun go down through the golden highlights of Charlie's windblown hair, deciding that he'd never seen a more gorgeous sight. "We should head back. The roads aren't well lit and the temperature is dropping." They were on foot this time, deciding to forgo the bikes for a nice hike to his cousin's house and then down to the shore to the shipwreck. It was a huge, rusted formation. Beautiful in its abandoned, disintegrating state.

He paused for a minute, looking a bit nervous. "I'm sorry, I didn't plan very well." She crinkled her brow, a questioning glance. "I grabbed the box of condoms when we stopped for petrol. After getting interrupted at the flat, I just wanted to have something. Just in case I was the luckiest man on the planet and you decided to make love to me. The problem is there's only one left, and you won't find something like that in any store that's open this time of year. I'm sorry. I know that probably seems strange to a woman from a big American city."

Charlie should tell him. Shit. She really should. There was no way she was going to stay two nights here with him and only have sex one more time. "Tadgh."

261

He cut her off. "I asked Mac, on the sly, but apparently his dry spell has been as long as mine." He laughed at her face. "Sorry, Charlie. I was desperate. It's not that I'm not clean. I had a check up, you know, after Brittney. And we used protection. I've always used protection. I just don't want to take the risk of getting you pregnant. I wouldn't do that to you."

"Tadgh, wait. Listen. I have to tell you something." She exhaled. "I didn't exactly lie, but I withheld information." It was his turn to be confused. "I swear, I told the truth about not being with anyone since Ted. It's just..." She closed her eyes, suddenly embarrassed that she hadn't said something earlier. "I'm on the pill. You don't need to use..." He almost jerked her arm out of the socket, pulling her wrist as he marched up the path. "Relax, Tadgh. I'm sorry. I should have told you. I didn't know how to bring it up." He stopped short and she banged into him, letting out a little oomph.

"You think I'm upset?" His laugh had an edge to it. He pulled her to him in one motion, his one hand cupping the back of her head and the other hand splayed across her ass. "I'm not upset. I'm getting you home and out of those britches." He kissed the hell out of her, then pulled away just far enough to speak. "I want to come inside you. Over and over again until neither of us can move."

The walk back was a blur. The wind picked up around them, and the island air was wild with energy. Then he opened the door and kicked it shut. He had her jacket off her shoulders in seconds. Her clothes came off in a flurry of activity, but he didn't bother with his. He freed his arousal from his jeans and lifted her as he pressed her into the door. She was completely nude, her hair spilling over her breasts and shoulders, and he pushed inside her with one thrust. He yelled like a wounded man, "Ach, Charlie." His face was in her neck. "I feel you. I feel all of you."

She cradled his head against her chest as his mouth found her breast. His clothes were rough on her skin. His stubble grazing the skin around her nipples. Something seemed to occur to him, and he covered her scarred shoulder with one palm, keeping it from rubbing against the wood of the door. Then he started rolling his hips. He pinned one of her legs wide against the wall and drove into her.

Charlie moaned in his ear as he pulled her hips to him, filling her. Then he walked to the couch, sitting with her astride him. He looked up at her as she rolled her hips. Having her totally undressed, while he'd simply pulled his cock out of his jeans, should have been absurd, but when she was like this, taking him, hovered over his mouth, taking what she needed, it was like being under some sort of spell. He was not a submissive man, especially in bed, but he watched the hunger take her over. She threaded her hands in his hair, pulling a little, and he moaned. He ran his hands from her hips to her back, loving the feel of her toned muscles as she curled her back, rode him, letting her head fall back as she made her own delicious sounds. She was the most beautiful sight he'd ever seen. His breaths became shorter and her eyes locked on his. His voice was achy, strained. "Charlie, I'm going to come. I need to come inside you." He felt a shudder go through her as her body warmed from the inside. Her face was pure ecstasy, her mouth open just a little. He felt her let go, releasing him to do the same.

* * *

THE NEXT MORNING, sunrise barely registered. The wind and rain was violent outside the cottage walls. They didn't care, though. Charlie was in the tub now. It was next to the shower, deep and filled with warm water and bath oils that Tadgh had pilfered from the linen closet. The red mandarin swirled around the room, lulling her into a deep relaxation. The tub was deep, but small around the circumference. Tadgh would never have fit in it with her. Probably best. She was sore, and she need a few moments to herself. He seemed to know that.

The night had been unforgettable. They'd made love again, slowly and in front of the glowing fire, taking the time to explore each other, taste and touch and tease. He was an incredible lover. So giving, never trying to steer her somewhere other than right where she wanted to be. He read her body, knew how to pleasure her. And she enjoyed the same privilege. He watched as she hovered on all fours, teasing him with her mouth, then he'd flipped her around and drove into her deep from behind. They'd fallen asleep in his bed, but not before he'd done as he promised. He took his time and there wasn't one inch of her that he hadn't kissed.

She woke again in the middle of the night and saw his pale eyelids from the light coming in from the neighbors house. Just a glowing bit of illumination that let her really see him as he slept. He felt her eyes on him, and smiled as he opened his lids. "I love you, Charlie." He pulled her close and she drifted off in his arms. She was so exhausted. She'd had more sex in the last twenty-four hours than the last five years combined. It was late morning when she felt his light touches on her nose, her cheeks, her chin, then her mouth. She loved kissing him. "I ran you a bath, darlin'. Have a soak and I'll get some coffee going."

She leaned on her knees, letting her body absorb the nourishment of the water and oils. She'd told him she loved him. And she did. It was horribly foolish and selfish, but she did. He'd said this would be enough, and she'd have to just accept it. He would never pick up and leave his family, job and country to come to some shitty American city.

He did love her, but he needed this place. All of it. The rolling hills, the sea, the people. He needed to stay near his mother, be there every year to go to his father's grave. And he was a good cop. This time here with him would have to be enough. And they still had Dublin, where he would climb down the fire escape and give her that mischievous smile through the window.

"Charlie! Your phone is ringing! It's an international number!" *Josh.* She jumped out of the tub and grabbed a towel. Tadgh opened the door and shoved it at her. "I answered it. I didn't want you to lose the call. It's your brother."

Charlie spoke with him briefly, then came out to set up her laptop. "He's at a friend's house. He's going to video call." Tadgh noticed she'd put some clothes on and tied her hair up on top of her head. He gave her the wifi information and the video conference program started opening.

"I'll give you some privacy." He started to duck out, and she caught his forearm.

"Hold up. He wants to know who the man was who answered the phone. Tadgh, he's suspicious of adult men. I know he's seventeen, practically an adult, but he has reasons for not trusting people. Don't be too hard on him, even if he's a little short with you."

Tadgh kissed her forehead. "I get it. He can ask me whatever he likes, as long as he's nice to you."

She called him, smiling as he appeared on the screen. "Hi Buddy. How was your holiday?"

Tadgh watched Charlie's demeanor change. She was very maternal and sweet to her brother. She also looked him over, asked the right questions. She was making sure nothing had happened since the last time she spoke with him. They talked about the lawyer as well, and he seemed so relieved. "I'll pay you back, Charlie. I'll get two jobs." Tadgh's heart squeezed. The boy had his pride. Charlie looked at Tadgh and he gave her a look and a nod. She understood.

"You're a responsible man, Josh. You don't have to pay me back. This is for both of us. You just need to pull your weight when you move in. We'll be two adults living together at that time. You can look into a community college and get a job. Then maybe you could help me with the bills."

Charlie watched her brother's chest inflate at the thought. "I will. I totally will. We'll do this together, and we'll be free."

She smiled. "Exactly."

Tadgh thought about Sean Jr. at this age. He was full of easy laughter, teasing. He'd inevitably start making cracks about *no threesomes on weekdays*. This kid was nothing like that. He held a quiet desperation in his eyes, like he didn't want to screw up or Charlie was going to decide not to bother with him. This was the fear of an abused child. The fear of hoping too hard.

"I want you to meet Detective O'Brien. Tadgh O'Brien. He's a good friend of mine and he's helping me with this case."

Tadgh appeared in front of the screen so that the boy could look him in the eye. "Are you my sister's boyfriend?"

Charlie sputtered. "Josh!"

"Yes, I am. She's a wonderful woman. Can you blame me?" Tadgh's face was passive, his smile genuine.

The kid's mouth twitched at that, then he got serious again. "Her last boyfriend was a jerk to her. I was too small to kick his ass. I'm not anymore. She's a good girl."

Tadgh gave a slash of his hand beneath the table, so only Charlie saw him. It said, *Don't interfere. Let him do this.*

"You're a good brother, Josh. And I'll be good to her. I'll watch out for her until this is done. Then she'll come home to you. I vow it."

Charlie hadn't even thought that her brother might be worried about her not coming back. After all, women moved all the time when they fell in love.

"Goodbye, lad. It was good to meet you. Call any time, Josh. I'm going to have Charlie send my information and my Uncle Sean's phone number. I don't want you to have to worry if you don't get in contact with her, okay? No matter what time it is, you can call any of us."

The boys eyes softened. "Thank you. I'd appreciate that. Are you the one that took her to the lighthouses? The green one that's hard to get to when the tide is up, and the red one that looks like a boss?" Tadgh laughed, looking at Charlie. "Yes I am, and if I spoil her fun and tell you what she saw yesterday morning, she'll likely kick my bum."

That's when Charlie came back. She told him about the whales and he thought she was lying. "I'm not! It was one at first, then I saw the calf and the daddy as well. There were others a little farther away. They stick together in pods, forever." Then she told him about the island and the castle.

"Do people live in it? Are you dating some kind of prince?"

"No, no. It's a ruin, but it's so cool. You can look over the island and the ocean from the hill where it was built. And, I think the island has a lighthouse as well."

Tadgh laughed, because when she mentioned the shipwreck, he

thought the boy's head was going to pop off. "Man, I wish I could see it. I wish I was there."

Tadgh walked back into the bedroom, giving them some privacy. But he heard the boy ask her. "Charlie, can you have a pod of two?"

"Yes, Josh. You can definitely have a pod of two."

THEY SPENT the day wandering the island. The rain stopped and started, but Tadgh had put their phones and Charlie's sketchbook in waterproof containers along with a couple of pencils. She liked the animals and the stone walls squared off as natural fences over the rolling green landscape. She also watched him, and he wondered if she was committing this day with him to her memory, because he was doing the same. They sat by the water's edge and watched the seals on a spit of land off the shore. He finally had to make her come in out of the weather, her protests coming through chattering teeth. The pub was not crowded, but there was music playing in the background and a few people having lunch.

The waitress was giving a family of tourists the kid-friendly options. The mother, tired and busy seating everyone, proclaimed to her children that they were not getting one more basket of fries and chicken fingers. Charlie smiled, because the server's accent was thick. The "baby bowl" consisted of boiled root vegetables with a *button o'butter*. A far cry from the mystery chicken-parts nuggets and fries.

The waitress was maneuvering the picky toddler's DaVinci code of dislikes and acceptable foods when she surprised the mother by offering the child something off menu. "I think I've got an orange in my lunch and some berries that we use for salads. I'll see what we can come up with for the lad. But I have to tell you…if he doesn't like potatoes, he doesn't have a lick of Irish blood in him, despite all those freckles and curls." She winked at the boy and went back to make him a mom-approved lunch.

"This is nothing like the bars my dad hangs out in. No kids allowed, for starters."

Tadgh nodded. "I haven't been to America, but Branna said the pub vibe is less kid friendly. These villages have had the social scene revolving around the small pubs for centuries. They're not nightclubs or dens of ill repute. Up until about nine o'clock, it's common to see the entire family come in. Local and tourist."

The server came to their table and Tadgh greeted her in Gaelic. "Dia duit, Tadgh. Long time no see. Who's your friend?" After the introductions were made, Tadgh ordered the fish and chips, and Charlie ordered the smoked mackerel plate with a side of boiled potatoes and root vegetables.

"Is the button of butter just for the kids?"

The waitress smiled. "Not at all. It's good, fresh Irish butter and sea salt. You'll love it. Ye' don't mind turnips do you?" Charlie shook her head. "All right then. You're in for a treat. And the mackerel is gorgeous altogether. Would you like a pint of something?" The question was for both of them.

"Are you going to have a drink? It's okay if you don't."

Charlie looked at him, understanding. They both had alcoholic parents. But she'd never had a problem with an occasional drink. He didn't seem to either.

"When in Rome, right? What do you have that's warm?"

The waitress assured her that she had the perfect thing, and Charlie left it up to her to decide. Tadgh ordered a hot toddy for himself.

When the waitress brought the creation, Charlie sighed. A steaming cup of cocoa with all the trimmings...including St. Brendan's Irish cream and fresh whipped cream. Tadgh laughed and looked at the waitress who was smugly satisfied that she'd gotten it right. "Sometimes a lass needs chocolate, Tadgh O'Brien. It fortifies a woman's soul."

"Amen to that, sister." Charlie took a sip, and groaned, coming up with cream on her nose. She noticed Tadgh watching her and took the cream off her nose. "Don't judge, O'Brien. You know I need my sweets."

* * *

"H ᴇ 's ɪɢɴᴏʀɪɴɢ ᴍʏ ᴛᴇxᴛs." Liam was shoving his phone at Michael.

"I told you to give him some space."

"He never ignores anyone's texts."

Caitlyn interrupted at that. "He doesn't want to spoil the weekend. He doesn't want to let anyone in. Surely you can understand that? Don't you get it, Liam? He's not angry. He probably blames himself!" She paused, reining in her temper. Liam was destroyed, and she couldn't lay into him about Tadgh. "Add that to the upcoming heart-break. He's just taking these two nights to forget that his heart is about to get ripped out. They are going to leave that island and he's going back to that police station to look over the files of those dead girls."

"You think I don't know that!" Patrick stood now, quiet. He felt bad for Liam, but no one raised their voice at his wife. Liam put both hands up. "I'm sorry. Christ, I'm sorry. I'm just so angry." He put his head in his hands and Caitlyn handed Brian back to Branna, who'd been quietly listening. She took her brother-in-law in her arms. "I know, deartháir. Believe me, I know. What did Eve's parents decide?"

Liam palmed Caitlyn's head, kissing the top of it, then he pulled away. "It's a closed ceremony. She'll be buried in the family plot. Her grade school will have a memorial service separately. So will Trinity. They said I was welcome. I'm the only non-family member that will go. They just can't take a big crowd right now. She was the eldest. Her siblings are not handling it well. No one is. They just don't want hoards of people around right now. I understand. I'm sorry, but you'll have to go to the Memorial mass at Trinity if you are inclined. It doesn't matter, really. She's gone. The only thing left is to avenge her."

Sean spoke quietly from behind. "After this break, I'll be living in Dublin until this is over. I'd like it if you stayed here with your mother."

"Not going to happen."

"Liam."

Liam looked at his father, and the anger in his eyes was palpable.

"Not going to happen, Da. I return to Dublin tomorrow, after I see Tadgh."

"You can't be involved."

"It's my right!" The words boomed through the room and Branna and Caitlyn jumped, causing Brian to start crying.

Liam put his hands through his hair. "I'm sorry. Christ, I'm sorry Branna." Then he turned and walked away. He said to Michael, over his shoulder. "Tadgh will be on the first ferry. Then it's back to Dublin. If one of you won't take me, I'll take the bus. You decide."

* * *

Sean went into his bedroom, and Sorcha was sitting at her vanity rubbing lotion on her arms and hands. He stood in the doorway for a few moments, just watching her. She was so beautiful. Yes, she had a sprinkling of silver in her hair, but not much. The benefit of being a redhead. He thought back to that day, just outside the teashop. When they'd run into each other, she'd been in a rare temper. Her hair had been longer then, almost to her waist. She and her friend had been being harassed by some local tossers. He'd sorted them out well enough. Then she'd sorted him out.

"You're smiling, a chuisle, but you're far away."

Sean looked at his wife. "Not so very far. It's good to have you home, love. I missed ye something fierce. I'm sorry, though, for the why of it. Did you make any progress?"

Sorcha shrugged, staring at nothing. "I suppose. It's a bit much to take, when you go back into the depths of your mind on purpose. I walked the streets and brought it all back. The bombings, the wounded, the fighting, and the men in the van. All of it. I'd like to say I've put it to rest, but I'm not sure you ever put those things to rest for good. It's just a compartment you keep closed off, and every once in a while, something springs the latch. Alanna said it's like that for Aidan sometimes." She shook herself. "Anyway, I think it's latched again for now." Then she looked at him. "And how is your latch holding?"

"I'm fine."

She put her hands out to him, and he took them, kneeling down in front of her. Her eyes misted. "You had to tell him. You and our boys had to tell him something that is so unthinkable, I can't even imagine it. Then Tadgh had to go identify the body. You're not fine. None of us are fine."

He put his head in her lap. "You're right. I'm not. I feel like I buried a knife in my son's chest. I feel like I killed him and that he's slowly bleeding to death."

CHAPTER 18

*A*idan sat in stunned silence. He'd picked his wife and children up from the airport an hour ago. When they'd unloaded the kids and luggage, and come inside, Alanna had put the children in their rooms so that she and Aidan could talk.

"Another cousin. He's my age, you say?"

"Yes, pretty close. It's so sad. Your uncle never knew. Apparently the mother, this Molly Price, didn't want to dishonor the man who had married her when she had nowhere to go. He raised Daniel as his own. Loved him no less than the other two children they had together. He had a good life. Apparently, the man who married his mother is on the birth certificate. No one knew, and he's the first son of a titled Scotsman. He was some sort of Baron. Now that he's gone, this Molly MacPherson is technically the head, but Daniel will inherit the Barony. His brother and sister are younger, and he says they don't want anything to do with the title or the taxes that come along with it."

"Is that why she left? Was my uncle too common for her ambitions?"

Alanna understood the bitterness. "No, I honestly don't think so. She told Daniel that her parents pulled her out of Northern Ireland before she knew about the baby. She knew if she revealed the father, they'd let him go. Jobs were hard to find during that time, and he was a Catholic. He'd have lost everything. She was only twenty, and she had nowhere to go. When they tried to force the abortion issue, that's when her childhood schoolmate, Robert MacPherson, stepped in. Robert Daniel MacPherson."

"So, she named the lad after both fathers."

Alanna nodded. "She did love John, he says. She made a life with Robert, tried to be a good wife and mother, but she never got over him. She told Daniel right after his adopted father died. And Aidan, he wants to meet you. He lives over the border, of course, but it's just a half day drive for him. He really wants to meet you. You'll be shocked, I think. Apparently he looks like a Mullen. Your grandda's build, Edith's nose, John's coloring." She laughed. "His hair is just like Patrick's. You know, that chestnut color that is brown and a little bit red. Curls up at his ears. He's rather handsome, actually." Aidan gave her a sideways glance. "I'm just saying that he got a lot of the Mullen good looks." She was smiling at his spark of jealousy. "So, will you meet him?"

Aidan nodded. "Aye, I will. He's family. We don't leave family behind."

Alanna got up from the couch. "I need to call Izzy. She'd want to know about Eve. They didn't spend much time together, but Izzy liked her. They hit it off the couple of times they were together. She'd want to know."

* * *

Tadgh looked over the water, dreading the shore. Once they were on shore, the road led straight to Dublin. He had responsibilities there so heavy, they threatened to suffocate him. They both did. Now one of their own lay among the dead. Charlie sensed the ending as well. The end to their small escape from reality. Did she mean what she'd said when she'd told him she loved him? He thought so. Last night, they'd made love again. It had been like nothing he'd ever felt. Every time with her was like that. But the last time, they'd been desperate for each other. Almost in pain from it. Holding out until they were both mad with it, not wanting it to be over. Then she'd finally let go and so had he, and it had been catastrophic. Like the earth had trembled. She'd shook in his arms, not speaking. She did love him, but in the end it wasn't going to be enough. Not with what she was in the middle of. And he understood. It's part of the reason he loved her. She didn't turn her back on the hard stuff.

She'd left a sketch for his mother. The first one he'd seen. It was of him sitting on the shore, watching the spit of land where the seals liked to sun themselves. She was very good.

"Charlie, I was thinking. Have you ever done sketches for any of your cases?"

"No, I've never tried it. Are you thinking of the girl in the hospital? The one Eve saved?

"Yes, maybe if she talks you through a sketch, it will help her remember more."

"It's worth a try."

The ferry approached the dock in Galway and Tadgh's body tensed. Two men stood waiting. "Bloody hell, just what I need. Another flogging."

Charlie looked up and exhaled. It was Michael and Liam. Patrick had texted them this morning, and he was off at o'dark thirty with Finn riding shotgun. Sean had driven up separately and had left as well. It was time to try to retrieve the data from Eve's phone. This little visit, however, was personal. She didn't know what had gone down between Liam and Tadgh, but they certainly didn't need an audience. She'd go warm up the car and leave them alone.

Tadgh approached his cousins and was shocked at the condition Liam was in. He was gaunt. Only three days had passed, but his face was ashen. Circles around his eyes and dry lips, like he hadn't been sleeping or even taking in enough fluid. Michael waved, but his face was tight. Shit. He didn't want Liam dragging Charlie into this.

"I'll leave you guys to talk. I'll take the bags to the car."

"I'll join you, if you don't mind." Michael took one of the bags from her shoulder and they discreetly left Tadgh and Liam to talk.

Tadgh readied himself for another round of mental blows. What he saw when he looked in Liam's eyes wasn't what he'd expected, however. The pain was fresh, his eyes bright. No tears. He hadn't cried since the night in the hospital, as far as Tadgh knew. But he saw the pain, nonetheless.

"I didn't mean it. What I said. I didn't mean it, brother."

Tadgh shut his eyes, unwilling to ease himself of the blame. "I've tried. I've worked every night. I'm sorry, Liam. Oh, God. I'm so sorry I failed her. I should have left work! I should have picked her up!"

Liam pulled him tight. "No." He whispered. "No, Tadgh. I should have left work. I shouldn't have left it up to a bloody cab. I should have watched after her more carefully. You warned me." Tadgh was shaking his head. "No, Tadgh. This isn't your fault. Ye stood there and took all I had to give, because it's your way. You've always been the best of all of us. But the truth is it's no one's fault but the three animals who are still out there somewhere in Dublin. And you're going to go back and find the bastards. You're going to win, because you're smart and you won't give up until you do."

* * *

CHARLIE AND MICHAEL loaded the trunk, heated the engine, and sat. "It's a good sign. Hugging and no punching."

Michael laughed. "Aye, it is. He's a good man, Charlie. Don't think less of him. O'Briens don't know how to…" He paused, thinking. "When they love, they love hard. Deep. Losing that, it's something we all fear. O'Briens don't have an easy time coming to their mates. They treasure them above all else. I look at Liam and wonder if he'll ever get over this."

Michael cleared his throat, his voice thick with emotion. "Thank you, Charlie. Thank you for giving him somewhere to go. Letting him have something that was his own, even if it's only for a little while." He was talking about Tadgh now, and she couldn't look at him. *Don't thank me. I'm going to leave him and break his heart.*

* * *

IN THE END, Michael drove Liam and followed Charlie and Tadgh to Dublin. The Memorial at Trinity was today and they would undoubtedly be followed by more of the family. As Michael broke off of the caravan, headed to Liam's apartment, Charlie and Tadgh went back to work.

By lunchtime, the task force was around the table again. All of the detectives who were currently working on the case were gathered together. Finn was in the tech area, utilizing their equipment, and the equipment that the FBI had overnighted to the Garda station. The software was superior, and they needed the best.

Tadgh grinned as he watch Detective Miller, aka Detective Hairy Ass bring in a cup of coffee and set it in front of Charlie. He gave her a wink and she turned that thousand watt smile on him. "Detective. Have you been surviving without your token female?"

"Just barely, darlin'. It's good to have ye back."

Those two had come a long way. The men respected her. Miller stood up and began briefing the group on the fruits of their labors. "According to the wrecking yards we checked, there are actually two salvaged taxi's missing from the lot out in Dublin 12. The lot's so big, and the security is not very good. They didn't miss it until now. I've got the VIN for both."

"Stolen. Shit. I suppose it was too much to ask to have them registered to the killers," Patrick said. "Any information on the body of the vehicle? Color, damage, distinguishing marks? Obviously the plates will be stolen as well."

"Yes, that would be more of a needle in a haystack. It's an embarrassment to the Garda how many license plates get stolen in this bloody county."

The meeting lasted another ten minutes and everyone was off. Charlie approached DC Sullivan and he had a smile for her. "The fresh air did you some good, I see. Glad to have you back, Charlie."

"Thank you Sir. I'm going to head over to the DCU Campus. It's one I haven't checked and it's not too far from where the last attempt was made."

"Aye, just keep the GPS tracker on you. I want to know where you are. I'd like ye to make an appearance at the housing complex where O'Brien and Sal are posted. You've been seen together, so it's time. Maybe you can make some progress with the women in the area." Charlie agreed with him. It was past time. As she went to leave, Tadgh approached.

"So, at the complex tonight? Sal's wife wants to meet for dinner beforehand, if that's all right with you? She'll likely interrogate you. She'd give Brigid a run for her money with the nosy questions." He was smiling, and Charlie could tell that he was fond of the couple. "Her name is Leyla. I think you'll like her."

"I'm sure I will." Their eyes met briefly, relaying an affection that could not and would not be shown in the workplace. "Be careful, mo ghrá."

* * *

CHARLIE WAS SITTING in the hostel common area talking Shannon Hath-away through the night of her attack. The trip around DCU campus had been brief. It was cold and the students were rushing from building to building. That's when she'd decided to take her sketch book and visit Shannon. The girl was tough. She wanted to help any way she could. "I'll go around with you. I'll help you look. I'm not afraid of them. They killed that poor woman. You have to let me help. I could go on the news."

"You need to heal. And you are helping. You really are. You have no idea how much. Please, continue."

"This was the only one I got a look at for any amount of time. Just the eyes and brows. The woman was shadowed in the car interior. The other guy came from behind."

She talked Charlie through his features, including the texture of the neck gator, the shape of the hat, and his jacket. After they were done, the woman started to walk her to the door. She stopped and hugged her. "Thank you. It's good to have another woman here, and an American. I just wanted to say that."

As Charlie walked down the street, toward the river, she got a text. *Finn did it. We have the video.* Charlie picked up her pace, heading toward headquarters. When she rounded the corner to the alley behind the police station, she slowed. About five blocks back, she'd noticed the man. Dark clothing, dark hair. He was good, though. She hadn't been able to get a good look at him. When she'd passed the Garda officer giving someone a ticket, the man ghosted. Disappointing, because other than the incident with the four refugee males, this had been the first real nibble she'd had. She looked all around her before entering in the back passageway that led to the connecting doors.

She passed Janet in the hallway. "Hello, lass. They're all in there. I was just grabbing a box of pens." As she waved to the woman, she nearly ran into another woman coming down the hall. She stopped short, then tensed. Brittney.

"Well, well. If it isn't our Yankee consultant. Had a meeting all weekend, I heard. Lucky you. I only got a taste, but he was absolutely..."

Charlie pointed a finger. "Shut your mouth before you finish that sentence. You will not discuss him like that with me. Ever."

Brittney stood up straighter. She was taller than Charlie by about five inches. Her brows were up in surprise. "Jealousy? Interesting."

"I'm not jealous. Quite frankly, I'm disgusted. It's bad enough you used him so poorly, then talked about him like some male whore you picked up on the street, but you are shameless about it even though you are wearing another man's ring. You don't deserve to lick his boots. I suspect you don't deserve the man who's marrying you either. Women like you make me sick. Now, move along before I decide to get angry."

"Charlie, the meeting is starting."

She jerked at the voice. She turned around, swallowing her embarrassment over the little chick on chick aggression she was throwing. Worse yet, she was bracketed in by Janet, holding a box of pens, awestruck by the display. "Thank you, Patrick. I'm on my way." She left Brittney standing there with her mouth open.

"Don't say a word. Seriously." She walked past Patrick who was, for once, not grinning or mocking.

"I think you said all that needed to be said, Charlie. Well done." His voice was soft. His eyes warm. "You love him enough to defend him. Where I come from, that makes you family."

* * *

FINN DIMMED the lights and projected the video to the screen that Sullivan had pulled down from the wall mount. "The image jumps around a bit. Likely her adrenalin was causing it. Now, see here. White Toyota van, taxi sign illuminated. Now this is where the woman is, but we can't see her."

"Godammit, why can't the steering wheel be on the right side! She's totally shadowed."

Charlie was feeling overly pissy, especially since the confrontation with Brittney.

"It is on the right side." Patrick was goading her.

"Correct side. You know what I mean." But her tone had relaxed a bit, a smile teasing the one corner of her mouth. "Okay, this is the main guy. Bigger, taking the lead as the aggressor. This is the one I have a sketch of. Just the build, clothing, and the eyes."

Everyone looked at the sketch she'd given them. "I didn't know we had a sketch artist on staff." Sullivan said in amazement. "How did I not know this?"

"We don't. Charlie visited the victim today. She did the sketch." The pride in Tadgh's voice warmed her.

"Well done, lass," Sullivan said.

Charlie had paused the video. "Okay, Finn. We're going to start the video again, but first…" She looked at Sean, Tadgh, Patrick, then back at Finn. "I haven't seen this in its entirety, but the tech team and DC Sullivan have. Eve caught part of the collision on tape. I'm not sure you should watch. You knew her. We can do this without you."

"I'm not leaving, lass." Sean said, his jaw tight. "But Patrick and Tadgh, you don't have to be here. We don't all three need to..."

Both men crossed their arms over their chest in a classic O'Brien move. Sean sighed. Charlie looked at Finn. He gave a single shake of the head. "Christ you're as bad as they are. Roll it."

The room was tense. The video audio was hard to make out. Eve was screaming at the top of her lungs. In the background, you could see lights starting to come on in a neighboring building. That's when the girl broke free. As she ran, Eve swung the camera to the van. The big male screamed at her. *You fucking bitch!*

"I am going to gut that mother fucker." The room turned to look at Patrick. His eyes were ice. As were Tadgh's and Sean's. The aggression rolled off the men as they continued to watch. The men jumped in the car. Eve's camera started to get farther away, like she was backing up. Then the van turned toward her. *No!*

The camera went sideways, like she'd dropped her arm to run. The thump of the car hitting Eve was deafening and the phone camera blurred with motion and went blank. That was obviously when it had hit the ground face down in the puddle. The room was silent. When someone finally turned the lights up, Charlie looked at the horror on the O'Brien men's faces. Finn was staring at the floor, unshed tears pooling in his eyes. She put an arm on him and he shuddered. "Jesus Christ. Ye've got to find these bastards. What can I do? Please give me a job or I'll go insane."

"Can you clean it up? Get some freeze frames? Maybe get a shot of even a partial face. Also, anything distinct about the vehicle. And try to isolate some of the sound. Whatever you need, equipment-wise, just ask. The bureau is helping foot the bill for this. I can't go nuts, but I can try to acquire what you need."

Charlie walked toward the back of the building, leaving the men to talk. Eve's Memorial was today. They were all going to attend. All but Liam. Tadgh said he just couldn't be in public with the way he was feeling, and she understood. He wasn't just hurt, he was broken. He had enough anger in him right now to burn Dublin to ashes. Her death had made the news. No one, as yet, had linked it to the murders, but it was only a matter of time. For now it was a hit and run. When this was all over, the city needed to know. Eve sacrificed herself to save another.

She walked to the garage where she parked her car and headed toward the scene of the latest attack. She wanted to walk through it one more time, after having seen the video. Her body thrummed with energy. She felt sick as she replayed the images in her head. The kidnapping had gone sideways, and they knew they had to flee. Too much attention had been drawn. From the video, it appeared one of the men had taken control of the steering wheel. The driver had gunned it. They'd mowed her down on purpose. It hadn't been planned, more retaliation. She hoped to God that Finn could clean the images up enough to zero in on the woman's features. Even with a ball cap, the bottom half of her face might help. Until then, there was nothing here on this street but sorrow. The foot patrol, alongside some detectives, had interviewed the neighboring residents and business owners. The traffic unit was pulling camera footage from the area surrounding the scene as well as large intersections where the taxi might have gone. Charlie took a deep breath. *I'm so sorry, Eve. I should have prevented this.*

As she drove back to the garage, she saw a church spire from the horizon. After she parked, she walked west, toward the church. St. Patrick's Cathedral stood before her, quiet and majestic. The skies were gray, except for a beam of light peeking through a hole in the clouds. She'd seen pictures of it in the full bloom of early summer. The lush gardens, sun shining through the stained glass. But in the quiet depths of winter, the stone was the main attraction. Hues of grey and specks of light and dark. Changing light cast from the clouds enhanced the layers of spires, carvings, nooks, and details that were unique to these old churches.

It hadn't occurred to her that she would have to pay to get in, although it should have. This was a tourist attraction, a historical site. It undoubtedly involved a great deal of upkeep between Sundays. She paid the fee, declining the tour. She walked into the quiet sanctuary and saw the font of holy water. The only time she'd done this was at her Aunt Cassie's funeral. She dipped her fingers, crossing herself as she looked up in wonder at the interior of the church. It was jaw dropping. Art, sculpture, detailed architecture, high, opulent ceilings with beams that arched and joined at the peak. She saw small altars with varying saints. Signs for tourists. "Decisions, decisions," she muttered to herself.

"Can I help you?" Charlie turned, facing the priest in surprise. The place had been empty, so she had thought she was alone. "I'm sorry, lass. I just thought ye looked less like you were in mind for a tour, and more like ye were in search of some guidance." The old priest's smile was warm. "It's a good place to come for it. If you need some help, I'll be happy to aid you. If not, then I'll leave you to your prayers."

"Thank you, Father. I was just...I needed to pray for someone. Actually, a few someones. I have a lot going on right now. I've witnessed a lot of pain. I don't usually go to church, but I saw the spire and it..."

"It called to you?" Charlie nodded. "Well, now. I guess that means you're where you are supposed to be. What is your name, child?"

"Charlie. Charlotte, actually, but I use Charlie. I have come to this city to help with something bad that's been happening. If I talk to you, do you have to keep it a secret?"

The priest gestured for her to sit at the front pew. "I'm getting old, I'm afraid. Sit, Charlie. Tell me what brought you here today."

Charlie gave him the abbreviated version. Nothing about the FBI, but enough to get the picture. "It's a heavy burden you carry. You feel like you must stand between this evil and the women of this city. It's a brave and noble thing you're doing, and now you're here to do what, exactly? Pray for help with this case? Pray for their eternal souls? Pray for their families?"

Charlie laughed nervously. "Is there an all of the above option?"

"Aye, always. So, let's start with these poor women. Five dead, one battered and in turmoil." He took her to a side altar where the Virgin Mary was placed over a row of candles and a kneeling bench. The priest handed her three candles and he took three, showing her how to stick them in the holders and light them. Then they began.

* * *

CHARLIE WALKED into Tadgh's apartment and jumped with a jolt as she saw Tadgh coming out of the bedroom. He set the highchair down and went to her. He wrapped her up in his big body and hugged her so warmly and completely. "Sorry. I need the baby gear. We've got a lot of family upstairs."

"It's okay. What can I do to help?" He kissed her then, deeply and thoroughly. Then he pulled back, eyes deep with emotion. "That helped. It helped a lot." His grin was boyish, positively boyish.

They walked up to Patrick's apartment with their arms full of gear and kid snacks. Patrick opened the door, taking Charlie's armload and giving her a quick kiss on the cheek. She stopped short as she realized the apartment was full. Brigid and Finn and their two kids, Caitlyn, Branna and Michael with the twins, Seany, Sean and Sorcha, and finally Sal and his family.

She reacquainted herself with everyone, and finally settled at Sal and Leyla who had a child in each arm. The older toddler wiggled out of Sal's arms as the twins invited him to play.

"It's good to finally meet you." Leyla was exotically beautiful. She put out her manicured hand and Charlie took it. "Sal has nothing but good things to say about the work you've been doing."

Charlie smiled. "He's doing some pretty amazing work as well. This is quite a crowd. I was going to come home, eat a sandwich, and head back out. I didn't want to intrude."

Caitlyn came beside her. "Not at all, darlin'. Leyla has made some gorgeous Egyptian food. Come in and have a proper meal. I suspect with the day you've had, you didn't get lunch?"

Charlie shook her head. "I'm afraid I eat like a savage when I'm working. I usually shove a garbage burger or danish in my mouth in the car."

Leyla took her hand. "We decided that instead of having you to the house for dinner, we would head over with some food for everyone. It's the only way I know how to help." Her voice was sad. Then she smiled. "Tadgh tried to ring you, but he didn't get in touch with you."

"I was at St. Patrick's Cathedral...looking for a little divine intervention. I turned the ringer off, briefly."

Tadgh turned around at that. His eyes soft. "It's a good idea. We need all the help we can get. Come, love. Sit and let me get you a plate."

The women gathered in one room, kids running around their feet. Charlie didn't have a lot of women friends. Her job was mostly males, and she didn't have much of a life outside of work. But she liked these women. All of them. Caitlyn hooked an arm in hers. "It's good to see you again. I'm sorry we didn't get to see you back home in Doolin, but I understood the why of it. Did you enjoy your time on the island?" Her look was probing.

Charlie swallowed hard then tried to keep her tone light. "It was nice. Restful." But she could feel the blush on her cheeks. Caitlyn's gold and green eyes were bright and knowing.

She gave a husky laugh. "Oh, my. I see now."

"What?" she said innocently.

"Don't even, woman. You are glowing. I've seen that look before. O'Brien men are particularly gifted at putting that look on a woman's face." She put an arm around Charlie. "And if he's anything like Patrick, you are done for, my friend. Absolutely ruined for any other man."

They walked over to the other women and Brigid took one look at her and the brows went up. "Well, well. Enjoyed your time on the island, I see."

Charlie threw her arms up. "Do I have something written across my forehead?"

Brigid was undaunted. "Aye, ye do. Plain as day."

"That's enough, girls. Give the lass her privacy." Sorcha's voice held a tone of command. "How are you, love? Did you get a bite to eat?" Sorcha hugged her then, and the hug was warm and motherly.

"I did. Tell me. Are you all sleeping here?"

"Sean and I will be at Liam's. He has a spare bed since his roommate moved out. Brigid will stay here and drive back with Finn tomorrow. I believe Michael and Branna will do the same."

"I'm alone downstairs. Please. Let me open up the flat to everyone. I have another double bed and a pullout. I can take the couch. One family can stay here and one downstairs with me. You can decide who takes the two rooms."

"With the shifts you're working? No, dear. You'll not be on the sofa bed. How about this. We'll put Brigid and Finn in this spare room, the kids on the pullout. We'll put Branna and Michael and the twins in the spare room in your flat, Tadgh on the couch, and you can stay put in your room. It's a kind offer, and it might solve a housing issue for the night."

"Sounds perfect." Tadgh was behind the women, and he gave them a wink. "Now, we better head out. The Memorial starts in an hour, and getting all of these kids moving is going to be tough."

Charlie hugged everyone goodbye for the time being. Leyla was her final goodbye. "Take care of him." Leyla whispered. Charlie looked at Sal then back at Leyla. "I've just had bad feelings. Please, take care of each other."

Tadgh walked her back to the flat, taking the pack 'n play back down with him, now that they were splitting the group up. After he put it away, he went for the door. He stopped and turned, smiling. "I'll see you in two hours, then we head over to Sal's second home and we get you seen." He was going to leave, but he changed his mind, turning to her and pulling her into his arms. He kissed her slow and deeply. He broke the kiss and said hoarsely, "Once they've gone to bed, I'll come to you."

CHAPTER 19

$\mathcal{T}$he turn-out for Eve's memorial service was big. She'd been in a current performance line-up. They'd given the performance a couple of nights off, letting the cast grieve and giving the ticket holders a raincheck, so to speak. But, the show would go on without her. The chapel at Trinity was full. The kids were passing out flyers, inviting people to walk to the performing arts building for a final farewell, and to join them to walk a portion of the St. Andrews 10K, holding signs in remembrance of Eve and the other women who had been killed. #WeStandWithOurAmericanSisters and #WeStandWithDublin were the new hashtags circulating. Twitter was exploding, according to Finn. It had been inevitable that the story would link itself to the recent murders. The witnesses in the neighborhood, the shop owner who had aided the survivor, hospital staff. Even police staff who disagreed with keeping it quiet. Someone on the inside obviously spoke to the media, because the details of the case were starting to emerge, including the Arabic writing carved into the victims. Tensions were high, but Irish were a reasonable people. Dublin was diverse. They'd get past this.

When they left the chapel, Tadgh was surprised to see a crowd standing outside. They were quiet, holding candles, signs, and flowers.

Many women in abayas and hijabs. The signs read, *We Stand With Dublin. Stop The Violence. You dishonor the Prophet* and other such things. The Muslim community had shown up, standing outside of the chapel respectfully, unsure of their welcome. He stood next to his family, watching the gesture affect them all.

The women teared, the men were still, but the emotion was palpable. These people were not to blame for the actions of a few. They were Dubliners now, and they felt the losses alongside the Irish citizens. They started the walk to the performing arts center, the two groups intermingling. Sal approached, having been with the other group. Obviously, keeping an eye out for trouble. Luckily, he'd found none. He blended well enough, spoke the languages and dialects. The gesture was genuine by all whom he'd come into contact with.

They stopped where the *Giselle* poster usually stood, large and advertising the current performance. Instead, they'd put a picture of Eve in her lovely costume. Her sweet face, honest eyes, delicate presence.People had put flowers, candles, cards, even old ballet slippers. That's when Tadgh broke. He felt Patrick's hand on his shoulder, Patrick letting his own tears finally come. They wept together in silence, feeling Sean come behind them. Michael and Finn comforted the other women. Sean Jr. held his mother. This was different for Patrick, Tadgh and Sean, however. This was their case. It was like a double punch, working so hard to find the murderers, only to lose one of their own. They felt shame and guilt and rage, enough to bring the walls of the city down to rubble. No one had worn their uniforms. They couldn't be seen with Tadgh or Sal in uniform. Sal put an arm around Tadgh's shoulder. "I'm sorry, my brother. We will end this. You and I."

He looked around, taking in the intermingled and unlikely crowd. Students, professors, citizens, children. "Zaid is the one who spread the word and got them to come. I thought you should know. He's taking this personally. He's fond of you. And, he has daughters of his own. He wants to see us tonight."

Tadgh wiped his eyes, taking a deep breath. "Okay, I'll be there as soon as I pick up Charlie."

* * *

CHARLIE WALKED into the housing complex alongside Tadgh, holding hands. The night was chilly, which was good. Her layers concealed the pistol she'd been issued. There were some men in the common area, smoking and talking. They watched her with interest, having never seen Tadgh with a woman. Tadgh gave a small wave, and they returned it. "They keep to themselves. Zaid said they are Yemeni. The fourth one keeps quiet, Sal hasn't picked up an accent or narrowed down a dialect on him. He's heard a few words of Arabic, but he doesn't think he's from Yemen like the others."

Charlie caught a glimpse of the fourth and something lingered in her mind. Recognition, but she was not sure from where. Not from her drawing. He was shorter, too, and slighter built than the main guy on the video. The other assailant had been so averagely built and had on winter clothing, so he could be anyone. They'd never gotten a clear look at his face. Where in the hell did she know him from?

They walked up to Sal's flat, being met at the door by him. "Zaid's family is waiting. They've made tea service."

Zaid's eldest son answered the door, respectful as always. The other children were scattered around the room. His eldest daughter was helping her mother set the tea out on the coffee table. Abdul, the middle son, was nervous. His eyes down. He looked at his father and Zaid nodded. He stood up, taking a tea cup and saucer in hand, and handed it to Tadgh. Then, he did the same to Charlie and Sal. He looked up, tears in his eyes. "I'm sorry. About your friend I feel sorry. I am not a bad boy. I am helping. I am watching for bad men."

Tadgh put his hand on the boys shoulder. "I know that, lad. It isn't so easy being young. You want to be a man, aye? You're a good man. I know you will help."

Charlie watched the exchange, then looked around at the other kids. There was a girl who looked to be about fifteen or sixteen. She wasn't dressed traditionally. She had a hijab on her head, covering her hair, but she had a long sleeve t-shirt that said Element. Her track pants were unisex. She had a skateboard propped next to her, like she couldn't bear to be off of it for long. Charlie smiled because the girl watched her, curiosity in her eyes. Her younger brother whispered something to her, obviously something less than complimentary. She didn't cower. She smacked him in the back of the head. She said something on a hiss in her native tongue. Charlie suppressed a grin. She liked this girl. She obviously didn't let her brothers push her around. Her father noticed Charlie watching them. He pointed. "That one is Rasha. She's giving me gray hairs. She likes to jump off things with the board of hers. She's always climbing things and wanting to play football in the yard."

"It's okay. In America we call them Tomboys. Girls who are a little tougher. They usually make very strong women." Zaid translated to the girl and her smile was huge and instant.

Zaid's family didn't know they were police officers, but he knew about the murders. Now, they obviously knew about Eve. That she'd meant something to Tadgh. The boys talked with Sal and Tadgh, Sal translating most of it. At nineteen and seventeen, these boys were still lads in the eyes of many. But they were military-age males in the eyes of others. It was good to have their eyes and ears open.

Zaid's wife came into the living room, carrying a tray of pastry. Nuts and honey layered between flakey dough and something that looked like the tea cakes that... "That's it!" Everyone jumped. Charlie covered her mouth. "I'm sorry. So sorry. I didn't mean to shout like that."

She turned to Tadgh. "The fourth man. I felt like I'd seen him before. I know where I've seen him. A bakery. Not like this type of stuff. A Russian bakery where Tatyana works. He came in while I was there. He was rude to her, demanding, so he made an impression. He spoke Arabic. She didn't seem to know him or understand him, but that's where I saw him."

"The Russian girl you told me about, from the church?"

She nodded. "It's nothing, probably. He just rubbed me the wrong way. I didn't like the way he looked at her...or me." She felt Tadgh tense. "It's nothing. I can take..."

"Care of yourself." He interrupted her sentence. "Aye, so you keep telling me." He turned to Sal. "Ask him if he knows anything about him."

Sal translated, but Zaid answered in broken English. "Yes. That whole bunch of them, number one bad. They are the men who tried to talk to Abdul. The one you talk of, he is saying he's Georgian, but he lie. He likes my daughter. Wanted to arrange a marriage. But he's a liar. He's quiet to me; he talk to my son more. But I hear him. I don't know where he's from, but he's not Georgian."

* * *

THEY DROVE BACK to the flat, and Charlie was uncharacteristically quiet. "You're thinking about the fourth man. The one you saw in the bakery."

"Why would he lie? Granted, some people lie for the hell of it. But why lie? I believe Zaid if he says he is. Why say you are Georgian? To make connections?"

"I don't know, but he's being watched now. While you were in the kitchen with the women, we decided. Sal's really moving in to the flat until this is done. He is packing tonight and moving to the housing area early in the morning. Leyla will be livid, but I think it's smart. Time to go to 24 hour surveillance, and he's the logical mole."

"Does Sullivan know?"

Tadgh nodded. "Aye, he agrees."

* * *

THE APARTMENT WAS quiet when they came in. It was late and everyone was emotionally drained. As they readied for bed, taking turns with the bathroom, the bedroom door creaked open. It was Halley. She had her pillow and a stuffed seal. She looked at Tadgh expectantly. He sighed, looking at Charlie.

"It's okay. I can wait." She smoothed her hand down his bicep and leaned in to kiss his cheek. Then she went into the bedroom alone, because family was forever and that little girl needed her uncle right now.

Charlie's dreams were a random mélange of stressors. Bad dreams about her brother, about harsh hands coming down on her, on Josh. Then her brother was in that housing complex in Dublin, and the *number one bad* guys, as Zaid had called them, were whispering in his ear. She woke suddenly. Nothing but an opening of her eyes. She looked at the clock. Two o'clock was way too early to get up for good but she needed some water. She went out of the bedroom quietly. She'd just meant to go into the bathroom, but curiosity pulled her toward the living room. The room where Michael and Branna were sleeping had a cracked door, where the little girl Halley had escaped.

She entered the living space and the moon was bright, coming through the window to illuminate the area. Dublin was cloudy often, especially in the winter, but now the air was crisp and the sky was clear. She looked on the sofa bed and clapped a hand over her mouth, stifling a giggle. Tadgh was covered. Not with a blanket, but with warm bodies. Halley was half splayed over his chest, her arm cradling his face. His chin was in the crook of her elbow and her hair was in his face. Duncan was curled around the top of his head, like a hat. Not on him, but more around him, making sure that he had prime seating while staying out of the strike zone of little limbs and grabbing fingers.

The final addition was little Brian. The adorable little boy with Branna's raven hair and Michael's eyes. Except for the dark hair, he looked as every O'Brien man undoubtedly looked at this age. Big for his age, fair skin, beautiful eyes. He undoubtedly would have the little girls swooning in pre-school. He was sleeping across Tadgh's shins, both of them. He'd actually laid a pillow across Tadgh's legs and pinned him to the mattress. It was the silliest sight she'd ever seen, and the most beautiful. It probably never occurred to their uncle to order them back to their parents' bed. And they obviously adored him. His hands, so big and strong, were cradling the children with tenderness so at odds with his size. One hand cupped in Halley's silky dark hair. The other holding Brian's little hand because that was all he could reach in their position. The entire scene was enough to explode a woman's ovaries. She'd never thought too hard about having kids. But when she looked at Tadgh, at his gentle hands and his beauty inside and out, she felt a tug she'd never felt before.

What had started as a bubble of laughter swung in the opposite direction. Her throat was thick, her eyes blurring, and a stuttering breath under her hand were all signals for retreat. She turned to go back to the bedroom and standing behind her was Branna. Her smile was big, having seen the pile of bodies on the sofa bed. Then she saw Charlie and her face changed. Sadness and understanding. Concern.

"Oh, Charlie." Her voice was so kind. So soft.

"I just needed some water. I'm sorry if I woke you." Her voice was hoarse. "Goodnight, Branna." And she calmly retreated to her room.

* * *

TADGH WAS WOKEN by bodies being lifted and cool air replacing the stifling heat of too many mammals sharing one space. The final retreat was Duncan, walking over his face, down his chest, stepping on his balls, and then jumping to the floor. He let out a grunt, but then settled and drifted off again. When he came awake the second time, he was shivering. He had no blanket on. He looked at the clock on the cooker. It was just after three. He realized that the children had been removed and his head cleared. *Charlie.*

She was certainly asleep by now, but that didn't matter. He'd said he would come to her, and all he really needed right now was to feel her. Curl around her and hold her for as much time as he could. He got up, being careful not to make too much noise. He loved his niece and nephew, but they didn't like to share him. He carefully opened the bedroom door, excited to see a light on. Maybe he'd get more than a cuddle.

She was sleeping on the bed, propped on a pillow. He approached to see what book she had open. He knew she liked his art books. Especially the pre-Raphaelite books he had. It wasn't a book, however. It was her sketchpad. It was off to the side, open. The pencils next to it. She'd obviously pushed them aside as she felt herself nodding off. He gently retrieved the book, curious what would cause her to sketch so late.

Hands. She'd been drawing hands. And as he looked closely, he realized they were his hands. He had a birth mark on his left hand. Just one of those dark dots, more than a freckle but not quite a mole. It was on the back of his hand, below his first knuckle. She was good. Hands were difficult to draw. There were several drawings on one page, like someone who had learned to conserve paper. The other was a small hand in his. The waves and wrinkles of fabric underneath. She'd drawn him holding Brian's hand. They'd fallen asleep like that.

His heart squeezed so hard in his chest, it actually hurt. It physically hurt. She'd come out and seen them, no doubt. He leafed through the pages of the book. It was thick, like she'd had it a while. These one's she'd drawn tonight were nearing the end of the thick tome. He wondered how many she had back at home. How long she'd been sketching.

He looked through it, ashamed at the intrusion, but too curious to pass up the opportunity. He started at the beginning. She had the sketches dated at the top right hand corner of the page. She had some of Josh, younger, and they were dated 2012. For 4 years she'd filled every inch of the book. There were some of birds. Some of people's eyes, just a sliver into the soul of a person. There were old people, children, animals, scenes in city parks.

He flipped one page and his blood ran cold. The date was 2013. The note at the top said "art therapy". For the next three pages, there were angry eyes, the tense mouth, clamped down in disapproval. The hands were almost gothic. Shadowed around the edges with shades. Fists coiled and ready. Boots. Some sort of work boots. A dinner pail. An iron that was so accurately drawn that it made him shudder. A man's belt. Then her mother. Had to be. Sad, empty eyes. Eyes that had given up.

"You shouldn't be looking at that." Her voice startled him. He looked up and her face was defensive. She snatched the book out of his hand. "It wasn't yours to see. Not without my permission." She shot out of the bed.

He whispered, trying not to wake the house. "I'm sorry. God, Charlie. I'm sorry. You fell asleep with it next to you. I didn't mean to...well I did. I didn't understand, though. Christ, I'm sorry." His arms came around her and she tensed.

"Don't. I don't need comforting. I did those drawings years ago. I'm not some hurt little girl you need to save! I'm fine!" She hissed the words just above a whisper, mindful of sleeping children. She wriggled and he let her go, putting his hands up. She met his eyes. "Don't look at me like that!"

His brows crinkled, a question in his eyes. "Like I'm some poor, white trash kid who got the shit beat out of her. I'm not some little broken piece of garbage! I came from a bad home, but I made something of myself. I take care of myself. I can take care of Josh!"

"Jesus Christ, Charlie. Is that what you think? That's not it at all. I hurt for you, yes. Of course I do. And I won't apologize for that. I won't apologize for wanting to kill that da of yours or for wanting to protect you. But I don't think less of you for where you came from, I think more of you. You're the strongest woman I've ever known."

Her chin was up, defiant. Everything about her said, *See me. See me. I am not weak.*

"I see you, mo ghrá. I see you."

She swallowed hard, her chin still up, but the tears were so involuntary. Like a dam that just couldn't hold back the leaks anymore. "I'm not what you need. If you see me, then you see that. I can't be what you need. People say love conquers all, but they're wrong. I am needed, Tadgh. My will is not my own. My wants come last."

He took her in his arms. "I know, Charlie. I know what you're saying. Just please don't push me away. If the parting is to come, let it come in its own time. Don't push me away a second sooner. Please." He kissed her face, soft kisses all over her face as his hands weaved in her wild, unruly hair. He stopped, burying his nose in it as he drew her sleepy scent into his lungs. She soaked in the affection, finding his mouth with hers. The kiss was deep, loving, like she was thirsty and drinking him in. He scooped her up, her legs wrapping around his waist. She pulled his shirt off, then her hands were in his hair and she was kissing him again. They made love slowly, savoring the connection.

"I love your hands. I love your hands on me." She moaned the words as he slid one hand behind her back, up to her shoulders. The other down her hip, under her ass to pull her hips up to meet his deep glides. When she came, it was a long, smooth, rolling climax. Taking its time as the waves of pleasure went through her. The sounds she made were low and erotic in his ear, as she ran her hand through his hair. Just for him. The sounds were just for him. "Come inside me, Tadgh."

Tadgh raised up on his arms, looking down at the most beautiful woman he'd ever seen. Her mouth was lush and pink from his kisses and her arousal. Her eyes held the hazy delirium of a woman who'd been satisfied by her man. And they held love. *I love your hands on me.* He was twice her size, but she'd never feared him. Even when he showed frustration with her. What she saw in him was everything her father wasn't, and for that he was grateful. She deserved to have men around her who treated her with loving hands. Not just as a lover, but as a father, a brother, a friend. Men who didn't want to control her, but celebrated her strength, her simple beauty, her dedication to doing good in the world.

"I love you, Charlie. Forever, I'll love you." His glowing hazel eyes bore into hers as he let go, his hips swinging as he spilled himself deep within her.

Charlie watched him as he let go, released himself to her. He was big and thick and so deep inside her. And as he looked down at her with utter love and trust in his eyes, another orgasm blasted through her, tackling her unexpectedly from behind. He felt her, his eyes rolling back as she started to contract around him, extending his orgasm as she milked him. He let out a guttural moan, no longer caring who heard them and she smiled at the sound returning with her own gasps and moans.

* * *

BRANNA TRIED to cover her ears as the moaning followed the bed squeaking in the next room. Michael pulled her hands off. "Oh no, Hellcat. You don't get to block it out. Listen up. That's what we could be doing right now if ye hadn't brought these two fiends back into the bed with us. Need I remind you that you're ovulating and the timing is perfect?"

She buried her face in the pillow and laughed. Trying not to disturb the children who were currently occupying the bed with them. Then he was laughing too. She leaned over and kissed him. "We'll be home tomorrow, baby. Then we'll try this again. I'll even pull out my little lavender lingerie set."

His eyes flared, remembering the night they'd spent in Dublin four years ago. The night she'd surprised him, in their little rented room, with a spectacular lacy bra and thong. "It's a date, mo chroí." Then he nipped her bottom lip and settled back down on the pillow, willing himself to wait until they were back in their cottage. Just when he started to drift off, he heard that damn squeaking again. That bastard was going for a twofer.

CHAPTER 20

*C*harlie walked toward the bakery in Ballsbridge, feeling lighter than the night before. That's what happened when the man you loved made sure he satisfied you numerous times before letting you fall asleep, curled in his arms. If she stayed single forever, she was grateful for this blessing. He was an amazing lover. He knew just when to be gentle, just when to turn up the dominance. Most of all, he paid attention. Guided by her movements, her noises, even her commands, he knew her inside and out. Knew just how to drag out the pleasure until she was ready to lose her mind. But, he never denied, never played games.

When they were together, he was one hundred percent engaged, and he always knew what she needed. The smile teased her lips as she thought about leaving him asleep, exhausted by their night activities, but also the stress of the week they'd endured. She'd left him to sleep, knowing he needed it. She wanted to probe Tatyana, to see if she knew anything about the man at the complex. The quiet one with the questionable background. She came to the bakery, and heard the ding of the bell as she entered. Then she looked around, and saw Tatyana sitting in a chair alone. It wasn't at a table. It was off the main eating area in the hallway leading to the kitchen and the public restrooms.

When the woman looked up, Charlie gasped. Her face was beaten. Charlie went to her immediately. She swung the kitchen door open and no one was there. "Are you alone?"

Tatyana nodded. "The woman who bakes already go. It's just myself."

She knelt down, taking in the state of Tatyana's eye and lip. It was not so recent as this morning. The bruising looked several hours old, the split lip having clotted and dried. She took her chin softly in her hand. "Who did this to you, Tatyana?"

The woman's eyes were remote. "It no matter. He no matter. He was just someone I was having to help me, to find my sister. It no mattering."

"You need to call the police. I can help you, honey. You have to let me help you."

She looked up, fear in her eyes. "No! You must not call police. He knows where my sister is. You don't call!" Her voice was harsher than Charlie had ever heard.

"Okay, okay. Let's just make sure you are okay. Where else are you hurt? Can you stand?"

The woman grunted as she stood, and she was guarding the right side. "I need to look at your ribs. Let's go into the bathroom." Charlie followed her down the hallway to the restroom.

"I need cleaning up. Just let me do it. I will look." Tatyana went in the bathroom, the swinging door closing behind her. Charlie let her have a minute, but she needed to see how badly she was hurt. Broken ribs could be tricky. She wasn't wheezing or anything, but she needed to see a doctor. Tatyana wasn't making any noise. She started to worry after a couple of minutes. She texted Tadgh and got no response. He was probably still sleeping. *Tatyana's been beaten. Badly. The Russian bakery in Ballsbridge.*

She forwarded the message to Patrick and Sean, hoping someone was around. After another minute she knocked lightly. "Tatyana, honey. Can I see your ribs?"

She pushed the swinging door open, and Tatyana's back was to her. It wasn't the bruising that made her blood ice over. It was the tattoo. Suddenly Cora's words came back to her.

"She was in the street screaming. There were wolves. Three wolves. They were big and mean. They wanted to hurt her. One had green eyes. Glowing green eyes." Cora was trembling now. "The other red. The last one had white eyes. Oh, Charlie. They were going to kill her. I should have told!"

The Chechen flag was on her lower back. There were a few versions of the red, green and white flag. This one was definitely distinct. Above the sitting wolf, the wolf of Chechnya, was the Arabic style sword and script. The symbol of the Chechen rebels. *Three wolves. Three killers.*

Tatyana whipped around, her phone in her hand. That's when Charlie saw the knife on the sink. It was a spring loaded knife and Tatyana grabbed it, flipping the blade out. She thought about the gun in her waist band, under a layer of coat and sweater. She was in too close of quarters to try to get it now. She had to talk her way into the open area, then she'd get it. Police 101. If someone has a knife drawn, and they are closer than sixteen feet, they will stab you before you are able to draw your weapon. She had maybe eight feet between her and Tatyana's knife, but she had about a foot to the door. She thought about her phone as well. Please God, let someone be on their way. She felt the buzzing of texts and was comforted by it.

"You're not Russian, and you are most definitely not a Catholic."

Tatyana grinned, and it was not the sweet and vulnerable girl she'd spoken with on the park bench. "Smart girl. You know your flags. Now, little Charlie, we just wait awhile, and you can meet my other friend. He's been anxious to know you." She slid her shirt back on as she kept the knife pointed at Charlie.

Charlie had to play dumb. Tatyana obviously didn't know who she was. If she played this cool, she might get two of the three in custody before she'd had her coffee. Her jaw tightened. This was who was driving when Eve had been killed.

She couldn't go there right now, though. She was just a simple, ditzy American girl. "I don't understand. I thought we were friends?

Why did you lie? Why are you holding that knife? I just wanted to help you!"

"I don't need help from some little American whore. You have no idea what you are dealing with. You'll find out though. Everyone will." They both heard the bell at the same time and Charlie darted for the swinging door. Tatyana was hot on her tail. She stopped short as she broke out of the hallway. Bracketed between two threats. One bigger than her, one armed with a knife. His smile didn't mask his dead eyes. The "Georgian" or more accurately, the second wolf in Cora's dream. How in the hell had this slipped by her? The truth was, most Chechens looked of Middle Eastern descent, maybe a bit lighter skinned. It was like her. If you looked at her you wouldn't know if she was Irish, English, Welsh, or French. The genetic markers that came out in someone's face often diluted with generations of border changes and mixing bloodlines. *Chechens. Just like in the case of the Boston Marathon bombing.* What in the hell had she stepped into?

"Nazha, this is the final one. We will take her to him and then…" He cut her off, continuing in Russian. If it had been Arabic, she'd have been able to follow some of it. He already knew that. She didn't know any Russian other than yes, no, and a drinking toast. She needed to get the upper hand. Distraction was going to be her friend.

"You can let me go. I won't tell anyone. I've already called the police."

He laughed. The little bastard laughed at her. "Shut up and sit down."

Screw you, buddy. "You think I'm lying? Someone beat her up, I called the Garda while she was in the bathroom. I thought she needed to report it."

He looked a Tatyana. "You let her call the Guardians?"

Tatyana cursed. "I didn't know, and she saw my tattoo. She knows I'm no Russian." She spit on the floor when she said it. "Disgusting pigs. I should burn this place with my boss inside it."

Ah, this was a Russian bakery. That must have chaffed, but they'd found it necessary. She had those more classic Baltic features. She was perfect. She'd been every bit as undercover as Charlie.

"They are coming. You don't have a lot of time." His face grew angry and just as he went to step toward Charlie, she looked over his shoulder. "Too late, they're here." Which was a total lie, but just enough to get him to look behind him and Tatyana to shift her eyes as well. She yanked up her sweater and brought up her pistol. "Don't move you piece of shit."

The look on the guys face was priceless. She backed up, looked at Tatyana. "I will blow your head off. Throw that knife down the hall. Like you mean it, or I will start with a knee cap."

She could tell the man was thinking about charging her. She was calm. She knew she could handle them both. "I will shoot him and you will never see your sister. Throw the knife down the hall now." The look she gave the man as the knife slid down the hall had him grinding his teeth.

"Thank you. Now, Nazha. That's your name, right? Yes, you are going to lay down on the ground, palms and legs out as far as you can get them." He paused. "I know you can speak English. Lay down, arms out. Now."

He obeyed and Tatyana was next. Following instructions and moving closer to the man, lying on the ground. Charlie palmed the pistol, pointing it at the male as she took her cell out. She hit the command button and the automatic voice recognition asked her *How can I help you?* "Call Sullivan." *Calling Sullivan.*

"Charlie, what's up?"

"Russian bakery, Ballsbridge. On Clyde. I need back up. Two suspects. One male, one female. Chechen nationals. I think it's them. Move fast, Sullivan. I don't want some Garda tasering me because I have a pistol."

"Jesus Christ, hold on lass. We are there in five."

"Send a tow truck. There's a taxi van parked out front. No damage, but we still need to grab it."

* * *

TADGH WAS DRIVING like a bat out of hell. He didn't know what the hell was going on, but he and Patrick had both received a text from Charlie. He'd woken up to Patrick shaking the bed. "Get up, Charlie needs us. Something to do with a girl at the bakery in Ballsbridge."

As he pulled up to the bakery, he felt Patrick tense. Then he saw it. A taxi van. He threw the car in park as they both jumped out. What he saw through the window made his body get thrown into overdrive, adrenalin flooding his bloodstream. Charlie had her weapon drawn. They ducked behind the only other vehicle on the street. Both of them took their pistols out. "What the hell is going on?" They spun around to see Sean and Liam. "Liam, get back in the car."

"The hell I will."

"Please. Charlie's in there. Something has gone wrong in there. Move!"

"Fuck.You. Is that the van that hit Eve?"

Tadgh closed his eyes. *Not now.* He spun around and grabbed him by the shirt with his other hand. "I don't know, but Charlie is in the shit right now. Stand down!" he hissed.

Liam blinked, that sinking in. "I understand. Go." They went single file, checking the van windows. No one was inside, and there was no damage to the front of the vehicle. Then Tadgh got a better look in the windows. One male, one female, prone position on the floor of the bakery, Charlie holding a gun on them like a goddamn boss. She saw them and gave a hand signal for all clear. They opened the door and came in just as the cavalry arrived.

Luckily Sullivan and his merry men were coming up the rear, because it occurred to Charlie that she was A. on foot and B. not in possession of handcuffs. Nor, she suspected, were the O'Briens. The two suspects were cuffed and searched, then taken out the front door of the bakery. Sullivan tossed a set of keys at the uniformed officer. "Likely the bakery keys are on that ring. Lock it up and go about finding the owners. We'll need to question them as well."

Just as he walked to the marked vehicle, prepared to stuff the male Nazha into the back, Liam came out of nowhere. Everyone jumped to high alert as he tackled the man, pulling him out of Sullivan's grip.

Sean and Patrick were on him immediately, prying him off the man. Liam was unglued. Cursing and hitting the man. Sean pulled him tight against his chest. "Have ye lost your bloody mind? We need him! We haven't found the third. Get a hold of yourself!"

Before Liam could come to his senses enough to respond, the man was secured in the vehicle. Sean whipped Liam around to face him. "We may have two of the three. The third is still out in this city. Calm down or I will put you in handcuffs as well!" He leaned in, anger flushing his face. "Do ye think I don't want to kill him myself? We need him, Liam. We need them both. Go home, son. Take the car and go home. I swear I will end this. We will end this. On my life, I vow it."

* * *

CHARLIE GOT in the car with Sullivan, not ready to deal with the O'Brien men. Their tempers were high, and Tadgh was particularly agitated. *We need to talk. Now.* Nope. She'd seen that look in his eyes and knew it was time to back away and let him cool off. As they pulled into the police station, she didn't bother with wigs or backdoors. Her cover was irrelevant now. This was all about interrogating and finding that third and final piece of shit. She would flip Tatyana if she had to beat it out of her.

Tadgh followed closely behind the line of officers that were walking toward the detectives' main offices. His temper was at a slow boil. The other men were patting her on the back and congratulating her. No one thought to address the obvious. She'd gone off on her own. Ended up outnumbered and one of the suspects had been armed with a knife.

When they walked into the large meeting room, he'd had enough of Charlie dodging him. If she wouldn't talk to him in private, then they would have it out here. He could give a shite who heard them.

"What the bloody hell were you thinking?" The room went dead silent as Charlie slowly turned. It wasn't caution that slowed her motion. It was like a female cobra, slowly coiling back, ready to strike.

Her face was thunderous, but he didn't care. "What kind of

cowboy shite was that, heading to the bakery to find a murderer on your own? You should have told someone where you were going, for God's sake! Do you know how that could have ended?" He was shouting, and Charlie's eyes were ice.

"Gentlemen, if you could excuse us?" It was Sean's voice that dismissed everyone. They didn't need to be told twice.

When Sullivan closed the door behind him, Charlie attacked. "Who in the hell do you think you're talking to? You are completely out of line! I didn't go there expecting to find the asshole! I went to question Tatyana! How dare you dress me down like that in front of the other men!"

Tadgh opened his mouth, ready to argue, when an unlikely ally spoke up. Patrick said, "She's right. Shut your gob, Tadgh. Seriously. Shut the hell up and think about it. She texted us and said the girl had been beaten. That was it. This obviously went sideways fast, and she was left to her own devices. Do you really think she'd jeopardize the case, take a chance of blowing her cover or losing the bastard in order to go off on her own? You're letting that O'Brien temper cloud your judgment, and you acted like a dick in front of the other men."

Tadgh turned on him, ready to pound on him, when Sean put a hand on his chest. "Easy, lad. How about we sit at this large, over-priced table and sort this out? You're upset and I understand the why of it, but Charlie is not who you're angry with right now. Sit down, and listen."

He pushed Tadgh into a seat and Tadgh exhaled, running his hands through his hair. "Do you know what it was like to pull up to that bakery and see that van? Then I saw ye through the window, your gun drawn. Knowing you weren't wearing a vest!" He shut his eyes, his jaw tight.

Her voice was steady, but her tone held a warning. "Are you ready to listen? Because, no shit. I will drop you if you raise your voice at me again. Cut the He-Man routine, O'Brien."

Tadgh's eyes burned with emotion. He didn't speak at first, but then his body eased a bit. He nodded, not trusting his own voice.

After she'd told them everything, she said, "Now, if you would kindly go brief the team. I need to sit and make some notes, get ready for the interrogation. I also need to call my boss."

Before he left, Tadgh stood, looming over her. She looked up and immediately softened. His regret was obvious. "I'm sorry. I was an arse," he said.

"Yes. You were." She went up on her toes and kissed him. "I understand you were scared for me. You just have to trust me. This is my job, Tadgh. Just like you."

When they left the room, she began tapping her pen on her tablet. But she realized Sean was still leaning against the wall. She just looked at him expectantly.

"Don't be too hard on him. He was out of line, but he just wants to protect you."

"Sean, I understand. I just don't need the protection. He needs to treat me the same."

"You don't understand. You should. Ye see the way he looks at you. Surely ye know he loves you. He's an O'Brien, Charlie. We protect our women whether they need it or not."

She sighed. "I know about the O'Briens. I see it. The amazing relationships you all have. But I'm different. I'm not one of you. I'm not his…"

"Mate. So he told you about that? The history of our family?" She wouldn't meet his eye. She just nodded. "And you're wrong. Ye may have no intentions of staying with him, but you're his mate nonetheless. We protect our women. To the last drop of our blood."

"I'm not like the other women in your family, Sean. That's why this won't ever truly work. The women in your family are amazing. I'm just not cut from the same cloth. Which is why Tadgh will end up marrying some sweet local girl who will give him a pile of babies. I don't fit the mold."

Sean laughed. The infernal man actually tossed his head back and laughed. "That, Charlie love, is a load of bollocks. If that's what Tadgh wanted, he would have married years ago. Ye think we like docile women? Shove them in an apron and keep them pregnant?"

She grunted in frustration. "That's not what I'm saying. Just look at them! They're beautiful and smart and altogether perfect women. You've got one teacher, a real estate investor, a social worker, and a nurse. They come from loving homes and wholesome upbringings. I'm a cop who came from an abusive home. I swear too much, say the wrong thing, and I like guns and kicking doors in. I don't fit into this world, no matter how..." She cut her words off.

"No matter how much you'd like to?" He said softly.

She said nothing.

"You're wrong Charlie. There's no mold. There's just love. There's connection. It's that tug that you feel behind your ribs that pulls you to him. Fighting it is like fighting the tide. We see you, Charlie. He sees you."

Her eyes clamped shut, her jaw tight. Tadgh had said the same thing. *I see you.* "You don't understand. This isn't just about me."

* * *

CHARLIE LOOKED through the glass as Tatyana sat, restrained to the table in an interrogation room. "You have to let me in the room with her. I know her, sort of. I can use what I know against her."

Sullivan and Sean were in the second room. Charlie knew very little about Irish laws, but she knew from talking to Detective Miller, that they didn't have the equivalent to Miranda rights. They had the right to stay silent, but that was as far as it went. They were nowhere near as accommodating to criminals in Garda Headquarters.

She walked into the room and Tatyana tensed, then looked away. "How are you, Tatyana? The officers took great care not to make your injuries worse, but I was told that you declined a medic." Nothing. "Was Nahza the one who beat you? You can still press charges, despite the tremendous amount of trouble you're in."

Her eyes shot to Charlie's, hate filled. Charlie sat down across from her. "So, did you make up the thing about your sister? Is that how you lured them in? Sympathy?"

The woman fidgeted, her jaw tight. "You didn't make it up, though, did you? Not all of it. Obviously you aren't Russian, but there was a thread of truth in there. What was her name again? Nika? Yes, that was it. You said she was nineteen. Who has her, Tatyana? Was it worth those women's lives? The blood on your hands? Did you get your sister back after all of this? For the love of God Tatyana, do you even know if she's alive?" She said with a snide tone.

"Western whores. They were western whores. They didn't matter. My sister was a good girl. Worth a thousand of them."

Charlie leaned in, menacingly. "Well, unfortunately the people of the United States and Ireland don't see it that way. You will die in prison and your sister will be stuck in whatever hell she's been in forever. Until you meet her in hell. After all, I doubt the people holding her are taking her to worship. Undoubtedly, she's been passed around and tortured. Human Traffickers are rarely picky about the origins of their product. As a matter of fact, they specialize in turning good girls into bad girls."

Tatyana dove at her, stopping short from the cuffs which were fastened to the table. "You bitch!"

Charlie slammed her hands down on the table. "You really think they will find her for you now? You got caught! Even if you never talk, they have washed their hands of you. Has it occurred to you that they don't even know where she is? That they played you? All those women! Do you think that your prophet will give this all a pass? Do you think that the gates of heaven are open to a trio of serial murderers and rapists? You will be lucky if you don't get extradited to the U.S. and hung for your war crimes! And, you will never..." Her tone was deep and guttural. "Never see your sister again."

The panic in the woman's eyes at the thought of extradition hit its mark. It was bullshit of course. Getting someone extradited for a crime committed on foreign soil was almost impossible. She didn't know that though. She'd been spoon fed anti-West propaganda from childhood, no doubt.

Tadgh watched Charlie through the glass, Patrick and Detective Miller beside him. "Damn. She's good. She is really good." Miller had stars in his eyes. He'd been won over, completely.

He was right, of course. Tadgh had heard about the FBI interrogation schools. They were well respected. She was brilliant to watch, as horrific as this whole thing was.

"Tatyana, I have connections. I have the U.S. government and Interpol at my fingertips. I can help you, but only if you cooperate. I can help your sister."

"I will not help you. You have no idea what you're facing. This goes beyond dead whores. We are many. I serve the one true prophet."

"Sell it to someone who doesn't have a younger sibling. I would crush the earth to rubble for my brother. You and I are not so different. You may be telling your partners that line, to get them to help you, but blood is blood. I can help you, Tatyana. I can help her. You think about that. Even if your sister isn't alive, she deserves to be found. She deserves to go home to her family."

A shudder went through Tatyana, her eyes focused on her hands. She didn't look up as Charlie left.

* * *

CHARLIE WATCHED Sean O'Brien unlock the cuffs of the male suspect. The cup of tea was slid in front of him. "I don't have to tell you to behave. Do I, Nahza? Nahza Akhmadov, 22 years old, Chechnya born. Brother to Khassad. 28 years old." Sean flipped a page in his notes. "I looked up his name, I'm the curious sort. It means cruel, unjust, the oppressor. It's fitting, given his nature."

Sullivan stood silent, arms folded. His presence held a quiet menace as he looked on, his eyes boring into the man.

"We know your brother did the worst of it. It's of little consequence unless you cooperate, however. You will rot alongside your brother. I am quite certain that your female associate has more than enough information."

"She won't tell you anything." Those were the first words they'd had out of him. "She has much to lose."

"Her sister, you mean? Aye, I suppose. That's why Interpol is already drafting an offer to aid in her recovery. We will find her sister, dead or alive. And, she will tell us everything."

"Then you don't need me." His grin made the hair stand up on Charlie's arms. "And, it won't matter. Very soon, my friend, it won't matter. You have no idea, Sir. You have no idea what you've got coming. Your streets will run red with Irish blood. You won't give those dead bitches a second thought."

Charlie knew when Sullivan stood, it wasn't due to his own anger. The menace was rolling off of Sean. The patriarch of the O'Brien family loomed over the suspect. "If that's true, then I've got nothing more to do than to throw you in an Irish prison, where you can be gang raped until you meet your brother in hell."

CHAPTER 21

Sean and the rest of the task force, minus the politicians, were in the conference room, ready to start the meeting. They began the briefing. Charlie was first, sharing what she'd learned from her interrogation of Tatyana. Sean went next. The common theme was that something else was brewing. These murders were a smaller part of a bigger plan. What they needed now was to find out where the third accomplice was. Where the other van was being stored. Where they were taking their victims to torture them. Neither of the suspects were talking, but they were letting them sit. Stew in their own juices for a while. Then they'd go back in and try to get them to talk. But Charlie needed some food. She hadn't eaten since the tea and cookies at Zaid's apartment. She excused herself, heading back to the flat for a break. She'd had no sleep and she needed to fuel up.

* * *

THE INTERCOM SQUAWKED in the middle of the meeting. "DC Sullivan. We've got a recording from dispatch. You have to hear this now, and bring O'Brien."

All three O'Brien's stood. "I think she meant Tadgh." Sullivan said, but it was pointless. None offered to stay back. That's when Finn came in. "I've got a voice isolated on the video."

"Come along. Talk on the way. Something is up." Sean said as they headed toward the dispatch center.

Finn played back a digital recording on his laptop as they walked. The male voice was cursing at Eve. But the recording had only had muffling background noise, chaos. Filtered, the voice was lower and addressing the other two in Russian and he called the woman by name. *Tatyana.* "We translated his words. We didn't catch it all. He was ordering them to get out of there and for the woman to drive. Then he said *run her over.*" That was it. They had them. Tatyana by name, and intent to kill Eve. They had them. "Well done, lad." Sullivan said. "Whatever we're paying you, it isn't enough."

When they arrived in the dispatch center, they passed Detective Miller leading an older couple into the interview rooms. He nodded. "The bakery owners. They're Russian, not Chechen. They have their paperwork in order."

Janet flagged the others down. "You've got to hear this. Something's wrong. This guy is all wrong. He mentioned Tadgh specifically."

The men leaned in as she pulled up the recorded line. "Eileen took the call, have a listen."

The dispatcher gave the official greeting, *emergency line, how can I help you...blah blah blah.* Then the man's voice came on line.

"I believe you have something that belongs to me. Your pigs have my brother. You tell them they take from me, I take from them." The voice was thickly accented and hauntingly familiar. "You tell the man Tadgh, if that is his real name, I take from him. Those dead American whores were just the start. You tell him that. He take what is mine, I take what is his."

Ice shot up Tadgh's spine. *Charlie.*

* * *

311

NORTH DUBLIN- GOVERNMENT SUBSIDIZED housing

Two hours earlier:

Sal was finishing putting the week's worth of clothes away in his borrowed dresser when he heard a knock on the door. The doorbell didn't work in this shitty apartment. He'd received a call from Tadgh a few hours ago. Apparently they had two of the three in custody. At this point they were looking for the brother. The name wasn't familiar, and according to the refugee records, he was supposed to be living with his brother. He wasn't, though. They'd obviously split up, which was probably a tactical move. If one got caught, one would stay free.

His instructions were to stay here, keep his eyes and ears open. He hated it. Hated lying to these people and hated that he couldn't be in on the interrogations. They had other interpreters if they needed it, however, and they thought he was best served here. He was to keep an eye on the other three assholes whom Nazha had been hanging around with. They weren't Chechen. He knew that. Nazha had kept quiet, blended in until Charlie had recognized him. The other three had distinct dialects and accents, and they had family in the complex that Zaid had discreetly probed for information.

It occurred to him it could be Tadgh at the door, although he'd have expected him to call or text first. He looked through the peep hole and cursed. He whipped the door open. "Abdul, what happened? Oh, God." The boy could barely stand, he'd been beaten so badly. He started to go over and Sal caught him. "Who did this to you? I'll call an ambulance."

The boy looked up at him, his eyes tearing. "I'm sorry. They said they'd kill my family." The shadow came right before a flash of pain ripped through his skull, and then darkness.

* * *

TADGH DIALED AS HE RAN. "We need to get her up on the GPS!" They flung the room of the tech office open. "Pick up, Charlie! God, please!"

Sullivan pulled the GPS software up on the computer as Tadgh hung up and redialed. "I've got her! She's in her apartment!"

"Hello?" Charlie's tone was light.

"Jesus Christ, lass. Are you okay?" He choked on his words.

"Tadgh, I was in the shower. What is it? What's happened?" He looked at the screen. Her GPS signal was strong, right where she was supposed to be. He also noticed that Sal was where he should be, right there in his flat. Relief flooded him. "We need you here now. Like right now. I have to go. Call Janet and she'll explain." He hung up, then thought about the message. He looked at Sean. "Call everyone. Call my mother, all the family. Sean Jr. at training, Liam. Everyone. Check everyone."

Sean took one set of names, Patrick the other. Finn interjected. "I've been researching this from a technical perspective. The phone can't be traced since it's a burner. However, these radical groups are known for running their gobs on social media. We need to start looking on Facebook and Twitter. Every major event has had activity before or after on social media. What were the hashtags from the memorial?" #WeStandWithDublin #WeStandWithOurAmericanSisters #StopTheViolence

Finn started doing his thing as the men made phone calls. He put them all in, searching for a hit. The men hung up their phones after making very brief, alarming phone calls. "Everyone is safe," Patrick said. The same results for Sean and Tadgh.

That's when they heard Finn curse. "Jaysus, I think I found something." Finn turned the screen around and Tadgh clapped his hand over his mouth. The video was dark, the room was dingy and nondescript. Like a shut up room with no lights or windows. The camera was in a man's face. He was bound, on his knees. The video was on a loop. A man punched his already beaten face.

"You take my brother, I take one of yours." He pulled Sal's hair back, forcing him to face the camera.

"Send a unit to Leyla! Take the family out of the house and somewhere secure!" He called her then. "Leyla, it's Tadgh. I'm sending a uniformed unit over to get you and the babes. You need to lock the door until they get there, and keep your phone with you. Pack what you need for the kids. I'm sorry, love. I can't explain right now. I will, I promise. I have to go. Please do as I say."

He hung up and noticed Charlie was standing over the computer, a look of disbelief on her face. She was breathing heavily. "Did you run all the way here?" She was bent over, nodding.

She inhaled and exhaled. "Tell me everything."

* * *

CHARLIE WALKED into the interrogation room where they'd brought Tatyana from her holding cell. She set the laptop down out of reach, volume turned up. She played the recording. The woman's eyes flared. "We have you on tape. The hair, a slice of your face, and him calling you by name. We can place you behind the wheel when the woman is approached, your voice on tape, and then you hitting the other young woman with the van. You are in such deep shit, they need to find a deeper pool. Now. Are you ready to talk? Because, so help me God, I will make sure you rot in prison and you will never find your sister. You will be rotting in your own private hell while she spends a lifetime as a slave."

Tatyana stared at the computer, her jaw tight. "You have to help me find her if I help you. They told me they heard about a trafficking ring. It was working out of the port. You find her, get her home. I will tell you all I can."

"Done. I'm listening. Where do they take the girls?"

"I don't know."

"Wrong answer."

"I don't. I just help them find the girls. He like the American girls more better than Irish girls. He say the devil is in America. He like to take the young girls living over here, because they are not near the families."

"Why does he kill them?"

"He used them to train. That's what he said. I don't know where they go. I just help him find them. We get them in the vans and they leave me at my street."

"You aren't giving me shit. Where? What direction?"

She was silent. That's when Charlie read it in her face. "You're lying. You know where. You think if you give me a few crumbs and play dumb, I'll help you? Forget it. I'll get his brother to talk."

"He will never tell you. Our purpose is larger than ourselves. He will not tell you. You are too late."

"Too late for what? If I am too late, it won't affect anything if you tell me." But the woman had shut down. "You've got five minutes. Get your priorities straight, Tatyana. These men are not worth protecting. They are murderers and rapists, just like the men who took your sister."

She walked out of the room, wiping the sweat off her forehead. "Damn it!" She kicked a garbage can across the room. She leaned on the table. Tadgh put an arm on her shoulder. "Try again. I thought you had her."

She shook her head. "She was toying with me. We're missing something. A connection to the location. We've been checking abandoned buildings and warehouses in the urban areas and industrial parks, but this damn city is huge. We need a direction. Abdul said that the men would head toward the harbor. The South end of the harbor. The bakery is in that area." Then something occurred to her and she ran back down the hall, leaving the O'Briens to scurry after her.

Charlie knocked on the interview room door and Miller waved her in. She nodded politely at the older couple. "Do they speak English?"

"We do." The man's tone was even. His face calm. "We are very sorry. This girl Tatyana. She seem like a good girl. She was never late, she clean up."

"Did she ever steal from you, maybe money to fund some of this activity? Have you had any money go missing?"

"No never. She live nearby, never late. Never trouble to us."

They were checking her one room apartment, but there was almost nothing in it. A mattress, a closet with a few sets of clothes. She didn't even have a TV. They were pulling everything from her phone, but it wasn't much. She had a burner phone as well. "Do you own or rent any other properties?"

"Yes, Madam. We have a storage area near the old power station. It is empty." Then he thought about it. "You asked if anything was ever missing. Our keys. They were gone for a day, missing. Then they reappeared. We think she took them home by mistake and didn't want to tell us. We let it go. The keys were all there, but..."

"But she could have made copies. Was the key to the storage facility on there?"

He nodded. "Yes. But she wouldn't know what it was. The tag was marked storage unit. In Russian, of course, but it didn't have any address on it."

The wife spoke then. "She does paperwork for the shop. She has access to all of our files, our bookkeeping. We write the storage unit off in expenses. The deed, the address, it's all there in our books. She could have taken the keys and copied them. Why would these bad people need our old storage unit? It's not in good condition. It's of no use."

* * *

"My strength is as the strength of ten, because my heart is pure."
Sir Galahad... Alfred Lord Tennyson

"You can make this quicker. Less pain. All you have to do is tell us where the armories are for the Garda. I know your Irish government likes to pretend they don't like guns, but you have them don't you? Where do they keep their weapons? It's a simple question. Answer these questions and we can end this."

Sal was so tired. He couldn't open his eyes; they were swollen and the blood had started to dry, stinging. His captor continued, "Okay, let's start with an easier one. What's the response time for your Armed Response Unit? Let us imagine the threat is at Trinity. How far? How long?"

"Piss off."

The blow was merciless, right to the side of the head. He felt a wave of nausea come over him, and kabluey. He vomited and heard the man curse. "My shoes! You pig! Someone get me a clean towel!"

Sal smiled internally. Externally, he would split his lip open further, so he stayed still. The vomiting hadn't been deliberate. He undoubtedly had a concussion, maybe worse. He lost count of how many times they'd hit him. They varied it, not wanting him to expire or pass into a coma. The asshole jerked his head back. This prick loved to grab him by the hair. "I am going to find your family. We already know you have one. Abdul told us. Apparently Zaid had designs on you for a match for his daughter. She should not have rejected my brother. You will be dead soon, so maybe I'll find your pretty little wife and marry her. Teach her how a proper Muslim woman behaves."

"Go to hell you piece of shit."

Wham! This time it was something across his back. A pipe, maybe, or a board? "You won't gain anything by attaching your loyalties to these people. They will never accept you. They won't mourn you. And you will not make a mess of these plans. Months of planning. Conditioning. You think this is about dead women? They were tools. Nothing in the big picture."

"Your English is very good. Were you born in Ireland like I was? Did you turn on the people who took your family in, and resettled them?"

"I studied in the West. In Chicago. It was a cold shit hole. But my heart was true. You are a traitor."

He hit Sal in the belly and he groaned. He had nothing left to vomit up. He was pretty sure he had several broken ribs. He was wheezing, which meant he may have a punctured lung. He couldn't tolerate much more, but he was not going to give them any information. He knew he would die here. His GPS was in his belt, woven into the loops of the jeans he'd worn earlier. When they'd ambushed him, he'd been in his track pants. No one was going to find him. One thing he knew for sure was that he'd gone southeast, near the water. He'd been able to hear the seagulls for a time, and then the sound of a barge calling to port. But he was underground, now. He smelled the dank, old air. He'd been taken down a ladder. It wouldn't be a subway, more like a sewer. But that wasn't right, either. It wasn't that dank. It didn't smell like bad water or mildew or waste.

"You said they were tools." He started to choke, coughing and wheezing. "Tools for what? What could you possibly gain by taking those women and torturing them? You're going to kill me, so there's no harm in telling me."

"Bring him some water. He's not looking so good and we still need him." He leaned in closely, whispering. "We will video your death. This social media is also a good tool."

They brought water and he held it to Sal's mouth. He took a sip, knowing these savages were too merciless to quickly poison him. They liked to break things. He coughed, blood coming out of his mouth. Yep, definitely breaking him slowly. The man poured water over his head, then he felt the towel wiping his face, around his eyes. It smelled like vomit.

"There, now you can see better, no?" This man had a slightly Russian sounding accent to his Arabic. This was the Chechen. The third. The main killer and the rapist. His big hands were the ones that had been wrapped around those dead girls' necks. "That's it, big man. Open your eyes."

He pried his eyes open, knowing the sick bastard would cut his eyelids off if he didn't listen. He stared at the man in front of him. He remembered Charlie's sketch. The eyes. She was good. Hopefully she'd get this bastard and be able to pat herself on the back. He looked around. There were the three men from the housing complex. There was one who always appeared to be in charge. That hadn't changed. The man standing in front of him was the muscle, a Lieutenant of sorts. He did the dirty work. Khassad Akhmadov, the horrible prick they'd been looking for. The first man, however, was the leader. The third man stood quietly, a look of disgust on his face while he watched them pulverize their victim.

Sal was surprised when the boss of the group answered his question instead of Khassad. "This business with the American women is not so good, yes. It is an ugly thing, but it had its purpose."

He nodded at the door where someone stood, but Sal couldn't turn his head. A man he didn't know brought in a young woman. Her eyes were down, her face gaunt like she'd been malnourished. "This is one of our soldiers. She is brave and serves us well." He walked over and the girl tensed, began to tremble. "She is proud to martyr herself. She will secure a good stipend for her family, assure their safety." He nodded. "The American girls were a training tool. It keeps the soldiers focused. Fear is useful."

"So you tortured and raped those girls, then killed them, all to scare your female captives into towing the line. Jesus Christ. You are completely mad. You think this is helping? You think this is securing a spot for your families in this city?"

The man laughed. "You misunderstand. We don't want to live among these people. We will occupy, we will conquer. We will send our soldiers out to wipe this slate clean. It starts in the morning. They are already in place. Leading the charge will be the strongest of my brothers." He put his arm around Khassad, and the man's brows furrowed. "You see, he exposed the whole of our group. He allowed himself to be recorded and he marked the girls most brutally. Which means they can tie all of the murders to him."

Khassad spat on the ground, then looked at Sal. "They dishonor their God as they dishonor their fathers and husbands. They deserve to be made examples of."

Sal croaked as he spoke. "You are a murdering psychopath who will never see the gates of heaven."

Sal groaned at the blow to the abdomen. He knew he wouldn't be able to take much more. He really did need to learn to shut his mouth.

The other man shrugged. "I'll admit I indulged his cravings too much. He has a thing for American girls. Small, young American women. So, I let him have his fun. But he got caught. The idiot's face is all over the news. So, he will lead the charge as recompense for getting sloppy." He turned to the man, then. "Now, my friend. Take your place outside the city. You know where. You have this night to set your soul in order. You will lead this attack. If you don't, I will find you. You will do this for our higher purpose, and earn a place of honor in the afterlife. Do you understand?"

Sal watched with a sinking, sickening feeling as a peaceful acceptance came over the man's face. "I do. I understand." The men hugged, clapping each other on the back, and doing a double kiss on the cheeks. "I will see you again, my brother." He left and Sal was left with one less asshole to beat on him. *Small favors,* he thought. But what in the hell were they up to?

* * *

SEAN ROLLED a map of the Dublin Port area out on the table in the conference room.

"So, Ringsend. Are we talking that big power station with the stacks? That's hardly low profile." Charlie was the only one in the room unfamiliar with the many districts of Dublin.

Tadgh shook his head. "No, she said the old power station. Let's have a look. It's a derelict station, lots of old buildings. Here." He pointed at it.

As Charlie read the name out loud, "Old Pigeon Power Station at Poolbeg." She thought about Cora's words. *I saw your Da. I knew him from the photos, but he told me he was my Uncle William. He said to tell you to follow the pigeons. The pigeons will show you the way to the wolves.* Charlie's voice was quiet. "Follow the pigeons." She looked at Tadgh. "Follow the pigeons to find the wolves." Then she pointed to the road. Old Pigeon Road in Ringsend.

* * *

THE TEAM of Garda moved closer to the old building, surrounding the cargo doors and the side entrance. Charlie was back with Tadgh and Sullivan. She'd wanted to go in with the special response team, but that had been shot down with fervor. She watched as Patrick took point, swallowing hard. There was a sniper on the roof of a nearby building, watching carefully. Patrick used the key, not wanting to boot the door unnecessarily. The owners were fully cooperating. His partner threw in a flash bang. Then they entered. Filing in one behind the other, Sean tensed as he watched his son clear the building. "You must be very proud." Charlie gave him a small smile.

"Aye. I'd ask ye not to relay the story to his mam, however. You'll turn that pretty red head of hers white."

Patrick surfaced, giving the all clear. "We've got van tracks. There's some equipment in here as well. You aren't going to like it."

They searched for a light switch, forgoing the high powered torches that the armed response team carried. They weren't done, and they needed the battery power. A single light illuminated the space from the ceiling. It was enough to see everything.

There were sliding closets with shelving lining the walls. There were pressure cookers, piping, wire, ball bearings, nails, crates of low impact fireworks, and digital timers. Other things as well. This was the storage unit that no police department wanted to find. Tables were set up, and had been used as work surfaces. The set up someone would need if they were making IEDs.

"Holy God, who the hell is this guy? This can't just be three people. What in God's name were they planning?" Sullivan's voice was tense, higher than normal.

"And where is the van?" Tadgh said with a tone of dread.

"There's more. There has to be more. If they are keeping the van and equipment here, this has to be the drop off for their prisoners. Do we have a map of this area? This entire area is ruined buildings. They could be a lot of places."

Tadgh spread out the map on the hood of a car. "Think about what we know. The rust, iron filings, copper wiring. All found on the victim's bodies. We are standing on the edge of an abandoned power station. We need to break up and start searching the area. There are several areas where they could hide. No one would hear them out here. They come and go at night, they're driving a taxi. They've gone completely under the radar."

Within ten minutes they were split up into teams. "Radio discipline. Nothing unnecessary. Succinct communication. I've split the property up into five sections. Teams of four will travel together."

He looked at Charlie, a sinking feeling in his stomach. She had a weapon holstered, a bullet proof vest under her coat and over her sweater. Her hair was bound back neatly. Her facial expression was all business. She was with Sullivan and two of the Armed Response officers who were armed to the teeth. She'd been adamant that they not be on the same team. Too distracting. She was right of course. Emotion had to be removed as much as possible. He looked up as he saw the Garda helicopter doing another pass over.

* * *

PATRICK AND TADGH walked through the main structure of the abandoned power station with the other officers on their team. It was eerily quiet. Derelict old buildings could be like that, as if the decay and deterioration managed to transport it to a plane of its own existence. Only the pigeons were in attendance, darting through the beams of intruding light that speared through old windows and holes in the roof's structure. The only other noise was a barge sounding off in the distance, a reminder that this old place was right on the sea. It was over a century old.

"We've been at this for hours. It's getting dark. This is the last place. We'll have to break off and start fresh tomorrow," Patrick said calmly.

"I'm not leaving until I find Sal. I will not leave him here overnight."

"He may not be here, Tadgh. And he may be dead already. You have to prepare for that."

"Shut your gob and focus. I'm not leaving."

Three wolves. Follow the pigeons. Three wolves. Follow the pigeons. He thought about the words. His father had come to Cora in a dream, specifically to give him that message. William O'Brien would not have left until he'd found his partner.

Tadgh looked up, watching as the birds fluttered in the beams of the old roof. Then something caught his eye. Periodically a bird would soar down and through a doorway, leading off the main area. The door had been removed, probably so no one would get trapped in there. He stopped, observing. The pigeons were flying in and out of the little nook, and he wondered if there was a nest in there, like a brooding barn that you saw for hens or a dovecot. He approached, and sure enough there were a series of pigeonhole compartments, maybe employee mail boxes or something. He walked into the side room, flashing his light around. Nothing.

"What are you looking for?" Patrick said. The other two men followed closely behind him. One said, "Careful, the floor is covered in bird shite." Just as he said it, Tadgh slipped a bit. Something clinked under his boot. He looked down. "Hold this, light up the floor." He handed his torch to one of the men. He swept away debris and cursed. There was a latch. "There's an access door. It leads underground."

"No one's been through that door in decades. You can see it, surely." Patrick eyed him, then the door.

"Yes, but this probably isn't the only way in and out." He pulled on the door and it screeched from lack of use, heavy and covered in filth and rust. Peering down, he took back his torch, illuminating the tunnels. "It's where they ran power lines underground. It's a tunnel. Call the teams. We can't do this alone."

* * *

NINETEEN MEN and one woman stood around the entrance to the tunnel. Charlie knew this was it. She looked at the pigeons cooing in the little nooks, and the others spiraling around, complaining. They didn't like having someone in their nesting area. But they'd been the clue Cora had told them about, leading the way. Cora and William. The hair on her arms stood up on end. *Please don't let us be too late.* One by one they went down.

It was about five minutes and several rats later that the first ladder appeared. Another hatch to get out. Good to know. "This is like being in some sort of rat infested hell," one of the men whispered.

They'd come across only one other door on the same level, and it had been so corroded shut, that it was obvious no one had gained entry to the room. As they kept going, the air changed. "Something is different. Stay sharp, stay quiet, kill the torches." The team leader was whispering, his eyes tense. He was a middle aged man. He was tall and thin, had come to Ireland as a twenty something year old man from India. Prior military. Patrick had commented more than once that the man had a sixth sense. He could detect subtle changes in the landscape, in the scenery. He also had a very acute sense of smell. He'd insisted everyone either put knit masks on or blacken their faces. They needed the element of surprise or they could blow something up or kill Sal. This guy didn't need much camouflage. He had a full beard, in the Sikh style, and a traditional turban on his head. He'd received a uniform waiver to bind his hair according to his religion. Tadgh followed closely behind him, watching the man's body language, yet trusting him to take the lead.

As they all obeyed and killed their lights, they were amazed to realize it hadn't gone to pitch black. There were less rats, too. This was it. Tadgh knew it in his bones. *Please don't let him be dead.*

They all smelled the cigarette smoke at the same time. Officer Rahn, the unit commander, gave the signal for them all to stop, then he did the damnedest thing. He handed off his weapon and torch to Tadgh. He peered around the corner, just quickly. He signaled for everyone to stay put. Then he proceeded. The noise was minimal. Tadgh did his own quick peek as the big officer had put one hand over the man's mouth, one arm around his neck. He squeezed with efficiency, and the man went lights out. The sleeper hold was a tricky move. Tadgh would have never tried it. But this officer moved like a Ninja. *Who the hell is this guy?* Tadgh started thanking God that the Garda had put this guy in charge of Patrick's unit.

He came in behind the man, cuffing the asshole as another man taped his mouth. He looked up and stared at Miller. His eyes said,

Duct Tape? Really? But you couldn't argue with the results. Detective Hairy Ass gave a wink under his bushy brows.

Tadgh was outside a lit doorway, the other officer having stealthily crossed to the other side. He could hear them. He was going in behind Rahn. Patrick was behind him, although they'd argued about it. Patrick had wanted Tadgh behind him since he carried a rifle and was trained to be on an entry team, but that was his partner. His brother of sorts. *You take from me, I take from you.* He prayed again, that Sal was still alive.

* * *

"Well, my friend. We've come to the final showing. Would you like to say anything before we carry out your sentence? You are, after all, a traitor. You will die like one. But, perhaps you would like to say some final words of contrition?"

Sal knew this was it. Another man had joined the party and brought a smart phone with him, turning on the camera. His only consolation was that he'd not given these pricks one useful piece of intel on the Garda's operational security. He wasn't going to go out like a sap. Leyla knew that he loved her. His kids would forget him after a time. They were so young.

"I would like to tell my partner something." He looked at the camera phone, trying to muster some strength. "This wasn't your fault, Tadgh. Don't ever let my family see this tape."

"That's it? Not so very original." When Sal took a deep breath, and opened his mouth, the man chuckled. "So sorry, please continue."

Sal cleared his voice and started the prayer. The man's eyes growing wide with astonishment, then realization.

"Saint Michael the Archangel, defend us in battle..." he was shaking with the effort, so much pain, so difficult to breathe. "Be our protection against the wickedness and snares of the devil; may God rebuke him, we humbly pray; and do thou, O Prince of the heavenly host, by the power of God, cast into hell, Satan and all the evil spirits, who prowl through the world seeking the ruin of souls. Amen."

The man let him finish, his eyes narrow, a wicked grin teasing the corners of his mouth. "An Apostate. You son of a bitch." He went over to the table, dropping the knife he held, and picking up a handsaw. "Hold his head back," he instructed one of the other men.

* * *

TADGH HEARD HIM. His eyes pricked with tears. It was Sal and another man. Sal's voice was weak but pure, and a shot of terror went through him as he heard his partner's prayer. *Cast into hell, Satan and all the evil spirits, who prowl through the world seeking the ruin of souls..."* He looked at Rahn. No waiting. "Go now." He mouthed. The flash bang went off as they all covered their ears. It was such a confined space. Then they were through the doorway.

Chaos. Bloody mayhem. The take down was fast. There were only three other men in the room besides Sal. Sean and Charlie were toward the rear of the line. Charlie came into the hazy, hellish tomb of a room and all she saw was Tadgh. He was cradling Sal in his arms. Someone was untying Sal's hands. Tadgh was screaming, "Oh, God. Get a medic down here!"

Miller yelled, "Already on it! We found a better way in! They're landing the helicopter on the green!"

He was hurt badly. Possibly fatally. It looked like they'd beat him from the time he went missing until now. Old wounds clotted, fresh ones freely bleeding. Tadgh was sobbing. "Get a goddamn stretcher down here!"

Sal was mumbling, trying to communicate. "Shhh, brother. We know about the bombs. You can tell us all of it when we get you out of this hellhole." He rocked him like a child. "I'm so sorry, brother. Oh, God. I'm so sorry I wasn't there."

Sal's voice was weak. "I didn't tell them shit. I didn't give them anything."

The medic showed up, put him on the stretcher, but the men from the task force shoved their way forward. "We take him out!" It was

Miller, his eyes barely containing the tears. "We take him out. He's ours!"

They did. Tadgh, Charlie, Miller, Sullivan. One on each corner. The other ART officers filing in behind them. The bomb tech had checked the area before sending the medics down the shaft, making sure there weren't any IED's hidden to secure their little torture chamber.

Sean looked around the room, sickened. It had more than Sal's torture team. It was full of evidence. This room was obviously where the girls had been taken and murdered. He looked at the table that had pliers, a blow torch, and the hair raised on his neck as he saw the X-Acto style knife. The knife that had been used to carve up the victims. To mark them. There was one missing in the group, the brother Khassad. These three suspects were from the housing complex, according to Tadgh. The men Zaid had referred to as *number one bad.* The ones who had tried to recruit the son, Abdul. Tadgh had told him that Abdul was a good kid who had attentive parents. Luckily they hadn't gotten their hooks into him. *One missing,* he thought. "Where are you, you bastard." *And where the hell is that second van?*

CHAPTER 22

$\mathcal{T}$adgh rode in the helicopter with his partner. It was a medivac situation because they were one hundred percent sure that Sal was bleeding internally, and that his broken rib had partially pierced his lung. "They've got something planned. Tomorrow morning, Tadgh. There are people in place. I don't know where. Jesus, you have to stop them!" He was tearing off his oxygen mask, half in shock, half pissed off. He had to be in unbearable pain, but he was too bloody minded to lie still.

The medic looked at Tadgh. "You need to keep him calm. He has multiple injuries and broken bones. I'm afraid to sedate him. His vitals are all over the place. We're almost there."

"I've got it, big man. I swear, I heard you. We know about the bombs. We're on it." Tadgh just patted his hands, clasping them in front of him so he'd quit trying to pull his mask off. The saline bag was swinging as they started to descend.

They were taking him to the best trauma unit in Dublin County, St. James Hospital, where Liam was currently on duty. He'd been told he could stop working when Eve had been killed, but he'd refused the gesture. He was not a trauma surgeon, but internal medicine and infectious disease, so he'd likely not even know they were there until Sean went to find him. He had a right to know what was going on.

They landed and the medical professionals took over, having a full team ready to care for Sal. Warrior-faced doctors and nurses who sprang into action just as they landed. He ran through the trauma chute until someone rerouted him away from the surgical wing. "We'll keep you posted, I promise. Your men are already calling and your boss is in the waiting room giving the nurses a ration o'shit. We'll take care of your partner. I swear it. My husband is Reserve Garda. He's in the best hands possible."

* * *

DETECTIVE MILLER WALKED in with Charlie behind him. Miller had gone to pick up Leyla and the children. Leyla's mother was ten minutes away, coming to help with the children. When Leyla walked up to Tadgh, she smacked him right across the face. Then she grabbed him, hugging him and sobbing with one hand on her double stroller. "I hadn't heard anything. They came to get me, took me to a safe place. They said Sal was missing. Then nothing! Nothing for hours!"

Tadgh wrapped both arms around her. "I'm so sorry, love. Oh, God. I'm so sorry. I was looking for him. Every minute that went by we were working to find him. He's alive. We found him and we got some of them."

He noticed that Charlie had taken the stroller, standing close by so that Leyla could see her children.

"Tell me what has happened. Do not sugar coat this. How hurt is he?"

Liam approached just then, standing next to Sean. "I'm Dr. O'Brien, ma'am. I'll go in and get a full account. All we know now is that there are broken bones, internal bleeding, and that he's very dehydrated. He's lost a lot of blood. They're likely taking care of that right now. I will go check and then come and tell you. We'll take care of him. This is one of the best trauma units in the country."

His absence was short. He came back within five minutes, because they were taking Sal into surgery. "If you want me to give it to you straight, I'm ready. You have a right to know it all."

Leyla kicked her chin up. "My husband's bloodlines trace back to the Lion of Babylon. He has warrior blood in him. Whatever you tell me will not matter. He will survive."

"You bet your ass he will." Miller was standing to the side, arms crossed.

"His lung is collapsing due to a broken rib. He has three broken ribs on one side, two on the other. His spleen is bleeding, but they think they can repair it. Bruised kidneys, a broken clavicle, a dislocated knee, and multiple facial fractures." Leyla's whimper underneath her hand almost undid them all, but Tadgh could tell this was taking its toll on Liam in a very personal way.

"The most urgent concern is brain swelling. He was beaten repeatedly. They've called in our best surgeon, another is video conferencing from the Level 1 Trauma unit in Cork. He's in the best possible hands. The brain injury is an unknown element. Tadgh said he was uncooperative in the helicopter, but lucid."

Leyla choked on a laugh. "He specializes in lucid and uncooperative." Tadgh put his arm around her, kissing her head. He looked over at Charlie, who was holding the baby. He'd heard a brief cry, but she'd taken care of it, making sure that Leyla could focus. An older woman who looked like Leyla came in, and Leyla went to her, starting to cry. The woman held her daughter, then relieved Charlie of the baby as they went to the chairs to sit down.

Liam watched them, his face tight with pain. "Please tell me you got them all."

"I wish I could," Tadgh said. Sean was silent, lost in deep thought.

Charlie and Sullivan approached the men then. Tadgh addressed the group. "Whatever is going to happen, it's going down in the morning. We need all hands on deck. We need to saturate the city with Garda before the sun comes up, including reserve, military, fire services, everyone you can call in, try the bloody trash collectors. Anyone who knows the city. Patrick is back with his unit. We need them out in force, and we need every bomb tech standing by. All major institutions need to go on lock down. College campuses, major cathedrals, large entertainment venues, cinemas, theaters. Activate an Interpol message immediately. We have no idea how many are on foot. These pipe and cooker bombs can fit in a backpack. That doesn't even take into account that the second van is out on the streets and probably full of explosives. We only have a few hours to prepare for this. We are in real time."

He turned to Liam. "You need to call the bosses. We need to beef up staffing at all of the city's emergency rooms. Just in case."

* * *

HORDES OF GARDA were pouring into the station. Every single able body. Even those usually pushing a desk like Janet were gearing up. They were in pairs, because they didn't actually have enough hand held radios. They were color coded throughout the city, each color taking a radio channel. Everything feeding into a main dispatch center.

Charlie was teamed with Patrick, Sullivan insisting she stay with a uniformed officer. They were coded the blue team, along with Sean and Tadgh who were also paired with uniforms. The other task force members were dispersed throughout the different teams. There were even cadets and fire services, Coast Guard and Army in the mix. Literally everyone they could pull in this short of notice, all paired up with officers. Some armed, most not, but every team had some sort of communication, and were armed with stunning, chemical, or impact weapons if they didn't have a firearm. It's the best they could do.

They'd split the city up into zones based on the same color system. The blue team was assigned to Dublin 2, 4, and 8 which were high tourist areas and contained Trinity College. As they split up their zone, assigning areas to the duos, Tadgh looked over at Charlie from his side of the table. She was hyper-focused, ready, bent over the map talking to his cousin about likely targets. That's when it hit him. She was going to be right on the front lines. They were all exhausted. Tadgh and Charlie had taken shifts sleeping in chairs in the hospital

331

waiting room, not wanting to leave Leyla. He watched Charlie now, going on about two hours of sleep. She looked so tired.

"Charlie, can I see you for a moment?" She looked up, doing a mental shake in order to redirect her attention. "Of course."

He led her down the hall, to the interview room that the bakery owners had occupied hours before. He opened the door, guiding her in. Then he deployed the blinds and he was on her. He pressed her to the wall as he kissed her roughly. His hands were in her hair, his mouth demanding, his body strung tight with lust and fear. She understood. She'd felt it too. That stabbing fear of watching him go out to do this job they'd both chosen. To try to put himself between those who would do mass murder, and the people he'd sworn to protect.

He broke the kiss. "I love you. God, Charlie. I can't do this!"

She was kissing his face, soft and comforting. "You can. Just like I'm going to watch you walk out that door. It's okay. I'll be careful. You and I will be careful and we'll meet at the flat tonight. When this is all over, we'll be together." He was shaking, both with suppressed arousal and an almost crippling fear. "You can do this because you love me and you know this has to be done. This is our job."

They took another moment, just to love each other. Soft kisses, passionate embraces. Tadgh had slipped into Gaelic. She was positive that he didn't even realize it. The island and the Western coast were bilingual, the children learned Irish in the cradle. She was really going to need a crash course. Then again, she wouldn't. After this case was over, she'd leave. That thought made her heart sink and she gripped him closer. "I love you too, Tadgh. Always."

* * *

Tadgh walked toward Saint Patrick's Cathedral, his head on a swivel. The Interpol system was pretty effective, as was the power of the radio. Sporting events inside stadiums, theaters, and concert halls had been contacted. Any who chose not to close up assured the Garda that no backpacks or large bags would be permitted in the building, barricades would be put out to keep people from parking near the buildings, and that the security guards would be on high alert. It was a horrifying thought that the suspects were unknown, other than the Chechen that was currently at the top of the *Dead or Alive* list. Were they men or women, young or old? Were they in traditional dress? Were they Irish converts who would blend in without a second thought, homegrown terrorists that had been recruited to turn on their own countrymen? They just didn't know. That's when he saw it. As they approached the church, there was a sign on the light post of the adjoining street. *Saint Andrews Day Charity Run- 10K thru the streets of Dublin.* How in the hell had he forgotten about the run? There were people from the performing arts department who were doing a walk for Eve, splitting the route up along the ten kilometers of the race. He'd seen the flyers at her memorial.

He stopped the officer beside him. "I need your radio. The charity run. We didn't contact the run committee!" They'd had no time. He was shocked that nothing had happened yet, because there had been dwell time to rally the troops, time when anything could have happened. There just hadn't been enough time to warn everyone.

As he put the information out on the radio, all he could think about was Boston. It had been Chechen refugees responsible for that horrible day. What if they'd decided to recreate it? Then he thought of the festival in Nice, France. The terrorist drove a truck right into the crowd. That bastard who had run Eve over was behind the wheel of the taxi van. There were so many taxis in this damned city. His access was staggering.

* * *

CHARLIE AND PATRICK ran toward the area of Dublin 2 where the run would be happening. Down Harcourt, through Saint Stephen's green, across the Ha'Penny Bridge. Ten kilometers where the attack could happen, assuming the run was the target. The major sites and buildings had been covered, but this was tourist central. Pubs, shops, restaurants, churches, and a major university. At any time, they could peel off and hit another target...improvise. Luckily they'd saturated the city.

She did a double take as she saw someone across the green. It was Zaid and his eldest son. She darted across the street, explaining to a trigger ready Patrick that they were friendlies. "Zaid, you should be home! Where is your family?"

"They are at hospital, Madam. The bad men beat my son. They beat him!"

"Slow down, Zaid. Who beat him?"

"They beat him, they make him go to Sal. They took Sal and beat my son! He wouldn't tell us at first, but I finally got him to tell me everything this morning. They threatened to kill our family. He's a good boy, but he is young. They threatened to kill his family."

"I understand. We have Sal. He's badly hurt but we have him. Now, there are very bad people planning attacks. You need to go to the hospital, wait with your family."

Zaid shook his head. "Yes, we heard security officers at hospital. They questioned us. We heard them talking. They're watching for bad guys. We are here to help. I know some of the languages. I was inter-preter for the British Army. I will help. We..." he gestured back and forth. "We will help. I will call Mr. Tadgh if I see anything bad. I can help."

Charlie paused for a minute. She couldn't just send him away. His son had made some mistakes, dishonored his family. "Okay. You call him if you see anything, or flag down an officer. You do not try to stop them. You follow and report. That's it. We are also looking for a taxi van with front, passenger-side damage. White van, Toyota. There should be a large twenty seven year old male driving it. Short black hair, brown eyes, medium skin. Do you understand?"

Zaid nodded, "I understand."

* * *

SEAN HEADED AWAY from the stadium area, toward the river. The officer that was with him was about twelve. Okay, maybe not twelve, but he was certain he had socks older than this lad. He stopped short as he saw a young woman. A girl, really, who looked to be about seventeen. She was Middle Eastern in appearance. She was on the corner waiting to cross, but as the light turned, she didn't go. As he approached, he saw that she was weeping. Her face stricken with fear. She was wearing a backpack. He stopped, and his partner did the same. "See there. Don't overreact. Just look at the young girl on the corner. Something's not right."

The uniformed officer tensed. "She's got a sack on her back," he hissed.

"Aye, I see that. You keep your weapon down. She can't be more that seventeen. Don't startle the lass. I'm going to approach her. Stay behind me."

"I'm supposed to stay with you."

Sean smiled. "And you will. You're going to let me go first, so she doesn't run."

Sean approached the girl slowly. She was shaking. She was absolutely distraught. "Hello, lass. Can I aid ye in some way?" The girls eyes were huge. "It's all right. I've got girls of my own. I won't hurt you. What's got ye so troubled?"

She seemed to take his face in, assess the threat. "Please, Sir. I don't know this place. I don't know anyone. I don't want to die."

"What makes you think you're going to die? Have you lost your family?"

"I don't know where this is. I want to go home. Please. They take me. I don't know this place. I will go back to my village."

"What's your name?"

"Halima. This is not my home. I want to go home."

"What's in your bag Halima?" Her tears came in earnest.

"Help me. I don't want to die. I don't want to hurt anyone."

* * *

THE CALL CAME over the police radio and Tadgh was about to lose his mind. His Uncle Sean had found one of them. A young woman who was piss pants scared and had essentially aborted her mission. They were using scared young women. They'd called from the hospital. The officer who was guarding Sal had relayed his message. They were using the tortured women to train soldiers. And by soldiers he meant other kidnapped young men and women that would do their bidding. According to Sean, they'd had this girl, a Sri Lankan girl, for months. They'd lured her to Europe on a housemaid visa, promising her good wages to send home to her family. She was eighteen, but Sean said she looked younger. They'd practically starved her, all part of her training. She said she was the first from the group to be used along with a young man who was carrying the same explosive device she was. She didn't know anything about the van.

The bomb techs had responded quickly, finding a timed pressure cooker bomb in her backpack. They'd cut the wires, then submerged it in a tank of sand, then took it to a secluded area.

The next call came in about ten minutes later. The second suspect had been on foot as well. Detained outside of Grogan's trying to leave a backpack in a trash can along the runner's route. Tadgh wondered if the pub had been chosen because it was a Garda hang out, or a tourist attraction, or was just some random trash bin on a major street. The run would have gone by the bin in ten minutes, but Tadgh's alert had assured that the runners were intercepted, the event abandoned. That left only the van and the monster driving it.

* * *

TADGH SAW THE VAN, even before his uniformed partner. "Call it in. Go in the shop where you can't be seen. Call it in."

"I'm not bloody leaving you!" Tadgh kept them hidden just around the corner of an alley. He looked at his phone. In fifteen minutes it would be the start of lunch time. The doors to the Leinster House would have people coming out to go to the pubs and shops for a midday meal. "Ye need to go. You're too conspicuous in that uniform. You'll likely scare him off. Go inside that shop and call it in. I need bomb techs here yesterday."

"He knows what you look like."

"No, his brother knows what I look like. He doesn't. I've shaved and I'm wearing a hat. He won't know me. Just go and do it. Now. He's waiting for the lunch crowd, most likely. We've got fifteen minutes at the most. Go, for fuck sake!"

* * *

CHARLIE AND PATRICK headed down a main avenue of Dublin 2, headed for Tadgh's location. According to the radio call by his uniformed partner, he'd spotted the van near the Irish Parliament building. Charlie's heart was racing. The bomb techs were on their way, but it was lunch time in a major city, and they were having trouble getting through the center of town. "Where would he go? If he drove the van to a safe place, where would he go?"

Patrick's eyes were wide. "You don't think he'd try to get it out of the city?" But as soon as he said it, he knew the truth. If it came down to blowing up on a crowded street in front of a government building, or trying to outrun the timer, Tadgh would do it.

Just as they rounded a corner, they smacked right into Zaid again. "I sent my son to the hospital. I go with you. I may know the man's face." Charlie didn't have time to argue, she just ran with Patrick and Zaid behind her.

* * *

TADGH APPROACHED the van from behind. It was running but idling. The parking lights were on, so all he needed to do was get the jump on the man, make sure he didn't put it in drive and hit the gas. He came along the driver's side and saw an arm hanging out with a cigarette. The man was talking to someone, but he couldn't tell if he was on the phone or someone was in the car with him. His pistol was out, his partner waiting impatiently at a distance.

He exhaled for one pause then snatched the man's arm, cranking down like a well pump handle until the man screamed bloody murder.

His pistol was at the man's temple before he could move. The sliding door of the passenger side swung open and someone ran, but he would have to leave him to his partner. He couldn't take his eyes off this one. It was him. The eyes were all he needed to see. That sketch had been amazing.

"You're too late. Even if you get the bomb men here. There are too many."

Tadgh ignored the comment. The bomb was not the immediate threat. "Put your other hand on the window or I will break this arm in two." He gave the arm a tweak, just to make his point. The man's face was pure hatred. Luckily, there was no sort of remote or detonator in the other hand. The man put his hand up, reaching toward the window.

"Now, reach to the outside door handle and open the door with that hand." The man's smile was evil. That was the only word that would sufficiently describe it. Just when Tadgh thought he would comply, he pulled something out from between his legs.

The muzzle was a surprise. Guns weren't easy to get in Ireland. The thought was clear, silly almost, as he pulled his own trigger, and heard the man's gun report in kind.

Tadgh kept his gaze steady on the man. He was slumped over the steering wheel, bleeding from his head. Tadgh reached in and took the weapon out of his hand. Then he opened the door, and pulled the man out. The man's body fell limply to the ground, eyes blank. Tadgh hope to God there was a hell, and that this man was in it. The voice he heard behind him was familiar. "Is this him? Is this the man who killed Eve?" Tadgh looked up and Liam's face was uncharacteristically stoic.

"Yes, it is. He gave me no choice. It was him or me."

"I understand. It should have been me who killed him. But if it wasn't me, I'm glad it was you."

* * *

CHARLIE WATCHED as the young Middle-Eastern man ran away from a uniformed officer. Before she or Patrick could even act, Zaid ran full force and clotheslined the guy in the throat with his arm. The kid was squealing on the ground, covering his face. The officer who had been pursuing him stopped, astonished. Then blinked at Patrick. "Take him, brother! I need to go back! O'Brien is alone with the other one!" Then he did an about face and ran back toward the Parliament building.

Patrick quickly cuffed the young man, calling for a vehicle to pick him up. He looked at Zaid who had his foot on the young man's neck. "You can let him go now."

Zaid looked at Charlie, shrugging casually. "He run. Now, he no run."

Charlie slapped him on the shoulder. "Stay with Patrick. And thank you. That was a Super Bowl worthy tackle."

Zaid laughed. "I like the rugby."

Charlie was running then, Patrick screaming for her to let him go. "Dammit, Charlie!" But, she was gone. Tadgh was facing off with that murdering monster. She had to get to him. That's when she heard the gun shot...no, not one shot. Two shots in rapid succession.

* * *

THE UNIFORMED OFFICER arrived to find Tadgh standing over the man's body. He was calling an ambulance and for a Garda escort to follow the ambulance. Then he looked at him. "Check in with dispatch as well, on the radio. Tell them we have the suspect, don't say he's dead. Just say we have him and ask for the location on the bomb techs. We need them now. Like right now. I need an ETA."

He did as he was told, and the dispatch answered. Ten minutes. Eight if they were lucky. He went around to the open sliding door. "Jesus Christ. There are at least two dozen in here. All on separate timers. You can't defuse them all at once. When one goes off, it will blow the rest." They were a mix of pipe and pressure cooker IEDs. Along with several gallons of fuel. Tadgh was afraid to move anything. The timers were counting down, detonation set for eleven minutes.

This was not going to work. He couldn't wait. The officer and Liam were next to him. "Tell them to head toward Sandymount. Take another route and head toward the strand. I can outrun this clock if I push it. I'll get as close as I can. And tell them to shut down the main road. Get everyone the hell out of my way!"

He closed the sliding door and as he went to sit in the driver's seat, he saw that Liam had climbed in the other door. "No! Get out! I do this alone."

"No, brother." His voice was soft, steady, like they were discussing their favorite book. "No. You go, I go." Then he saw Charlie running toward them. No way was she going to get in this van. Liam saw her too. "She'll try it, you know she will. Hit the gas, Tadgh. Go!"

* * *

CHARLIE WATCHED with horror as the van pulled away with Tadgh driving it and Liam in the passenger seat. The officer was left at the scene with the suspect's body. He was calling for a transport as well as instructions to close the main road and send the bomb techs to the Sandymount Strand. He was also screaming at the gathering crowd, because this had gone down in the middle of the work week in a big city. People had seen the confrontation.

The beach. They're taking it to the beach. She grabbed her phone and dialed, but Tadgh didn't pick up. Liam did. "You tell him to wait for the bomb techs! You tell him, Liam!" She was screaming now.

"There are too many and not enough time, love. I'm sorry. This is the only answer."

"NO! You stop that van and both of you get out!"

"I'm sorry, love. I'll take care of him." He hung up on her.

Charlie was screaming at her phone, even though he'd hung up. That's when two different marked cars showed up. One with Patrick and the young accomplice riding along, the other was for this piece of shit at her feet, but he didn't need a ride. He needed a body bag. The ambulance was right behind them. She looked at Patrick. "We have to go after them."

Patrick didn't hesitate. Charlie hopped in the back seat of the second police car and he got in the front. "Drive to the strand," he told the uniformed patrolman. "As fast as you can."

* * *

TADGH WAS WEAVING in and out of traffic at an obscene rate of speed, when they got farther out, closer to the water, the roads began to clear. "I can't believe you followed me." Tadgh growled. "How long?"

"Since the hospital. I'm rather impressive at it. I may have missed my calling." Tadgh snorted, ready to come back with a retort.

That's when he noticed the police and fire vehicles blocking intersections, police with bullhorns telling people to get off the street. *Thank God.* He winced when they hit a bump, his eyes watering. That's when Liam saw the blood.

"Holy God, you're hit?"

"He got a shot off. It went straight through the door. Luckily I'm a better aim." He was smiling.

"It's nothing to bloody smile about. How bad is it? Where did he hit you?"

"Just at the waist. I don't feel like I'm dying, if that makes ye feel better."

Liam was digging under Tadgh's coat, mumbling something about him being an eejit. "It looks like it went through. Ye've got an exit wound. That's not good, but it's better than having the bullet bounce around in there and not come out. I think it missed the kidney. Jesus Christ,. there was an ambulance on the way, you daft bastard! What were you thinking?"

Tadgh swerved around another car, honking as he went up on the sidewalk. "Hold on!" He clipped a trash can as he righted the vehicle. "I was thinking kaboom. In case you haven't noticed, there's a shit ton of explosives back there. Check the timers and quit pecking at me!"

Liam unbuckled, turning around. "We've got three minutes and twenty seconds. How far are we?" Tadgh laid on the horn, and then gunned through an intersection. "We're almost there. It's going to be tight." His phone was ringing. "Answer it."

"Aye, I see you!" Liam was looking in the mirror. "The bomb guys, they're behind us. They said to stop at the strand and they'll take it from there."

"Tell them to hang back. When we hit the sand and jump out, this whole thing is going up. Tell them there are a couple dozen separate devices and ten gallons of petrol in the back."

They reached the access road to the Sandymount beach and Tadgh was relieved to see no cars. It was about 35 degrees and drizzling, so the weather had worked in their favor. No beach combers. He slowed down, right before the beach. "Get out."

"Piss off. Drive."

"I got this. Go. Now."

"Push on, Tadgh."

Tadgh looked at him fiercely. "You'll get out as soon as I hit the water. Promise me."

Liam, looked back. "One minute, brother. Tick tock."

"Promise me. I won't be able to live with it, Liam. Promise. Eve would want you to keep going. Promise me or we're both dead. I won't leave you."

Liam nodded, exhaling on a shuddering breath. "Aye. I'll get out. Now finish this." That's when Tadgh drove over the concrete walkway, hit a bench, and gunned it right into the surf. Both doors flew open at once, Tadgh got out and his feet sunk into the surf. The wound in his side screamed for attention as he made his way through the water and wet sand as quickly as he could, his jeans tugging at the waves. Then Liam was next to him, hoisting an arm under him. They ran and Tadgh saw the bomb techs pulling up.

"Get back! Get the hell back!" They ran toward the concrete building, that housed the public toilets, just as the van exploded. One loud boom, then the bigger one to follow, when the rest of the bombs followed, igniting the gasoline. Tadgh turned around just in time to see the rolling ball of fire go up, and shrapnel fly outward. He swung Liam around the building as it flew by them. He looked at the bomb tech vehicle as the screws and ball bearings that had been inside the pressure cookers were now embedded in the glass and metal of the front of their truck. They threw it in reverse as the third explosion happened.

* * *

THE EXPLOSION ROCKED the core of the city. Charlie screamed as she saw the ball of fire go up in the air. She'd heard the communication on the radio. The bomb team had been told to back off, that there was no time. "Oh, God! Patrick! Did they get there? Did they get clear?" Patrick was dead quiet, watching the fire and smoke. The officer screeched to a halt when he saw the bomb technicians throw it in reverse, a third explosion going off. Patrick jumped out of the vehicle, opening the back door for Charlie. She looked on in horror as she searched in vain for Tadgh and Liam. Patrick's wail of agony shot like ice water up her spine. The van was fully engulfed.

Patrick's hands were in his hair, eyes blurring. "Oh, God no!" He ran at the burning van and the police officer who had driven them grabbed him in a bear hug from behind. "No, O'Brien. You can't. That fire is too hot. You'd never get near it."

That's when Charlie saw Tadgh and Liam come from behind the small concrete building. She ran and Patrick was right behind her. She launched herself at Tadgh. Liam was saying something, telling her something, but she didn't care. They were on the ground, in the sand and she was kissing him all over his face. "You're an idiot! You're so stupid! I love you so much! Oh, God! You jackass! I love you!" Tadgh was laughing and groaning.

"For God's sake! Charlie!" Liam yelled it and everyone stopped, looking at him.

"Don't stop her, this is just getting good." Patrick was smiling.

"Oh, for the love of Christ. He's been shot!"

Charlie was struck dumb. Then she looked at Tadgh, sprawled out under her, smiling. "Don't listen to him, darlin'. Give us another kiss." He moved in and she put a hand over his face, then looked between them. Blood, lots of it. She jumped back, rolling off him. Then she smacked him. "You're so stupid! You took off like some sort of action hero with a bullet hole in you? What were you thinking?"

"There's a paramedic on the way, oh and look. Here's Da," Liam said casually.

Sean was running, and stopped short, looking at the van, then at all three of his boys. "I can't take my eyes off you three for a minute. Never could."

Then they were laughing, Tadgh wincing as he turned in on his wound. "Ach, Christ. Don't make me laugh!"

Sullivan was next. He took in the hysterical group, the rubble, the van that continued to burn the fuel off that had been in the interior of the van as well as in the gas tank. "Well, now. There'll be no keeping this out of the news." That's when the ambulance pulled in followed by a camera crew from the BBC Ireland.

CHAPTER 23

*T*adgh was wheeled out of recovery, drowsy and thick headed. They'd taken him to St. James Hospital on Liam's insistence. When they rolled him into his hospital room, he looked over at his roommate. His throat ached, thick with emotion. Sal looked awful. He was bandaged and had tubes sticking out of him. He was out of ICU, however, which just proved how strong he was. Sal stirred and Leyla took his hand. "Hello big man. You have a new roommate."

"Aye, I heard you were layin' about while I did all the hard stuff."

He saw a shake start in Sal's body. He was laughing. He croaked in his strange, unique accent. Part bred from his Iraqi parents, part learned from his Irish neighbors. "Don't make me laugh, you bastard." Then Tadgh was laughing, groaning as his stitches pulled. He got out of bed, making sure his ass wouldn't flash Sal's nearest and dearest. He wheeled his IV cart alongside him.

"Tadgh! Your doctor will have a stroke if he sees you! Get back in bed."

He waved her off. "I'll do. It's easier for me to move than for you to roll him."

He came around the bed and she gave him her chair. Sal took in the sight of him. "You're way prettier than me in the aftermath. She wouldn't tell me what was going on. What the hell happened?" His words were muffled, his jaw and lips swollen from the beating he took.

"I took a 9mm round in the side. It's fine. It didn't hit anything important."

Sal's eyes were grim. "You might be dead if he'd gone a few inches inward, you daft idiot. What were you thinking?"

"I was thinking a great many things at the time, but the main one was that I wasn't going to let him hurt any more people."

Sal listened as he got the full telling of the race for Sandymount Strand. "Have you lost your mind?"

"Not at all, brother. And it was all grand in the end. I felt like quite the action hero. The explosion was a hell of a sight, and no one was hurt. That alone was worth the risk."

"Where's Charlie? Is she okay?"

"Aye, she is. A bit put out with me, but fine."

This is when Leyla interjected. "And who can blame her? You two running around getting beat and shot and doing car chases. You're lucky she didn't box your ears in front of that news camera."

Sal laughed and groaned in pain. "I'm lucky I'm so injured or she'd likely beat me."

"Don't worry, she bashed me a good one when she showed up to the hospital." Tadgh's voice was dry.

"You're takin' a piss." Sal looked at him, then at Leyla who had the good sense to look contrite. "You hit him?"

She shrugged. "I was emotional."

Tadgh moved on, shaking his head."And as for Charlie, she's at the police station now. Her boss got on a plane yesterday, when she got the first two. He's dropped his family off in Kerry for a holiday while he takes care of the FBI's press release and sees her through some of the red tape this will involve."

Sal's mouth was dry, so he licked his lips. Leyla helped him get a sip of water. "Did you get the other girls?"

"Other girls?" Tadgh shook his head, trying to clear the memories

SHADOW GUARDIAN

of right before he was shot. The girl Halima, the other captives. Leyla and Sal cursed in unison as Tadgh began removing the IV from his arm.

* * *

CHARLIE STOOD outside Sullivan's office and turned when she heard clapping. She peered down the hallway as she saw the men and women of the department lining the hall clapping for...she did a double take. "WHAT are you doing out of the hospital?"

Sullivan got out of his chair, looked out of his doorway and cursed. "Jesus wept. Deliver me from O'Briens."

Sean and Patrick were walking into the room and gave a simultaneous curse as well.

Tadgh walked with purpose, ignoring the burning pain and pulling stitches in his side. In the blur of being shot, a race to beat the clock, and an exploding van, he'd pushed the thought of other captives to the recesses of his mind.

"I'm fine. It's just a flesh wound."

"Aye, and did your doctor release you or did you leave AMA?" Charlie asked, hands on her hips.

"Not to mention that you're supposed to be on administrative leave until you're cleared for duty and they take a full account of the shooting." Sullivan said. He came in front of Tadgh's line of vision. "Ye took a life. You need time. You need to see the department shrink. Did you file the report, even?"

Tadgh ignored the question. "I understand that I took a life. Normally that would really screw with my head, but the man killed Eve and he shot me. I'll sleep at night. Better now, because he's dead." He shook himself. "As much as I love this psychobabble bonding, it's not why I'm here. There are more girls. Like the one Uncle Sean found."

Sean nodded. "I interviewed the girl. She confirmed she was the one that they brought in to Sal while they worked him over. She and the other lad, the boy that Patrick arrested, were the only two who had been kept underground. She doesn't know where they are keeping the rest. They kept her hooded when they transported her. She thought she was still in England, the poor lass. We're taking a quick break, then we'll interview the young man. He was in the van with your suspect. Although, we don't think he was one of the main members of this group. He shows old bruises, some electrical burns. I think he must have been subjected to their training as well. I think he'll talk."

Tadgh watched through the glass as the young man was interrogated. If it was discovered that he'd been kidnapped, forced into this situation, they'd send him home. If his family was here, if he'd been recruited, he would be tried and punished along with the others.

As it turned out, the boy's family lived in Dublin. He was nineteen and had gone to work to help support them. That's when he'd been recruited. He was scared, and he was cooperative, which would work in his favor. The only thing they had on him was that he'd been in the van with Khassad. He swore, of course, that he hadn't wanted to go. He was used at several points in the city, to go ahead on foot, then would report back to Khassad. They'd apparently meant to target Trinity, but when the security measures had been too high, they'd gone to both Christ Church and St. Patrick's. But, the Garda had anticipated the targets and been ahead of them. The Parliament had its own security and some barricades. They'd agreed to handle their own building security, freeing up the Garda to handle softer targets. It hadn't been enough, though. Tadgh had been there and seen the layout. Right at lunch time, the casualties would have been catastrophic.

This young man was from Syria. The others, however, were lured in from other war torn or developing countries. They checked the rest of the underground tunnel. They hadn't found the other people. But according to Halima, the young girl that Sean had found wearing a bomb on the street corner, there had been thirteen of them. She said that they'd been moved back and forth a few at a time, and one girl had gone missing after a while. According to Halima, they'd always been hooded and in the confines of the van. They'd been kept in the unused storage area in the basement of an apartment complex. No light, barely fed, given buckets to use for a toilet. There was one area for the women, another for the men.

Tadgh shook his head, overcome with weariness and sadness. "Most of these young people just needed jobs, money to send home, or a safe place to live and start over. I don't want this whole thing to color relations between the Irish and the refugees. Most of them are good people. Look at Zaid."

Charlie understood. A few bad apples and all that. The problem was that the bad apples recruited and sometimes they did worse, like they'd done with these poor people. Tricking them and holding them prisoner until they didn't know who they were, where they were. They only knew fear and obedience. They'd been trafficked as slaves for the purpose of making them martyrs. Tadgh looked at Charlie. "Is it possible that they have Tatyana's sister? That they played her? She did say she tracked her here."

"It is possible."

* * *

TATYANA SAT motionless as Charlie laid out the facts for her about the other women and men who were being "trained." Apparently the instructors used the American women by torturing them in front of the group of captives. *This will happen to you if you don't do as you're told.* They'd also lied, told them they'd send money home to their families. Using the age old method of withholding food, stopping any outside contact with the world, and fear mixed with propaganda, they'd worked to condition them into murderers. It hadn't worked on Halima. Tadgh suspected, however, that it had worked on the young man who had been in the van with Khassad. He'd been able to come and go since he'd not been smuggled into the country, so as to not raise suspicion, while the others were held captive. He was cooperating, however, and that was something. Now, the question was, would it work on Tatyana?

"Your sister could be among them. Did you ever see this group of women? Do you know for sure they aren't the ones who have her?"

Tatyana shook her head. "No, he wouldn't do that. Not to his own countryman."

"Ah yes, but Nika wasn't a man. Neither are you. No offense, but I'm not buying the gender equality line from these guys. Not after what I've seen."

Tatyana wasn't sharing, and Charlie suspected it was because she didn't really know. She'd also had suspicions that there had been a sick sort of romantic entanglement with the elder brother, Khassad. If her sister was among the captive *trainees*, they'd have never let her in the same room with her. Tatyana jumped as someone pounded on the door. Sean opened it, and she saw the other men behind him. "We don't need her. We've got the location. You'll think I'm takin' a piss when I tell you where they are."

* * *

RIGHT UNDER THEIR NOSES. Three buildings to the east of Sal's surveillance flat. That was the problem with locked buildings. Safer for the inhabitants, but they'd never had access to the interior of any of the other buildings. Even the owner hadn't known Sal's true identity. They'd put the flat under a false name.

When Charlie had interviewed the young man they had in a cell at headquarters, he'd described two more key players who lived in the area. He was positive that the rest of the residents in the area had not been involved other than the ones they knew about. Recruiting hadn't bore a lot of fruit among most of the refugees. *Because of men like Zaid who watched their sons. Taught them to embrace their new life.*

They were looking for two more, three counting whoever guarded the captives they were trying to find. There was a man in his mid-twenties and his wife, who was actually an Irish citizen and had converted. They maneuvered through the building and then followed the east stairway down. The door was out of view, past the residential part of the building. A closed off, leaky storage area that the landlord said they never used. There weren't boilers or any other plumbing access that might have a maintenance man coming in to check. The landlord was being questioned, of course, because they'd gained access to the area somehow. When the unit commander of the entry team, Officer Rahn, tried the key, it didn't work. "They changed the lock. It looks like they forced their way in and changed out all of the hardware."

Just as he started to go full door kicker with the battering ram, someone came down the stairs. Charlie and Tadgh were in the back of the line, per the boss's orders. Armed Response Team officers would lead the charge with them in the rear. It was those two, and one other officer, at the end of the row of Garda officers. They saw the man, and it had to be the one described by the younger bomber that they had in custody. He bolted like a startled rabbit and the chase was on.

"We've got him, stay put!" Charlie yelled. The young ARU officer and Charlie took off behind Tadgh, pursuing the man. He cut through the buildings, weaving through the various walkways and Tadgh was slowing down. "You're going to pull your stitches. Stand down!" Charlie screamed as she ran. She was fast for such a small woman. The younger officer was also fast, but weighed down with weapons and armor. They still had the little piece of shit in their sight, though, and he tried to cut through the garden area of Sal and Zaid's building. Abdul, Zaid's son, saw them coming and jumped in front of the man, but he knocked him down.

That's when Charlie looked in horror as he ran straight for Zaid's younger daughter, Rasha. She was coming through the walkway, and she saw him knock her brother down. Charlie didn't even have time to scream. The man was coming at her and she took her skateboard like a baseball bat, slamming him in the face. His feet went over his head. It was a thing of sheer beauty. He landed with a thump and was out cold.

The officer running with Charlie yelled. "Nice shot, lass! Holy shit!" Zaid had joined the fray just in time to see the take down.

The girl stood over her victim, looked at her father, then at Charlie and shrugged. "He run. Now, he no run." She looked at Zaid and his face was priceless.

"Like father like daughter," Charlie said with a grin.

He looked at Charlie, then back down at the man his fifteen year old daughter had just flattened. Then he burst out laughing. "Yes, she's my warrior."

Tadgh was next to them, holding his side and laughing as well. "Well, officer if you would be so kind as to cuff this bastard and call for a transport, we've got to get back."

Charlie looked back as the people came out of their houses. They were cheering. She wasn't sure if it was for the Garda or little Rasha, but she was sure that kid was going to be talking about this until she was a grandmother.

THE SMELL IS what hit them first. Charlie was sickened as she saw the foam, the cardboard, the old blankets, all used to muffle sound. Rahn had taken out, with frightening efficiency, the man they'd posted guard inside the storage area. The flash bang had sufficiently stunned him and he hadn't put up much of a fight. Then slowly she started seeing the movement, heard the chains. There was a makeshift barrier between the males and females. Tarps hung from rafters and tied into place. The human waste and unwashed flesh was pungent. There were air fresheners everywhere, bleach soaked cloths that made the air almost toxic. They'd been trying to mask the smell of a dozen people being held captive. The air was stagnant, no vents or windows. No wonder they didn't use it for storage anymore. No ventilation and a leaky foundation made for mold and mildew and damp rot. There were five men and seven women. Barely, given their ages. The officers were horrified. To be kept in such conditions. They were all dehydrated, malnourished, and terrified. Such darkness in their eyes, like they weren't sure what new devil had come to torture them. Charlie was shaking with rage, but they needed to act. Now. The medic they had with them determined who needed an ambulance, and who could be taken in a Garda wagon. The guard was quick to rat out the other man and his wife. They'd caught the man, now they needed to get his wife. Charlie went up to the apartment with Tadgh and Sullivan.

The appearance of the woman who answered the door was a surprise, although it shouldn't have been. Fair hair, blue steely gaze. She was in full abaya and hijab. Her Dubliner accent at odds with it all. When Charlie saw the young girl hovering in the bedroom, she went mental. The girl was only about sixteen, and she was, after speaking with her, determined to be the man's second wife. Charlie noticed that she had a swollen abdomen and a black eye. She was very pretty, which is undoubtedly why she'd been taken out of the population to serve as a spare wife. Charlie went over to the woman who answered the door. "Who hit her?"

"She's disobedient. She must be taught. A wife's place is to submit. Both to her husband and his first wife."

Charlie looked at her knuckles and saw the abrasions. "You hit a pregnant girl?"

The woman's jaw tightened. "She was dis…"

The punch came out of thin air. The woman went flying across the room, landing on the sofa. Tadgh grabbed Charlie as Sullivan grabbed the woman. "She struck me! I want her arrested!"

"You shouldn't have resisted." Sullivan said calmly.

"Filthy pigs!" The woman spat on the floor.

"Aye, I've been called worse. Now, let's get some ice on that cheek and get you to your cell."

CHAPTER 24

*C*harlie walked into the police station, waving at Janet who was working the front desk. "Ye did good, lass. I'm sorry to see you go, but I'm glad it's over."

Charlie didn't want to think about that...about leaving. She just hugged Janet, handing her the bullet proof vest she'd taken on loaner. As she walked into the main area of the detective headquarters, she saw her boss talking to DC Sullivan. "Assistant Director Schroeder, so glad to see you." She shook his hand. He was beaming.

"You did well Special Agent Ryan. You made ten apprehensions and rescued thirteen victims of human trafficking. Are you bucking for a promotion?" He was all smiles, and she warmed at his approval.

"We. I couldn't have done this without a huge and amazing team of local officers. And one particularly gifted tech guy. Oh, and a psychic eight year old."

He was laughing at the last bit, until she cocked a brow. "Really? Well, I can't wait to hear all about it. However, I have enough for the press conference. Rumor has it that you haven't slept in a while."

She looked at Sullivan. "Go home, lass. And take this lunatic with you. He looks ready to fall over." She looked behind her, her face softening. Tadgh's eyes were bright, looking at her boss then at her. *I'm leaving. I'm sorry I have to leave you.* She smiled sadly. "I am, for once, not going to argue with you. Let's go, O'Brien."

"Are you living in the same area?" Schroeder asked, his gaze speculative. He narrowed his eyes at Tadgh.

Charlie cleared her throat. "Yes. Practically neighbors."

"I think my city has rather grown on the lass. You'll be lucky if I don't lose all scruples and try to poach her right out from under your nose." Sullivan gave Schroeder a wry look.

"Oh, no. You are not getting my best and brightest. You'll leave me with a bunch of tax attorneys and all their paperwork skills." Schroeder said dryly. She heard Sullivan laugh as she left for some well needed rest.

* * *

THEY'D GONE to separate flats, both needing a shower. The filthy conditions that the captives had been kept in were like an unholy entity, needing to be cleansed off their bodies. Each apartment only had one small shower. Charlie took her time, letting the tragedy of the last few weeks rinse off of her. She'd grabbed a large t-shirt from Tadgh's drawer, wanting the soft cotton and feel of him on her skin. She rubbed lotion on her body, needing to nourish her skin and feel human again. When she came out of the bathroom, pink and clean, he was waiting at the kitchen counter, propped on a stool. He had pajama pants on, but no shirt. He was so beautiful, his hair wet and spiked like he hadn't bothered with a comb after he'd toweled himself off.

"How are your stitches?" She looked at his side, noticing he'd changed the bandage.

"They're fine. I barely notice them." He looked her up and down. "Christ, Charlie. You're so beautiful. Your hair is in a wet tangle, your skin's flushed." He got up and walked to her. She wrapped around him, taking his kiss. His breath was labored, his noises hungry.

"I need you. I need all of you." His voice was hoarse, edgy. He backed her up against the other bedroom door, kissing the hell out of her. Then he flipped her around. "Grab on to the bar. Both hands. Please." His voice was pure sex in her ear, half pleading, half demanding. She looked up and saw what he meant. The pull-up bar that was mounted in the doorway was above her head. "Both hands, Charlie."

She did it, because she knew whatever he had planned was going to blow her mind. He was undoubtedly going to slip inside her from behind. Then she was surprised when he got on his knees behind her. She groaned as her head fell back, knowing where this was headed. He slid her panties off and then he was there, right where she wanted him. He split her thighs with his hands as he tasted her from behind. She arched, pressing into him shamelessly. He loved it. She could feel his moans vibrating on her core as he drank her in, penetrated her, drove her wild. When she came, she screamed his name, hanging on to the bar so that she didn't sink to the floor in a puddle. He held her up, relentless as he kept going, spinning her into a mindless tornado of sensation and pleasure. Then he was turning her around. She was limp, using the door for support as he hoisted her off her feet, impaling her with one thrust.

* * *

"I'M SORRY, MO GHRÁ." He whispered against her neck as he curled around her in the bed. "I know you were tired. I just couldn't wait. I needed ye so desperately, I thought I'd die from it."

She burrowed against him as he clicked the light off. "Don't ever apologize, Tadgh. You're the most beautiful thing in my life."

Then don't leave me. I don't want to live mine without you. His heart was breaking. He couldn't ask her to stay, he knew that. He'd be a selfish bastard if he did. She wouldn't, and it would spoil their last days together. But, a little part of him wanted her to think outside the box. He'd finally found his mate, and the losing of her was going to be a sort of death. Even as he said it in his mind, he thought of Liam. At least he knew that she'd be out there somewhere, living her life. Alive. Liam had truly lost Eve forever.

He'd belonged to someone for a time. Someone who had loved

him completely. Who'd really seen him down to his soul. He was grateful to have had something that was his alone. He just didn't know how he was going to get through this with his dignity intact. How he was going to keep from throwing himself at her feet before she got on that plane, begging like the pathetic sod he was. *Keep me. Please keep me.*

He kissed her hair. The room was cool, the blinds shifting with a wintery breeze. "I can shut the window, it's probably too cold for you." she said, getting up to tend to it. He pulled her to him, stopping her.

"No, my love. Leave it. I'll keep you warm. It feels nice. It feels clean." Then he fell asleep against her, surrendering to the pain pills and the bodily trauma, and to the complete exhaustion he felt, having loved her so thoroughly. He slept and so did she.

CHARLIE WOKE TO MALE VOICES. She put her hand on the place next to her in bed, and the sheets were cool and empty. She climbed out of bed, closing the window as she shivered. She liked a cool room at night, but morning was different. Leaving the warmth of her nest, the cold was less inviting. She looked out at the morning sky and her heart sank. The grey skies reflected the current mood. She'd be leaving. Not right away, of course. They had to deal with the red tape of prosecution and the process of interviewing the thirteen people who had been held captive in that dark basement. She needed to find out about the human trafficking ring, if there were any more coming, or somewhere else in the city, and if any of them were American citizens. But she would leave, and a piece of her heart, a large, important piece, would be forever wandering this wet and ancient city. It would be housed within a set of golden, hazel eyes.

Charlie couldn't remember the last time she'd slept so late. It was ten o'clock. She walked out of the room, hearing Tadgh's voice as he spoke to his cousin. "I'm sorry. I know it was a difficult evening. I can't even imagine. She's laid to rest, then?"

Liam's voice was rough, tired. He'd gone to Eve's family service the night before. She was from County Cork. Her funeral had been at seven this morning. A quick and painful affair that had done more harm than good, by the sounds of Liam's voice. Then he'd come straight here, to see Tadgh. To talk to him. She didn't want to interrupt, and as she started to retreat, she caught their conversation.

"You need to find a way to make it work with Charlie. You never know how long ye've got in this world. I should have married Eve two years ago. She'd been afraid of upsetting her parents. She was young to marry and there's a bit of an age difference, but we loved each other. I should have convinced her. Moved into married housing at the university. Now I'm left with nothing. Ye need to make it work."

"She can't leave her job, Liam. And, this thing with her brother is serious. He needs her. What I want, and what I can ask of her, are two different things. She's the breath of my body, brother. But she's not free to stay."

She leaned against the door jam. She shouldn't be listening, but she couldn't make herself move. That's when Liam said something that surprised her. "So, why don't you follow her? If you love her and she loves you, you can quit this bloody job and move to America. I don't want to lose you, brother. It'll kill all of us. But she's your mate. You can't just let her walk away."

"I can't do that." Charlie's disappointment was an ache in her belly.

"And why the bloody hell not?"

"Because, Liam. She never asked." There was a large pause, and Charlie put her hand over her mouth. The tears were pouring down her face.

"Would you say yes?"

"Aye, I would. I'd leave it all and marry her. I'd help her fight for her brother. I'd wait tables again if I had to. Aye brother, I'd say yes."

* * *

Tadgh cracked the door to the bedroom and saw that Charlie was awake, lying on her side with Duncan curled up with her. She was just staring at the wall, stroking the purring cat. "I made you breakfast, darlin'. Are you ready to eat? I know it's been a while."

She looked at him and smiled. "I'm starved. Thank you."

She could smell something divine wafting from the kitchen. "Is that pancakes?"

"Waffles, actually. My ma makes them better, but I think you'll like them."

She looked at the stacks of waffles and moaned. Some had preserves and cream, some had Nutella and bananas. He'd also made rashers and bangers. "You, Tadgh O'Brien, are a keeper." He smiled, but it didn't reach his eyes.

"Well, not so far, but thank you." He poured her a cup of coffee. She thought about the men in his family, so good to their wives, their sisters, their mothers. She couldn't ask him to leave his family. No matter how badly she wanted to stick him in her suitcase and tote him off to America.

"It's hard to believe how little time has actually passed since I came here. Weeks. It seems like much longer. It feels like home here." She looked at him. "I wish my life was different. I'm sorry for both of us that it isn't." She shrugged. "Now, I go back to an awful set of parents and try to take my brother from one crappy city to another. Not that Cleveland is all bad, but the area they're living in is rather depressed. You're lucky, Tadgh. Your life is your own."

"I understand. You don't have to explain. I knew where this was headed when I fell for you." He wiped down the counter. "Are you done with that, then?" He motioned to her empty plate.

She nodded. "Stuffed." She stood up, walking around the breakfast bar to put her plate in the sink. He came behind her and pressed into her.

"It's occurred to me that you'll go back to America with an image of my cousin's spectacular ass having sex in the kitchen." He turned her around and hiked her up on the counter. "We need to remedy that. Erase it with a new memory." Then his mouth was on her as he pressed his hard cock between her legs. He fumbled with his bottoms and she felt a rip as he tore her panties aside. He met her eyes as he filled her. He made a strangled sound. "You're always ready. Bloody hell!" He moved inside her as she took her shirt off. She leaned back on her hands, stretching back and arching as he thrust into her. His eyes fixated on her flushed nipples, her smooth skin, her glossy eyes as she succumbed to the pleasure. His face was pained as it looked her over. Like he was memorizing her. "Tadgh," she groaned, the tears starting to pool in her eyes.

He ran a hand over her ass and under, feeling where they were joined. Tadgh touched her taught skin as he felt the presence of himself taking her, filling her, gliding deep. "I feel us, Charlie. We're one. Right now, we're one." His chest quivered, his breath stolen.

Then she put her palm over his heart. "And, here. Here, we're one. Tadgh." He cried out and let go, feeling her follow him with her own climax. When they were spent, completely destroyed, he kissed her. She wiped the tears from his face, and he kissed hers away in kind.

CHAPTER 25

*C*harlie sat across from Tatyana. The woman's face was blank of emotion. "These questions again? You are starting to bore me."

"No, I think you're going to want to hear this. I won't mince words. I found your sister."

"You lie to me."

Charlie took out the freshly printed copy of the photo she'd taken in the hospital. Tatyana shot upright. "Nika! I want to see her! Why is she so thin?"

"They starved them. There were thirteen in all. So far. Eight women, five men. All in their late teens and early twenties."

"Russian pigs!"

Charlie put the photo in front of her, then slid the collage of men's photos next to it. "Guess again. It wasn't Russians. You lied about a lot, including her age and the fact that she was at business school in a Russian city. That was all crap, because you were orphans. She was seventeen when she disappeared, living in an orphanage in Chechnya. You were working, too old to live there, I'd imagine. She disappeared and they told you Russians invaded? Is that right?"

Tatyana's look of horror was something Charlie was going to

remember for a long time. Despite all of the horrible things she'd done, she'd once just been a big sister. That was one thing Charlie understood. "They had her the whole time. They were training her to be a terrorist, just like the girl who carried the bomb a couple of days ago. They targeted young people looking for work visas and orphans that no one would miss. They took them out of several countries, but she was among them. They starved her, beat her, and did other things. I'll let her tell you if she wants to, what those other things were. It's not my place. You're right, by the way. It was one of the things you did tell the truth about. She's a good girl. She didn't deserve this."

The door cracked open and the slender girl walked in. Tatyana's wail raised the hair on Charlie's neck and arms. "I can give you ten minutes, but I can't leave. Do you understand?" Tatyana was sobbing, the girl's head in her lap. She looked up at Charlie. "If what you say is true, I will give you the information you need. You just take care of her. Promise me you'll take care of her."

"She did nothing wrong. If you don't have family back at home, the Irish government will help resettle her. You need to help me, though. You will hold nothing back."

She nodded and squeezed her sister closer.

Charlie leaned against the wall, trying to block out the crying. They had a translator on the other side of the window and the video recording would catch it all. She just needed to block out Tatyana's wailing, and the whimpers of another young woman who'd learned to stay quiet.

Tatyana's voice was hoarse, and Charlie looked up, meeting her eyes. "You never asked why he beat me. Khassad beat me."

"Why? Was it because of me?"

She shook her head. "No. The girl in the street. He wanted me to run her over. I wasn't going to. I was just going to go. He grabbed the wheel. He shoved me against the door and grabbed the wheel and pushed the gasoline pedal. He beat me because I didn't want to run her over with the car."

"We saw a partial video. I have to tell you, though, Tatyana. It won't matter much in the long run. Their deaths are on your hands as well. You weren't a spectator or a victim."

She nodded. "I understand. I just...wanted you to know. I didn't want to kill that girl."

* * *

SCHROEDER WATCHED his favorite agent across the room as the Lord Mayor and the Prime Minister gushed over the job the task force had done. She was tired, sad, and she looked like she was being eaten alive. She'd confided a couple of months ago about her brother, and he knew this overseas assignment had been a hard thing to manage. But something else was amiss, and it had to do with that pretty boy detective. He had the same look of deep despair, and he rarely took his eyes off of Charlie. Not good. Charlie was single and beautiful in a very natural and appealing way. It wasn't any wonder half of the Garda headquarters had fallen for her.

Sullivan leaned over to Assistant Director Schroeder. "It's been going on for a few weeks. The connection was instant. It happens like that with those O'Briens. I'm sorry she's hurting, if it's any consolation. She's a good lass. The best."

Schroeder gave him a sideways glance. "And he's a good man?"

"None better. I knew his da."

"Yeah, well she's got a lot going on back home. Besides a promising career. I hope he's ready to let her go, because she won't be staying."

Sullivan just sighed, because what could he say?

* * *

CHARLIE SAT across from DC Sullivan's desk and he was speechless. "Does your boss know you're talking to me?" She shook her head. "Well, now. He'll likely have my bloody head if this goes the way I think it's going."

"The Prime Minister said anything I needed, that he was in my debt. All I want to know is whether I could legally move to Ireland and get a job with the Garda."

"You're not a citizen, and it's not as easy as you might think to get that done. Unless of course..."

"What?'

"Unless you married an Irishman."

She said nothing and his brows lifted. "Well, then. I guess I'll have a chat with the Prime Minister."

"I'm just inquiring. Nothing's been proposed if you catch my meaning. But if it does happen, I don't want to start at the bottom. I'll do the training, but I keep my seniority."

He laughed. "Do you really think after you stopped a terrorist plot, a human trafficking ring, and caught a serial murder that we would have you in Parking Services?" She smiled. Then she got up to leave.

* * *

THE SUN HAD SET EARLY, December in full swing. Tadgh turned the steaks in the cast iron skillet. Charlie had requested steak tonight. He loved cooking for her, so he didn't mind. She was still interviewing the victims and had taken a thorough statement from Tatyana. The Garda and Coast Guard would take over from there. There was a ship expected, carrying imported goods and ten more victims of human trafficking. This time from Asia. Potential soldiers for the unsavory elements that still hid in Dublin.

He'd visited Sal in the hospital, and was happy to know that he'd be released by the end of the week. Apparently the Prime Minister had gone to him and thanked him personally. Then he'd extended the same offer he'd given Charlie and Tadgh and other key members of the task force. He'd even sent Disneyland Paris tickets to Cora.

Sal had thought about his request, and it had been simple. He wanted to improve the living situation for Zaid and his family. Tadgh had brought Zaid to the hospital that afternoon. His words stuck in Tadgh's brain.

"I don't want more help from the government. They've been very good to us, don't misunderstand. But my friend, I want to be able to take care of my family on my own. I want a well paying job. I am a good interpreter. I want a job so I can move my family out of the flat, get them a garden and a space to play. I want to be independent."

So it was settled. Sal was going to make sure that the Prime Minister found a decent paying job in the government for Zaid. His sons would go to college. His daughters would go to college too, if they wanted. All he wanted was a normal life. To acclimate out of refugee status.

Charlie came through the door smiling. She seemed lighter than she'd been that morning. He was glad. He didn't want her to be sad. He wanted her to be happy. "Did you talk to your brother?"

She nodded. "We have a court date. They want to clear the docket before the new year. The court date is in a week. Two days after I get home."

"I'm glad, Charlie. Good for you. Now, hang on to your hat because this is the best steak you will ever eat. Herb butter, garlic, medium rare."

She sat down at the table. "Have I told you that I love you? And steak? I love steak almost as much."

He leaned down, kissing her as he put a plate in front of her. He poured them both a glass of champagne "We need to celebrate."

They sat down and he toasted. "To emancipating Josh."

She clinked his glass. Then she sipped. "Thanks again for dinner. It was a busy day. I'll make it up to you. I can actually cook, I swear. I make a really good pot roast."

She sawed off a piece of the gorgeous steak he'd made and bit. "Ah, God. This is heaven. Marry me," she groaned.

He smiled as he always did when she teased him like that. His voice was rough, though, less lighthearted than the other exchanges. "Don't tease me, lass." He cleared his throat, suddenly aching and thick. "I'll hold ye to it."

She put her fork down, looking at him. "I'm counting on it."

He looked at her, becoming cross. "Don't, Charlie. It's not so funny anymore."

"I wasn't joking." He looked up into her face and her eyes were intense. "I love you, Tadgh. I don't want this to end. Ever. I want to be the one who keeps you."

His face was unfathomable. "What are you saying?"

She started to get a little worried. "Unless. I mean. If you don't feel the same, I haven't done anything that can't be undone."

He jumped up and pulled her out of the chair. He pulled her face to his. "Are you asking me to come with you?"

"Would you? Would you leave everything and come to America? Leave your family and job and be my husband?"

"Yes." He said it without hesitation.

She smoothed her hand over his face. "And that's why I can do the same for you. I asked Sullivan to cash in my favor with the Prime Minister. If we get married, I'm a citizen. The Garda will start up a Human Trafficking division."

"What about Josh? Charlie, you can't leave him, even for me."

"I won't. If he's emancipated, he'll be part of the package. He goes where I go. If you can't..."

He didn't let her finish. He was kissing her and they were holding each other with a desperation that was born of unimaginable joy. "We'll be brothers. He'll be my family, Charlie. I'll protect and love him like my own blood. I vow it."

She hugged him so tightly around his neck that he could barely breathe, but who the hell needed air anyway?

* * *

CHARLIE LOOKED up as Schroeder came through the door with a scowl on his face. She felt Tadgh and Sullivan stiffen around her. "Isn't this nice? Another meeting I wasn't invited to. So when were you going to tell me that you were poaching my best agent?"

Sullivan stood up and put his hands up. "Now, now. Calm down. I've just given the lass some options. It's not like you've given her any. She's getting married or she's keeping her job. I'm offering her both. Surely you can understand me not wanting to waste such talent. She's going to be a great asset to our department. I was overjoyed when she came to me."

Charlie looked at him like he was insane. He seemed to actually be gloating, which didn't seem his style. "Look boss, I'm sorry but…"

Schroeder put a hand up. "Well, since this meeting is about offering up some options, how about this one? You can't have her."

Charlie looked at him, seeing a side she hadn't before. He was being territorial. "Do you know how rare it is to find an agent with her instincts? I've spent the last twenty years trying to teach lawyers and business majors and linguists how to run an investigation! So, let me repeat myself. You.Can't.Have.Her."

He looked at Charlie, shaking some of the aggression off before he spoke. "I've gone up the chain of command. Our division needs a liaison in Europe. You are officially transferring to an overseas assignment as the American Liaison to Interpol for the International Human Rights Crime Division of the FBI. Nice long title that I made up on the fly, right before the brief. The assignment is for at least three years. Maybe longer, but I bought you three years. They wanted you to live in London or Munich, but I convinced them that the Republic of Ireland would suffice. You've got some leeway as to when, depending on what goes down with your brother, but the position is waiting for you."

Charlie's jaw was practically on the floor. "You did that for me?"

"I did it for the FBI. We need you. And I won't let you go without a fight. I just don't have a long term plan, I'm sorry. You can't stay in Ireland forever."

That's when Tadgh spoke up. "We'll cross that bridge when we come to it."

Schroeder said, "The good news is, we've got three years to sort it out. Now, you'll be on call. It will mean traveling. You need to understand that. You might be in Dublin one week, Barcelona another, Paris the next week. You'll have a broad territory."

She looked at Tadgh. "We'll make it work." Then she hugged her boss for the first time ever. She looked at Sullivan, suddenly guilty that she'd… "Don't go worrying your pretty head about it, lass. I knew once I leaked your defection to his secretary, he'd make his move."

Schroeder looked at him hard, then his face cracked and he laughed. "You bastard. You knew I wouldn't let her go."

Sullivan gave a small shrug. "And, I won't give him up without a fight. So in three years, it's back in the ring, old boy."

* * *

CHARLIE WAS quiet on her way back to the flat. Tadgh wasn't sure why, but as they went into the flat she turned to him. Her face was flushed, but her eyes were direct and her chin up. "What is it, love?"

"I just...I wanted to give you the opportunity to back out of this. When I asked you to marry me, I meant it. But you may have felt pressured, knowing my new job depended on my citizenship. We have three years now. Some time. If you don't want to rush things...I just didn't want you feeling like you got backed into this."

He stalked toward her. Sometimes he was so sweet, so caring. He knew when to give her room, when to ease back and let her work through something. There was nothing of that side of him now. *This. This is the O'Brien male that I've been hearing about. This is the O'Brien man who has only one true mate.*

"How about we scratch the initial deal?" His voice was deep, husky. Then she absorbed his words. He wanted out of their deal. She tensed, trying to back away.

"Okay then. We'll just see..." He kissed her then, rough and demanding.

"This was never about a job," he said against her mouth. "This is about you and me not willing to live apart. Not willing to waste a minute of our lives without each other. So, let me renegotiate."

He pulled her to his body, his arousal hard against her stomach. "Will you marry me, Charlie? Will you stay by my side no matter where we bloody live or no matter where we bloody work? Will you love me forever? Even when I'm old and gray and sagging and have ten grandchildren? Because, that's the only deal that matters to me, mo ghrá."

Tadgh started to laugh as Charlie climbed him. She actually climbed up his body like a little monkey until she was kissing his forehead, perched in his arms, hands in his overgrown hair. She kissed him and squeezed him like someone had just handed her a big puppy. "I love you! Oh, God. I was worried there for a minute you big jerk! I love you!" He smiled against her mouth as she kissed him, and this time it wasn't the same. It was a lover's kiss, and he turned and marched to the bedroom to seal the new deal.

CHAPTER 26

"*I think a child should be allowed to take his father's or mother's name at will on coming of age. Paternity is a legal fiction.*"
James Joyce

CUYAHOGA COUNTY JUVENILE **Court House**
Cleveland, Ohio

"I'm scared, Charlie. Dad's been really bad at home. He's been keeping his hands off me. I think he was afraid of putting a mark on me. But mom's been crying a lot. I think he's been on her while I'm at school. He said he'll never let me leave. He said he has rights. That I'm his."

"You belong to yourself. Do you hear me, Josh? He's never been a real father. We were never his. This is going to happen."

Josh looked at Tadgh. He was steady, his face calm. "She'll stay as long as she has to, brother. Then you'll come to Ireland. Your life will change and your pod will grow bigger than you ever imagined. You've got this, Josh. As long as it takes, we'll be together."

Josh's eye misted, but he clamped his jaw down, not wanting to cry in front of Tadgh. He nodded.

They entered the courtroom and Tadgh felt the eyes on them. One set in particular drew his. It was the father. Christ, he looked like Charlie. Short for a man, lean, the same coloring. But there was no spark of intelligence or purpose in his eyes. They were tired, angry, resentful eyes, and they were fixed on Charlie. He stopped as they took a seat, and he turned his body to the man, causing him to look away from his daughter and at Tadgh.

That's right, asshole. Take a good look. Never again. You will never hurt them again. The man tried to hold his gaze, but in the end he looked away first. As was the way with most cowards. His wife's eyes were downcast, but she snuck a peak at Tadgh and her children, the slumped shoulders of a defeated human being.

They called the room to order and the lawyer Charlie had hired gave the request to petition for the emancipation of a minor. The judge was an older, stern looking man. Charlie had been hoping it was a woman, but this judge had a good reputation. He'd been a Marine. He was strict and fair. He looked over all of the players in the room. It was a small court room, closed to the public.

"We don't take emancipation of a minor lightly in this county. You can't just leave your parents when you don't want to live by their rules. Is that what this is about?"

"Exactly, and a meddling sister." Mr. Ryan had interrupted, not being directly asked a question, and the judge bristled.

"When I have a question for you, Mr. Ryan, I'll address you directly. Until then, keep quiet in my courtroom."

That's when the lawyer laid it all out. The lifetime of domestic abuse, the mental abuse, the alcoholism. Everything. The judge listened, jaw tight. The lawyer for the parents tried to object, but he wasn't having it.

He looked through all of his paperwork. "I'm sorry, son, if all that is true. I just don't have any evidence to back up this claim. I have a few domestic disturbances on record to the household, but no charges. I have one child services case, but it was dropped. Two DUIs. Nothing substantiating your abuse claim."

"Could I say something, Your Honor?" Charlie was respectful, calm.

"Can I assume you're the meddling older sister?" He said, a grin turning up one corner of his mouth.

"That would be me. I'm Special Agent Charlotte Ryan. I'm his sister. I'm also prior CPD." Brows shot up.

"Special Agent? As in FBI?"

"Yes, Your Honor."

"And is this your husband?"

Tadgh stood up, "Detective Tadgh O'Brien, Your Honor. An Garda Síochána, and very soon to be her husband."

"Well, this gets more compelling by the minute. All right, Special Agent Ryan. Say your piece."

"She's not his parent. She's got no say in…"

The judge didn't bother with the gavel. He pointed his finger menacingly at Charlie's father. "Mr. Ryan. You will shut the shut, or I will have my burly bailiff remove you from this room. Do you copy?"

Tadgh suppressed a smile. *And there's the Marine coming out.* He thought of Alanna's father, Hans. He was liking this judge more and more.

He turned back to Charlie, "Continue. I'll have questions and I'll want to hear from your brother most of all, but you have the respect of this court, given your profession and your time with the Cleveland Police Department, and you will get a say."

Charlie spoke clearly, holding her emotions at a distance. Tadgh was so proud. This was a woman who was familiar with giving a solid account. Of painting a picture. Someone who had experience as a first responder who knew exactly how to put things in perspective, legally. She'd undoubtedly testified in court during her time as a police officer.

The judge listened, then he asked Josh some questions. The final one being the most compelling. "Why do you want emancipated?"

"I just want to be free. Not free because I want to do whatever I want. It isn't like that, Your Honor. I get good grades, I work, I stay out of trouble. I just want to be free to be happy. I don't want to be afraid. I don't want to watch my mother put up with this abuse anymore. I don't want to live my life wondering if every adult man I meet secretly treats his family like garbage at home. I want to be normal. I just want a house that isn't full of anger."

"Son, that was very well said. But the law is clear about this. You have to prove that you can actually take care of yourself. Your sister isn't taking custody of you. You are taking custody of yourself. You'll be a man. No safety net."

Tadgh was fidgeting, which didn't go unnoticed. "Do you have something to say, Detective, or are you suffering from a case of fleas?"

Tadgh smiled, waiting. "Go ahead."

Charlie's father started to open his mouth, but his lawyer put a hand on his arm and the judge shot him a look.

"He won't be without a safety net, Your Honor. He's got a big family waiting to love and support him. We don't leave a man behind anymore than you would have in the Marines. I've got a job lined up for him. We're ready to start the process for a student visa in Ireland. He can have a good life. He will have a good life."

"Everyone would love to think they can chuck the crap family they got stuck with, but that's not how these proceedings work. There's no real proof of abuse. I can tell by the downcast eyes and silence on the mother's part that she's not willing to stand up and be counted in all of this." Charlie's mother looked up for the first time, her eyes sad and feeling the full blown weight of her failures.

"What do you have to say about all of this, Mrs. Ryan?"

She looked at her son, then at her husband. "His place is at home with us. His sister should have never started this. It's an embarrass-ment. He's almost eighteen. She didn't have to do this."

"I did, and you know why!"

"Easy there, Special Agent. Wait your turn." Then he turned to her mother. "What does she mean? She said you know why? Am I in the dark about something?" Mrs. Ryan squirmed uncomfortably in her chair, but said nothing.

He looked to Charlie for clarification. "Your Honor, if I could see you in private with my attorney?"

"I'm sorry, that's not appropriate. Whatever you have to tell me, you'll have to do it in the courtroom in front of the other counsel." That's when Charlie and Josh's attorney asked for a moment to speak with her.

She whispered something to him, low and just for him, and his face blanched. Then he rubbed his forehead. Tadgh watched as his face twisted in anger as he looked at Charlie's father. "You're going to want to see this, Your Honor. It's a bit out of the norm for evidence, but necessary."

Charlie stood and approached the bench with permission. When she started to unbutton her blouse, the judge raised a hand to stop her. "I have another layer underneath. It's okay. I just…I didn't want to put my brother through any more pain." She didn't meet his eyes, and his face softened.

Tadgh took Josh's hand as he stiffened. "I don't understand. What is she doing?"

"I'm sorry you had to find out this way. Please, just be strong. None of this is your fault."

She took down the back of her shirt and the judge hissed. "Jesus Christ. Is that from an iron?" Charlie nodded, replacing her blouse.

"That was the child services call you have on record. The doctor at the ER called. My mother persuaded me to lie. I lied and I shouldn't have. These are my records from that incident. Then underneath those are more records during my physical and medical screening for the FBI. I have a healed fracture from blunt force trauma to the shoulder blade. I'm sure if it came down to it, they could pull the polygraph from my interview. It was addressed at that time as well. If not, I'll take another one. I'll pay for it if I have to. I doubt you could get either of my parents to pass a polygraph on the incident."

The judge's face was pale, tight, and full of barely contained anger as he looked over at her parents. "When this happened, what were the circumstances surrounding the attack?"

She turned, looking at Josh who had tears coming down his face. She didn't want to say. So he did. "She was protecting me. I remember the injury. She told me to go in my room and lock the door. He was coming after me. I'd been in his shaving cream." He shuddered, the tears free flowing. "I heard the screams. I poked my head out and heard the crying. My father was headed out the front door. He told my mother not to take her to the hospital. I didn't know what happened. She came home with bandages, had to go back to the doctor a few times. She said she'd had an accident. She said she tripped over the cord and fell and the iron came down on her back. I never thought....Jesus. He was mean. He hit us. He hit mom. But I never thought he'd done that. Oh, God. It was because of me."

Charlie went to him. "No! No, buddy. I should have told. I didn't want us getting separated. I should never have lied. This is not your fault."

The judge tapped his gavel. "I need a five minute recess." He looked at Charlie's parents and their lawyer. "Take them to the common area. We need a degree of separation right now. Come back in five."

Tadgh suspected that the judge needed five minutes to rein in his temper. He looked ready to kill. He knew how the guy felt. Charlie's father had finally removed that icy glare away from her. On some level, he knew that what he'd done was unforgivable. Even if he went to his grave denying it.

"We'll fight as long as we have to. I'll take out a loan for the fees, buddy. We won't stop all the way up until your birthday. I'll try to get appointed as an emergency foster parent, I'll take leave from the FBI if I have to. We will find a way. I promise."

"You won't have to worry about that. I'm returning your retainer. This is pro-bono. Put the money in his college fund." The lawyer was obviously dealing with a little male aggression himself.

"Thank you. I don't have the words to thank you." Charlie said.

* * *

EVERYONE WAS IN PLACE AGAIN, the judge's face was less flushed. He had wet wisps around his hairline, and Tadgh suspected that he may have gone into his private judge's chamber to splash cold water on his face. This was good. They needed his righteous anger.

"Now, I've heard from everyone but the father. Let's hear it, Mr. Ryan. Why don't you explain to me why I should leave this young man in your custody?"

He cleared his throat, a little less spark in his face now that Charlie had outed him for the horrible bastard that he is. "The boy belongs at home. He's ours to care for. He's my child. When he's eighteen, he can prance off to Ireland or wherever the hell he thinks he belongs. But for now, he belongs to me."

"He belongs to no one. He may belong with someone, but he belongs to no one." Charlie said, menace in her tone that she'd kept out until this point.

His lawyer objected to the interruption. "Duly noted counselor. Now, if the juvenile in question would stand before the court."

Josh stood, his body language more sure. He looked at his father, chin up, then at the judge. This was the moment, Tadgh thought, that he became a man. He was ready for whatever life was dishing out that day, because he wasn't going to quit fighting. "As you can understand, I'm not comfortable putting you in the care of your parents. I'm also, however, not convinced I can just emancipate you. You work part time. You don't have anything settled with a student visa in Ireland. You haven't even graduated from high school."

"If I could interrupt, Your Honor." Josh's lawyer stood. "He's finished the required coursework to graduate. This semester, all he has left are electives. He's in all honors and advanced placement classes. He could walk away tomorrow with his diploma. His passport will be processed as soon as he doesn't need a parent signature."

"But he's got no way to support himself. Student visas can be denied. Jobs can fall through. There are a lot of what ifs."

"I could adopt him." Everyone's head swung to Tadgh's. "If he were emancipated and he moved to Ireland, I could adopt him. He'd be a citizen immediately. He would be an adult in America, but I could adopt him as a minor in Ireland. I checked into it before I left. The Prime Minister of the Republic of Ireland owes me a favor. A big one. He said he'd push it through. He'd be a citizen as my son, and no one could put him off the island."

"You'd do that for me?" Josh's face was shocked.

"I would. You'd be my brother, but on paper you'd be my son until you turned of age. It's unorthodox, but I think we could make it happen. Regardless, you'll have a home with me. No matter what. If I have to leave Ireland and move to America to take care of you, I will. I will never abandon you, Josh."

Charlie's father stood up. "Wait one damn minute!" The judge cut him off, signaling for the bailiff.

That's when a small voice spoke up. "Let him go." They all stopped and looked at Charlie's mother. "Your Honor, he's not safe at home. Please, let him go. Emancipate him... free him."

"You bitch!"

The bailiff grabbed Charlie's father and he submitted, given the size of the man. "This is my family. You can't do this," he growled.

The judge looked at Tadgh, at Charlie, at Josh. "No, Mr. Ryan." He pointed at them. "That's a family. Take him outside and let him cool off, James."

He turned to them. "I hereby rule in favor of Joshua Albert Ryan. You are emancipated by this court by close of business today." He clamped the gavel down on the bench and Charlie screamed with joy. She was hugging Josh so tightly, she was likely cutting his air off. Then she pulled Tadgh in, and her lawyer. As she calmed, she looked over at her mother and saw a rare smile. "Thank you. Thank you, Mom." Tadgh stood then, big and strong and walked over to Charlie's mother. She shrank a bit, but he knelt down, below her eye level, making himself smaller.

"I'm sorry for it. All of it. I'm sorry ye've suffered so." The woman's face twisted with grief. "I'll take care of them. I swear it. And if you ever need a safe place to land, Mrs. Ryan, you've only to call. You've got some place to go if you ever decide you've had enough."

* * *

TADGH AND CHARLIE sat across from Josh in the donut shop, a plate of delectables disappearing by the minute. It had been six days since the court date. Tadgh had shopped in the city, getting some local gifts for Christmas presents. The local art museum, the science museum, and the Rock 'n Roll Hall of Fame all having the dual purpose of sight-seeing while shopping. Cleveland was actually a pretty cool town. They secured connected hotel rooms in a local suburb, Tadgh giving Josh the space he needed to get to know him without the intimacy of sharing a room.

He'd kept out of their hair as Charlie and her brother had prepared for Josh's departure. His high school had agreed to a study abroad program with the local school near their flat in Dublin. They'd been aware of the situation with Josh, and the counselor had smoothed the way to supersede enrollment obstacles, calling the Dublin high school personally to set up the unorthodox arrangement. They'd had other errands, more trips to another court house with their lawyer. Tadgh didn't pry. He was just happy to know that it was happening. Josh's passport was being rushed. He'd packed two suitcases of his favorite clothes and books. That's all he took with him. His father had been ordered to leave the premises while he moved out and said goodbye to his mother.

"You'll like an O'Brien Christmas."

Josh smiled at the thought. "I saw the cliffs on the internet. I can't believe I'm going to see them."

Tadgh put his arm around him. "You'll see everything. Anything you want. Every time we've got a couple of days off, I'll take you anywhere you want to go, lad. Ye've got the guide book, aye? Just start mapping it out. And you'll get to see my island, where the castle and the shipwreck lie."

Josh looked at him, a question in his eyes. "Would you really have adopted me? I know we got the visa sorted out, but would you have done it?"

"Absolutely, brother. Regardless, your family just got a whole lot bigger. My cousin Seany is beside himself at the notion of another young man. He's twenty, just joined with the fire services. He's ready to have a younger side kick."

"Will they like me, do you think?"

Charlie reached for his hand. "They'll love you. I've met them all. They're the real deal, Buddy. You don't have to worry. You are going to get a whole new outlook on the family thing."

Tadgh watched the two and his heart squeezed. Josh was taller than Charlie's father. Apparently his maternal grandfather had been a big man. His hair was a bit lighter like his mother's. Not blonde, but the sandy color of Charlie's highlights. His eyes were blue, not hazel. He was a handsome boy, fit and strong. Tadgh had watched the boy's demeanor start to transition in the last couple of days. A weight removed. Hope replacing fear and despair. He was young, and with counseling, he'd recover from the damage his father had done.

CHAPTER 27

$\mathcal{T}$he luggage area of Dublin Airport was filled with O'Briens, Murphys, Carringtons, and Donoghues. Even Alanna and Aidan had made the trip for Christmas holiday as had Aunt Maeve and her husband. When Charlie came through the arrivals gate with Josh and Tadgh bracketing her, and walked to the luggage carousel, the sight of all that family nearly undid her. They had signs. Lots and lots of signs. *Welcome to the family Josh! You can share my room Josh! Merry Christmas Josh!* along with *It's a boy! Welcome Home!* Josh was blushing like mad. It was Tadgh's mother Katie who approached first.

"Well now, aren't you a fine looking lad. Welcome to Ireland, my boy." And she hugged him so sweetly, like he was the most precious thing in the world. Behind her they all lined up with hugs and good wishes.

* * *

İT ẇᴀꜱ Cora who snuck in to wake Josh. Charlie heard the little footsteps. She'd been sharing Aidan and Michael's old room, two twin beds, with Josh. It had been Tadgh's idea. Josh was in a new place, and he needed his sister despite his recent adult status. They had some catching up to do. They'd talked and laughed until all hours, like they'd done when they were young. Now Cora was tickling his nose, trying to wake him. "Father Christmas has come. You need to wake up, Josh. You've got presents waiting."

Josh came down the hall of Sorcha and Sean's house, rubbing his eyes. Everyone was there, despite the hour. Some were staying at Michael and Branna's cottage, some with Brigid and Finn, others at Granny's, more with Hans and Mary. There were so many people, big and little, crammed in the house, they could barely fit. And a new addition. Tadgh had filled Charlie and Josh in on the recent occurrence in Belfast. Apparently Sorcha had a nephew, Daniel MacPherson.

Josh walked in and noticed that Tadgh, Michael, Seany, and Patrick were standing in front of something. "Merry Christmas Josh!" Cora yelled as the men parted to reveal a beautiful, high speed bicycle. "You'll need a bike in the city, since ye can't drive for a while. It's got a good lock and Charlie said you liked blue."

Tadgh was so adorable. He didn't realize that he could have given Josh an old shoe and he'd love it. He had some serious hero worship going on with his brother-to-be. "It's the best bike I've ever seen. You didn't need to do this. I'm used to taking the bus."

"You're a man, now. And a man needs his own wheels." Patrick smiled and winked at him.

"Does that mean I can drive your motorcycle?' He looked at Tadgh, teasing.

"Oh, no. No way. You won't be putting him on that motorbike ever!" Katie was full mother mode now. Josh hugged her. "Just kidding. This bike is just my speed. It's perfect. Everything is perfect."

As the festivities continued, Tadgh watched Daniel stand up and walk over to his mother. He thought it odd, because technically speaking, they weren't even related. He spoke to her and then handed her something. Her mouth was agape and then she hugged him. Tadgh stood, curious. But he didn't need to walk across the room, because Daniel came to him. He handed him a wrapped gift. Then one to each couple in the room. They all stilled as he stood in the middle.

'I've been talking to Auntie Sorcha about the family. She mentioned the troubles with the cottage in Inisheer being sold. I've recently sold some land to the village crofters that were leasing prior to now. If ye'd open the small parcel I gave everyone." His accent was a mix of Manchester, England and Scottish. Having been exposed to both during his upbringing, the Scot bur only came out when he was excited and unguarded.

They did, and they all held up an identical set of keys. Tadgh inspected them. They weren't to his mother's cottage. He had a set of those and these keys in his hand were totally different. These were skeleton keys. He looked at Daniel.

"I decided that since I had family here, I should look into some local property. I couldn't buy the cottage Katie was living in, ye ken. The owner wanted more than it was worth, it wasn't a good investment and I didn't much care for the man." He gave an easy shrug. "I did find another place, closer to the water. It's got a fine view and it's much older, classic. It's a good holiday cottage. Wee Branna's the expert, so to speak. It was her idea actually. I thought Katie could live in it during the tourist season, sell her knitting and rent the other rooms out like a proper guest house for me. She's agreed to it. When she goes to the mainland in the fall, I leave it open for the family or as a self catering cottage. I can use it too. I just...well, I thought it would be a good solution to the housing problem and a nice bit of property for the family. My new family. And I can bide there when I choose, bring my siblings to meet everyone. My sister's a writer, so she'll likely go any chance she gets. So, then. Ye've all got keys."

Tadgh stood up and grabbed the man. "Thank you! God, ye've got no idea how this has been weighing on me."

Sorcha came next. "Well done, lad. You've got your father's heart. It'll be good to have ye visit more often, now that you've got a place of your own."

Aidan hugged him next. It was uncanny to look at them. Sorcha had been pregnant at the same time as Daniel's mother. Aidan was only eight months older than Daniel. But Daniel hadn't married and she knew there was a story there. She just didn't know what it was.

She'd find out in time. For now, she was amazed to have a little piece of her brother back.

He'd spent Christmas Eve morning with her parents, then driven down last night to stay in a bed and breakfast. He was hesitant to impose, she knew that, and he was a grown man. Used to his own space. When he'd told her about the cottage he'd been considering, she'd known that this was the beginning of a new familial attachment. A new volume in a book she thought had been closed upon her brother's death. And for that she was grateful.

* * *

"Peace, peace; she cannot hear, Lyre or sonnet; All my life's buried here, Heap earth upon it."
Requiescat, Oscar Wilde

LIAM SAT IN HIS APARTMENT, looking at the parcel that had come internationally from a Naval base in Virginia. He opened the box, and there were other parcels wrapped individually. All numbered. The first was a simple envelope. *Open first!*

He opened the letter after taking a sip of whiskey. The only person he knew in that area was Alanna's friend Izzy. He hoped to God it wasn't something that had been caught up in international mail that had been meant for him and Eve. He really wouldn't be able to handle it. He looked at the letter, addressed only to him and he read.

DEAR LIAM,

The news of Eve's death reached me across the ocean. I can't tell you how sorry I am. No matter what I say, it won't make a shit bit of difference. So, I'm going to save the platitudes. Nothing I can say to you is going to ease your suffering, and honestly, I barely had a chance to get to know either of you. Eve was good people, though, and I'm sorry I'll never get the chance to know her better.

I just wanted to send you something, Doc to Doc, because that's the only medicine I can offer you right now.

I hope your opportunity in Brazil brings you the distraction and purpose you need. So, I've compiled a treasure chest of helpful gifts and advice. Enjoy.

Izzy

LIAM WAS SMILING, laughing to himself. Izzy was a piece of work. Blunt, unapologetically American, bigger than life. Eve had liked her immediately, admired her. He opened the first package. It was a waterproof map of the Amazon region of Brazil. The note said. *So you don't get lost and cooked by native cannibals.*

The next had been a bottle of essential oil based bug repellant. She'd replaced the label with one that said *Zika Be-Gone.*

The next was a book of dirty limericks called *Potty Humor: The Bathroom Edition.* The note said, *"In case you end up with dysentery and have a lot of time to kill in the head."* Liam barked out a laugh. The next was a bottle of water with a note that read, *"Don't drink the water and you won't need the book."* Liam's hand was over his mouth, stifling his laughter. It was the first time he'd laughed in weeks.

The next thing he opened shocked the hell out of him. It was a condom. *"Your O'Brien manliness is probably going to send those nuns into heat. Just in case."* Then there was an arrow, instructing him to turn the note over. *"I'm just kidding. Don't you dare bang a nun!"*

He was fully belly laughing now. There were two more tiny gifts left. The next one was a comb. A small comb. The label said *Sandalwood Beard Comb.*

Seriously bro, those nuns and their vows of chastity are going to be tested. You need to go full ape man. Dread locks, a beard, no deodorant. Think of the sisters. They're only human. Funky is your only defense.

Liam shook his head. He'd never failed to shave a day in his life. Not since he was nineteen. The woman was nuts.

The final one was a small, thin, square package. An international calling card. *Call your mother. I'm not kidding. She's a good lady. Call your*

mother, or I'll hunt you down in the jungle, put you in a headlock, and make
you call her. Have fun in Brazil, Doctor O'Brien.

Your friend, Izzy.

He stared at the final note. Somehow she knew. His desire to flee, to disconnect from everyone and everything to do with his family, his home. He needed away. He wasn't sure how long he'd be gone or if he'd ever be ready to come back. All he knew was that the Mother Superior, who had arranged his medical mission, had bumped up his departure per his request. He walked over to his duffles, finding a place to store all of the small, silly gifts that she'd paid God knows how much to ship internationally. Of all the sympathies he'd received, she'd gotten it right.

He took his key off the ring, leaving the car keys, the title he'd signed over to Tadgh, the spare flat keys he'd left for Seany. He left a general note, then one for Seany about the apartment, and finally one for Tadgh.

Then he picked up his bags and left his flat, locking the door behind him.

CHAPTER 28

$\mathcal{T}$adgh and Charlie walked with Sal into the cluster of townhouses on the outskirts of Dublin. It was two days after Christmas, and they'd all been invited to Zaid's new digs. He'd been busy. He really was a resourceful man. Upon starting his new job, and with a reference letter in hand from none other than the Lord Mayor of Dublin, he'd moved out of the government subsidized housing. They didn't have much, for such a large family, so the move had been quick.

Zaid worked as a civilian contracted interpreter for the city of Dublin. He was called out for emergency services, government offices, even the Coast Guard if they needed an Iraqi or Arabic translator. He was fluent in both. The Lord Mayor had caught wind of Rasha's part in the take down, and ordered the immediate construction of a skate park in the nearby city park. They had a set of the plans with them, to show her. The skate park was Charlie's idea, just a nudge in the right direction that she'd given the mayor. A good way to keep them off of the sidewalks and public steps.

Zaid smiled at Charlie who was talking to the women. Zaid's wife didn't know English like the others who got to go to school, so he translated for her. "She says you've ruined that one!" he said laughing.

He was pointing to Rasha. "She wants to be police, now. Thinks she is some sort of tough girl."

"Well, she is a tough girl! I think she'd be wonderful. That's why you came here, right? So that you would all be safe and have the opportunity to follow your dreams?" Charlie said, winking at the girl.

"Yes, Madam. Yes. My daughters will have many choices." He spoke the words both in Iraqi and English. His wife smiled at him, a knowing smile between people who loved each other. And Charlie knew that one day she might very well see this skateboarding little tomboy taking down bad guys.

After a huge lunch where Zaid's family had stuffed them to bursting, they broke off from Sal and headed to Liam's. No one had heard from him since they'd seen him on Christmas Eve. He hadn't answered his phone, and he'd lied about picking up shifts over Christmas. Tadgh had called the hospital, only to find out that Liam hadn't worked in the last week. Seany was on liberty and was meeting them at the flat. He had a key, because he was moving in as soon as his training was over.

As they approached the door, Tadgh read the fear in Seany's face. All he kept thinking was that Liam had been tempted to stay in that van. When they'd driven it to the strand, driven it into the water, he'd made him promise that he'd jump out with him. Even then, he'd felt his desperate despair. He'd like to think Liam would never hurt himself, but then again, none of them had ever lost their woman. Family lore held a few cases of it, women who died in childbirth. One story of a woman who'd died in a shipwreck that had drifted too close to the rocky cliffs. But nothing recent. Not until now.

Please God. Let him be drunk and sleeping it off. Please don't let him have killed himself. Sean Jr. opened up the apartment and Tadgh's heart jumped as he looked at the note. "Liam!" he raced through every room in the apartment, expecting the worst.

"He's gone, brother. It's okay."

He went back to the living room and Seany held up the note. "He's gone to Brazil. He left two months early." Seany's face grimaced. "Why the hell didn't he tell anyone? I thought I was going to find him hanging in the bloody shower!"

"Because he wasn't thinking clearly, Seany. I'm sorry, but it's as simple as that. He didn't strike me as the theatrical type. He just bugged out." Charlie's tone was level, compassionate.

"An interesting turn of phrase considering what he'll be doing in Brazil." Tadgh said absently. Then he sighed, a huge sigh that said he was also glad he hadn't found his cousin hanging. "Has he left a number?"

"Just one for Mother Superior at the hospital. I'm on it."

Seany thumbed the number into his phone, confirming with the sisters at the medical mission that Liam had landed in Brazil yesterday in the wee hours.

"All right. How in the hell am I going to tell Mam and Da?" Seany asked.

"He's alive. He's doing what he needs to do right now to survive. He'll come home when he's ready, Seany. He'll come home when he can bear to be here again."

He looked at the car title. There was a sticky note. *Since you can't get three people on that motorbike, I figured you'd be needing a car. I love you, mo deartháir.* Tadgh dangled the keys, smiling at the gesture. "I love you too, brother."

EPILOGUE

*T*he breeze of late June swept over the landscape of Inis Oírr. The day had been speckled with intermittent showers, and Branna had assured Charlie that it was good luck to have rain on her wedding day. Now the sky was relatively clear, the afternoon sun warming the stones and surf of the island. The women were buzzing around Daniel's cottage, getting ready for the big event. Sorcha swept into the room, carrying the dress that Charlie would wear down the aisle. She wasn't much for dresses, but when she'd seen Granny Aoife's collection, she hadn't been able to take her eyes off the gauzy cotton and breezy feminine lines of the Gunne Sax vintage gown. It wasn't the dressiest or most elegant. Circa 1978, it had a Bohemian feel to it that just spoke to Charlie. Perfect really, for a wedding on the beach. As Sorcha helped her into the dress, Alanna and Branna sighed.

Brigid walked in and put her hand to her chest. "Ach Christ. Look at her. She's gorgeous altogether." All of the women, the grannies, the cousins, and finally Katie gathered around her. Sorcha started to zip up the back and stopped, stroking the scar on Charlie's back. Charlie froze. Then Sorcha zipped the gown and turned her around to face her. All she did was put out her arm, showing the long deep scar on her forearm. Then Alanna came too, lifting a lock of hair to show her scar above her brow. The one that had been made by a piece of shell that had cut her brow. Another story on another island.

"We've all got our battle scars, love. Some ye can see, some not." She gestured to Branna and Katie. "But we've all got them. 'Tis the way of women. It's part of our lives, taking these wounds and finding a way to be stronger for them. And we're stronger in numbers. You've got a tribe now. A tribe of rare, strong women to hold you up, love you the way only other women can. You'll marry an O'Brien man today, and that's a hard and wonderful thing in equal measure. But you'll get us in the bargain, and we take our own sort of vows. The vow of sisters. The vow of a mother to a daughter. And that, my dear Charlie, is also 'til death do us part."

The women circled around her and she looked at all of their beautiful faces. Caitlyn's hand rested on Branna's swollen tummy, her blonde head pressed to Branna's dark head. Such amazing women, all unique in their beauty and strength.

Katie came forward with a box. "Ye've got Sorcha's dress. Now, if you'd do me the honors, this is a bit of the Donoghue tradition." Charlie sat on a bedroom chair as Katie put the veil in her lap, her eyes blurring with unshed tears.

* * *

TADGH STOOD on the flat rock that overlooked the stretch of sea between Doolin and Inis Oírr. They'd opted to marry on the island. A tea time wedding that his cousin Beverly had been overjoyed at the prospect of catering, with every type of tea time dish she knew how to make. The women on the island had pooled sets of china for the event, they'd closed the tea shop to the public, and spared no amount of effort to put on a uniquely Aran experience. Irish linen, bone china, local delicacies.

They'd decided to host a dry event other than a simple champagne toast. This wasn't just for his mother. It was for Josh. The kid had come a long way. He was loosening up, getting settled. He'd had the lasses at the school in Dublin swooning in their knickers. But he'd grown up in a violent home with a mean drunk. He was still getting acclimated to his altered reality. Still struggling with the idea of being safe and being in a loving home.

He'd been accepted to three major universities, but he'd opted to take it slow. He would work and take a couple of classes. He'd never had such freedom. He loved Ireland. Loved their weekend excursions. He rode his bike to the port on some days, just standing on the edge of the city. One lighthouse or another at his back, he looked out over the water, reveling in the possible places he'd go. The new things he'd see.

Tadgh felt a nudge and it was Josh. "You're not getting cold feet, brother. You're stuck with us." Tadgh laughed. His sense of humor was developing as well, a little more comfortable letting his mouth fly with the other O'Brien men. He'd started hanging out with Seany in his apartment, when he thought that Tadgh and Charlie needed some alone time.

"Not a chance, Buddy. I'm in this until I'm old and in my grave. Are ye ready with that ring?"

Josh patted his pocket, having a matching linen sport coat to the other O'Brien cousins that were lined up behind him. The processional started, and the women all came down the pathway to the beach. The wedding was well attended. Sal and his family even helped Zaid's family find their way to the West coast. Tadgh smiled at the sight of Rasha. She'd submitted to a dress, but she was wearing Vans with little sharks on them, her only rebellion to the girly dress code.

The women were lovely. Mac walked Tadgh's mother down and seated her first, in a place of honor. Patrick walked Aunt Sorcha and sat her beside his mother. She was a sort of mother to him as well. She'd picked up the slack during those few dark years when his mother had succumbed to her grief. They cuddled each other, more like blood sisters than in-laws. Then, Sorcha smiled at him, reading his thoughts. They were so beautiful, his two mothers.

The line of women came down to the shore, all dressed in some sort of pale blue cotton sundress. Each chosen to fit their figures. Caitlyn's short and leggy, Brigid's fitting her postpartum softness, Alanna's accentuating her athletic beauty. Branna's tented over her expanding waistline, six months along in her pregnancy. She glowed with impending motherhood, smiling through unshed tears as she looked at him. He kissed each one of them as they took their place alongside the bridal party. Branna whispered to him. "I told you she was out there, mo cara."

Then the music changed, Jenny's fiddle and Robby's guitar starting a bridal march of sorts, and suddenly he couldn't breathe. His Uncle Sean led his beloved out of the seaside cottage, through the garden gate, to her O'Brien mate. He'd seen the dress so many times, in the living room photo gallery at his Uncle Sean's. It was Aunt Sorcha's dress, some sort of seventies style. It was stunning on her. The flouncy, gauze skirt blowing in the sea air. The peasant style bodice and sleeves fitting her earthy, tomboy personality better than lace and sequins. She had on simple sandals and her little pink toe nails were bright against her golden skin. It was the veil, he reflected later, that did him in. The Donoghues had their own ideas when it came to weddings on the island. His mother had worn the veil when she'd married his da. The wreath around Charlie's head was made of tiny shells, threaded with thin strands of local yarn. They'd intertwined freshly picked heather into her hair. It fit perfectly with the vintage dress, the Irish lace trailing down her back. She had small shells and flowers adorning her wild hair, with all its colors and waves.

It was the only thing he'd asked. He didn't want her binding her hair up in one of those bridal up-dos. All tight pins and hair tonics. He wanted to see that beautiful unruly mane blowing with the sea air and the strands of sunlight that poked through the clouds. His Feisty Pants in all her untamed glory. Her smile was radiant, obviously noticing the complete adoration on his face. He didn't care if he looked like a sap. She looked like the Fairy Queen, come to take a mortal husband. She came to him, taking his hands in hers. She stole a look at her brother. A look that said, We're home. *These people are our home.*

* * *

THE TEA TIME wedding reception was in full swing. Josh had burst out laughing when he saw the spread. It was like something out of Alice in Wonderland. Tarts, pies, scones, jams, chocolate éclairs, finger sandwiches with bacon and thinly sliced beef. "Wow, it looks like they catered this spread specifically for my sister."

Women were hired for extra help from around the island, because work was scarce in such a small community. They filled tea cups, and the little girls running around in frilly dresses commented that it was much better than the boring weddings where everyone ate chicken and drank wine.

Mac had taken Tadgh and Charlie on a horse drawn carriage ride through the island, people coming out of their houses and businesses to wave at the happy couple. They'd taken pictures by O'Brien castle and near the shipwreck. But the reception at the tea house was really where the magic happened. Beverly had gone all out to make the gardens perfect. Indoor and outdoor seating and a spot for the musicians. All the women pitched in with the preparations, decorating tables, putting fairy lights all through the inside and outside for when the sun went down. It was the heaviest meal Tadgh had ever had during tea time, the dishes reappearing full and rolling into an early dinner.

There was music of course, because music was what O'Brien's did best. The evening sky dimmed to the sounds and rhythm of a traditional Irish session. They all sang, taking turns playing and making jokes. And they'd danced the O'Brien set. He'd been worried about his mother, but Daniel had taken her hand and asked her to help him learn it. He wasn't an O'Brien, but Tadgh knew that he'd felt her loneliness. The loneliness of a widow like his own mother, and had wanted to draw her into the fun. And Josh...well, that was another story. The Donoghue teenage girls, Caitlyn's younger sister Madeline, and every other young girl under the age of nineteen had been swooning in their sandals, vying for his attention. He'd taken Cora, however, and she'd taught him how to do the steps, as well as an eight year old could.

Then Sorcha had taken the microphone and asked Katie and

Tadgh to come to the dance area, and have a proper mother and son dance. "You've got a rare lad, Katie darling. And your William would be proud. Now, take the boy in your arms and have your dance."

She looked at her husband and he started to play the guitar. Brigid joining him on the fiddle. And Sorcha sang. Her voice was clearer, less ragged then the iconic sound of Stevie Nicks, but the song was so perfect, it made both Tadgh and Katie sag into each other. Holding on for dear life.

I took my love, I took it down
I climbed a mountain and I turned around
And I saw my reflection in the snow-covered hills
'Til the landslide brought me down

Oh, mirror in the sky, what is love?
Can the child within my heart rise above?
Can I sail through the changing ocean tides?
Can I handle the seasons of my life?

Well, I've been afraid of changing
'Cause I've built my life around you
But time makes you bolder
Children get older
And I'm getting older too

THEY'D BEEN through so much together, this mother and son. A crippling loss, almost too large and tragic to bear. But they'd survived, and in the long run, they'd been closer because of it. "My sweet lad. I can't stand to part with you."

He squeezed her tight. "You'll never have to, Ma. I will always be here for you. Nothing will change that. And now you've got the daughter you always wanted. Someone to teach to knit and bake. And, there's the boy. You've got the three of us now."

* * *

It was a lull in the activity, the musicians taking a break, when the champagne flutes were being passed around. They'd bought sparkling grape juice for the children, and Katie and Josh as well. Josh took his fork, as Seany had shown him, and clinked it on his glass. That's when he stood for the toast.

"I want to thank everyone for coming today. I've never been a best man before. Actually, I've never been to a wedding before." Everyone chuckled as he shrugged sweetly. "What you all did for my sister today, this was really beautiful. Everything was perfect. I'd like to toast to my sister first, because she's the best sister anyone could ever ask for. She protected me, she loved me, she gave me hope when I didn't think I had anything good to look forward to." He blushed, smiling at her. "Anyway, I just wanted to say I love you, sis. Tadgh's lucky to have you." Everyone whooped and took a sip.

As the group quieted, he spoke again. "I'd also like to thank my new brother-in-law." He looked at Tadgh, straightening his back and holding his chin up. "You didn't have any reason to take me in. No one falls in love and expects to get the little brother in the bargain, but you made room in your life for me. You gave me a safe and happy home. I don't have anything to give you. I just have me. But I set something in motion before I went away from Cleveland. So...um, I got something in the mail from my lawyer last month and I wanted to give it to you. Kind of like a present. So..."

He took an envelope out of his pocket. Tadgh looked at Charlie and she shrugged. She had no idea. "What is it, Buddy?"

He was blushing scarlet now. "It's nothing really. Nothing you can touch. It's just, like I said, I don't have anything to give you but me, but you've got all of me. I hope it was okay." Tadgh put an arm on the young man's shoulder. "It's okay, lad. Whatever it is, it will be perfect because it's from your heart."

He handed the envelope to Tadgh. "In America, if you're an adult, you can change your name. Like if you don't like the name you have or you have some other reason to do it. It's not really that hard and the lawyer helped me. I hope it's okay. It's my wedding gift to you guys. So, we can all be the same."

Tadgh looked down at the letter and choked on his words, emotion flooding him. "Ye changed your name to O'Brien?" There were gasps in the crowd, women starting to cry, but Tadgh's eyes never left Josh's.

Josh nodded. "Yes, just like you and Charlie. I'm Joshua Albert O'Brien. My old name will stay on my old records, but I changed it legally." Tadgh pulled the boy to him. He felt Josh melt into the embrace. He'd been so shy those first few weeks, not being used to getting affection from male family members. He was learning though.

"I'm glad you're my brother, Tadgh. Thank you for bringing me into your family." Tadgh felt the tears on his shirt. Then, he felt Charlie's arms around both of them. She was crying so hard she could barely speak, as her two men held her. They all held each other, really, their heads pressed together. Supporting each other, because that's what O'Briens did.

Author Notes and Acknowledgements

This book was the most challenging so far. Not that I don't love a challenge. Tadgh is a beloved character from the O'Brien Tales series, and I wanted to get it right. Not only is he beautiful, as all O'Brien men are in their own way, but he's smart. This book was about his loyalty, his brains, and his big heart.

Mo Ghile Mear is a traditional Irish song and poem written in the eighteenth century by Seán "Clárach" Mac Domhnaill. *The Parting Glass* is older, early 1600s in its original form. Originally Scottish, but sung widely by both Irish and Scottish musicians.

It was important for me to handle the subject matter of the killings and the refugee challenges with grace, dignity, and fairness. Unlike most Americans, I have lived in the Middle East. I loved it actually, and spent two years learning about the cultures in that region and the people. Unlike most people in the world, I have actually helped settle a refugee family. My husband, a United States Marine, obtained political asylum for his Iraqi interpreter, his wife, and his six children. They live about an hour away from us, and they are as much like family as our own blood. Bonds forged in war have no race, color, or religion. The character Zaid is loosely based on my Iraqi brother and his family. The only real name I used was that of a certain, spunky teenage girl who liked to play soccer and hit bad guys with her skateboard. Because girl power is a very real thing.

I had to do some research both on the FBI and the Garda to prepare for this book. I know that people often play fast and loose with reality when writing fiction, but I didn't want to do that if it wasn't necessary. So I went to the source, researching on both those agency websites. Between those two sites and the research I did on bombs, the Middle East, and other parts of this story, I'm probably flagged on some sort of watch list!

I was a police officer in my younger years, before I married the big Marine. I wanted to get the basics right, because there are real women and men that do those jobs every single day. The International Human Rights Crime Unit of the FBI and the National Security Surveillance Unit's Armed Response Team of the Garda do exist and have specific jobs that keep the two countries and their citizens safe. The Special Detectives Unit is also a real branch of the Garda.

The character Charlie came to me slowly. I wanted her to be tough and smart, but have a vulnerable side that she'd inevitably be able to show to her O'Brien man. Having been a police officer, and currently volunteering in a domestic violence shelter, I have worked both as a first responder and support services for the victims. Domestic violence happens in every branch of our society. Every race, religion, and every socio-economic background. The victims are men, women, children, heterosexual and same sex couples. I think it's a real problem. If you get this book free during a promotion, please consider donating to a domestic violence safe house. Those safe houses can mean the difference between staying and leaving.

The modern shame of our current generation is the widespread human trafficking that is happening on a global scale. Slavery, sex trafficking, illegal pornography rings, exploitation of minors, the oppression of other human beings on every possible level. If you are moved to do so, I encourage you to research how you can affect positive change with regard to the human trafficking epidemic in your own country.

As always, I would like to give a special thanks to my beta readers and my cover designer, Christine Stevens. They are behind the scenes with me, helping me get these books out on time and looking spectacular.

My final thought is this. I know it was a hard thing for the readers, losing Eve. I understand your grief. I had a beta reader and dear friend of mine send a selfie of herself crying and flipping me off. I get it. The only explanation I can offer is that Eve was supposed to die. It was how the story came to me. But don't worry. Liam will get his story.

Made in the USA
Las Vegas, NV
12 June 2023

73314927R00226